PRAISE FOR
CHILDREN OF PARANOIA

"A generations-long war that's claimed thousands of lives, waged in perfect secrecy beneath the clueless noses of people like me? Oh, hell yeah. *Children of Paranoia* is a claustrophobic, relentless, fascinating ride that will have you eyeballing everyone you pass in the street. I can't wait for the sequel."

—Marcus Sakey, author of *The Two Deaths of Daniel Hayes*

"Trevor Shane's *Children of Paranoia* is a gripping journey into a secret war where literally anyone could kill you. Like *The Bourne Identity* turned inside out, his protagonist navigates a world where banal choices like going to the ATM have life-and-death consequences. Filled with sharp plotting and vivid action, this book will stay with you long after you've raced to the end."

—Chris Farnsworth, author of *Blood Oath*

"What keeps the reader relentlessly glued to *Children of Paranoia* are the unrelenting suspense and complex characters. It is definitely a roller-coaster ride that one won't soon forget."

—New York Journal of Books

"Shane's work here is impressive. He certainly knows how to stage an action scene and how to ratchet up tension. If you're in the market for an exciting, propulsive read . . . *Children of Paranoia* would make an excellent choice."

—The Saturday Evening Post

"*Children of Paranoia* functions neatly as a surreal variant on the noir thriller where evil lurks in every shadow and happiness either remains tantalizingly just out of reach or could be snatched away in an instant."

—Shelf Awareness

continued . . .

"This story is heart-stopping one moment and tear-jerking in another. Shane has created a masterpiece you will pick up and not put down until the final word and then you will say, 'Wow,' and sit back to contemplate this story and then want to tell your friends all about it."

—*Midwest Book Review*

"An action-packed story of war, intrigue, and twists and turns."

—*News and Sentinel* (Parkersburg, WV)

"[*Children of Paranoia*] is an interesting but poignant metaphor for the senselessness of killing, be it by rival street gangs, feuding families, or entire countries . . . a powerful story." —*Suspense Magazine*

"Well-written and exciting . . . the plot takes some interesting and unexpected turns." —Geek Speak Magazine

"Fast-paced . . . a thought-provoking, enjoyable read that will stay with readers when the last page is done." —Monsters and Critics

"An exceptional story." —Fresh Fiction

"[*Children of Paranoia*] will please lovers of adventure and action."

—Examiner.com

"*Children of Paranoia*, the first installment of a planned trilogy, never flags and kept this reader's attention rapt until its end, by which time Irene's winds had died down and the rain had long since stopped."

—*Psychology Today*

CHILDREN OF THE
UPRISING

THE CHILDREN OF PARANOIA SERIES

TREVOR SHANE

NEW AMERICAN LIBRARY

New American Library
Published by the Penguin Group
Penguin Group (USA) LLC, 375 Hudson Street,
New York, New York 10014

USA I Canada I UK I Ireland I Australia I New Zealand I India I South Africa I China
penguin.com
A Penguin Random House Company

Published by New American Library,
a division of Penguin Group (USA) LLC

First Printing, October 2013

 REGISTERED TRADEMARK—MARCA REGISTRADA

LIBRARY OF CONGRESS CATALOGING-IN-PUBLICATION DATA:
Shane, Trevor.
Children of the uprising: the children of paranoia series/Trevor Shane.
p. cm.—(Children of Paranoia ; Book 3)
ISBN 978-0-451-41964-4 (pbk.)
1. Children—Fiction. 2. Paranoia—Fiction. I. Title.
PS3619.H53465C45 2013
813'.6—dc23   2013018663

Printed in the United States of America
1   3   5   7   9   10   8   6   4   2

Set in Janson Text

To my wife, Carly,
for years of inspiration, support and love
and for putting up with me mumbling to myself
in the middle of the night while I write.

And to my son, Van.
You and Leo are what gave these books meaning.

CHILDREN OF PARANOIA—BOOK III
CHILDREN OF THE UPRISING

"Are you ever going to tell me how the War started?"
the young girl, growing antsy, asked the old woman.
"Patience," the old woman responded. "There's still a
lot of story to tell."

CHILDREN OF THE UPRISING

One

They waited until Christopher turned eighteen before they tried to kill him.

Ever since Christopher was a small child, he'd known that someone was watching him. Even though he couldn't see them, he could feel their eyes burning into his skin. He could feel people lurking in the shadows, watching his every move. They were waiting, but Christopher had no way of knowing what they were waiting for. He never told his parents that people were watching him. Christopher was trying to protect them. They knew that Christopher had problems. They knew that he wasn't a normal kid, but they assumed that everything related back to something that had happened to Christopher when he was a baby, something that he had no memory of. Christopher heard his parents whispering about it late at night when he was supposed to be asleep. Whatever had happened to him when he was young didn't matter. He wasn't afraid of his past. He was afraid of his future. Before he learned anything else, Christopher learned how to be paranoid. That was his birthright.

Since Christopher didn't know who was watching him or why, he did what he could to prepare for the unknown. He took karate lessons. He learned to box and to wrestle. He took tae kwon do classes. He took every fighting class the little town he grew up in had to offer, and then, when he got his driver's license, he took every class offered in the surrounding towns. He didn't stick to any one thing for very long. He never felt like he was learning fast enough. He'd get frustrated and quit and then try something new, each time hoping that this time he would learn fast enough. Even though he moved around, he learned. He integrated skills. He was a misfit, but he wasn't afraid of bullies or jocks or any of the kids in his town. He had other things to be afraid of. Even among the outsiders, Christopher was an outsider. Christopher had only one close friend. Even before Christopher had felt strangers' eyes watching him, Evan had been his friend. They were different. Christopher was practical. Evan was a dreamer. Evan saw something bigger in their future, something more than what their little town offered people. The other kids feared Christopher because he was different. Evan reveled in the fact that Christopher was different. That was what drew him to Christopher in the first place. Christopher was more than this small-town high school life full of jocks and nerds and cheerleaders and Evan knew it.

Maybe everything would have turned out differently had Christopher remembered the key that he received on his sixteenth birthday or the note that came with the key that he never read. He'd hidden them at the bottom of one of his dresser drawers and tried to forget them. As sure as Christopher was that he was being watched, he was just as certain that the key would unlock answers for him, but he wasn't sure he wanted answers. As afraid as he was of the people watching him, he was even more afraid of why. Sometimes Christopher did his best to pretend that he was merely imagining things. Maybe it would have been better that way. Maybe it would have been better if he was crazy and the rest of the world was sane. But he wasn't crazy. Someone was watching him. They were watching him and waiting for his eighteenth birthday.

It was the evening of Christopher's eighteenth birthday, and he was driving home from Evan's house. He was in his own car, a beat-up, rusty heap of junk that he'd bought for three thousand dollars the day he got his license. The evening was already dark. Christopher had gone to Evan's house to show Evan the gift that his parents had given him for his birthday. It was an autographed baseball bat, signed by David Ortiz. Big Papi. "The man who killed the ghost of the Bambino," Christopher's father, a die-hard Red Sox fan, used to tell him when he was growing up. It meant little to Christopher. No matter how hard his father prodded him, Christopher couldn't find any interest in team sports. They seemed pointless to him. He had other things on his mind. Even so, his father supported the sports Christopher did play. Christopher's father went to his son's wrestling matches and karate matches and everything else. After every match, win or lose, Christopher's father always said the same thing. "Helluva of a match, kid. Just don't forget to have fun, you know."

The bat that Christopher got from his parents was the color of wood near the knob but shifted to a dark, shiny black near the barrel. His father told him that it was exactly like the ones that Big Papi used to use in games. Christopher genuinely thanked his father. He knew that his father was giving him a piece of himself. He loved his father. He loved both his parents. Before they cut into Christopher's birthday cake, Christopher wanted to drive to Evan's house to show Evan the bat. Evan was a huge baseball fan. Evan's brain wasn't filled with the distractions that Christopher's was. "Do you know how much this thing probably cost?" Evan asked as Christopher handed him the bat.

Christopher shrugged. He had no idea. "No. Do you?"

Evan paused, running his hand up and down the polished wood. He shook his head. "I bet it cost a ton."

"Do you want it?" Christopher asked Evan. He knew that Evan wanted it. He could see the desire in Evan's eyes. He didn't care. Having the bat wasn't important to him—not as important as making his only friend happy.

Evan stared down at the name signed in the wood on the beige part of the handle. He shook his head. "Your father would be really upset if you gave it away." Christopher hadn't even thought of that. Evan handed the bat back to him. "Do you want to go out tonight?" he asked Christopher. "To celebrate? I can probably get Tracey to get one of her friends to come out with us."

Christopher thought about it. Maybe he should celebrate. It was his birthday. He'd had fun with some of Tracey's friends before when he didn't scare them away too quickly. He shook his head no, though. It was a Tuesday night. He didn't want to put anybody out. Christopher looked out the window. It was getting darker. "I should go home. My mother made a cake."

"Okay," Evan said. "I'll make Tracey give us a rain check. How about Friday?" Evan eyed his friend, never exactly sure what was going on in Christopher's head.

"Friday," Christopher agreed, knowing that it was the easiest way to end the conversation.

"Well, Happy Birthday, man." Evan got up from his chair and wrapped his arms awkwardly around Christopher, patting his friend on the back with one fist.

"Thanks."

"See you at school tomorrow," Evan said.

"Yeah," Christopher answered, thinking it was true when he said it.

Christopher left the house. He waved good-bye to Evan's parents on his way out the door. Evan's parents waved back, not un-happy to see their son's odd best friend go. Christopher walked across the gravel driveway toward his car. Everything seemed normal. Christopher was even relaxed. He opened the car door and threw his bat in the passenger seat. Then he sat down, started the car, and flicked on his headlights. Night came fast this far north.

Christopher looked to his left before pulling his car out onto the long, windy road. This stretch of road was free of streetlights. He would be able to see the headlights of any oncoming cars from miles away even as the light darted through the trees. Cars drove fast on this stretch of road at night, though. When Christopher looked, all he saw was miles of empty road, surrounded by trees and darkening, hollow spaces. Seeing nothing, Christopher stepped on the gas and inched the car forward onto the road. The road in front of him was as empty as the road behind him appeared. His headlights cut through the darkness, reflecting off the yellow lines in the middle of the street but otherwise being swallowed by the dense forest around him. Christopher looked in his rearview mirror again. Still nothing. He looked down to turn on the radio. He began to tune it away from the station he usually listened to, the talk radio station full of shows about UFOs and conspiracy theories where people from all over the country called in to tell strange stories about secrets hidden right in front of us. It was his eighteenth birthday. He wanted to listen to music. He found a station playing an old Bruce Springsteen song. Evan always made fun of Christopher for liking old people's music. Christopher turned up the volume and then glanced up again. The road in front of him was still empty. Then he looked in his rearview mirror again, expecting to see darkness. Instead, he saw them. They had finally come for him.

The headlights of the car chasing him were already large in the rearview mirror and they were getting bigger, bearing down on him. The car had come out of nowhere. It couldn't have come all the way down the road. Christopher would have seen the headlights—tiny specks of light in the darkness—miles before they got this close to him. The only explanation was that the car had been parked in the woods waiting for him to drive by. Christopher heard the engine of the car behind him rev as it closed the gap between them and neared his rear bumper. The moment that Christopher had feared ever since he was a child had finally arrived.

For a split second, the only emotion that Christopher felt was relief—relief that the moment was finally here, relief that the waiting was over, relief that his paranoia wasn't madness, relief that his paranoia wasn't worthless. Had he known them, Christopher's birth mother and birth father could have told him that there is no such thing as worthless paranoia. Christopher knew that well enough now. His paranoia had value. It was a currency that, if he was lucky, he could cash in to buy his life. The relief lasted only a split second. After that, the relief was chased away by the sudden feeling of inadequacy. Christopher began to question every decision he had ever made. Why hadn't he stuck with one fighting style? Why hadn't he trained harder? Then, after deeming the feeling of inadequacy to be a waste of time, he was left with only one emotion. Fear. So much fear that it drowned out everything else.

Christopher looked at the dark, empty road in front of him and did the only thing he could think to do. He slammed on the gas. The road wound back and forth through the dense forest. Even as well as Christopher knew the road, he couldn't floor it without running the risk of driving off the road and into a tree. All he could hope for was that whoever was in the car behind him didn't know the road as well as he did and would have trouble keeping up. The problem was that they didn't have to follow the road. They only needed to follow Christopher's taillights. The car behind him moved in closer. Christopher felt a heavy tap on his rear fender. It jolted him forward. Christopher began turning the steering wheel later and later as he neared oncoming turns, hoping to lose his tail. He would wait until the last possible second, then jerk the wheel to one side, barely avoiding driving into the woods. The wheels of Christopher's car skidded on the road as he turned. He held his steering wheel tightly to try to keep from losing control. Still, the car behind him stayed on his bumper. Whatever they were driving, it was faster and handled better than the piece of shit Christopher drove.

They pulled their car up beside Christopher's. Their car was dark, with tinted windows. Christopher couldn't see inside. Then they suddenly rammed their car into the side of Christopher's, and he almost lost control. As long as he was on the road, he was outmatched. Christopher knew it. He had to get off the road. It was his only chance. If he could just stay on the road a few more miles, he could get to the woods close to his house, the woods he'd virtually grown up in. If he could make it that far, he knew he'd have a chance of surviving.

The dark car bumped Christopher again, sustaining the contact this time, trying to push his car off the road and into the trees. They were going over sixty miles per hour now. Christopher clutched the steering wheel, trying to hold on, trying to keep his car from veering off into oblivion. He could feel his pulse in his hands. He could feel his tires skid sideways. Then the road bent suddenly. Christopher cut his steering wheel as the road curved. When he did, the cars separated. He heard tires screeching again, but they weren't his this time. The dark car skidded, trying to stay on the road as it almost missed the turn. Christopher stomped on the accelerator. His foot touched the floor. He only needed to make it another two miles or so. In seconds, the other car was back alongside him again, moving in to try to ram him off the road.

This time Christopher had a plan. As the passenger-side door of the dark car was about to ram Christopher's door, Christopher slammed on the brakes. The dark car flew by him, going at least fifty yards in front of him before it pulled to a stop. The dark car skidded sideways as it stopped, blocking the entire road. The car was lit up by Christopher's headlights like it was being shown in a spotlight. Christopher waited, wanting to see what the people inside the car would do. He half hoped that another car would come speeding from the other direction and slam into them, but he knew that this was unlikely. People didn't often drive this road at night. He watched the car. He felt like he was watching an animal, a predator. He felt like he could see the car breathing. Then the car's passenger-side window, the window facing Christopher, began to go down. Christopher didn't wait to see what horrors the descending window would reveal. Instead, as soon as the window began to go down, he floored it again.

Christopher knew that he would have to go off the road to get around them. His wheels screeched before they caught, and then he launched his car onto the dirt on the side of the road behind the dark car. He prayed that he wouldn't hit a hole in the ground or a tree before he was able to get past the dark car. His car rattled over the unpaved ground, but it made it past the other car. When he could, Christopher turned back onto the road, without taking his foot off the accelerator. Then he heard the screeching of tires as his pursuers started up the chase again. The dark car was only seconds behind him, but seconds were all that Christopher needed. He knew where he was now. He watched the trees as he zipped past them. The other car was gaining on him again, coming right up to his rear bumper. He spotted the landmark he'd been looking for, an old felled tree, its roots sticking up into the air like the tentacles of a giant sea monster. Christopher counted the seconds. One. Two. The car behind him was about to ram him again. On three, Christopher cut the wheel hard to the left, launching himself into the darkness of the woods. He felt the wheels of his car leave the ground as he catapulted off the paved road into the wilderness. As he flew, he turned off his headlights and then he felt himself plummeting into darkness.

Christopher's car hit the ground hard and kept moving forward. He slammed on the brakes again. The car skidded, unable to gain traction on the dirt and leaves on the forest floor. The brakes couldn't stop the car; they could only slow it down. Still, the car slowed down enough that by the time Christopher sideswiped the tree, he felt little more than a jolt.

The tree that Christopher hit pinned the driver's-side door shut, so Christopher leapt over the middle console and opened the passenger-side door. On his way out, he grabbed the David Ortiz autographed baseball bat. He got to his feet outside his car at the same moment that the headlights from the car chasing him shot through the darkness at him. Christopher held the bat halfway up its barrel and ran from the light. Even as he crested the hill in front of him and found his way back into the darkness, he knew that he wasn't going to be running for very long. He hadn't spent the majority of his youth training to run. He'd spent it training to fight. He heard the dark car's doors slam behind him as he raced deeper into the forest. *Bang. Bang.* Christopher hoped that the two bangs meant that there were only two of them.

The two men assigned to kill Christopher this time should have watched him disappear into the darkness of the forest and gone to his home. They knew where he lived. They knew that he couldn't get very far now that his car was wrecked. They easily could have waited him out. They didn't need to chase him blindly into the woods. They could have killed him tomorrow or the next day or the day after that. It was only their pride that made them chase him. He was just an untrained, unarmed kid, a nuisance by reputation only. Forget karate and tae kwon do and all that other shit Christopher had done. He still wasn't trained the way that everyone in the War was trained. He still wasn't trained to hate. So they chased Christopher into the woods because they were more afraid of telling people that the kid got away than they were afraid of the kid. They should have known better. They both knew Christopher's story. They knew that he'd witnessed the killing of two of his fathers before he turned a year old. They knew that he'd been ripped from the arms of two different mothers. Even if he didn't remember those things, they stick with you. Sometimes, anger is as good as hate. It may be less directed, less targeted, more blunt, but it will do the job. Besides, they also knew what type of blood ran in Christopher's veins. They knew that his father had been a gifted killer and that his mother, at the age of nineteen, had been the only person in the history of the War to break in to an Intelligence Cell and make it out alive. They knew that the blood that pumped through the kid's veins was dangerous blood. They chased him anyway.

Christopher stood behind a tree, his chest silently rising and falling as he breathed in through his nose and out through his mouth. He could feel his heart racing. This was it. The woods were dark, only slivers of moonlight breaking in through the forest canopy. Christopher waited. There was space between the trees. He'd have space enough to take a full swing. He listened, holding the bat close to his chest with two hands. He could hear their footsteps rustling over the leaves. He hadn't run very far. He wasn't trying to get away. The two men chasing him didn't split up, but they weren't walking next to each other either. They were walking about twenty feet apart, canvassing the forest, trying to make sure that they didn't walk past the kid while he was hiding in a hole or behind a tree. They knew that they would have heard him if he had kept running. They knew that he was close. Their mistake was their failure to realize that he was actually waiting for them.

The two men began shouting as they walked, trying to flush Christopher out of his hiding space. Their voices echoed back and forth between the trees, making it sound like they were a whole army of men even though there were only two of them. "Come on out, kid!" the first man shouted. Christopher could hear him fumbling through the darkness, trying not to walk into a branch or trip over a rock. "We just want to talk to you," the other man yelled, his voice higher than the first man's and closer. "There's no reason to be afraid," the first man yelled and, almost before he finished, Christopher could hear the other man begin to laugh under his breath. They were moving slowly, but they were close now. Christopher twisted his hands on the handle of the bat to make sure that he had a solid grip. It was about timing and accuracy. He remembered the batting lessons his dad had given him as a kid. Christopher silently rolled his shoulders, loosening up his muscles.

"Here kiddie, kiddie," the man with the higher-pitched voice shouted into the night. The man was on the other side of the tree Christopher was hiding behind. The man with the deeper voice was still only about twenty feet away, but they were twenty feet of comforting darkness.

"Where the fuck are you?" the man with the deeper voice yelled, anger seeping into his voice.

"Maybe he ain't here," the closer of the two men said to his partner. Christopher took advantage of the fact that the man had turned away from him. He slipped out from behind the tree. "Maybe we should just wait," the closer man started to say. He never finished the thought. Christopher swung the bat hard. He took the first swing with everything he had, every ounce of torque he could generate. It was dark, but Christopher could see enough.

He plowed the bat into the front of the closer man's knees. He could feel one of the man's knees give way and start bending in the wrong direction as he followed through with his swing. The man shouted, a primal scream of pain echoing through the night. Then he fell to the ground on his now useless knees. Christopher looked at the man's hands. He was carrying what looked like a nightstick in his right hand. Christopher lifted the bat and swung it down hard on the man's right shoulder, determined to disarm the man no matter how many swings it took. It took only two bone-crunching swings before the man dropped his weapon, his right arm now as useless as his knees.

Christopher heard the footsteps behind him. The other man was coming for him. Instead of immediately turning to fight, Christopher ran. He ran deeper into the dark forest. He knew where to plant his feet. He knew when to jump and where the holes he needed to avoid were. In only about twenty steps, Christopher was hidden again, ducking behind another tree. Christopher listened. He could hear the injured man moaning in the darkness. He didn't care about that. He only cared about the other man. Christopher was ready for anything. If the man came after him, he was ready to fight. If the man ran, Christopher was ready to chase him, to hunt him down through the darkness. In between the moans of the first man, Christopher heard a twig snap off to his right. He was holding the bat in front of him now, more like a sword than a bat. He wondered what type of weapon this guy had. What if he had a gun? Christopher heard another twig snap, this time even closer to him. Christopher spun, swinging the bat out in front of him, leaping out from behind the tree. Not as sure where his target was this time, he simply swung at the level of a man's chest. He swung hard, but the man was standing perpendicular to him, so the blow merely landed on the side of the man's arm. The man grunted when the bat hit him, but he didn't buckle. He didn't fall. Instead, he turned toward Christopher and swung at him with the bright silver hatchet that he held in his right hand. Christopher stepped to the side, barely avoiding the hatchet's sharp blade. Then the man threw a punch with his left hand and Christopher felt cold metal strike his cheekbone. The man had a hatchet in one hand and brass knuckles on the other. The punch was listless, the man's left arm weakened by the swing from Christopher's bat. If the man hadn't already been hurt, Christopher's cheekbone would have been smashed to pieces and Christopher would be on the ground being hacked to death by this psychopath.

Christopher was trying to regain his vision after taking the metal punch to the jaw when he heard a whizzing sound coming toward him through the air. Without thinking, he grabbed the bat with both his hands and lifted it up. As soon as he got the bat in front of his face, he felt the hatchet bury itself deep into the wood. Still slightly dazed, Christopher could feel the man trying to wrench the hatchet out of the baseball bat. One pull. Two pulls. Before the man could pull again, Christopher yanked the bat toward his chest, drawing the man in close to him. When the man was only an inch or two from him, Christopher lifted his knee and jammed it as hard as he could into the man's groin. He heard all of the air go out of the man's lungs. Then Christopher pushed the bat away from himself, creating distance between himself and the man, and he turned on the ball of his left foot and kicked the man hard in the chest. It was instinct mixed with training. The man flew away from him, toppling to the ground, the hatchet still buried in the bat that Christopher was holding in his hands. Christopher was in no mood for games, in no mood to gamble. He already had the informer he needed in the kneeless man still moaning into the darkness. He stepped forward as the first man tried to get to his feet. Christopher swung the bat again, this time with the hatchet still stuck in it. The bat connected solidly with the side of the man's head. It was the crunching sound even more than the feel of the skull giving way that made Christopher sure that he wasn't going to have to swing the bat again.

The man fell motionless to the ground. His body didn't even twitch. Christopher stood over the body for a second, looking down at it. His chest was heaving. His fingers were still wrapped tightly around the handle of the bat. He reached up with one hand and, with two hard tugs, pulled the hatchet out of the barrel of the bat. He could still hear the other man moaning alone and he knew he needed to move. He needed to get to the moaning man before the coyotes did. Christopher looked down at the body at his feet one more time. The head wasn't a normal shape anymore. Christopher wasn't going to have to worry about being followed through the darkness. With the bat in one hand and the hatchet in the other, he made his way back toward the kneeless man, following the sounds of pain.

The kneeless man had struggled, pulling himself up against a tree so that his back was leaning against it, his legs splayed out unnaturally in front of him, his right shoulder hanging loosely from his body. He saw Christopher coming at him through the darkness. Even through that darkness, Christopher could see the fear register on the man's face when he realized that it was Christopher coming back to him and not his partner. Christopher rested the bat on his own shoulder and stepped carefully toward the injured man. He knew that even an injured man could be dangerous. He looked at the injured man's hands to make sure that he was unarmed. Pitifully, he was.

When he got to within ten feet of the man, Christopher pointed the bat at him. "What do you want from me?" he asked.

"Nothing," the man answered, shaking his head, speaking through the pain. "It's just a game," he lied. The man knew that Christopher didn't know anything. He also knew that he wouldn't be able to explain anything to him, at least not in a way that would make Christopher spare his life.

"You've been watching me for ten years as part of a game?" Christopher asked, stepping closer to the man, almost brushing the man's nose with the tip of the bat.

"We weren't watching you," the man said, not lying. They weren't the ones who'd been watching him. Others were.

"Don't lie to me," Christopher shouted into the night air, yelling more loudly than he could ever remember yelling before. Out here in the woods, the yelling didn't matter. Then Christopher swung the bat, knocking the injured man's head hard enough for him to feel but not hard enough to do any lasting damage. The man flinched before the bat hit him.

"There's nothing I can tell you that will make you understand," the man said.

"Try me," Christopher answered.

The man swallowed hard and bit down on his lip. "Your father was a member of a War that you know nothing about. Your mother was a child when she gave birth to you." The man took a moment to catch his breath. "They didn't follow the rules, so now you're being punished."

"So you came here to punish me?" For the time being, that was the only thing that registered, the only thing that Christopher could make any sense of. He could understand being punished for his sins, even if he didn't know what they were.

The man shook his head. His head and his left arm were the only parts of his body he could still move. "We came here to kill you," he said with a touch of ironic relish in his voice.

"And now that you failed?" Christopher asked, his voice trembling as if he already knew the answer.

"There will be others," the man said. Christopher looked down at his watch. It was almost ten o'clock. His parents would begin to miss him soon. They would call. His phone was back in his car. If they didn't reach Christopher, they'd call Evan. Then they'd start looking for him. He couldn't let that happen. He couldn't let them find him like this.

Christopher walked up to the injured man. He tossed the hatchet on the ground about ten feet from them. He kneeled down and grabbed the man's one good hand by the wrist and held it tightly. Then he reached down and patted the man's pockets. "What are you doing?" the man asked. Christopher felt the bulge in the man's right pocket. He reached inside and pulled out a cell phone. He turned it on to see when the last phone call was placed, making sure that the injured man hadn't already called someone to tell them that he'd lost. The last call, sent or received, was hours ago.

Christopher stepped back, away from the man. "What are you doing?" the man asked again. Christopher threw the phone into the air and swung the bat at it, shattering it into countless tiny pieces. Then he began to walk away. "What are you doing?" the man asked one more time, nearly shouting this time. "What? You don't even have the guts to finish the job?" the injured man yelled.

Christopher motioned toward the hatchet on the ground. "I might see if I could reach that if I were you. You'll need it to try to fend off the bears and the coyotes, because nobody is going to find you here. If you're lucky, the bears will come first. They'll be a lot quicker than the coyotes." Christopher turned and walked away again. This time he didn't turn back.

He walked for another fifty yards or so. Then he started to jog. Then he started to run. When he got back to his car, he opened the car door, reached inside, and grabbed his phone. He called Evan.

The phone rang twice before Evan picked up. "Yo, man, what's up? You change your mind about Tracey?" Evan spoke into the phone before Christopher said a word. Christopher could still hear the man in the woods crying out for help, but it was a quiet, distant sound.

"No," Christopher answered, trying to control the panic in his voice. "I need a favor."

"Okay," Evan said, a bit confused. Christopher wasn't one to often ask for favors.

"I need you to call my parents and tell them that I'm staying at your place tonight. Tell them that you're taking me out as a surprise or something. After you talk to them, call me back."

"What's going on, Chris?" Evan asked.

I just killed two men in the woods, Christopher thought but didn't say. "I'll tell you later. This is important. Will you do it?"

"Why can't you just call your parents?" Evan asked. But Christopher couldn't. He knew it. He'd break down on the phone with them.

"I don't know," Christopher answered. "I just can't. Will you please call them?"

"Okay. I'll give you a call right back." Evan hung up. While Christopher waited for Evan to call him back, he assessed the damage done to his car. The whole driver's side was still clinging to the tree he hit, the metal bent around it. He couldn't drive the car anymore. Even if he could get the car to run, it would be like driving a neon sign. Christopher lifted his head and eyed the other car. He walked over to it. The keys were still inside. The car had some scratches on the door but was otherwise in remarkably good shape. Christopher opened the driver's-side door and got inside. His phone rang.

"Evan," Christopher said, picking up the phone before the first ring had finished.

"Dude," Evan said, "is something wrong?"

"Did you talk to my parents?" Christopher asked.

"Yeah," Evan answered. "They bought it."

"So they were okay?" Christopher asked. He was breathing more heavily now than he had been when he'd been hiding in the woods.

"They're fine," Evan said, frustration leaking into his voice. "Are you going to tell me what's going on?"

"As soon as I can," Christopher said. "I promise. Not now, though. Not tonight. I promise to call you tomorrow."

"Okay," Evan said. "I hope there's a good story behind this." *So do I*, Christopher thought before hanging up the phone. He turned the key in the car's ignition. The engine began its low rumble. Then he pulled the jet-black car back onto the road and headed for home.

Christopher parked the car a mile from his house and walked the rest of the way. He didn't dare bring the car any closer. He didn't dare tell his parents what had happened in the woods. Somehow he knew that he needed to keep them in the dark to protect them. When he reached the edge of his yard, Christopher stopped and stared into the brightly lit house. He watched the shadows of his parents as they moved from room to room. After only a few minutes his parents began to turn off the lights in each room. First the living room went dark. Then the kitchen. Then the upstairs bathroom. The dim light coming from their bedroom stayed on the longest, but that too eventually went out. Christopher waited for another half an hour after the lights were turned off before he walked the rest of the way to the house.

The birthday cake Christopher's mother had baked for him was still on the kitchen counter, covered in plastic wrap. It was a

German chocolate cake, Christopher's favorite. He was tempted to lift the plastic wrap and cut himself one slice—just one. He didn't do it, though. He didn't want to mess with his parents' heads any more than he was already about to. As quietly as he could, Christopher made his way up the stairs toward his bedroom. He moved through the darkness in his house even more easily than he had through the darkness in the woods. He knew every inch of this house. He knew which floorboards to step over to avoid creaking. He knew to lift the door to his bedroom as he opened it to keep the hinges from making noise.

Christopher walked into his bedroom. When the men had started chasing him, Christopher remembered the key and the note. He opened the top drawer of his desk. He silently pushed aside the papers that were lying inside. He reached for the back of the drawer. His fingers felt the envelope. The envelope had some weight to it. Christopher pulled it out, being even more careful now not to make noise. If his parents heard him now, he would have no way of hiding what he was doing. He opened the envelope. He found the key inside with the note that he had never read. He took out his cell phone so that he could use it as a flashlight. He thought the note might have answers for him. To his dismay, it didn't contain any message at all. The only thing that was written on the paper was an address in Montreal and a number.

Christopher took the key and the note and put them in his pocket. Then he gathered up a few changes of clothes and his cell phone charger and threw them in a backpack. Even if the note was a bust, he figured the key had to lead to answers. He looked around the room to see if he should take anything else, not knowing when he would be able to come home again. His breath began to tremble over his lips. He was almost overcome with a surge of emotion, but he willed it to stop. He'd spent his whole life training to never let himself break like that. Even as a child, his parents told him, he rarely ever cried.

Christopher took a deep breath and walked out of his room. He walked past his parents' bedroom, stopping for only a moment to listen to them breathe. Then he walked silently down the stairs and out the front door.

Two

Christopher sat in the café across the street from the bank. He ate his breakfast and eyed the other people in the café. He listened to the sound of forks and knives clinking on cheap china. He felt like he could hear every spoon that rattled against the edge of a coffee cup. No one appeared to be looking at him. They were looking at their plates, at their food, at the waitress. They talked to each other. Christopher could still feel eyes on him. Somebody was watching him. He just couldn't tell who. He had hoped that the feeling of being watched would end after he faced down the men in the woods. He'd hoped that he'd already seen enough, that it was now over. But it wasn't over. Christopher knew it. He stabbed his fork into his eggs and felt eyes on him. The guys in the woods weren't alone.

Christopher felt his phone vibrate in his pocket. He took it out and looked down at the message on the screen. It was from Evan: "where the hell r u? this story better b epic . . ." Christopher put the phone back in his pocket. Epic didn't begin to describe it. Christopher wouldn't even know how to describe it. Terrifying would be a start. Confusing. Christopher looked out the window toward the bank. People were beginning to move around inside. It was almost eight in the morning. Christopher hadn't slept, hadn't even considered it. He wasn't tired. The way he felt, he wasn't sure if he'd ever sleep again.

Christopher ate the last two bites of his breakfast. He reached into his pocket again, reaching past his phone, and ran his fingers over the cool metal of the key. A real key to a safe-deposit box. It seemed so antiquated, like trying to kill someone with a hatchet. Christopher stood up. He had already paid. He eyeballed the room one more time before leaving, trying to see if anyone looked like they were going to follow him. Nobody moved. Christopher knew that this didn't mean that no one was watching him. It only meant that they were good at it. His phone buzzed in his pocket again. He ignored it. He didn't have anything to say yet, but the answers were close. He could feel it. He only needed to survive the next hour.

Christopher stepped toward the door to leave. Despite the noise and chatter in the café, everything seemed calm. As he stepped closer to the door, someone in a booth near the exit stood up behind him. The stranger began to follow right behind Christopher. The stranger was close, close enough that he could reach out and touch Christopher if he wanted to. Christopher made it to the door and pushed it open with one arm. Then he stepped aside, holding the door open for the stranger behind him, motioning politely for the stranger to exit first. Christopher had never liked being followed, but he really didn't have any stomach for it today.

"After you," the stranger said to Christopher, his tone oddly formal. The stranger was relatively young, no older than twenty-seven or twenty-eight. He was at least six feet tall, a good two inches taller than Christopher. He had dark hair and dark eyes and was wearing a light jacket despite the warm summer weather.

"No, thanks," Christopher replied. "I left something at my table," he lied.

The stranger took a deep breath and shook his head. "I spend way too much time in this business sitting in cafés." The man looked straight at Christopher. "What do you think you forgot, Christopher? There is nothing at your table."

Christopher felt his heart speed up again, the same way he'd felt it last night while being hunted in the woods. "I'm not going outside with you," Christopher said to the stranger. He didn't even bother asking the stranger how he knew his name. He had half expected the man to know it. The man scared him, maybe even more than the men in the woods. The way the stranger carried himself scared him. The stranger was calm. Everything in the woods had been utterly insane, but the stranger was the picture of sanity. To Christopher, after all the waiting and the paranoia, after what he'd done to those men in the woods, nothing was more frightening than sanity. "If you're going to kill me, you're going to have to do it right here in this restaurant."

"I'm not going to kill you, Christopher," the stranger said, not at all surprised that Christopher thought such a thing.

"Then what are you here for?" Christopher asked him. The stranger's words didn't make him feel any better.

"I'm here to keep you from going inside that bank," the stranger said, motioning over his shoulder at the bank across the street.

"Why?"

"Because if you go inside that bank, you'll be dead within half an hour of leaving it," the stranger said calmly and quietly. The two men stopped speaking for a moment as an elderly couple walked out of the café. Christopher stood there, barely breathing, still holding the door open with his outstretched arm. The old man tipped his hat to Christopher as he walked by.

"I don't understand," Christopher whispered to the stranger once the old couple was gone. The confusion was almost as bad as the fear.

"Follow me," the stranger said, "and I'll tell you as much as I can."

"Why should I trust you?" Christopher asked the stranger.

The stranger shrugged. He leaned in toward Christopher and spoke in a low whisper. "If I want you dead, you're dead whether you follow me or not. If I'm telling the truth and I actually want to help you, then following me is your only smart move. You don't have to trust me. You just have to realize that you are outclassed and extremely short on options." When the stranger finished speaking, he looked into Christopher's eyes. "Either way, it's been an honor to meet you," he said. Then the stranger walked past Christopher's outstretched arm and through the open door toward the street. Christopher only waited a second before following the stranger outside.

The stranger was already at the end of the block when Christopher stepped out of the café. He timed it so that Christopher caught only a glimpse of him before he turned the corner, just enough so that Christopher would be able to follow him. It was clear to Christopher that the stranger had experience with this, meeting people, persuading them to follow him, and then leading them away. The stranger had, in fact, done this dozens of times before but never with someone exactly like Christopher. After all, no one else was exactly like Christopher.

Christopher looked both ways down the Montreal street. He saw the stranger turn and Christopher followed him. Instinctively, Christopher matched the pace of the stranger. He didn't rush to catch up. He tried to walk calmly, to appear to be moving without the agonizing purpose he felt in his gut. He did his best to control the adrenaline pumping through his veins.

At each corner, Christopher turned in the direction the stranger had gone just in time to see the stranger turning again. Together, they walked farther and farther from the bank. Christopher put his hands in his pocket and ran his fingers over the key again. He remembered the stranger's words. *If you go inside that bank, you'll be dead within half an hour of leaving it.* He looked around to try to see if anyone else was watching him. He glanced behind him to see if he was being followed. Nothing. He saw nothing. He knew how little that meant, though. He made it to the corner and turned toward the stranger again.

It went on this way for another fifteen minutes, the two men weaving through the city streets. Eventually, Christopher saw the man walk into a hotel on Sherbrooke. Christopher could see the lush green of the hills running up toward the top of Mount Royal and the miles of park running down beneath it. He still didn't speed up. For a second, he doubted whether or not he should really be following this stranger inside. What if it was a trap? Sometimes you have to take your chances. Christopher kept walking. He couldn't listen to his paranoia every time it told him not to do something. If he had, he wouldn't have been able to move for the past ten years.

Christopher entered the hotel. The lobby was buzzing with people. He looked around to see if he could see the stranger. People all around him were sitting beside their luggage on the lush furniture, waiting to check in or waiting to check out. Christopher's eyes darted over them. A small queue of people was at the front desk. Then Christopher's eyes moved to the elevator bay. He saw the stranger standing alone inside an elevator. He got only a quick glance at the stranger before the doors closed. The stranger made eye contact with Christopher and held up four of his fingers.

Christopher walked quickly over to the front desk, cutting in the line of people waiting. "Can you tell me where the stairs are?" he asked the closest person behind the desk, a short woman with neatly done hair.

"The elevator bay is just over there, sir," the woman said to him before turning back to the queue of customers.

"The stairs," Christopher said. The woman looked back up at him, annoyed. "I have a thing about elevators," he finished.

"Keep going past the elevators," the woman said. "The stairs are on your right."

"Thanks," Christopher said and began moving quickly toward the stairs.

Christopher ran up the first two flights of stairs, taking two or three steps at a time. When he got to the third floor, he began to walk again, trying to calm down. His head was spinning. The bank. The mystery safe-deposit box. The men in the woods. The stranger. He felt his phone buzz in his pocket again. Evan. His parents. What was he going to tell his parents? He blocked it all out and counted the steps as he climbed them. He tried to decide if he could take the stranger in a fight if it came to that. He didn't know. He could usually size someone up pretty quickly. With the stranger, he had no idea.

The stranger had chosen a room close to the elevator so that he could get in and out quickly without being seen. Christopher was still climbing the stairs when the stranger reached the door to his room. He unlocked the door with his key and stepped inside. The stranger wasted no time. He walked into the bathroom first. He pulled the shower curtain back, revealing the empty bathtub. He opened the cabinets under the bathroom sink and peered inside. Then he walked back into the main room. He opened the closet doors, staring into the closet's dark corners. He dropped to the floor and lifted up the bed skirt, peering under the bed. Finally, the stranger walked over to the windows. He pulled the thick curtains wide open. Light cascaded into the room from outside. The stranger pulled the bunched-up curtains away from the wall at the bottom, running his hand along the insides of the folds. He felt nothing. Then he let the curtains drop back into place and pulled them closed again, shutting out the light. The room was clean. The stranger walked back toward the door, finally ready to greet his guest.

When Christopher got to the fourth floor, he slowly pushed his way through the door leading from the staircase into the hallway. It was a long hallway. The carpet was an ugly golden color with a maroon pattern crisscrossing over it. The doors on either side of the hallway were evenly spaced. Christopher couldn't see any windows, only the dim lights from the ceiling. There were so many doors. Christopher stood alone in the hallway. He didn't see any sign of the stranger. He was unsure of what he was supposed to do. He thought about moving down the hallway, placing his ear on each door, trying to figure out which door was the right one, but that seemed absurd.

Christopher was about to take a step forward when he heard a clicking sound coming from one of the doors at the other end of the hallway. His first instinct was to hide, but the only place to hide was the stairwell and Christopher refused to ever go backward. Instead, he girded himself, readying to charge like a bull. The door swung open. The stranger stepped out from behind it, into the hallway. Without a word, he waved Christopher toward him. Christopher moved silently toward him. As Christopher approached, the stranger stared down the hallway toward the elevators. Finally, when Christopher was only a few steps from him, the stranger looked at Christopher again. "Get inside," he said, his voice barely above a whisper. He held the door open as Christopher slipped past him.

The room appeared to be in a shambles. The closet doors were all open. The bathroom door was open too, and the shower curtain was pulled back. The room appeared empty. The curtains were drawn. The only light in the room came from a small lamp sitting on the desk. The stranger closed the door behind him. "Can I get you something?" the stranger asked Christopher, stepping around him to get to the minibar.

"No, thanks," Christopher answered.

"You sure?" the stranger asked again. "A water? An orange juice?"

"I'm fine," Christopher said again. He didn't want a drink. He wanted answers.

The stranger pulled a bottle of water out of the minibar for himself. "Okay, then let's get started. Take a seat." The stranger motioned to the plush chair across from the desk. Christopher sat down in it. The stranger sat at the desk. He began strumming his fingers on the desktop's dark wood. "Where to start?" the stranger asked himself. He looked back up at Christopher and smiled slightly. "You know I do this. I convince people to come and talk to me and I tell them about what I can do for them, what we can do for them." The stranger shook his head and smiled. "But I've never talked to anyone like you before."

"What does that mean—someone like me? What did you mean when you said it was an honor to meet me?" Christopher asked. He had an endless list of questions running through his head, but these were as good a place to start as any.

The stranger started talking. He enunciated every word to avoid any more confusion than was necessary. "Your father was a soldier in a War that you've never heard of. He met your mother when she was very young. Your mother gave birth to you in contravention to the rules of your father's War. Because of this, your mother decided that she couldn't raise you herself. She thought you would be safer if she hid you with someone else, but hiding from the War is not that easy—especially in your case." The stranger spoke the words as if he'd rehearsed them.

Christopher stared blankly at the stranger as if the stranger had just told him that the sky was bright red at nighttime. "What are you talking about?"

The stranger paused and then started back up again. "Your father was a soldier in a War that you've never heard of. He met your mother when she was very young. Your mother gave birth to you in contravention to the rules of your father's War. Because of this, your mother decided that she couldn't raise you herself. She thought you would be safer if she hid you with someone else, but hiding from the War is not that easy—especially in your case," he repeated, word for word.

"My mother and father are back in Maine," Christopher told the stranger. He knew the words were only partially true. He'd known it his whole life.

"I'm not going to argue with you about that," the stranger said. "Instead, I'll put it this way: your parents in Maine are actually your third mother and your third father. Your first father was killed when you were less than a month old. He was shot in the chest by his best friend. You were in the car with him at the time. His name was Joseph. The man who killed your first father took you away from the woman who gave birth to you and gave you to your second set of parents. You lived with them for less than a year before your birth mother found you again. She stole you back and gave you to your current parents because she was afraid."

Christopher forced out a laugh, trying to pretend that he didn't believe the stranger's story. It was a weak bluff. "What was she afraid of?" Christopher asked.

"Who," the stranger said curtly.

"Who what?"

"*Who* was she afraid of?" the stranger corrected Christopher.

"Okay, who was she afraid of?" Christopher asked on cue.

The stranger leaned in toward him. "Everyone," he whispered. The word floated through the air toward Christopher. "When I said that I had never worked with anyone like you before, that's what I meant. I usually deal with people born on one side of the War or another. They could stay in the War. It's my job to convince them that it's not worth it. I try to convince them that they can have a better life if they run away."

"And me?" Christopher asked.

The stranger shook his head. "You have no side. You have no-where safe to go. You're as innocent and ignorant as your mother was when she met your father. Except—" The stranger stopped and stared at Christopher.

"Except what?"

"Except you're not," the stranger finished.

"Is any of this supposed to make sense to me?" Christopher asked.

"We think we know what's in the safe-deposit box in the bank," the stranger said to Christopher without answering his question.

Christopher's hand nearly flinched toward his pocket, toward the key, but he controlled it. "How do you know so much about me?" he asked the stranger. The stranger ignored his question.

"We think it's journals that your mother and your father kept. I can get them for you. Maybe they will help you understand."

"Why don't I just get them myself?"

"I told you before. They'll kill you. The only thing they want more than whatever is in that safe-deposit box is your head on a stick."

"Are you talking about the people that attacked me last night?"

The stranger smiled at Christopher. "Same make. Better model. They thought that you were a big problem with an easy solution. They underestimated you. They sent a couple of two-bit thugs after you. Don't be a fool and think that they will underestimate you again. Ever."

"So there are people here in Montreal looking for me?"

The stranger shook his head. "Waiting for you like a hunter watching a snare trap. Both sides of the War are here. But there are people everywhere looking for you. You're the War's most wanted man."

"And you're here to help me?"

"If I can. I think I can get into the bank. They're not looking for me, and they know almost nothing about the safe-deposit box other than the location of the bank."

Christopher thought about it for a second, unwilling to relinquish the key in his pocket just yet. "If you're so eager to help me, how come there was no one there to help me last night?"

"That's a fair question. We'd sent someone. We thought that sending more than one person would draw attention to you."

"What happened to the person you sent?"

"We don't expect to hear from him again. The men they sent after you were thugs, but they weren't completely incompetent. Not everyone is blessed with your instincts."

Christopher swallowed, not wanting to believe that someone he had never met had already died on his behalf. "Why are you helping me?"

"You wouldn't understand, even if I tried to explain it to you. Not yet." The stranger strummed his fingers on the desk. "All the answers are in that safe-deposit box. So will you give me the key to helping you understand?"

Christopher reached into his pocket and pulled out the key. It shined brightly in the dim light from the desk lamp. Christopher placed it on the desk in the middle of the small halo of light. "At the diner you said that it was an honor to meet me. Why?"

"Because flattery works better than you'd think," the stranger said, lifting the key off of the desk. "And because you're a legend," he finished. Christopher felt a chill run down his spine. He didn't feel like a legend. He felt like a frightened child.

The stranger returned to the hotel room a little over an hour later. Christopher had spent the hour trying to organize all of the new information that he'd learned in his brain. He checked his phone. He had four more texts from Evan. The last one read, "where are u? your mom is looking for u. i need info if u still want me to cover for u." Christopher also had a worried voice mail from his mother. He didn't have time to think about how the stranger was already putting his life on the line for him.

When the stranger returned, he had two tattered bound books with him—the one on the top more worn than the one below it. The books were filled with page after page of handwritten notes. The handwriting in the two books was different. The more worn book had sloppier handwriting. The handwriting in the other was neat, perfectly spaced, and slanted. On the top of the two books was a note. He began to read, barely able to breathe as he did so.

> *Christopher,*
>   *You need to know who you really are. You need to know where you come from. It's the only way you'll be able to fight Them if They come after you.*
>   *Love, always, Your Mother*

Three

Addy pushed the Power button on her computer and the light from the screen cut through the room's darkness. Her face glowed in the light, her skin appearing pale and soft, her light brown hair nearly glowing. She knew that she'd gotten the e-mail. She saw the e-mail come in on her phone during the day, but she didn't dare click on the link, not with other people around who might see her do it. She couldn't risk having someone see where the link embedded in the e-mail went. She was careful. She knew the game that she was playing. It was a game within a game within a game, but it was more than that. It was life versus death. Freedom versus paranoia. She opened up her e-mail. Before clicking on the link, she took a deep breath and listened. She knew she was alone in her apartment, but she also knew that you can never be too sure. She heard nothing and then she clicked on the link.

The site the e-mail linked to loaded almost instantly, being free of pictures, graphics, videos, animation, or any other bells and whistles. Addy felt her pulse quicken as her computer screen filled with words, nothing but words. She risked her life almost every day searching for people who were on the run from killers and yet her pulse quickened like this only when she opened up this Web page. The text on the page was dark green. The background was bright yellow. Those were the colors of the Uprising. The site wasn't password protected. Anyone could get on it if they knew where to go. That wasn't an easy task, though. The URL changed almost daily, like a code, from one random selection of twenty-two characters to another. The only way to know the URL on any given day was to receive an e-mail with a link. Addy had been getting the e-mails for nearly two years now. Someone had found her after she'd been talking to others in a chat room. The message they gave her then was simple. *What you're doing isn't safe. Nothing is safe. This is safer.* Then she started getting e-mails.

Something was different now. In all the time Addy'd been working at this site it had never been buzzing like this before. Even though what was talked about on the site had always felt real to Addy, now it felt somehow more *real* even if she didn't know what that meant.

Addy scrolled down the page. The middle of the page was filled with long messages voted there by the page's visitors. New messages appeared on the left-hand side of the page, ready to be read and voted on. Most messages would never be promoted to the page's center. There was so much fluff, so much conjecture, so many rumors. You could only count on your own instincts to find the truth. On the right-hand side of the page were various discussion boards. Addy glanced over them, looking to see if anyone whose handle she recognized had posted anything recently. These people were Addy's friends. Sometimes she felt like they were the only real friends she had. That's because they were the same as her: young, frustrated, and angry at the older generations for failing to make the world any better and, in a lot of ways, making it worse. To Addy, it seemed as if nothing in the history of the War had ever changed and, worse, that nobody had ever really tried to change it. It wasn't that she wasn't appreciative of what Reggie had done for her, plucking her out of the War to work with the Underground. She simply didn't believe that they were doing enough.

The site was alive. Addy could see it change as she watched, hitting Refresh over and over again. She didn't recognize anyone on the discussion boards. Addy skipped over the new messages. They were coming quickly, a new one posted every few minutes. She went to the center of the page. A new message from Dutty had risen to the top. His posts always rose to the top, but they were coming much more frequently now. Every one of his messages made Addy's hair stand on end.

> *Children of Paranoia,*
>
> *Don't be afraid. Fear is how they control you. They teach you that paranoia is your friend, that paranoia is the only thing keeping you alive. Even if those words ring true, ask yourself if a survival through paranoia is a survival worth clinging to.*
>
> *They want you to be afraid because it's the fear that keeps us apart. It's the fear that separates us. It's the fear that keeps us from talking to each other and realizing that the Emperor, while maybe not yet naked, is wearing tattered robes that are frayed at the edges and loose in the seams. Pulling one loose thread might not do anything, but if we all grab a thread and pull at the same time, those threads will unravel.*
>
> *I know that some of you are itching for a call to action. I know that you're eager to stop what you're doing, to stop fighting, to stop running, to stop hiding, to stop hiding others. All I can say is "Soon." For now, you can only do one thing to help the revolution: stop being afraid.*
>
> *As always without fear,*
>
> *Dutty*

Addy felt a chill run down her spine as she read the post. When Dutty wrote that people were eager to stop hiding others and to act, it was like he was speaking directly to her, like he knew about the work she'd been doing with the Underground. Addy had decided to stop being afraid years ago, though. Now she was merely waiting, trying to figure out what role she might play in the big things that she was sure were coming. Addy looked at Dutty's words, trying to find some specific meaning for her, trying to find a direction in them, even though she knew that there was no secret message for her in the words. Addy was unsure of what she could possibly have to offer the Uprising. She was only twenty-two years old. She'd run from the War when she was nineteen, when Reggie personally recruited her into the Underground. She'd been helping to hide people since she was twenty, but she was still green and raw. Before she ran away, Addy only had a desk job in the War, and an entry-level one at that. She had one kill under her belt—during a botched pickup for the Underground. The man they were trying to pick up had been followed. She barely remembered killing the man who had followed him. She'd read rumors that Dutton was only twenty-six. Maybe changing the world was a young person's game.

It was Dutty's third post that week. Already, multiple conversations had broken out on the sidebar about what it all meant, especially about what Dutty meant when he said "soon." Addy skimmed a few of the conversations. The sidebars were so full of rumors that Addy never bothered to spend too much time on them. Tonight, new comments popped up by the second. Addy had never seen the message boards this alive before. Her eyes could barely keep up. She scanned the stories. Almost all of them were about the Child. Conversations were raging about how *he* had turned eighteen. Addy knew that a lot of people had been waiting for this day for years, though she didn't understand what they expected to happen. The rumors ran rampant in front of her. Arguments erupted about what had happened to the Child. One camp of people claimed that both sides had sent people to recruit him to their side. Offshoots of that camp argued over which side he would join and why. Other people restated rumors that the two sides had both sent people to kill him. Some even went so far as to say that the two sides had joined forces to try to rid themselves of the troublesome boy forever. Then those people who believed that the Child was being hunted went on to argue about whether he was currently dead or alive.

It had been a long time since Addy had paid much attention to the stories about the Child. She had listened to them when she was a kid, but she worried that people were putting too much faith in fairy tales. She worried about what would happen to the Uprising when the Child, if he was even real, turned out to be one big disappointment. The contingent on the message boards who argued that he must already be dead pointed out the unassailable fact that he was essentially an innocent who had little chance in a fight against real soldiers. More than a few suggested that he'd be dead before he even knew why. Addy didn't want to agree with them, but she did. What chance did the Child have? She wanted desperately for everyone to stop searching for a savior and just get up and fight. But she kept reading. She read the messages by the people who believed that Christopher was alive for no other reason than because they wanted to believe it, because that belief gave them hope. Soon the messages were popping up faster than Addy could read them. She began to feel overwhelmed. For the first time in over an hour, she took her eyes off the computer screen and stared into the emptiness of her room. Then she closed her Web browser.

Addy hit a button, completely wiping her hard drive of every potentially personalizing keystroke and cookie. It took a couple of minutes before the computer was clean. She wiped the computer before turning it off every time. You couldn't be too careful. Then she powered off. A second later, the screen went dark and her room went completely dark with it. Addy sighed and stood up to get ready for bed. She went to sleep that night trying to focus on Dutty's message. The problem was, no matter how hard she tried, her brain kept coming back to a question that was posted in one of the chains about the Child. *If Christopher is alive, where is he now?*

Four

Christopher was in the passenger seat of the car, heading south. The only thing slowing them down was the rain. Max, the stranger, was driving. Christopher was asleep, his head bouncing lightly against the passenger-side window. Christopher had spent two full days and nights in the hotel room in Montreal. He barely slept. Max stayed with him, leaving only periodically to pick up food. Max refused to use room service. He didn't trust it. Holed up in the room with Max, Christopher eventually asked the stranger, "Who are you?"

"Max," Max answered without saying any more. Max knew that it wasn't worth telling Christopher anything until Christopher finished reading the journals. So Max gave Christopher the journals and then sat quietly in the room with him for two days as Christopher read every page.

Once, when Christopher was alone and Max was out getting them something to eat, Christopher dared to call his mother. Even as he dialed, he wasn't sure what he was going to say to her. He didn't want her to be worried or to think that he'd run away from them. He loved them. He loved them even more after reading about his birth parents, after having it confirmed once and for all that his parents didn't bring him into this world. If they had brought him into this world, he'd have that to hold against them.

But no, all they did was love him and try to protect him. Love they could do. Expecting them to be able to protect him from what he was up against wouldn't be fair.

"Mom," Christopher said when she picked up the phone before it had finished even its first ring.

"Christopher, where are you?" His mother's voice was trembling. He could tell by the sound of her voice that she'd been on the verge of panic for days. "Are you in trouble?"

"I'm okay, Mom," Christopher said. He began to stammer, almost unable to get the words out. "I can't tell you where I am."

"There were bodies here," Christopher's mother said. "They found three dead bodies and you disappeared. Have you been kidnapped?" Christopher could hear the sound of his father's voice saying something to his mother in the background, like they'd been doing nothing since he'd left but sitting in that room together waiting for him to call.

He thought about lying for a second. It would be a useful lie. He could tell them that he'd been kidnapped. It wasn't too far from the truth. "No, Mom," he said instead. "There's just some stuff going on. Some stuff I need to take care of."

A moment of silence passed between them while Christopher's mother decided whether or not she should say what she eventually said next. "Did you have anything to do with those men who were killed?" she asked him. "You can tell me if you did, Christopher. We'll love you no matter what."

A lump developed in Christopher's throat. He wanted to lie to her now even more than before, but he didn't know how to lie to his mother. "It's not what it looks like, Mom. Please trust me."

His mother cut him off before he could say anything else. "Come home, Christopher," she ordered with a force that Christopher hadn't heard since he was a little boy. "We can help you. Whatever it is, we can help you. We love you."

"I love you too, Mom. I'll come home as soon as I can. Don't worry about me. I'll call. I promise."

Muffled voices came through the line for a few seconds. "Your father wants to talk to you," Christopher's mother said.

"Okay," Christopher answered and then waited for the phone to be passed.

"Chris"—his father's voice was hoarse—"whatever problems you're having, we can help." *No you can't*, Christopher thought. *Not this time.* "Whatever it is, we'll stand by you."

"Dad," Christopher said, letting the tears flow now but doing everything in his power to keep his voice steady. "I need to handle this on my own. I promise I'll come back. I promise everything will be okay."

"You're still a kid, Chris. I know that you don't think you are. I know how smart you are and how independent you are, but you're still only a kid. Come home, please." It had been years since Christopher felt like a kid, but he felt like a child again now, talking to his father on the phone.

"I'm sorry, Dad. Not yet. Soon, but not yet. I love you both so much. I want you to know how much I appreciate everything you've done for me." He could hear his mother's muffled voice in the background now, saying something to his father. "Please don't say anything else. I have to go." Christopher waited for a moment and then hung up.

Later that same day, when Christopher finished reading the journals, he had a million questions, too many to organize in his own head. So he asked Max only one. "So what now?"

"We need to leave the city. I need to get you out of here. We've been here too long already. It's too dangerous to stay any longer."

"If I go with you, where would we go?"

"Florida," Max answered. "There's someone there who knew your mother, someone who wants to help you."

"And then what?" Christopher asked.

"We think we can clean you. We think that we can keep you safe."

"What does that mean?"

"We think we can keep you hidden from all the people chasing you."

"For how long?"

Max didn't have to answer. Christopher knew what Max's silence meant. He'd read the journals. "So I run and hide for the rest of my life?" he asked.

Max put his hand on Christopher's shoulder. It was a brotherly gesture. "That's true whether you come with me or not," Max replied. "That's true for all of us. You don't get to pick between running and not running. Your only choice is between running with us and running alone."

Christopher slipped his phone out of his pocket and looked down at it. He was up to fourteen unanswered texts from Evan. The last one read, "i talked to your parents. now I'm worried too."

"Okay," Christopher said to Max. "Let's go to Florida."

The rain splattered on their windshield. Their headlights reflected off the wet asphalt on the highway. The drive from Montreal to Florida would take more than twenty-four hours, but Max didn't plan on stopping. Somewhere in upstate New York, Christopher woke up for a second. "Do you know what happened to Maria?" he asked, almost certain that he already knew the answer.

"You mean your mother?" Max asked.

"You know who I mean," Christopher said.

"She went to prison in Ohio for killing some kid. I heard that she turned herself in after giving you away." Max squinted, peering through the rain pelting the front windshield.

"And then?"

Max looked over at Christopher, trying to make a judgment call about how much the boy could take. "They killed her the day she was released. They couldn't let her live," Max said. "She meant too much to too many people. She was too big a liability."

"How so?"

"It's what she represented. To a lot of people out there, your mother was more than merely the girlfriend of a martyr and the friend of a traitor. She's a legend in her own right and the mother of a hero."

"I'm no hero," Christopher said to Max.

"I know. That's why I'm taking you to Florida."

Max believed that he was telling Christopher the truth when he told Christopher that his mother was dead. He had no reason to think that Reggie would have lied to him. Christopher had no reason to believe he was being told lies either. He put his head back against the passenger-side window and slowly went back to sleep.

Max kept driving through the rain.

Five

Addy felt the buzz in the compound before she had any idea what was going on. All she knew was that something was happening. As usual, she felt out of the loop. Everyone else seemed to be talking to each other in quick glances and secret whispers. Even though Addy couldn't make out the words being whispered, she could hear the excitement in the voices of the whisperers. She thought that maybe the excitement had something to do with Max's return. Before he left, Max had told Addy that he was going on an important job, but she thought that he was teasing her. That was what Max did. Addy never minded being teased by Max. It reminded her of her older brother before her older brother was killed.

Addy walked down the hall toward her desk. She eyed the others as they spoke under their breath. About thirty people total worked at the compound. She counted more than twenty of them there today. She'd never seen the compound so crowded before. Addy looked for someone, anyone, that she might have the courage to ask what was going on. If Max had been there, she would have asked him. She thought about asking Reggie but didn't have the courage. Whenever she thought about going to Reggie recently, she worried that he would somehow sense that she'd been reading about the Uprising. Addy wondered if Reggie would make her leave if he found out she'd been reading Dutty's postings. Since she couldn't find anyone to ask, Addy simply decided to wait. Whatever everyone was whispering about was going to happen whether Addy was in on the secret or not.

Six

Evan stood in the hallway in front of his open locker. He'd told his English teacher that he had to go to the bathroom. She knew he was lying. He knew that she knew that he was lying. Even so, she sighed and told him to be quick. The issue was that the school had a no-leniency policy on the use of cell phones in classrooms. Students making phone calls wasn't the problem. The problem was the texting and the cheating and the porn. The school officials might even have looked the other way if it was just the texting and cheating, but when the third teacher caught one of her students watching porn on his phone during class, the ban was instituted. Students could keep their phones in their lockers, but bringing them into the classroom was an automatic suspension. Evan considered risking it. It was absolutely killing him, sitting in class, not knowing if Christopher had texted him or e-mailed him back yet. He needed to check his phone.

So instead of going to the bathroom, Evan snuck to his locker and pulled out his phone. He looked down at it. He was up to sixteen unanswered texts and four unanswered e-mails. Christopher was beginning to piss him off. Evan wasn't getting mad at Christopher for not getting back to him. He was getting mad at Christopher for making him look like a bitch. Evan almost felt like he was stalking his best friend. How could he still not have a message? Evan took his phone and banged it against the wall, trying to see if he could force it into action. He turned the phone off and back on again. He half hoped that it was broken, but the damn thing worked fine. He'd been getting messages from his other friends. Only Christopher was absent.

Evan knew about the phone call that Christopher made to his parents. They'd called Evan right after they got off the phone with him. They tried to use the fact that Christopher called them to get more information out of Evan. They assumed that Evan knew something. They didn't believe Evan when he told them that he knew even less than they did. Evan could barely believe it himself. That pissed him off even more, the fact that Christopher took the time to call his parents but didn't make time to call his best friend—correction, his *only* friend.

Evan looked up at the clock hanging above the lockers. Only five more minutes before the bell rang. He thought about sending another text to Christopher, blistering him, trying to guilt him into a response, but he controlled himself. He had to keep a little pride. He knew that Christopher would get back to him eventually. He also knew that whenever Christopher did, whatever Christopher was going to tell him was going to be huge. Evan knew that Christopher kept some secrets from him, but Evan always figured that he'd learn everything in due time. Evan wasn't even sure if Christopher knew his own secrets. That was what made all of this so painful. Evan hadn't been waiting for answers for three days. He'd been waiting for years.

Evan also knew about the bodies in the woods. They had to be connected to Christopher's disappearance somehow. Stuff like that didn't happen every day—not in their little shit pan of a town anyway. Despite everything, Evan couldn't imagine Christopher doing something like that, at least not unless he had to, but Evan had no idea what Christopher was capable of if he were ever cornered. The thought of it scared Evan a little.

So Evan stood in front of his locker, lost in thought. He heard the droning sound of the bell in the clock over his head—the hum that preceded the actual bell. He'd been staring at his phone for five minutes, waiting for a message. "How long is this going to fucking take, Chris?" he muttered to himself. The bell rang. The other students began to flow into the hall. He watched them stream out of their classrooms, grinning and giggling. "Fuck it," Evan said to himself and slipped the phone into his pocket. "It's not like I'm going to be watching porn during history class."

Seven

The buzz in the compound didn't die. It only grew, like a balloon inflating to the verge of exploding. Then Max and Christopher arrived. Addy was sitting behind her desk when the two of them walked in. She was working with mapping programs, evaluating new locations to pick up people running from the War. She had options—Palm Beach, Miami, Orlando, even Tampa. She had heard that the close proximity to so many cities was one of the reasons that Reggie had decided to put the compound outside of Port St. Lucie. Still, she was having trouble concentrating. She was trying to ignore the excited, secretive whispers around her, but she was failing miserably.

When Max walked into the building with the stranger, the whispers stopped. The talking stopped. Everything stopped. The room became completely still and silent. Everything but Max and the stranger was put on Pause. Everyone stared at the stranger. Addy, still confused, stared at Max. Max caught her glance for a moment and smiled. Then he wordlessly escorted the stranger through the building towards Reggie's office.

Addy had had enough. She needed to know what was happening. She got up from her desk and walked over to a woman who had named herself Angelina after some obscure Bob Dylan song.

She was sweet, and though Addy wouldn't say they were friends, Addy liked her well enough. "What's going on?" Addy whispered to Angelina once Max and the stranger had walked past them. "Who is that?" she asked.

"That's the *Child*," Angelina said. Not even her whisper could cover up the excitement in her voice.

"The child?" Addy asked, confused. "He doesn't look like a child to me," she said, following the stranger with her eyes. He was young and not very tall, but she wouldn't have called him a child. He looked like a man. He looked strong and fierce and his eyes glowed.

"*Christopher*," Angelina said. "*The Child with the parents.*" Angelina's words were little more than nonsense, but Addy finally understood. She could barely believe it. He was here. Max hadn't been teasing her when he had told her that he was going on an important job. She wished she had known what was going on before they walked through the door. She would have watched Christopher more closely. She would have joined the others and stared at him unabashedly. Christopher. The Child with the parents. Addy would have killed ten men at that moment for the chance to talk to Max. Not only was Christopher real and alive but *he* was actually *there*. Addy had no idea what it all meant or what it all would mean. All she knew was that her life now felt larger and more important than it had felt only moments ago.

Maybe it was a good thing that Addy hadn't known that the stranger that Max brought into the compound was the Child. If Addy had watched Christopher closely when he walked through the door, she wouldn't have seen the person she had heard stories about since she herself was a child. Instead, she would have seen a confused and scared eighteen-year-old boy. She didn't get a close look, though, so she didn't see reality. She only saw the legend.

Eight

Christopher felt uncomfortable being marched through a room full of strangers. Hell, he would have been uncomfortable being marched through a room full of people he knew. He hated being looked at. He hated being watched. He'd spent his life trying to avoid being watched by people he couldn't even see. Now Max was marching him past people who were standing right in front of him, staring at him. He had to believe that another route existed. He was sure that the building had a back door. He and Max could have come at a different time. He wondered if Max was doing this on purpose, if Max was trying to prove some sort of point. But what point could it be and who was he trying to prove it to? Christopher didn't know and couldn't figure it out. Max barely seemed to notice the oglers. Or at least, he didn't seem to care about them. He made eye contact with only one person, the confused-looking woman in the corner with the light brown hair. Christopher had an urge to run from all of this, to cut back out the door they'd just walked through and never look back. He didn't run, though. In the few days he'd known Max, he'd begun to trust him. He figured he had to trust somebody.

Christopher had slept for almost the entire twenty-six-hour drive from Montreal to this strange building hidden in the Florida swamps. He'd tried to catch up on the sleep that he'd lost over the two days after he killed the men in the woods. To Christopher, those moments in the darkness in those woods already seemed like an eternity ago. His memory of that night was dim and impersonal, like the memory of a movie he'd seen when he was a kid. This two-day emotional roller-coaster ride had him all off-kilter. He wasn't ready when Max pulled the car up to the building, put it in park, and told Christopher that they were "here." Christopher didn't even know what he wasn't ready for. And where the fuck was "here" anyway? Max sensed Christopher's unease. In a lot of ways, Christopher was the same as all the other people Max had found and brought to this building to be cleaned and sent back out into the world. Max knew that the ways that Christopher was the same weren't important. All that mattered was how Christopher was different. "It's okay, Christopher," Max assured him. "You're safe here. The guy I'm going to introduce you to, he's someone you're going to want to meet."

So Christopher followed Max into the compound and felt the eyes of all those people staring at him. Instead of meeting their gazes, Christopher put his head down and walked. No one made a sound. When they were a few steps into the hallway on the other side of the crowded room, Christopher asked Max in a whisper, "Is it always this quiet?"

Max looked at Christopher. Christopher still had no idea who he was or what he represented. "No," Max answered.

Nine

Reggie could hear Christopher and Max coming down the hall. He could hear the wall of silence that surrounded them. Reggie was nervous. He could barely remember the last time that he'd been this nervous. He'd been scared plenty of times, but the last time he could remember being nervous was more than eighteen years ago when he was hiding in a tiny apartment in New York with a woman he didn't know while running from the War for the first time. That felt like a very long time ago.

Max led Christopher into Reggie's office. Like all the others, Reggie stared at the boy. He had a different reason for staring, though. Even though Reggie had never seen Christopher before, he would have recognized him instantly, anywhere. It was the shape of his eyes more than anything else. It was like looking at a shadow of a reflection of someone he knew a long time ago. Reggie tried to reconcile the image of the boy standing in front of him with everything else that he knew. He tried to really look at the person standing in front of him, forgetting about the boy's history, forgetting about the power that the boy unknowingly had at his fingertips and what someone could do with that power, remembering only a promise that he'd made a long time ago.

Reggie stood up from his desk and took a few steps toward

Christopher, meeting Christopher halfway across the room. "Christopher," Max said as Reggie approached them, "this is Reggie. Reggie, this is Christopher." The two of them—one a tall thirty-six-year-old black man with graying hair and one a powerfully built but scared white boy three days past his eighteenth birthday—shook hands. "I believe Reggie knew your mother, Christopher," Max said by way of introduction.

Christopher recognized Reggie from the description in Maria's journal, focusing on the startling green color of Reggie's eyes. "I read about you," Christopher announced.

Reggie nodded. "Would you mind leaving us alone for a few minutes, Max?" Reggie said to the man who had already become the second best friend Christopher had in the world.

"Sure thing," Max said. He backed out of the office, closing the door behind him.

"So what did you read?" Reggie said to Christopher once they were alone.

"Maria talked about you in her journal," Christopher answered him.

"So you know that your mother saved my life. In fact, if it wasn't for her, neither of us would be here. So we have at least one thing in common." Reggie laughed at his own joke, trying to be simultaneously casual and authoritative. He waited for some sort of response from Christopher, but none came. "Do you know what we do here?" Reggie finally asked Christopher after waiting out the silence.

Christopher nodded. "Max told me."

"Before or after you got in the car to come here?"

"Before."

"That's good." Reggie walked over to a cabinet that was pushed up against the far wall. "I'm going to have a drink," he said as he opened the cabinet door. Inside were a bottle of whiskey and a few glasses. "Do you want to have a drink?" Reggie lifted two glasses into the air.

Christopher shook his head. "I don't drink."

"That's probably smart," Reggie said, sounding more like a father than he wanted to. "Will you be offended if I still do?"

"No," Christopher said. "I'm a pretty hard person to offend."

Reggie poured out a half glass of whiskey and carried it back to his desk. He sat down in the chair behind the desk. Following Reggie's lead, Christopher took a seat in one of the other chairs. Reggie leaned back in his seat and took a long swig from his glass. "So you read your parents' journals. That's good. After reading them, do you think you understand how dangerous this War is? How big this War is?"

Christopher thought about his answer, rehearsing it in his head before saying anything. He knew that saying "yes" or "no" wasn't adequate. "I've spent every single day of my life afraid, without having any idea what I was afraid of. Everything I've done in my life was done out of fear. The other night, two men tried to kill me in the woods outside the house where I grew up. Instead, I killed them, but I know that I got lucky. Everything else that I know, I read in the journals of the people that you guys keep calling my mother and father, but I get the impression that they didn't know how big or how dangerous the War was either. Do you know how big and how dangerous the War is?"

Reggie picked up his whiskey and finished it in two massive gulps. "I only know that it's too big and too dangerous for anyone to make it alone." Reggie lifted his eyes over the rim of his glass and looked at Christopher. "Especially you."

"Max already gave me this speech."

"Yeah, but he didn't know your mother. Your mother wanted to get you out of the War, and I think I can do that if that's what you want. I owe her that much." Reggie stood up and walked back to the cabinet to refill his glass. It would be more than he'd had to drink at one sitting in years. Normally, he kept the whiskey and the glasses in his office only for ceremonial purposes. Today, he needed it. He poured another three fingers of whiskey into the glass. He wondered if he should tell Christopher that the War was getting bloodier, that more people were running away, that more people were getting killed, that some people were even talking about revolution. He wondered if he should tell Christopher about the plans that he already knew about. He wondered if he should tell Christopher what the people talking about revolution said about him. Reggie drank half of the second glass before stepping back toward the desk. He could feel the alcohol already rushing through his veins. Reggie could see Maria in Christopher's face. He looked at Christopher and remembered drinking with Christopher's mother and her friend Michael in the apartment in New York. Maria and Michael were famous now. Famous and dead. "Will you let us help you?"

"What if I don't want to run?" Christopher asked. Reggie held his breath during the pregnant pause that followed the question, waiting to see what Christopher would say next, trying to think of how he would respond if Christopher told him that instead of running he wanted to fight. *If he asks to fight*, Reggie thought, *do I still have to keep the promises that I made or can I tell this boy who he is? Can I tell him that he alone possesses the power to end this War?* But the dilemma that Reggie was almost wishing for never crystallized. "What if I just want to go home?" the boy said, and Reggie once again remembered that Christopher, with all the power he had, was still a boy, and he remembered why he'd made the promise in the first place.

"You can't. You run with us or you run alone."

Christopher knew what that meant, but he didn't know what to say. He didn't know what choice he had, but he wasn't ready to forsake his parents in Maine or Evan without thinking about his options first. "I need to think about it," Christopher finally answered.

Thinking is dangerous, Reggie thought. "Okay," he said. "You can stay with Max tonight. I'll let him know. But you don't have a lot of time. Staying in one place for any amount of time is dangerous. I can't guarantee that you'll be safe here."

"I understand," Christopher said.

Reggie stood up and walked toward the door. His legs were already wobbly from the liquor. He girded himself and walked out the door to find Max. Reggie closed the door behind him. Christopher watched the door close and then he was alone in the dimly lit, windowless room. He had an urge to get up and pour himself a drink from Reggie's whiskey bottle. He fought it. He knew that it wouldn't do him any good. He didn't know anything that would.

Ten

Alejandro scooped up a handful of sand from the beach and let it slowly sift through his fingers. The sand was as fine and white as baby powder. It was still cool from the night before. The sun would heat it up soon enough. Before long, the sand would be so hot that you would barely be able to walk on it.

Alejandro looked down the beach. It stretched out in front of him, curving around the blue water of the Pacific Ocean. The waves came crashing onto the shore, endlessly battering it into submission. Dozens of palm trees lined the back of the beach where the white sand turned quickly into jungle. From where he was kneeling Alejandro could see the entire mile-long beach. He was alone. The beach would get more crowded later, but not by much. The tourists hadn't discovered this beach yet. Alejandro knew that they would find it eventually, but probably not for another few years. Still, plans were already being drawn up to move the Intelligence Center. The fact was that they'd put the Intelligence Center where it was, in the jungles of Costa Rica, specifically because of how remote the place was. As the world encroached on them, the relocation plans would have to be taken more seriously. After fifteen years working at the Intelligence Center, Alejandro had heard all the talk. He also knew that if everything went according to plan, moving the Intelligence Center would become a moot point. They wouldn't have to move it. They could simply stand by while the jungle reclaimed it.

One way or another, it would all be over in less than seventy-two hours. All of what? Alejandro couldn't be sure. He tried to stay positive but couldn't imagine the world without the War. So instead, he focused on what he had to do. He knew that he couldn't control anything else or anyone else. He had to play his part and then have faith. Whether the War ended or not, this was going to be something.

Alejandro stood up. Some of the white sand still clung to his hands so he wiped it off on his jeans. He looked out over the water. A boat would be coming soon—a boat full of people and weapons—and Alejandro would be there to greet them, to pull them ashore and to tell them the plan. Before that, Alejandro said a silent prayer to himself and hoped that Christopher knew what he was doing.

Eleven

It was well past midnight when Christopher first heard the noise. He had been drifting in and out of sleep for over three hours, but the sleep wouldn't stick. Christopher kept thinking about the decision he was supposed to be contemplating. He kept hearing Reggie's voice saying over and over again, *Staying in one place for any amount of time is dangerous. I can't guarantee that you'll be safe here.* So Christopher was awake, lying on the pull-out couch with his eyes closed, when he heard the light knock on Max's condo door. Christopher opened his eyes and looked at the clock. It was a quarter past one in the morning. The knock wasn't loud, but that didn't make Christopher feel any better. For as long as he could remember, the sound of knocking on a door had terrified him. It was fear bordering on a phobia. He lay still for a moment, trying to make sure that he was actually awake and wasn't merely having a nightmare. He heard the faint rapping sound again and knew that this was real. His heart began to pound, his body excited by the confirmation that it was right not to let him sleep. Christopher had to remind himself that he really couldn't trust anyone. Dangers lurked everywhere and now one of them was knocking on Max's door. As quietly as he could, Christopher stood up and tiptoed toward the hallway.

Max had heard the knock too. Christopher peeked through the crack in his door and saw Max already standing in the hallway. Max had offered to let Christopher sleep in his bed, but Christopher refused. He was pretty sure that he wasn't going to be able to sleep anyway, so he figured there was no reason to waste the bed. All the lights in the condo were off, but enough light came in through the windows for Christopher to see in blacks and whites and grays. Christopher looked over at Max and stepped into the hallway. Max looked scared. Seeing the fear in Max's face jumpstarted Christopher's heartbeat again.

Max's condo didn't stand out in any way. It was on the edge of the development. You had to make a few turns to find it. You wouldn't stumble upon this place if you were lost. Whoever was knocking on the door had found them. It was a two-bedroom condo, with both bedrooms upstairs. Max had turned the second bedroom into an office with the pull-out couch. The office, the bedroom, and a bathroom were the only rooms upstairs. The stairs ran down into the living room. The ground floor had the living room, dining room, kitchen, and another bathroom. From the window in the upstairs bedroom, you could climb out onto the roof.

Max walked over to Christopher. His footsteps were silent. "Go into my bedroom," Max whispered. "If anything sounds suspicious, leave through the window. When you're safe, call Reggie. Here's his phone number," Max said, handing Christopher a slip of paper. Max looked Christopher in the eyes and then gestured at the piece of paper. "Nobody has that. Nobody gets that. Die before anyone else gets to see that number."

"Who do you think is knocking?" Christopher whispered back.

"It's probably nothing," Max answered, "but just because they knock doesn't mean that they're going to wait for an invitation to come inside."

Max made his way down the stairs. Christopher walked toward the door to Max's bedroom. Then he stopped. If they had found him here, if they had come for him here, he wasn't going to be able to escape out the bedroom window. If they'd come for him here, there would be no escape. Maybe he could escape if they didn't know that he was there, if they'd only come for Max. *So*, Christopher thought, *the only thing that escaping would mean would be that I was too chickenshit to help my new friend.* So instead of walking into the bedroom, Christopher waited until Max had gotten all the way down the stairs and then he followed him, checking each step ahead of time to avoid any loose or creaky floorboards. Once he was halfway down, he stopped and listened.

He heard Max open the front door. He could only assume that Max had looked outside to see who was there before opening the door. Still, every muscle in Christopher's body tensed when he heard the hinges squeak as the door swung open. The paranoia didn't stop now that Christopher knew who was watching him. It only became worse.

Then Christopher heard Max speak. "What are you doing here?" he whispered to whoever was on the other side of the door.

"Why didn't you tell me?" Christopher heard a woman's voice respond.

"Why didn't I tell you what?" Max asked.

"Don't be a jackass." Even standing in the darkness around the corner from her, Christopher could hear the frustration in the woman's voice. "Why didn't you tell me you were going to pick *him* up?"

"Reggie wouldn't let me. He wouldn't let me tell anyone. He didn't want to take any chances." Max sounded apologetic.

"Because you're the only one Reggie really trusts," the woman said. Max didn't respond, making Christopher wonder if what the woman was saying was true. "Why are you acting so weird?" the woman asked Max, followed immediately by, "Why won't you let me inside?" When Max still didn't answer, it finally hit her. "He's here, isn't he?"

"I'm sorry, Addy," Max said. "I'll tell you everything as soon as I can, but you really should go. It's dangerous."

"You want to know what's dangerous, Max? Not letting me into your fucking house. That's what's dangerous." And that was that. Christopher could hear the woman step inside and could tell from the silence that Max had done nothing to stop her.

Christopher didn't move. He stood still in the darkness on the stairs, not knowing what else to do. He noticed that neither Max nor the woman made any sound as they walked. They moved liked ghosts, like they didn't even exist. Christopher saw them before he heard them. They walked beneath him, past the bottom of the stairs and toward the living room. They sat down in the darkness, Max in a chair facing away from Christopher and the woman on the sofa with her shoulders square to Christopher but her face turned toward Max. Even through the darkness, Christopher recognized her. She was the confused woman from the compound that Max had made eye contact with.

"Tell me what he's like," the woman said as soon as they sat down.

Max didn't hesitate before answering. "He's like the rest of us were when we were sixteen and we first heard about the War except that he's two years older, twice as smart, and three times as paranoid. Oh, and he's the only person I ever heard of who got their first two kills before their eighteenth birthday was over."

"He what?" Addy asked. Max simply nodded in response to her question. "Two kills?" Addy asked, barely believing it.

"Yeah. They went after him. He lived. They didn't."

"What are you guys going to do with him?" Addy asked.

"Reggie wants us to clean him."

Addy wasn't sure if she was surprised. She understood. He was merely a boy, but it seemed such a waste. "What does he know about the War?" Addy asked. Everybody wanted to know what he knew.

"His parents left him journals. I've told him a little bit. I don't know what Reggie told him."

"So he got most of the information from those journals?" Max nodded. "So most of the information that he has is eighteen years old?" Addy asked. Christopher hadn't even thought about how things might have changed since Maria last penned an entry in her journal. He'd been too focused on how crazy the world in the journals was to think about how the world might have gotten even crazier. "Shouldn't someone tell him what's been going on for the last eighteen years? Shouldn't someone tell him about everything that's happened?"

Christopher listened to Addy's question and his nerves made his body twitch. It was only one slight twitch, but the movement was enough. Addy caught sight of him out of the corner of her eye. She looked up through the darkness toward the stairs. Christopher saw Addy's whole face, her sharp features, her thin lips, her pupils enlarged by the darkness. "Maybe you should tell him," Addy said to Max while motioning toward the stairs. Max turned until they were both staring at Christopher through the dim light.

"Chris, why don't you come down here so I can introduce the two of you?" Max stood up and took a few steps toward Christopher. The lights in the room were on a dimmer. Max turned it up just enough for the three of them to be able to see in color but left it low enough that it wouldn't draw attention from anyone outside.

Addy stood up. Max led Christopher over to her. She held out her hand. Christopher shook it.

"Christopher, this is my friend Addy. Addy," Max said, now

stretching out each word as if teasing them out of his mouth, "this is Christopher."

Addy stood there, speechless. "It's nice to meet you," Christopher said to her before she could find the right words to say.

"It's nice to meet you too," Addy echoed.

The three of them sat down. Max moved so that he was sitting on the couch next to Addy. Christopher sat in the leather chair. "I didn't mean to eavesdrop," Christopher began, apologizing to Max.

Max waved off Christopher's apology with a flick of his hand. "It's not my job to keep secrets from you, Chris."

"He needs to know," Addy said to Max, her voice stern.

"I need to know what?" Christopher asked the two of them, not caring who answered.

"Addy believes that the War's been getting worse since your parents wrote their journals," Max said.

"I'm not the only one," Addy argued.

"What does that mean? Worse?" Christopher asked.

Addy answered before Max had a chance, before he could sanitize what she was going to say. "More people are getting killed. People are getting killed younger." Addy looked at Max. "More people are running," she said. "You *know* that's true, Max. You can't deny that."

Max nodded. "Yes, more people are running," he agreed. "But there are a lot of reasons for that." Max glanced at Christopher when he spoke those words.

Addy kept talking. This was her chance to do something noteworthy, something worth a posting on the Web site. "And the more people run, the angrier both sides get and the more violent. And the angrier both sides get and the more violent, the more people get scared and run. Third verse, same as the first. It's a snake eating its own tail." Addy glanced over at Max. "Tell him about Englishman's Bay."

Christopher looked at the two of them, scared that he wasn't going to be able to keep up. "What's Englishman's Bay?" Christopher asked.

"I'm not sure that it's really relevant," Max said. "It's more a story about poor planning than anything else." But it was too late. Addy had planted the seed in Christopher's head and now Christopher needed to know. Max could see that on Christopher's face. "Englishman's Bay is a small bay on the island of Tobago, just off of South America. It leads up to a steep, crescent-shaped beach. To get there by anything but boat you had to hike or drive through miles of jungle." Christopher listened without any clue as to where any of this was going. "Anyway, a few of the different groups in the Underground decided that, instead of trying to clean certain people by changing their identities and hiding them in normal society, they should send people to Englishman's Bay and let the exiles start their own community there, inland from the water, where no one would find them. The idea was to create a community that the two sides of the War didn't know about, a place where people could live unafraid."

"Some sort of utopia?" Christopher asked.

"No." Max shook his head. "Just a place with less fear. The truth is that they were scrounging for other options because there were so many refugees from the War that it was becoming almost impossible to hide them all. So the Englishman's Bay community had grown to about thirty-five people. It went well at first. They built buildings, dug a well. It was turning out exactly like they planned, a new world hidden away from the paranoia of the War." Max paused, not wanting to tell the rest of the story. Christopher stared at him, unwilling to let him stop. "But it turns out that you can't keep a secret like that. One night, after they'd been there for about five months, the hunters came. They came by boat. They anchored near the shore and waded through the water onto the beach. They were trained. They were armed with machine guns, flamethrowers, and night-vision goggles. The community had set up a night watch, but the hunters came too fast. The night watchman was merely the first one they killed. When they got to the little village the people had been building, the hunters used flamethrowers to raze it. Some people say that a few of the buildings were set on fire with people still inside. More members of the community were killed trying to fight the hunters as they flooded in. It wasn't long before the hunters outnumbered the remaining villagers. Those that weren't killed in the raid were taken away and never heard from again. The only people to make it back out into the world were two kids who were under the age of eighteen. The kids' parents had run away with them, trying to save them from the War." Max shot Christopher a knowing look. "After the raid, the kids were allowed to rejoin the War. They were given new homes and new names, but they didn't forget what happened. They were the ones who told the stories, exactly like the hunters wanted them to."

"And the hunters were from both sides of the War. They were working together?" Christopher asked, remembering how Max told him that the two sides were working together to try to kill him.

"We don't know," Max answered.

"Did you guys know any of the people that were sent down there? Were any of them people you saved?"

Max shook his head firmly. "No," he said. "Reggie never sent anyone there. He always thought it was too risky."

"Where does Reggie send his people?" Christopher asked, but everyone in the room knew what he meant. He wanted to know where Reggie might send him.

"It doesn't matter where they go," Addy answered him. "They just keep running—forever."

They kept talking until Addy left about an hour later. Max suggested that Christopher try to get some sleep, as if that were even a possibility. Instead, Christopher waited until Max went to bed and then he took out his phone. "you there?" Christopher texted to Evan.

He got a reply in a matter of seconds. "yes," was all it said. Christopher closed the office door and dialed Evan's phone number.

"What the fuck, man? This is not how you treat a friend," Christopher heard Evan's voice say before he even heard the phone ring.

"I'm sorry," Christopher said, happy to hear Evan's voice even if he was angry.

"What the hell is going on?" Evan asked, the anger in his voice already slipping away.

"You'll never believe me if I tell you," Christopher said, staring at the empty walls around him.

"Don't give me that shit," Evan ordered.

"I can't even really talk," Christopher said to Evan. "I wanted to get back to you so that you would know that I wasn't ignoring you. Things are a little crazy now."

"You can't leave me hanging like this," Evan said, his voice full of nervous excitement. "At least tell me one thing—did you kill those guys in the woods?"

Christopher thought for a second about how to answer. He knew that he was eventually going to tell Evan everything, as soon as he figured out how. Maybe this was a good place to start. "Yeah," Christopher said, "but only because they tried to kill me first."

"Holy shit." Evan spoke half into the phone, half into the air.

"Listen, Evan, I'll try to call you again soon. Check in on my parents for me. Don't tell them that you talked to me, but try to make sure they're okay." Christopher hung up the phone without waiting for a response. What response could he hope for anyway?

Then he eased himself back down on to the pull-out sofa and put his head on his pillow. Since sleep wasn't coming anytime soon, he stared up at the ceiling and began to count every day of his life that contained at least one distinct memory. He'd been alive for roughly six thousand five hundred days. He finished counting the ones that he could actually remember long before he fell asleep.

Twelve

Addy marched straight into Reggie's office early on the day after she'd met Christopher in Max's apartment. She hadn't been invited, never mind summoned. She wasn't about to sit around and wait for an invitation this time. Reggie was surprised when he saw her walk through his door. Reggie always claimed to have an open-door policy, but no one ever took him up on it—until Addy that day. "Addy?" Reggie said as she closed his office door behind her.

Addy got right to the point. "If he agrees to let us hide him, I want in. I want to be a part of it" were the first words out of her mouth.

Reggie was caught off guard for a second, but only a second. "Christopher?" he guessed.

"Of course, Christopher," she answered him. "Who else would I be talking about?"

"You know that he hasn't even agreed to let us help him yet, right?" Reggie asked her.

"I know. But if he does agree to go, I want to be on the team that helps hide him."

"And if he doesn't agree to let us clean him?" Reggie asked. Addy swore that Reggie was more than staring at her—he was staring *into* her. Reggie had known for quite some time that Addy wasn't happy. He did what he could to make her happy. She was good at what she did, but she was also so young and so hungry. Addy understood what Reggie was asking her. Reggie was asking if she was planning on going with Christopher even if he refused to let them hide him.

"I hope I don't have to answer that question."

"Me too," Reggie agreed.

Thirteen

The three of them drove away from the compound in a car that same afternoon. Max drove. Addy sat in the passenger seat. Christopher sat alone in the back. They were driving farther south. For now, they were only headed to Palm Beach. The drive took about an hour and a half—door to door—from the compound to the house where they were supposed to spend the night. They didn't know where they'd be headed after that. Reggie didn't want to waste any time. As soon as Christopher told Reggie that he was willing to be cleaned, Reggie started working the phones and making arrangements.

Christopher wasn't sure when he actually made his decision. He wasn't even sure that he actually made a decision. He just didn't see any other options. He did negotiate one point, though. He told Reggie that he was willing to be cleaned only if Max went with him. Christopher was surprised when he learned that the girl from the night before, Addy, would be going with them too. He wasn't upset about it, just surprised.

Even though it was hot out, Max drove with the windows open and the air conditioner off. It wasn't something Christopher would have ever done, but the wind whipping by him felt good on his skin. Without saying a word to Max, Addy leaned forward and turned on the radio. She had to turn the volume up really loud so they could hear it over the sound of the wind.

About ten songs later, they pulled up to the house where they were staying. It was the biggest house any of them had ever seen. "See, Chris," Max said as the three of them stepped out of their car, "running ain't so bad." But Christopher could still hear the surprise in Max's voice.

"Holy shit," Addy whispered to herself as she stared at the mansion in front of them. It was set back from the road, surrounded on all sides by ten-foot-tall bushes. Until you pulled into the wide U-shaped driveway, you couldn't tell how large the house was. It was seemingly as wide as a city block and three stories high. Even with the tall shrubs surrounding it, you could see the entire expanse of the Atlantic Ocean from the upper two floors.

"Welcome!" a voice shouted from the doorway. "Welcome, welcome, welcome." A tall, tan man walked out of the house. He had on loose-fitting linen pants and a long-sleeved white dress shirt with the sleeves rolled up. His hair was silver and slicked back but hanging loose at the sides. The man walked up to Addy first. Christopher half expected the man to bend down and kiss Addy's hand, but he shook it instead. "It's a pleasure," he said to Addy. Then he turned to Max. "My name is Jay," the man said as he shook Max's hand. He didn't wait for either Addy or Max to answer him before he turned toward Christopher. He took Christopher's hand in his. "And you must be Christopher," he said slowly, staring at Christopher as if studying him. Christopher nodded in response. "Where are your bags?" Jay said to the three of them without taking his eyes off Christopher. "I can get one of my men to carry them inside."

Max opened the trunk of the car and pulled out all three of their duffel bags. "I think we can manage," he said, slinging the bags over his shoulders and walking toward the open front door.

"Barry," Jay shouted into the house without moving, "can you come and show these folks to their rooms?" At that, a big man in a blue polo shirt and khakis stepped into the doorway, blocking Max's entrance.

"Sure thing, boss," Barry boomed in a deep, resonant voice. Then he took the duffel bags from Max without any further objections on Max's part.

"We'll have dinner in an hour," Jay informed them. Then he nodded to Barry and Barry led Max, Addy, and Christopher to their respective rooms.

Their rooms were on the same floor, spread out along a long hallway. In between their guest bedrooms were sitting rooms and studies and a pool room. Addy was dropped off first, then Max, and finally Christopher. "So you're the kid," Barry said to Chris as he led him into his room. Christopher's room was at the far end of the hallway, at the corner of the house. The massive room was bigger than the entire ground floor of the house that he'd grown up in. Christopher walked over to one of the windows. It looked out over the ocean. The sky was turning pink, and he could see white-caps out in the water.

"I guess so," Christopher answered. Barry smiled and nodded and walked out, leaving Christopher alone.

It was new to Christopher, this sudden aversion to being alone. For most of his life, all he'd wanted was to be left alone. Circumstances had, however, changed. Christopher waited until he could no longer hear Barry's footsteps in the hallway and then he went to the door of his room and peered outside. He stared down the hallway in the direction of Max's and Addy's rooms, though he couldn't even remember which doors they were stashed behind. He was hoping that they, like him, would open their doors and they would all look toward one another for comfort. Christopher waited like that for a few minutes, but neither Max nor Addy opened a door, so Christopher went back into his room. The room was large but cold. There were paintings on the wall, but they were abstract paintings and there were no pictures of family or friends. Christopher figured that maybe it was impolite for rich people to put personal pictures in their guest rooms. He walked over to the north-facing windows. From there he could see the road that they had driven down on, winding north along the coast until it disappeared from sight. Then Christopher went into the bathroom attached to his room to wash his hands and face. He honestly wondered if the next hour would actually pass or if he would be alone in this giant room forever.

While Christopher stared out his window, waiting for the time to pass, Addy, having never seen a bathroom as large and luxurious as the one attached to her room, took a bath. Max spent the time rummaging through his room, unsure of what he was looking for or even whether he would know it if he saw it.

Barry came to get them when it was time for dinner. Another member of Jay's staff, a woman named Alice, served them while they ate. They could see a third servant in the kitchen cooking. None of the servants spoke as they worked, but Christopher caught each of them staring at him when they thought no one was looking. Christopher, Addy, Max, and Jay all sat at a rectangular table in a large dining room on the ground floor with the view of the courtyard and the fountain in the back. Jay and Christopher sat at the head and foot of the table, with Addy and Max facing each other on the shorter ends.

"Well, I hope you all like your accommodations," Jay said to them as they were served the first course.

"Your house is beautiful," Addy told Jay. Christopher could smell Addy from a few feet away. Her scent wasn't overwhelming. It was simply noticeable. She smelled like rose petals.

"It's amazing," echoed Max, looking around him.

Jay looked at Christopher, waiting for his approval. "It's big," Christopher said.

"Yeah," Max agreed. "How did you come by your money?"

"Speculating," Jay said with pride. "It's amazing how simple the rest of the world seems when you grow up in a system as fucked up as ours. More wine?" Max, Addy, and even Christopher all nodded. Alice came out of the kitchen and refilled their glasses. "Though the wealth wasn't the original goal, it's merely a necessary means to an end."

"So what's the end?" Christopher asked, staring across the long, shiny table.

"Avoiding having to fight in the War." Jay swirled his wine in his glass before taking another sip. "It's something my father taught me. If you make yourself valuable in other ways, they won't ask you to fight. So I made myself valuable by literally becoming valuable."

"How does that work?" Max asked.

"Are you kidding?" Jay laughed. "I pay more in tithing to the War than I do in taxes and nobody from the War ever comes to fill in the potholes on my street."

"So what do they do for you in exchange for all that money?" Addy asked. This was new to all of them. Max and Addy knew about tithing, but this was different.

"They leave me alone and they try to keep the other side from finding me and ruining their sweet little deal."

"Are you married?" Christopher asked Jay, somewhat out of the blue.

"Divorced," Jay answered.

"Why'd you get divorced?" Addy asked, her lips loosened by the wine.

"My ex wanted to have children," Jay answered.

"And you?" Christopher asked.

Jay shook his head. "I didn't want to bring anyone else into this War."

"You have pretty strong opinions about the War," Max said.

"I hate it. Why do you think the three of you are here?" More food came out. As Alice pushed the kitchen door open, bringing out slabs of red meat for the diners, the cook glanced at Christopher again over the steaming pots and smoking burners in the kitchen.

"You're a way station. The first stop in cleaning Christopher," Addy answered over a forkful of food.

"Sure," Jay said. "I'm also paying for you to run. Your hotels, gas money, food, plane tickets if you need them. I'm paying for it all. The Underground needs money too."

"So what's in it for you?" Christopher asked the silver-haired man.

"You are," Jay answered, the levity dropping entirely out of his voice. "I just wanted to help keep you alive." He stared at Christopher. "My one condition before agreeing with Reggie to pay for your little escapade was that you stop here first so I would get to meet you."

"And have I lived up to your expectations?" Christopher asked, his face a stone.

"Have another glass of wine," Jay said to Christopher. "You have to realize that just by being alive, you mean so much to so many people. Your life is proof that the bastards aren't perfect."

"My life means a lot more to me than that," Christopher said.

"Just remember, boy, only the real crazies like the War, the ones that want to be heroes and bleed for a cause. The rest of us merely tolerate it because we don't want to be killed. Dessert, anyone?"

They were all drunk when dinner ended, all four of them. They'd gone through five bottles of wine. "I'm off to bed," Jay declared with some panache, throwing his napkin on the table and wavering only slightly when he stood. "It's been an honor to meet each of you. And you, sir," Jay said, staring at Christopher. "I didn't get this house making bad investments." And with that, he exited the room as if he were walking off the stage.

Barry led Addy, Max, and Christopher back to their rooms, and this time, when Christopher peeked out his doorway, Max and Addy were peeking out theirs as well. "It will be safer if we all stay in the same room," Max announced with only a slight slur to his speech. They all knew that it was merely an excuse to stick together. Since Christopher's room was the biggest, they all piled into it, Addy and Max carrying sheets and pillows from their beds.

Once they were all inside, Christopher closed the door. He felt an uncertain level of giddiness that he could never remember having felt before. "So what did you guys think of our host?" he asked, not entirely sure if in this crowd, Jay was the weird one or he was.

"Dude's nuts," Addy offered. Then she began to lay her blanket down on the floor on the opposite side of the room from Max.

"I'll sleep on the floor," Christopher said to Addy. "You can have the bed."

Addy laughed at him. "I don't do chivalry," she told him.

As they were settling in, Max had a sudden idea. "I know what we should do, Addy."

"What's that?" Addy asked. She was sitting next to one of the windows looking out over the ocean. Christopher couldn't see the waves, but he could hear them.

"Let's give him a name," Max said.

"Who? Christopher?" Addy asked.

"Yeah. Everybody needs a name."

"What do you mean?" Christopher asked, growing dizzy from listening to how quickly Max and Addy spoke to each other.

"Your name. If you're going to be part of the Underground, you need a new name."

Even though he'd read about it in his mother's journal, it hadn't dawned on Christopher that Max and Addy weren't his new friends' real names. "So you guys picked your own names? And you just forget the old ones?"

"Yeah," Max said. "Try to forget anyway. No one's called me anything but Max for almost ten years." Then he laughed before instructing Christopher, "Ask Addy how she got her name."

"Shut up!" Addy yelled across the room to him. Christopher felt like he was on the outside of an inside joke.

"Why, where'd you get your name?" Christopher asked meekly, hoping not to offend anyone.

"It's not a big deal," Addy said. "It's short for Adelaide—like Saint Adelaide. She was a princess, the daughter of a king, and her father arranged for her to be married to a man she didn't want to marry. When she refused to marry him, they threw her into solitary confinement in the Castle of Garda. But she was rescued by a priest who dug a tunnel under the castle walls and snuck her out."

The room was quiet for a moment and then Max stifled a laugh. "God, you take yourself so fucking seriously, Addy."

"It's better than your name," Addy shouted at Max. "At least I didn't name myself after a children's book."

Christopher looked at Max and tried to remember his favorite books from when he was young. He really had only one favorite. *"Where the Wild Things Are?"* he asked Max.

Max nodded. "Of course."

"But why?"

Max grinned a grin that could have made even his worst enemies fall in love with him. "Because I'm the king of all wild things."

"Jackass," Addy muttered, but the word was full of warmth.

"So, what name should we give Christopher?" Max asked, staring at him. And for a moment Christopher wanted nothing more in the world than to have these two people he barely knew christen him with a new name.

"I don't think he should have a new name," Addy said. She was staring at Christopher too, but she was looking at him differently than Max was. "I think he should stay Christopher."

"But everybody gets a new name," Max protested. Christopher sat up in the bed, looking from Max to Addy and back again and saying nothing. The effect of the wine was wearing off and he was becoming tired.

"Yeah, but he's not everybody," Addy said. "He's different from the rest of us. The world needs him to be Christopher."

Christopher began to feel uncomfortable beneath their gazes, particularly Addy's. "I'm tired, guys," he said, trying to end the conversation.

"Fine," Max said. "We'll have plenty of time to talk about this later." Then Max stood up and turned out the light. The room became dark except for the incoming light of the moon. "Good night, you two," Max said and lay down on his makeshift bed.

"Good night," Addy answered.

"Good night," Christopher said last. Then they all lay there silently, waiting for sleep to creep up on them. Christopher was the last one to let go of consciousness.

Fourteen

"There are people here asking questions about you."

"Who?"

"I don't know. I mean, the police have been asking everybody questions, but there are other people too. I don't know who the other people are."

"What have they been asking?"

"They've been asking if anybody knows how to get in touch with you or if anyone has any clues as to where you are or might have gone."

"Who have they asked?"

"Everybody. You'd laugh if you saw the people they were asking, people you wouldn't have been caught dead talking to. But mostly they've been concentrating on your parents, your teachers, and me. I think people might be following me. This town is getting really weird." *They can't hurt you*, Christopher almost assured Evan, remembering the rules that he'd read in his birth parents' journals. He stopped himself, though. He didn't have any faith in those rules. They seemed ludicrous. He wondered if he was putting Evan in danger merely by talking to him. They'd developed a system. Evan would text Christopher some sort of cryptic message that would have meaning only to the two of them.

Then Christopher would call Evan the next chance he had to sneak away from Addy and Max. Christopher had turned the ringer off his phone. He was getting too many strange calls. He was nervous that people might be able to track him by his cell phone, but he wasn't ready to give it up. It was the only connection he still had to home.

"When did it start?" Christopher asked Evan.

"The police have been asking questions since the day you left. The others came, I don't know, three days ago, two days after the police."

"How long have they been following you?"

"Ever since they got here, I think. Maybe before I even knew they were here."

"Has anybody threatened you?"

"No. They're nice, just fucking creepy. When are you going to tell me what's going on?"

"I can't now, not if people are asking you questions. It would make it too dangerous. How are my folks?"

"The same." Christopher felt his chest tighten. The same wasn't good. He supposed it could be worse, though. He hadn't called his parents since he and Max were holed up in the hotel room in Montreal. That was more than five days ago. Now that Christopher knew that people had been questioning them, he was sure that he'd made the right decision. He could only imagine what people would do to them if it seemed like they knew something. He'd have to wait. He didn't know how long.

"Tell them that you're sure I'm okay."

"I will," Evan assured Christopher. He paused, then said, "Are you okay?"

"Maybe we shouldn't talk for a while," Christopher answered. "Maybe it's too dangerous."

"Fuck you," Evan replied, to Christopher's relief. "I'll text you if anything happens."

"Okay." Evan hung up first. Christopher listened to the dead air for a minute or two and then went back to join Addy and Max.

Fifteen

They were all supposed to change their look. Addy chose to dye her hair red. She didn't go for just any red, though. Her hair became the color of a burning ember. Her head seemed to glow like the tip of a lit candle. Christopher and Max could barely move when they watched her come out of the bathroom. It wasn't only her hair color that changed; so much else seemed to change with it. Everything about Addy looked different. She looked stronger and more dangerous, and that was all Christopher would let himself think for now.

"Jesus, Addy," Max said when he could speak again. "They told us to try to look inconspicuous."

"No, they didn't," Addy replied. "They told us to look different. I looked inconspicuous before. That's what they told me to change."

The order had come in the day before. The three of them were at their fourth stop, if you counted the night they spent in Palm Beach. They'd been staying with random people. Max would be sent their destination and they'd go. Each of their hosts treated Christopher like he was an exotic animal, like he was either the first or the last of his kind. So he was excited when they were finally given the order to make a stop without a host. Then they were also ordered to change their appearance and Christopher wasn't so excited anymore. Now he was nervous. He figured it meant that somebody had spotted them or maybe one of their hosts had turned on them.

Max had gone first. They'd already talked about what each of them should do before sending Addy off to the store to get the supplies that they would need to make it happen. Addy came back with hair clippers, bleach, and two different colors of hair dye, one for men and one for women. She gave Max the hair clippers and gave Christopher the men's hair dye. The box he had in his hands said DARK BLOND on the label. He had trouble wrapping his head around what the words meant.

"We'll have to bleach it first," Addy said as Christopher looked down at the box. "We'll have to take your natural, darker color out before we can put the new color in." Christopher didn't say anything to her. He just stared at the picture of the smiling man on the box.

"Who's going first?" Addy polled the room.

"I'll go," Max said, pulling the clippers from their box. Max hadn't shaved his face since they left Palm Beach. The clippers weren't for his face, though.

Max walked into the bathroom. They were somewhere in Kentucky, all three of them sharing a room in a weird medieval-themed hotel near the Cincinnati airport. Max left the bathroom door open so Addy and Christopher could watch him sacrifice his hair for the cause. Max plugged the clippers into the wall socket and turned them on to test them. They buzzed with eagerness. They made the sound of a lawn mower as they cut the hair on Max's head down to little more than scruff.

Christopher and Addy watched in silence. Christopher kept thinking about Maria's journal. He remembered the details about how she took out a knife and carved off her hair one bunch at a time, how she went back two or three times to make her hair shorter, how the front was easier to control than the back, how much she seemed to change after she cut her hair like that. It was how much she seemed to change that Christopher remembered the most.

It didn't take long for Max to shave his head. After seven quick passes with the clippers, all he had left to do was tidy up. He asked Addy to help him at the end, to make sure he didn't miss any spots. His hair was piled up on the bathroom floor like the pelt of a small, dead animal. Max looked at Christopher. "What do you think?" Only a thin layer of dark stubble remained on Max's head. The hair on his face was longer than the hair on his head now. Without the hair on Max's head, Christopher noticed the gray in his beard for the first time. Christopher thought the gray must be new. "So, how do I look?" Max asked again.

Addy answered. "Bald."

"Screw you guys," Max said, staring at his reflection in the mirror. "I think I look kind of like a pirate."

"Do you want to look like a pirate?" Addy asked.

"Who the hell wouldn't want to look like a pirate?" Max turned back toward Christopher. "Wouldn't you want to look like a pirate?"

Christopher didn't answer, unable to tear his eyes away from the ridiculous picture on the side of his box of hair dye. He didn't want to look like that. He didn't want to look like anything.

"I'll go next," Addy said, grabbing her hair dye and walking toward the bathroom. "You can leave now," she said to Max, pushing him out the bathroom door.

While Max's transformation took only minutes, Addy's took well over an hour. "I don't think I can do this," Christopher said to Max as they waited. He held up the men's hair dye, showing Max the smiling face on the front of the box.

"What do you mean, you 'can't do this'?" Max asked.

"I know they told us to change our appearance, but—I don't know—I feel kind of sick."

Max shook his newly bald head. "I fucking shaved my head and you can't make your hair a little lighter?"

"I'm sorry," Christopher said to Max. And he was. He wished he could go through with it, but he knew that he couldn't.

"First you don't change your name and now this," Max said to him, shaking his head. "Look, kid, I get it. You don't believe that this is your War, so you don't want to have to change because of it. But it's going to change you. In more ways than you can imagine, it's going to change you. Your hair? Your name? They're nothing compared to what's in store for you. I'll try to protect you from it, but I won't be able to stop it."

"Okay," Christopher said. "But I still don't want to dye my hair."

"Let's wait to see how Addy looks. If she looks different enough, then maybe you dyeing your hair won't matter." So they waited for Addy to step out of the bathroom. They barely recognized her when she did. They all agreed that maybe it was enough. Maybe nobody would notice Christopher now after Addy and Max had changed so much.

"But what do you guys really think?" Addy asked Max and Christopher after they discussed their plans.

"I think you should have dyed your hair that color a long time ago," Max told Addy. Christopher, never having been wordy to begin with, was speechless. Addy took Christopher's frozen tongue to be the compliment that it was. She looked fierce.

They had the rest of the night to rest. Addy and Max had one night to become the new people they'd changed into. Christopher had one more night to try to ignore the insanity around him and try not to change. Tomorrow, the three of them would be on the road again, seemingly destined for nowhere.

Sixteen

Katsu looked around, trying to make sure no one was following him. The Tokyo street behind him was busy. In the few seconds that Katsu spent focusing on the traffic passing by the end of the alley, he counted eight scooters, four bicycles, and five cars. Katsu did not believe he'd been followed, but he knew that any secret can be ruined if a single whisper is heard or a single misstep is seen by the wrong person. He stood motionless for a moment. More scooters, bicycles, and cars passed the entrance to the alley, but Katsu saw nothing suspicious. The city was so full of people, but most of them knew nothing about the War. Then he reached deep into his pocket for the keys.

Katsu's hand trembled slightly as he dug through his pocket. He had lived a hard and violent life, but he could never remember being this anxious or this scared before. This time he knew that, one way or the other, he was close to the end. He heard the keys jingle in his pocket before he felt the metal with his fingers. He took one last look around him, and seeing no one else, he pulled out the keys. The door in front of Katsu didn't look like much. It was merely a rusty metal door in a wall halfway down a skinny, dank, dead-end alley. Nevertheless, Katsu slid the key into the lock and opened it.

Once the door was open, Katsu stepped quickly through it into a windowless room. Then he closed the door behind him and locked it. The lights were off inside the room. The room was empty except for a flight of stairs leading down into the cellar. Katsu didn't bother to turn the lights on. He knew the way through the darkness. He made his way to the stairs and went down them. At the bottom of the stairs another door blocked his way. Katsu took out another key and unlocked the second door.

"Katsu," a voice called out as soon as he opened the door. Testing the visitor.

"Takeshi," Katsu responded. "How is everything?" It was quiet in the room at the bottom of the stairs. The noise from the city was gone. Katsu closed the second door behind him and locked it as well.

"Perfect," Takeshi responded. "Everything is in perfect order. How did your end of the transaction go?"

Katsu stepped toward Takeshi. Covering the floor of the room were twenty-five state-of-the-art machine guns, ten long-range rifles, eight flamethrowers, and four shoulder-launched multipurpose assault weapons. Katsu had never seen that much firepower in one place before—one weapon for each of his men. It pleased him and frightened him at the same time. He hoped that they would be able to avoid, or at least minimize, civilian casualties. His eight best men would carry the flamethrowers. They would have to move quickly. Even with all this firepower, Katsu knew that it wouldn't take long before they would be outmanned and outarmed. They would simply have to reach their target fast. Even then, they'd be lucky if any of them made it out alive.

"How did the transaction go, Katsu?" Takeshi asked again.

"Fine," Katsu answered. Earlier that morning he had delivered the cash to pay for all the weapons, cash that had been collected over the course of years. "There were no problems." Katsu eyed Takeshi. "You've checked the weapons?"

"Every one," Takeshi confirmed.

"When do the men get here?" Katsu asked. He knew the answer to *his question but wanted to make sure that Takeshi knew too, that every man knew every detail of the plan by heart.*

"*Tomorrow morning, before the sun rises,*" *Takeshi answered.*

"*And they are ready?*"

"*We are all ready, Katsu. We've been ready. We're simply waiting now.*"

"*We have to wait. Everyone needs time. This isn't only about us.*" *There would be more waiting tomorrow. They weren't supposed to make their move until early in the afternoon.*

"*I know,*" *Takeshi assured Katsu. "Do you think everyone else will do their part?*"

"*They have to. So it is senseless to think otherwise.*"

"*It's a lot of faith to put in a boy,*" *Takeshi said.*

"*I've met him, Takeshi. Christopher is not any boy. He's the only one that could bring us all together.*" *He looked down at the weapons on the floor. "Which one do you want to carry?" he asked Takeshi.*

"*We all want the flamethrowers, Katsu sama, but we trust that you will choose our weapons for us wisely. What will you carry?*"

"*Hand me one of the machine guns,*" *Katsu said to Takeshi. Takeshi stepped over the rifles and picked up one of the machine guns. He handed it to Katsu. Katsu held it in his hands. Katsu had killed many men in his day, but he had never held a weapon like this before. He was relatively sure that none of his men had either. But the game had changed. Katsu wished that his men had found time for training, but it was easier to get the guns than to find more time. They had to trust the plan. "I will carry this," Katsu said, holding up the machine gun, "and hope that I don't have to fire it.*"

"*It will all be over soon, friend,*" *Takeshi said, echoing Katsu's own thoughts.*

"*I'm going to go home and try to get some sleep,*" *Katsu said to Takeshi.*

"*I'm going to stay here tonight to make sure everything is safe.*"

"See you in the morning, then."

"Yes, see you then."

The two men bowed to each other. Then Takeshi retraced his steps—back up the stairs, through the two locked doors, and into the alleyway, where the world, for a little while longer at least, seemed unchanged.

Seventeen

"Should we turn off the lights so that no one knows we're here?" Addy asked Max. They should have been completely off the radar by now. They hadn't stayed with anyone since Addy dyed her hair and Max shaved his head. That was five days ago. They'd kept moving since then, though not in a straight line. They spent three of the five nights in roadside motels. The other two they slept in the woods near their car. This was supposed to be the last of their one-night stays. They were supposed to get on a flight the next day. All three of them were supposed to board a flight that would take them halfway around the world to Sydney, Australia. None of them knew what would happen after that. Christopher was anxious. He'd never been on a plane before. Addy seemed anxious too, but for different reasons. She didn't seem eager to leave.

"The lights are fine," Max said to Addy. He was growing impatient with her. "You know that you don't have to come with us, Addy. You've done your part. You can go back to Reggie."

"Do you really think that's what I want, Max? Do you really think I could go back to that after all this?" Addy glanced quickly at Christopher. Christopher still hadn't gotten used to the way Addy looked with her dyed hair. He felt his skin tingle whenever their eyes caught each other. They looked at each other with a need bordering on hunger, though Christopher wasn't sure if they needed the same thing.

They were in a cabin in the mountains, only a couple of hours outside of Vancouver. Their flight left at one in the afternoon the next day. They were planning to head for the airport at around eight the next morning to make sure they didn't run into any problems catching their flight.

"If you don't want to go back to Reggie, then why are you acting so weird about coming with us?" Max asked Addy. Christopher didn't say anything. His role in the conversation was as an observer only. He knew he had no real role in it.

"I'm not acting weird," Addy answered, and all three of them knew that she was lying. Then she walked away from them, into another room. Christopher watched her as she went, wishing that he could understand her. His eyes trailed down her back, starting at her red hair and slowly making their way down to the soles of her bare feet. Addy never wore socks around Max because she knew he had a thing for them.

Max and Christopher were left alone in the main room. They were sitting in chairs, across from each other. They had a fire going in the wood-burning stove, which made the whole cabin smell like pine and made it feel almost cozy. Christopher was surprised at how well he and Max got along after all this time. Before Max, Christopher had been able to maintain only one friendship, with Evan. Christopher attributed his friendship with Max more to Max's patience than to anything he brought to the table.

"So what's the deal with you and socks?" Christopher asked Max.

Max laughed. "There's nothing sexier than a hot woman in socks." He leaned back in his chair and put his feet up on the wooden coffee table between them. "And not stockings either. Real socks, wool or cotton, and the longer the better. I mean, I'll take those cute little ankle socks, the ones that they fold down at the top with the frill, but really, the longer the better."

"Where did that come from?"

"Hell if I know. And don't you go digging around in my head to try to figure it out. If I ever find out that it's because my mom used to wear long socks when she nursed me or some fucked-up shit like that, it'll ruin the whole thing for me. This is not a joy that I want to give up." He paused. "I've got too few joys already."

"I won't go digging around in anything," Christopher promised.

Max looked at him with a crooked grin. "You a virgin?" he asked. Max rarely asked Christopher personal questions, and Christopher appreciated that—but here we were anyway. Besides, Christopher had started it.

"No," Christopher answered. He thought back to the two times he'd had sex, with different girls, neither girl even hinting that there was any chance for a repeat performance. The first time, he and Evan were hanging out with two girls at Evan's house while Evan's parents were away. Evan took one of the girls into his bedroom, leaving Christopher and the other girl alone in the living room. Everything that happened was stilted and awkward and Christopher was pretty sure it happened only because the girl couldn't stand the silence. The second time was with a girl whose only motivation was clearly to rebel by sleeping with the weird kid at school. Christopher was pretty sure she regretted it as soon as it was over. Christopher had been nice to both girls. At least, he thought he'd been nice.

"That's good," Max said. His voice carried more relief than joy. He took his feet off the coffee table and leaned toward Christopher. He started talking more quietly, to make sure that Addy didn't hear him. "I was with this girl once. She knew about my thing for socks. So she bought these rainbow-striped cotton socks that went all the way up to the top of her thighs. Holy shit." Max pronounced the word *holy* as if it were two separate words. He told the whole story with pure joy, like his telling it was a gift for Christopher. "I didn't let her take those socks off the whole fucking time. She took everything else off but those socks. I was so into it, and she really ate it up. She was laughing and giggling the whole time, but she loved it."

Max's story *was* a gift. It made Christopher happy.

That was when everything came crashing down. The door to Addy's room flew open. It swung open so hard that it banged against the wall next to it. Addy stood there, her face flushed. For a second Christopher wondered if she had heard Max's story and was somehow offended by it, but he knew how ridiculous that thought was. Something else was going on. "There are people outside," Addy said, her chest heaving. "I saw them. They're heading this way."

Max was on his feet instantly. "How many of them are there?"

"I couldn't tell," Addy answered. "At least five flashlights, but who knows how many people."

Christopher followed Max's lead and jumped to his feet. He'd been comfortable fighting the men in the woods back in Maine, but since then he'd been pulled so far out of his element that he felt lost. Besides, some of the words that Max had said to him the first time they'd met kept running through his head. *Don't be a fool and think that they will underestimate you again. Ever.*

"What should we do?" Addy asked Max. Max was the elder, the natural leader, and Addy was scared—though not half as scared as Christopher.

"Is there any reason why a group of people might be coming up here at this time of night?" Max asked.

"Besides to come after us? No," Addy answered. "And they must have seen the light and the smoke from the stove by now."

"Then the woods," Max said. "We'll take to the woods." Christopher and Addy shot each other a quick glance. Christopher had used the woods for shelter once before, but he didn't know these woods. "Now," Max added for emphasis. It worked. They moved.

Addy was right. They were coming. Christopher and Addy could see the light from their flashlights bouncing off the leaves on the trees around them. They came swiftly but silently. Christopher and Addy, believing they hadn't been spotted yet, darted off, searching for shelter in the darkness. Addy hadn't even taken the time to put her shoes on. It wasn't until they were a few hundred yards from the house that they realized Max wasn't with them.

While Addy and Christopher ran out of the cabin, Max went back into his room for his gun, the gun that he had promised himself years ago he would never use again. Once he found it, he stopped and listened. He knew he didn't have a lot of time. He'd known that even before he ran back for the gun. Now he could hear them. They were quiet but not silent. Max could hear the sounds of snapping twigs and rustling leaves as their pursuers marched closer to the cabin. The front door was no longer an option. Max ran to the window of the bedroom. The window faced the mountain. The pursuers were coming from the opposite direction. Max pulled on the window's lock. The rust on the old metal lock kept it from budging. Max thought about breaking the glass but couldn't risk the noise. The sounds of their footsteps were getting closer. There were no other sounds. The pursuers didn't say a word to each other. They simply moved as a group through the darkness. Max gave the lock another strong yank. The rusty metal dug into his skin and it tore open, leaving blood on the lock, but the lock moved. Max pulled again and the lock came free. He could hear sounds not far from the cabin's front door. He knew that they would likely surround the house before coming inside. He only had a minute. He pushed the window open. The window wasn't big and it was a good six feet from the ground. Still, Max jammed his body through the tiny space and fell. He didn't care about the pain of landing. He only cared about the noise. He hit the ground hard, rolled forward, and came up aiming his gun at nothing. Then he heard footsteps coming toward him from around the corner of the cabin. He saw a beam of light from a flashlight flare against the side of the cabin. Then he stood up and ran.

Christopher and Addy didn't stop running until they heard the shouting. The shouting was coming from back at the cabin. They turned. The cabin was now no more than a flickering of color between the forest's trees. They had been running away from the cabin, higher up the mountain, toward the rocky crags. Then they heard the shout. "Got one!"

"Is it him?" a second man shouted.

"No! It's the man!" the first man yelled back.

"Bring him back here. He'll know something!"

Addy and Christopher stopped running and the shouting stopped too. The forest went silent. They were too far away from the cabin to hear the footsteps. They were too far away to hear the men enter the cabin. "Where's Max?" Addy said in a panic when they heard the shouts. Christopher looked around them. It was dark, but not so dark that they would have missed Max if he had been with them. "Do you think they caught him?" Addy asked Christopher.

"I don't know," Christopher replied, feeling like he could drown in the ocean of what he didn't know.

"I'm going back for him," Addy said, without any hesitation in her voice.

Christopher wanted to tell her how insane that was. They were outnumbered. They had no weapons. Hell, Addy didn't even have shoes. Instead, the words "I'll go with you" slipped out of his mouth.

"No," Addy ordered Christopher. "This was all to keep you safe. Don't fuck that up for us. Keep running. I'll catch up."

Christopher gave Addy a look, a pleading, desperate look. "Don't worry," she said. "I have no plans to die today."

Christopher nodded this time. No matter what else happened, he didn't plan on dying either. Then Addy turned and ran back toward the cabin. She virtually flew over the ground, her bare feet making no more noise than a gust of wind. Christopher watched her disappear around the trees and then he turned and plodded farther up the mountain, in the other direction.

Addy rushed back toward the cabin, dodging trees in the darkness. She didn't know where she was going or what she was going to do when she got there. She felt helpless. There was nothing in the world that Addy hated more than feeling helpless.

Christopher turned again when he heard the faint and unnatural whistling sound. He'd managed to scramble up the face of a giant boulder. He decided, since he had no real idea where he should go, that he would keep going up until he no longer had any more up to go. Then he would go down. But the strange whistling sound made him stop. Christopher turned in time to see a flash of light. The flash made him flinch backward. It was only that flash of light, the moonlight catching metal in midair and the flinch it elicited from Christopher, that kept the arrow from piercing Christopher's chest. Instead, it clanked against the rock next to him. Sparks flew into the air as the metal tip of the arrow collided with the rock.

Christopher looked down the mountain. He could see three people below him, all dressed in black. All three were carrying bows and arrows. It was surreal. From where he stood, Christopher could see that it was two men and one woman. Their black clothes seemed to be some sort of uniform. Christopher stood for a moment, frozen by the utter madness of it all. Then the woman pulled out an arrow and strung it in her bow with lightning speed. She pulled back and the bow bent like a striking snake. Christopher moved again. Up. The woman's arrow whistled by his feet. He crested another rock and ran.

He heard them this time—not only the sound of their arrows whistling through the night air but their feet too, stamping along the forest floor. He heard the ground crunch with each of their steps. He couldn't look back. They were keeping pace with him, if not gaining ground. An arrow whizzed by his ear and stuck in a tree two feet in front of him. A second later he was past the wounded tree and still running, moving from side to side to become a harder target. White cliffs shined in the bright moonlight to his left. Perhaps he could find a crag to hide in. He turned left without slowing down.

They split up after Christopher disappeared on them. They tried to make sure they had every escape route covered. They knew they couldn't go back unless they finished the job. They didn't need the other two. The Child was their only target, and he had disappeared somewhere on the cliffs. Sonny ran ahead, around the cliffs and to the other side, trying to cut off any escape in that direction. Jesse stayed behind so she could ambush the Child if he backtracked. That left Arnold to venture onto the cliffs to try to flush him out.

It was much lighter on the cliffs. Without the trees, the moon shone down and reflected off the sheer rock, giving the impression of permanent dusk. The cliffs were steep. Dirt paths twisted along cracks in the cliffs. Arnold could walk along them, stepping carefully with one foot in front of the other, like walking on a balance beam. The paths were thin enough that he had to reach out and run one hand along the rock so he could grab it to keep his balance when he started to slip. This made his bow useless, maybe worse than useless because of its weight. He was walking along a sheer cliff, virtually defenseless.

In the last moments of Arnold's life, he wondered how he had ended up where he was. He wondered why he wasn't on the other side, fighting with the Child instead of chasing him through the darkness. He knew it wasn't because he believed in the War. He just believed in the Child even less. And Arnold was smart enough to know that when you don't believe in anything, all you can do is try to pick the winner.

A piece of the rock jutted out and the path grew thinner. Arnold wouldn't be able to walk normally here. He'd have to belly up to the stone and shimmy his feet, especially if he didn't want to drop his bow. The drop wasn't especially far, maybe thirty feet, but the bottom of the cliff was littered with jagged rocks. Arnold settled his feet. He strung an arrow in his bow. With one smooth motion, he shot the arrow like a missile into a tree opposite the cliff. He listened to see if he could hear any rustling. He thought that maybe the Child would see the arrow and run, but he heard nothing, so he stood up straight and began to shimmy around the jutting rock.

He was almost to the other side when he felt a hand hit his shoulder. He looked down. It wasn't a fist. A fist wasn't necessary. What Arnold felt was the heel of Christopher's palm. It didn't hurt, but Arnold still felt the force behind it. His shoulders flew away from the rock and he stared straight at Christopher, who had been patiently waiting around the other side of the jutting rock. He wondered what type of game Christopher was playing, why he hadn't hit him harder, why he hadn't taken him out when he had the chance. Then Arnold realized that his feet weren't on the ledge anymore. And he fell.

Christopher watched Arnold's body twist once in the air as he fell. Then he watched it smash on the jagged rocks. Arnold could have survived the fall had he landed better, but luck was not on Arnold's side. Not that night.

Arnold had managed to shout on his way down, to let out one last, dying wail. Christopher knew that his cry would alert the others. Christopher had already used up the one hiding place on the cliff and even that hid you from only one angle. He didn't suppose they would make the same mistake the dead guy did and follow him back on the rock. Instead, they would stand at the bottom of the cliff and shoot arrows at him until one hit its mark. So Christopher did the only thing he could think to do. He moved back in the direction that he'd come from. At least he knew that he could get off the cliff that way.

Jesse was waiting for Christopher when he made his way back off the cliff. She'd heard Arnold scream when he fell, but she didn't chase the sound. She was too disciplined for that. Her role was to cover this exit and make sure that Christopher didn't slip away, no matter what the cost. So she stayed, half hidden behind a tree, her bow in one hand and a titanium-tipped arrow in the other. She could string an arrow onto the bow, draw the bowstring back, and fire, all in one motion. The whole process took less than two seconds, and she could still hit a bull's-eye from more than two hundred feet away. The bow and arrow was a weapon particularly suited for this War—not in cities, but it was perfect for the woods. It was efficient and it was quiet. That was why they'd been sent—for their efficiency and their ability to be discreet. Jesse controlled her breathing, pressed her back against the cool bark of the tree, and waited.

At first all she saw was movement. Christopher was being careful. He was trying to stay hidden, moving only in short stretches before ducking back into the cracks in the cliff. Jesse was impressed. Watching him move along the giant rock was little more than watching a shadow dance across the cliff. If Jesse had been doing anything other than watching and waiting, she might not have seen Christopher at all. But she did see him. She caught a single glimpse of movement, and once she caught that glimpse, she could follow it. There would be no escaping now. Now it was all a question of when to shoot. They hadn't asked Jesse or her team to bring the Child back alive. They didn't even ask for his body, only proof that he was dead. Jesse took her arrow and placed its notch on the string of the bow. She pulled the bowstring back a single inch, just enough for her to feel the tension.

Christopher ran and waited, ran and waited. He'd expected them to come running after him once the man he'd pushed off the cliff screamed, but no one came. In the back of his mind, he wished they had. Then he would know what he was dealing with. Instead, he was running and hiding from shadows. Unless he could find Addy or Max, Christopher didn't even know where he was supposed to be running to.

Jesse waited until Christopher was off the cliff. She waited until he'd stepped back onto the solid, slanted earth of the steep hill. He was only about fifty feet from her when she stepped out from behind the tree, drew back the bowstring, and let the arrow fly.

The arrow whizzed by Christopher's head, missing him by inches, and slammed into a tree only a few feet behind him. He heard the arrow hit the tree. It was a thick thud, like the sound an ax makes when chopping wood. He tried not to think of what that arrow would have done to his skull if it had hit him. His instinct was to run, but he stopped himself. He stopped himself because he knew that whoever shot that arrow had missed him on purpose. He knew that if he ran, the next arrow would hit him in the back of the head. Christopher didn't want to die, and he was particularly certain that he didn't want to die this way. So he stopped and stared in the direction the arrow had come from.

Jesse had already strung another arrow onto her bowstring before the first arrow hit the tree. She stepped out from behind the tree and aimed the arrow at Christopher's chest. She would shoot the arrow. She had no doubt that she would shoot the arrow, but she wanted to see Christopher closer up first. She wanted to see the Child while he still had air in his lungs and was still standing on his own feet. He looked young and scared and, somehow, dangerous.

Christopher wanted to say something to this woman with the arrow pointed at his chest. He wanted to tell her that she didn't have to do this. He wanted to tell her that he wasn't worth it. He wanted to make her know that he wasn't what everyone made him out to be. He wasn't special. Despite the want, the words never came. Not from him anyway.

The voice came from above them, deep and resonant like the voice of God. "Put the bow down," it commanded. Christopher waited for the woman's eyes to move toward the voice before he looked too. There was Max, standing on the hill above them, pointing his gun at Jesse.

Christopher only glanced at Max before looking back at the woman aiming the bow and arrow at his chest. He thought that she would do as she was ordered. He couldn't understand the insanity of not listening to a man who was pointing a gun at you. But Jesse didn't put her bow down. She didn't budge. Christopher wondered what it took to make someone that crazy, what made someone care more about killing a person she'd never met than saving their own life. *Please put the bow down*, he thought to himself, afraid to say the words out loud. "Put the bow down and I let you walk away," Max said to the woman instead. He took one step closer to her without lowering his gun. Christopher knew that Max meant it. Christopher knew that Max didn't want to shoot her. Max wasn't like that. Christopher looked back at Jesse, trying to figure out how this was going to end. His only guess was badly.

Christopher stared into the woman's eyes. They were cold. He didn't see her twitch. He didn't even see her breathe before he heard the gunshot. He liked to think that Max saw something that he himself didn't. Christopher simply heard the gunshot and, before he saw anything, dove to the ground. The arrow missed him by less than an inch, but it did miss him and disappeared into the darkness of the forest behind him. Christopher got back to his feet. He wondered if the woman had let go of the arrow before or after Max shot her. He wondered but didn't want to know. Max was already standing over the woman. Christopher walked toward him.

"She's dead," Max announced.

Christopher could see by what was left of the woman's head that Max was right. "I'm sorry," he said to Max as they stood over the lifeless body.

"About what?" Max asked.

"I made you kill her."

"Don't apologize for the things that people do for you," Max said to Christopher. Then they both heard a sound, a twig snapping behind them. They turned, moving in almost choreographed unison, Max swinging his gun over Christopher's ducked head. Max fired another shot and another body fell to the ground. Christopher didn't even know how he'd had time to aim. Sonny fell backward with little fanfare. "Fuck," Max whispered with frustration. Sonny's body lay still. Christopher and Max walked over to it. He wasn't breathing anymore either.

"Do you know where Addy is?" Max asked Christopher as they stared down at the second dead body.

"She went to find you," Christopher told Max.

"I never saw her," Max whispered again.

"How many more of them are there?"

"These two"—Max pointed with his gun at the two bodies—"and three more."

"I killed one on the rocks," Christopher told Max, trying not to sound proud.

"Okay, so there are two left. Do you want to go back for Addy?"

"Me?" Christopher asked, unsure of why Max was asking him.

"You," Max told him. "You're the hero. You decide."

"I'm not a hero."

"I know that," Max told Christopher, "but nobody believes me so you still have to decide."

"Fine. Then let's go back and find Addy."

Twenty-two steps. Christopher counted. That's how far they made it with Max running behind him before Christopher heard another whizzing sound zip past him through the air. He didn't see anything. He only heard the noise. Then he heard another sound, like the sound he'd already heard of the arrow striking a tree, but softer and wetter. Christopher turned toward the noise. The arrow was sticking out of Max's neck. Max's hand had reached up toward it and was already covered in blood. Even in the gray moonlight, Christopher could see how red Max's blood was. Christopher froze. He saw Max's mouth move as he tried to say something, but the hole in his neck made it impossible for a sound to come out. Instead, Max lifted his gun and aimed it toward Christopher. He pulled the trigger and Christopher saw the dirt fly up a few inches from his feet. That's when he realized what Max was trying to tell him. *Run.* So Christopher ran.

Christopher ran away from the arrows, back the way that they'd come. As Christopher ran past Max, a second arrow struck Max in the chest. Then Christopher ran faster. He heard the footsteps coming after him, chasing after him. He turned and the footsteps turned too. He could tell that two sets of footsteps were behind him. He could hear them as they parted and came back together, dodging trees. All he tried to do was run fast enough that neither of them would have the time to stop and shoot another arrow, but there was no endgame with that plan. There was no escape. Only running.

Carl and Bill stayed after Christopher, doing their best to chase him down like a pair of hunting dogs, waiting for him to slip so they could pounce. They knew that they were the only two left, the only chance left of the mission succeeding.

Christopher turned again, unsure of where he was going, unsure that he wasn't running in circles. All he concentrated on was not tripping. He flew through the darkness like he'd practiced in the forests near his home in Maine hour after hour. That was when he heard it—a third set of footsteps even though there were only supposed to be two of them left. At first he thought that Max had been wrong about how many of them were out there. Then he heard a crash and the sounds of bodies tearing through leaves and branches snapping off trees.

After that, Christopher could hear only one set of footsteps following him. He guessed at what to do next. He purposely ran in a long, large circle. The footsteps stayed behind him. It took him nearly five minutes to circle back to where he'd heard the crashing sound. He felt like his heart was going to explode. He didn't know how long he'd been running, but it felt like forever. He didn't have much left in him. Fortunately, he didn't need much.

Christopher saw her hair, her new hair, like a flame in the darkness. She leapt out from behind a tree as he ran past. She had something in her hands. Christopher turned and watched as Addy grasped an arrow that she had pulled from a random tree and impaled Carl on it, using his own force and speed against him. It was the same titanium-tipped arrow that she had used to slit Bill's throat after leaping on top of him from an elevated ridge. The arrow went all the way through Carl, entering below his chest and coming out his back. Christopher looked away, trying to regain his breath. It took a few minutes for Carl to die. Christopher and Addy waited. For some reason, Christopher didn't feel bad about making Addy do what she'd done the way he'd felt bad about making Max kill. Addy didn't feel bad about it either.

Once Carl died, Addy and Christopher went back and found Max's body. His body still had three arrows sticking out of it. Addy reached down and picked up Max's gun and dusted the dirt off it. Then she put it in her pocket.

"What now?" Christopher asked Addy as he stared down at the body of the second best friend he'd ever had.

"It's time to stop running," Addy said to Christopher. Her words were strong, but her face was sad.

"What's the alternative?" Christopher asked, knowing that going home wasn't one.

Addy's face and shoulders were covered in specks of blood from the men she had slain. Her shoulders heaved with each breath she took. "Fighting," she told Christopher.

Eighteen

"I didn't want any of this," Christopher told Addy, unable to shake the image dancing in his head of Max standing in the woods, covered in blood, with an arrow jutting from his neck. "I didn't want anyone to die for me. I only want to live a normal life."

"First, there is no normal life, so forget that," Addy said. They were standing on the side of a road somewhere in the mountains of Washington State. Addy had her phone out. They'd been driving for some time, trying to find a spot where she could get good enough reception to check some Web site. She held her phone up in the air above her head and looked at it again, visibly frustrated. "Besides, nobody gets what they want, and the people who do decide they want something else as soon as they get it." Addy slammed her phone into her free hand three times, as if she could jostle it into getting reception. "We've got to get closer to a city—or at least somewhere with a cell tower."

"Is that what you were doing all those times when Max and I didn't know where you were? You were checking some Web site on your phone?"

"It's not just some Web site."

"Then what is it?"

"It's the Web site of the Uprising."

"I don't know what that means," Christopher shouted at Addy.

"Some of us have gotten sick of running and sick of hiding. We know that the world's gotten too small for this War. Either that or the War's gotten too big. There's nowhere to hide anymore."

"So what are you going to do? Fight to try to stop a War? That doesn't make any sense. And what does any of that have to do with me anyway?"

Addy looked at Christopher. He could tell that some of whatever it was that made Addy think he was so special was slowly wearing off. Max's dying had changed things. "We tried Max's way and it got him killed. Now we'll try the other way. And what does the Uprising have to do with you? The people in the Uprising, you're the reason that they have the courage to fight. You can't let them down."

"You're all nuts," Christopher said. "I'm not going to let anyone else die for me."

Addy put her phone back in her pocket. She walked over to Christopher and pointed a finger in his face. "Let's get one thing straight," she told him. "Max didn't die for you. He wasn't a martyr. He took chances for you, but he died because he was a little bit too slow and a little bit unlucky." The tip of Addy's finger was only an inch from Christopher's nose. "People are going to fight and people are going to die whether you come with me or not. The only question is whether or not they get to fight and die with a little bit of hope."

"I'm not the person that you think I am," Christopher protested, wishing Max was still around to agree with him.

"Yes, you are," Addy said, walking away from Christopher and back toward the car. "You just don't know it yet."

"What are you going to do when you finally get on that Web site?" Christopher called after her.

Addy stepped toward the driver's-side door of the car. "I'm going to tell everyone in the Uprising that you're alive and that you're with me and that you're everything that every single one of them dreams about. Now get in the fucking car," she ordered Christopher.

Nineteen

"You're where?" Evan asked, pulling aside his blinds and looking out his window to see if the strangers were still out there watching him. He couldn't see them, but he didn't find much comfort in that. Sometimes they chose to be seen. Sometimes they didn't.

"I'm not really sure. Oregon, I think." Christopher had lost track. They'd spent so much time moving forward and then backtracking again. He wasn't sure if Addy was trying to protect them or if she was stalling.

"That's crazy," Evan said, dropping the blinds back in place.

"I know," Christopher whispered into his phone. Addy was sleeping. Christopher didn't want her to know that he'd been calling Evan. "These people, apparently they think I'm some sort of hero."

"So be a hero," Evan told Christopher. Christopher didn't say anything. He didn't tell Evan about Max. He didn't tell Evan about the arrows or the blood. "Where are you guys going? I want to come out there. I want to meet up with you guys. After everything we've been through together, you can't do this on your own now."

Christopher hesitated, knowing that he was about to make a mistake, but then he went ahead and made it anyway. "I think we're going to Los Angeles but I'm not sure. I'll try to find out. I'll let you know."

Twenty

Evan sat in the airport terminal waiting for them to announce his row for boarding. He was doing his best to stand off to the side without looking suspicious. Mostly, he stood near the window, staring out at the planes, blocking his face from everyone else in the airport. Still, every so often, he took his eyes away from the window to scan the terminal and try to find out if anyone was watching him. He was pretty sure that he hadn't been followed. Even if they had followed him out of Maine, he was pretty sure he would have lost them by now. He'd pulled out every trick that he and Christopher had practiced growing up. He drove. He took the train. He traveled on foot much farther than he needed to. He used misdirection, going the wrong way more than once, then secretly turning back and retracing his steps. All that and he never saw anyone behind him. Not a single person.

He had followed Christopher's instructions. He'd done everything Christopher told him to do, but he was still nervous. He purchased the plane tickets with the credit card that Christopher had glued to the bottom of the desk in his room. Evan had found two of them down there and noticed the glue marks from where a third had already been pulled off. He'd thought that he knew almost everything about Christopher, but he didn't know about the credit cards. The credit cards that Evan found were in two different names, neither of them Christopher's. He had no idea if they were stolen or fake. As long as they worked, he didn't care.

They called Evan's row. He took one last look around to make sure that he was what he'd always been, unnoticed. He knew that this was his last chance to run. He walked toward the woman who was collecting the tickets and handed his to her. He tried to act calm. He tried to act like he'd done this before, even though he hadn't. It wasn't merely the running and the fake credit cards that were new to Evan. He was also walking onto an airplane for the first time in his life.

Evan stepped through the gate and walked down the short hallway toward the plane. It was a direct flight, Boston to Los Angeles. Christopher had confirmed that he was going to L.A. He didn't know where exactly, but he and Evan figured that they could contact each other once they both had their boots on the ground in the same city. Christopher tried to protest, but Evan knew that Christopher wanted him to come out. He knew that whatever else this War that Christopher kept blabbering about was, it was what the two of them had been training for since they were little kids. Evan wasn't going to let Christopher ditch him right when things started getting good, not after putting up with all the crap they'd been through together for the last seventeen years.

Evan found his seat, a window seat near the back of the plane. He checked his phone one last time before powering it off for the flight. Nothing. No news from Christopher. No messages from his parents wondering where he was. Evan felt his stomach drop as the plane sped down the runway and lifted off the ground. He stared out the window as the city of Boston became smaller and smaller below him. The plane circled once before straightening out and Evan had a clear view north toward Maine. From that high in the air, all he could see was thick forest and a few roads cutting through it like veins.

Evan didn't sleep on the flight. He didn't watch a movie. He did nothing but stare out the window at the clouds.

Twenty-one

Christopher and Addy were in a motel room outside of Fresno. Their car was parked only a few feet from the door to their room. The red neon light from the motel sign cascaded through their window, drenching everything in lush red color. They were finally heading to Los Angeles the next day. Addy had noticed a change in Christopher ever since she'd told him where they were going. She liked what she saw. She couldn't be sure, but she thought that maybe Christopher was beginning to accept who he was.

Christopher still hadn't told Addy about Evan. He didn't know how. He didn't think it made much sense to tell her until Evan actually made it to L.A. Christopher was looking forward to seeing his friend. He missed Max. He liked Addy, but there was something blocking any sort of friendship between them. He felt it every time Addy looked at him. She never saw him. She always saw something else, something that he wasn't. When Christopher looked at her, all he saw was the fire of her hair and the image of her face covered in specks of other people's blood. She had saved his life, but even that hadn't brought them together.

"Were you and Max ever a couple?" Christopher asked Addy. He was lying on one of the beds. She was standing behind a closet door, changing into the clothes that she would sleep in. The clothes Addy slept in weren't much different from the clothes she wore during the day. She wore black stretch pants and a gray T-shirt to bed. *You always have to be ready for them*, she'd told Christopher, *even when you're asleep.*

"No," Addy answered. "Max and I were always just friends," she finished with more than a hint of sadness in her voice.

"I miss him," Christopher confessed to Addy.

"Nobody in my life has ever stuck around for very long," Addy said to Christopher in lieu of agreeing with him.

"But you believe that we can change that?" Christopher asked, still unclear about what the Uprising was all about.

Addy stepped out from behind the closet door. She was wearing a white tank top this time instead of her usual T-shirt. Christopher could see her nipples poking through the fabric of her shirt in the red glare shining through the window. "Stand up," Addy ordered him.

Christopher stood up. When he did, she walked toward him. She lifted her hands to his face. She pulled his face closer to hers. Then she kissed him, softly, on the lips. The first kiss lasted only a second. Then she pulled him in again and kissed him harder. When their lips separated, they stood there, staring into each other's eyes. But there was nothing. They both knew it. They both wanted there to be something for their own selfish reasons, but merely wanting it wasn't enough to make it happen. "Yes," Addy said to Christopher, her voice straining to hang on to even the slightest sliver of hope. "I believe we're going to change that."

Twenty-two

Umut sat outside the café and sipped his tea. It was hot and sweet. He swirled it in his glass and watched the last bits of sugar spin in circles before it dissolved in the heat. The men sitting behind Umut punctuated their game of backgammon with bouts of shouting and eruptions of laughter. Umut wasn't listening to their words. He merely liked the sounds of the game—the dice shaking in the cup and being thrown onto the board, the clicking of the stones as the players moved them, the voices of the players as they taunted each other and, of course, the laughter.

Umut rolled his shoulders. The muscles in his back were tight. His trip to the baths earlier that morning, the first time he'd been to the baths in months, had done little to relieve the tension in his body. He watched as another ferry left the terminal, this one headed farther up the Bosporus before crossing over to the Asian side of Istanbul. The ferry was teeming with people. The passengers filled up the inside of the ferry and then flowed out onto the outer benches that ran along the ferry's sides. Umut counted three women in burkas. Many more were dressed in the fashionable clothes of American television shows. Umut wondered how many of the women in burkas were going to get off in Üsküdar. He wondered if he and the others would stand out when they got off the ferry in Üsküdar later that day. Each of the fifteen of them was coming on a different ferry, but all were wearing burkas to hide their faces and to hide the fact that eleven of them were men. Umut had tried his burka on earlier that morning. He stood in front of the mirror wearing it, staring at his own reflection. He walked past the mirror, slightly hunched to disguise his height, and noted the disguise's effectiveness. Then he strapped the guns and the knives that he would carry with him later that day to his chest and legs. The burka provided ample space to conceal the weapons, even for Umut, who had volunteered to carry a double load of weapons so that he could meet up with Tor Baz, the Afghani, in Üsküdar and arm him too. Tor Baz was too tall to be mistaken for a woman in a burka but was too brave a fighter to be left out of this battle.

The burka disguise was an old trick and one quickly losing its utility in a westernizing city like Istanbul. The fewer burkas there were, the more likely someone would look into your eyes and know too soon that they should be afraid. Nevertheless, Umut and his fighters were counting on the ploy working one more time. If the plan went right, each of them would cross the river separately and then they would descend upon the Intelligence Center together, all draped in black like vengeful ghosts, armed to the teeth, only their eyes showing their fearlessness.

Umut watched as another ferry pulled into the terminal. The passengers got off the boat, their eyes gazing past Umut at the fountains and the pillars surrounding the Hagia Sophia. Umut loved this city. It was a shame what they were going to have to do to it. An unexpected friend walked by as Umut took another sip of his tea. "Umut," the friend said. Umut stood to embrace him. "May I sit and join you?" the friend asked.

"Of course," Umut replied and motioned to the café owner to bring out another tea. Umut's friend was an innocent, at least as far as Umut knew. He was one of the few innocents that Umut had ever been friendly with. They'd met haggling over groceries. Umut was happy to see his friend. He wanted to forget about the War and enjoy the next few hours. Then he would have to go home and start getting ready.

"What brings you here, Umut?" his friend asked him as he dropped sugar cubes into his tea.

"I like to watch the ferries," Umut said, motioning toward the water. Umut's friend laughed at Umut's childishness, but Umut was not ashamed.

Umut had lost his sense of time and was surprised when the midday call to prayer echoed in the air. He did not move from his seat but instead silently mouthed the words as they were sung from loudspeakers all over the city. If he survived the day, he promised himself, he would wash his feet, enter a mosque, and pray. Until then, Umut put all his faith in the Child and was determined to follow him either to heaven or to hell, if there really was a difference.

Twenty-three

They were chanting his name, fifty or more of them. Christopher had never heard anything like it before in his life. It thrilled him and scared him at the same time. "If they can't stop a single boy," Dutty shouted to the crowd, who ate up every word, "how can they stop an entire movement?" The building was nearly shaking as the crowd stomped their feet and shouted back at Dutty. Dutty had been speaking for more than twenty minutes. Christopher stood, hidden from view of the crowd but still able to see Dutty as he spoke. Christopher wondered how anyone could talk for that long, let alone drive the crowd of people into a frenzy with nothing but words. He wished that he could see the crowd, but they were hidden from his view. All he could see was Dutty and Addy and Evan. But he could hear the crowd. He could hear them shout his name. Christopher was so enthralled by the sounds of the crowd that he could barely remember more than a few sentences that Dutty said, but that was okay. The speech wasn't for Christopher anyway. It was for the crowd. It was *about* Christopher.

The one person in the room who might have been more shocked than Christopher by Dutty's speech and the crowd's reaction was Evan. Everything Christopher had told him turned out to be true. Evan had never admitted to himself that he didn't believe

Christopher's story, but deep down, it all seemed far too insane to be real. Then Christopher showed up at the airport with the sexy redhead, and the insanity started to feel less crazy. Evan had so many questions that he wanted to ask his old friend, but the questions had to wait. For now, Evan merely tried to take everything in. He listened to Dutty. He listened to the words that Dutty shouted over the crowd, and even though Evan had no dog in this fight, he liked what he heard. He liked the message about taking control of your destiny. He liked the message about not being afraid. And he heard about how his friend—his crazy, obsessive, loner, loser friend—had finally come to show them all how to do this. To Evan, it all felt right. He barely understood any of it, but it all felt right. Suddenly all that time that he and Christopher had spent together, training to fight unknown enemies, seemed justified. It seemed like all the faith that Evan had put in Christopher when no one around him believed that Christopher deserved any faith was going to pay off. They were chanting Christopher's name, for Christ's sake. They were cheering for Christopher, and Evan took his natural place next to his friend.

"Should I bring him out?" Dutty shouted to the crowd and the crowd erupted. Fifty people sounded like a thousand people.

It had not been easy for Christopher to get Addy to accept bringing Evan into the fold. She told Christopher that Evan didn't belong, that he wasn't part of the War, and that he was unnecessarily endangering the life of his friend. Christopher didn't deny any of that, but he threatened to walk away if Addy didn't bend. Addy knew that he wasn't bluffing. She also knew that he wouldn't survive two weeks if he walked away on his own. They met up with Evan at Venice Beach. Evan had already been there for two days. He'd slept on the beach one night and in a cheap motel room the other. He'd nearly lost faith. Nearly.

"Do you want to meet the proof of our impending victory?"

Dutty shouted to the crowd. Addy remembered something she'd once read about rock bands, that they waited until the crowd was on the verge of a mass revolt before coming onstage because people are never more enthusiastic than when they are on the edge of rebellion. The response to Dutty's question was utter insanity. It was loud enough that Addy worried that the sound would travel out of the building and down the block until somebody on the outside heard and began to wonder what was going on.

From the stage, Dutty looked over at Christopher. Dutty was a powerful-looking man. He was tall, with broad shoulders. His skin was tanned dark and his black hair ran in waves away from his face. He beckoned to Christopher, motioning for him to step out from the shadows where he was standing and face the crowd. Christopher hesitated for a second. He felt like he was about to step into some sort of chasm that he would never emerge from. Dutty motioned for him again, nodding to Christopher as if to tell him that, yes, this was his purpose—this was what he was meant to do. Christopher still didn't have the courage to step forward on his own. He didn't need it, though, because before he could build up the courage to step forward, he was pushed. Addy and Evan, without even looking at each other, simultaneously reached out and pushed him gently toward Dutty. As they pushed Christopher, their fingers brushed against each other.

Christopher almost stumbled as he stepped toward Dutty, but he was able to catch his balance before careening to the ground. He took two stutter steps forward and then stopped, only halfway to Dutty. Before moving any closer, Christopher turned and looked at the crowd. When the crowd saw Christopher, a roar went up and fists rose in the air. It wasn't a huge crowd, but they made up in enthusiasm what they lacked in numbers. They came in all shapes and sizes, though they appeared to be disproportionately young, most of them about Addy's age. A few older members stood out. Other than their age, the crowd was a nearly perfect cross section of the people on the streets outside.

"You're almost there," Dutty whispered to Christopher, urging him closer. When Christopher was close enough, Dutty reached out and grabbed his hand. Dutty got a good grip on Christopher's wrist and lifted his hand high over his head, which had the effect of pulling Christopher closer to him. Christopher's eyes didn't leave the crowd as they cheered each step he took toward Dutty.

"Speak!" someone in the crowd shouted once Christopher and Dutty were standing next to each other. "Speak!" another echoed. The room went silent as everyone waited for Christopher to say something. They hadn't asked for a speech. They merely wanted to hear him speak. "Go ahead," Dutty said to him. Christopher stepped forward, toward the crowd, unsure of what he was going to say, unsure if he was going to be able to say anything at all. The silence went on. Christopher wondered when it would end. He wondered when they would realize that he had nothing meaning-ful to say. Dutty stepped closer behind Christopher. Christopher could feel his presence. They had spoken earlier that day, but only for a moment. Dutty didn't want to waste any time. He wanted to get Christopher in front of his people as quickly as possible. He told Christopher that they would have time to talk later. Then Dutty turned to Addy and said, "I knew you were going to be spe-cial as soon as they told me about you, Addy. I knew that you were going to do something special for us."

Christopher began to get nervous that the crowd would turn on him if he didn't say the right thing. Then he heard Dutty whis-per into his ear. "Just tell them that you're one of them. That's all they want to hear."

The silence didn't stop. The crowd kept waiting for Christo-pher to speak. They all felt that they'd been waiting for a long time for this—their whole lives, in fact. They were willing to wait a few minutes more. Christopher coughed, clearing his throat. He looked into the crowd, at their faces. Their eyes met his. "For eighteen years," Christopher finally said to the crowd. He still didn't have the courage to yell like Dutty had, but he didn't need to. The silence that they'd given him was amplifier enough. "For eighteen years, I haven't had any idea who I was. But now I know." Christopher was going to finish by telling the crowd what Dutty had told him to tell them, that he was one of them, but he never had the chance. The roar that went up from the crowd after Christopher merely told them that he now knew who he was drowned out every word after that.

Dutty stepped up next to Christopher, grabbed his hand, and again pulled it up toward the sky in both victory and defiance. "Now go meet them," Dutty said to Christopher. He wasn't whispering anymore, but Christopher knew that no one else could hear what he was saying over the din of the crowd. "They're your people." Then Dutty began to pull Christopher toward the crowd. As Dutty and Christopher neared, the crowd parted, creating a path for them through the middle. Once they stepped into it, the people closed in around them. People began reaching out so that they could touch Christopher. They didn't crowd him. They didn't move to crush him. They merely reached out to try to run their fingers over his skin, to touch his shoulders. The room became quiet again, almost eerily so. Christopher tried to look into the eyes of all of them. He wanted to remember each of their faces, but there were too many. Then one of them spoke. "I'm Ryan." Christopher looked at the man's face. He was a short, blond man of about thirty years old, with striking blue eyes. He smiled when Christopher looked at him. "I'm Sarah," another voice called out and Christopher turned his head to see an olive-skinned woman who seemed to be in her early forties with dark, curly hair. "I'm Patrick," another man called out. He was a tall man with red hair and freckles. The older ones spoke first, as if more entitled to speak, but the young people followed. "I'm Jennifer," a black woman with short cropped hair yelled. When Christopher made eye contact with her, tears rolled down her face. "I'm Michelle," another woman called out. "I'm Steve." Christopher stopped walking. He stood in the middle of the crowd as it circled him and, one at a time, they each called out their name to him and, as each person did, Christopher looked at them without saying a word. More than one of them cried when Christopher looked at them. "Why are they crying?" Christopher whispered to Dutty as he looked from face to face.

"Because those are their real names," Dutty whispered back to him. "Most of them haven't used their real names in years."

It took almost twenty minutes for all of them to shout out their names to Christopher. A few more reached out and touched him with gentle, grazing fingertips. One, a black man nearing fifty, who was easily the oldest person in the room, stepped forward to actually shake Christopher's hand. He introduced himself as Brian. As they shook hands, Brian reached out with his other hand so that he was cradling Christopher's hand in his. "I knew your father," the old man said. Christopher wanted to say something to him, but Dutty kept Christopher moving forward through the crowd until every person had their chance to greet Christopher.

When it was over, Christopher met up with Evan and Addy again. Dutty led the three of them out of the building. Dutty knew the secrets. He knew not to give the crowd too much exposure to Christopher, not yet. "That was insane," Evan whispered to Christopher as they followed Dutty down the empty L.A. street, Addy a few feet in front of them, next to Dutty.

In all the time that they'd known each other, Christopher had never been so happy to have Evan by his side. Max had done his best to keep Christopher grounded, but only Evan could help him keep his head amid the insanity. "Fucking crazy," Christopher said back to Evan, and simply having someone there to tell him that the madness was madness made Christopher feel better.

"You're like a god to these people," Evan continued, his voice full of confused awe.

Christopher glanced at Addy and Dutty, hoping that they hadn't heard Evan. Either they didn't hear him or they chose to ignore him. "Like you said," Christopher answered him, "that was insane."

Twenty-four

The four of them eventually got on a bus and made their way to an apartment in Santa Monica, only five or six blocks from the beach. "The three of you will stay here tonight," Dutty informed them. It was a small apartment on the second floor of a two-story building, which surrounded a murky swimming pool. There was a bedroom in the back of the apartment with a window facing the street. The front room contained a small kitchenette, a pull-out couch, and a TV. "The TV doesn't work, but you should be safe here as long as you don't let Christopher leave the apartment."

"Is this your place?" Addy asked Dutty.

"I stay here sometimes," Dutty answered, "but I can find someplace else to go tonight. It could get pretty crowded in here with four of us. When things settle down, I'll take you guys to one of our buildings to stay. I don't think they're ready for that right now. If we take Christopher there now, we're never going to get anything accomplished."

"What are we trying to get accomplished?" Christopher asked.

"Let's get some dinner and we can talk about it," Dutty said, staring at Christopher. Christopher could feel the difference between his stare and the stare of all the others. Unlike the others, Dutty wasn't in awe of Christopher.

"Is Dutty your real name?" Christopher asked.

Dutty smiled. "I named myself Dutty after the Haitian priest who prophesied the New World's first slave revolt, and I will never again answer to any other name. Now I'm going to go out and get us some food."

"So what is the plan?" Addy asked Dutty after they finished eating. Dutty and Evan had scarfed down their burritos. Addy ate half of hers. Christopher barely touched his.

"We have to strike soon, while the excitement is still high. We have to make sure that everyone knows that not only is Christopher alive, but he's changed things." Dutty looked at Christopher. "The people you met today, they're only a small sample. There are more people all over the world waiting to see what you're going to do. So I'm going to tell you what I think you should do."

"Okay," Christopher said, not sure if he had any options in any of this.

"There's an Intelligence Cell in Nevada, just outside of Death Valley. We know where it is. One of the people you met tonight used to work there. It's isolated. There's barely anything around it."

"And?"

"I think we should take it down," Dutty finished.

"What do you mean, 'take it down'?"

"I think we should attack it. I think we should show them that we've got some fight in us, that we're more than a bunch of talk. It's time for action. Right, Addy?" Dutty looked toward the one person in the room he expected to be his ally.

"What are we going to attack it with? Guns? Army tanks? How is this going to work?" Christopher looked around at the others to see if anyone else was confused.

"He's right, Christopher. You came here to stop running, right? Well, the only way to stop running is to start fighting," Addy told him

"And if you're there leading us," Dutty said to Christopher, "think of the message that will send to the whole world. We've got the firepower. We can make the plans. You merely have to lead the charge. This cell is in the middle of nowhere. We have at least an hour before their reinforcements show up. All we need to do is send a message, so we fight for an hour and then get the hell out of there."

"And the people who work there?" Christopher asked. He looked over at Evan, who was sitting silently, his mouth agape, taking everything in, trying to believe what was right in front of his eyes.

"If they run, we'll let them run. If they want to stay and fight, well, we fight them. We're all children of this War, Christopher. We know how to fight."

"If you're the one with the idea and the plan, then how am I the leader?" Christopher looked to Dutty for an answer, but Addy answered for him.

"Because the leader's not the person with the idea or the plan. The leader is the person that the others follow."

Dutty laughed for a moment and then he stopped laughing. "So are you in?" he asked Christopher.

"I'm in," Evan said, surprising them all. Christopher looked at Evan. He didn't want to drag Evan into any of this, but he also knew that he had to let Evan make his own choices. Besides, if he was going to fight, he wanted Evan beside him.

"If this is how it's got to be," Christopher said and his voice trailed off.

"Two days," Dutty said, holding two fingers up. "I need two days to get everything together. Then we move."

Christopher felt tired. Everything was happening so fast. He looked at the faces of the people in the room. Dutty looked satisfied. Addy looked excited. Evan looked scared. Christopher simply looked tired.

"I'll leave you three to get some rest," Dutty said. Then he left.

Twenty-five

The first time that Addy kissed Evan, she did it only to see if kissing him would feel different than kissing Christopher. She needed to know if that empty feeling that she had when she kissed Christopher was because of him or because of her. She hadn't planned it. It just happened. She and Evan had gone for a walk on the Santa Monica pier. Christopher essentially demanded it. He was feeling guilty. He said that just because it wasn't safe for him to go outside, that didn't mean that the two of them should stay cooped up in the little apartment. It had only been one day, but it felt like much longer. The three of them were nearly bouncing off the walls with nervous energy. Some people would say that the plan had been years, maybe even decades, in the making but to the three of them, everything was going to start in one day—whatever that everything was.

The night was dark, but the pier glowed beneath the lights from the vendors' stalls. Addy and Evan bought ice cream. The Ferris wheel lit up the sky with crazy, swirling patterns of light. The pier was crowded. Evan and Addy passed bands playing and people dancing, some for tips, some to the music. Beneath the sound of the music was the sound of the ocean, churning and crashing on the other side of the white-sand beach. And the screaming, the shrieks of joy from the people on the Scrambler and the pirate ship ride. It all made Addy feel young, like she was the sixteen-year-old that she'd never had the chance to be because, in reality, two weeks before her sixteenth birthday she was told that the world was a horrible place and no one was ever safe. But that night she was with Evan, and Evan was so young and innocent that it made her feel younger and freer than she'd felt in a very long time. She felt like she was on a first date.

"Let's go feel the water," Addy said to Evan after they finished their ice cream. They walked by a belly dancer twitching her hips and shaking the rattles that hung low on her stomach.

"Huh?" Evan said. He could barely hear Addy speak over all the distractions.

"Let's take our shoes off and walk down to the beach and put our feet in the water and see how cold it is." Addy's voice was full of fire.

Evan's head spun. He wondered how he'd found himself with this bizarre woman in this bizarre place. He wondered if Christopher liked Addy, if there had been anything between them. Christopher hadn't said anything to Evan, but Christopher rarely said anything to anybody. Evan wondered if he should go with Addy, if he should take his shoes off with her, if he should walk with her into the water, but he couldn't have said no if he'd wanted to. "Okay," he said.

So they followed the sound of the ocean and they took off their shoes. They stepped onto the sand. It was cold. Addy felt the cold sand slide between her toes as her feet sank into it. Then she ran. She ran toward the water. It took a moment for Evan's mind to catch up with what was happening. Then he ran too. He caught up with Addy just as her feet splashed into a small incoming wave. Then she laughed. She hadn't laughed in a long time. She looked over at Evan. He looked scared and innocent. That was part of it too. If he hadn't looked so scared, she might not have done it. But that was when she decided that she needed to know. Was it her or was it Christopher? Was she lost forever or was there still a chance for her? So she walked over to Evan and she kissed him. It was a long kiss, long enough to fill the moment. When the kiss ended, Addy knew that it wasn't her. She was still capable of feeling whatever that feeling was that you were supposed to feel when you kissed someone for the first time—excitement mixed with giddiness mixed with despair. She looked at Evan. She knew that it wasn't her and she knew that she wanted more.

Evan was still afraid when they stumbled back to the apartment. He was afraid of what would happen next and even more afraid of what would happen because of whatever happened next. Most of all, though, Evan was afraid of the crazy red-haired woman who fought wars, joined rebellions, and seduced strangers. He was too scared to even try to make her stop. That's not to say that he wanted her to stop. He didn't.

They walked past Christopher, who had fallen asleep on the couch, pausing for a second to see if the sound of the door was going to wake him up. When he didn't move, they slipped into the bedroom like young parents trying to find moments to make love without waking their sleeping children. Evan wasn't a virgin. He'd had girlfriends and a couple of onetime flings, but this was different. He'd never been so overwhelmed before.

They were quiet, as quiet as they could manage. Despite their efforts, Christopher woke up before they were finished. He could hear them through the thin door to the bedroom. He didn't say anything. He didn't stop them. He knew he could. He knew that he could tear into that room and shout and shame his best friend and this woman who worshipped him and also hated him for not being the person that she worshipped. He knew he had that power, but he didn't want it. He had no idea what he wanted. So he turned his back on the sounds coming through the bedroom door and tried to go back to sleep.

Dutty came back the next day. Nobody said a word about what had happened the night before. Evan and Addy didn't even speak about it to each other. Whatever spell Addy had seemed to be under disappeared with the sun. "So are you guys ready?" Dutty asked the three of them, though only Christopher's answer mattered to him. "We move tonight."

"I'm not going to get any more ready sitting around here," Christopher answered him.

Twenty-six

The sound of machine-gun fire ripped through the desert night. The desert didn't allow for darkness. The desert lacked the shadows needed to suck up the light. So Christopher could see it all, even the things that he wished he couldn't see.

Thirty of them made the attack. Almost all of them were given guns—a hodgepodge of semiautomatic weapons and hunting rifles. "God bless America," Dutty said as he handed out the weapons. In the end, the only ones not given guns were the ones driving the cars. The thirty of them packed themselves into five different vehicles ranging from beat-up, windowless vans to state-of-the-art SUVs. They all drove from Los Angeles, though the plan was to split up into three groups after the attack. Christopher, Addy, and Evan were all supposed to head back to L.A. with Dutty and about thirty others. Half of the rest were to head to Vegas and the other half would drive to Texas.

Christopher, Addy, Evan, and Dutty rode in one of the SUVs, with a driver and a Hispanic woman who looked to be about Addy's age. The drive took more than six hours. For the first few hours, nobody said anything. Evan and Addy sat next to each other, their shoulders touching. They were closer to each other than they needed to be, Christopher noticed. He didn't think that anybody else did. He didn't even know if Evan and Addy noticed themselves. It came naturally. The driver and the Hispanic woman kept glancing at Christopher, then looking away as quickly as they could when Christopher caught their eyes. They spent the first two hours trying to look anywhere but at Christopher and failing. It was especially awkward because the Hispanic woman was sitting next to Christopher. The driver glanced at him in his rearview mirror so frequently that Christopher began to worry that he wasn't keeping his eyes on the road.

"So what are you guys' names?" Evan finally asked the driver and the Hispanic woman long after the silence began careening toward absurdity.

"I'm Kevin," the driver said and waved meekly toward the back of the car.

"My name is Soledad," the woman answered.

"I'm Evan," Evan told them. Both Kevin and Soledad started laughing. "What's so funny?" Evan asked, turning a light shade of pink.

"We know who you are," Soledad said. "We know who all of you are." She peered at Christopher again as she said the words.

"You hear that, guys?" Evan said loudly. "We're famous!" Everybody laughed this time, even Christopher.

"There was a Soledad that I used to chat with sometimes on the Web site," Addy said. It wasn't quite a question, but it demanded an answer anyway.

"That was me," Soledad said and she smiled a broad, toothy smile. "I didn't want to say anything in case you didn't remember me."

"I remember," Addy said. "I remember everyone who talked to me on that site. You all gave me hope. Thank you."

"Don't thank me," Soledad said. "I hope that I can do as much for the movement as you have." Soledad snuck another glance at

Christopher. He gave her a wan smile, then turned and stared out the window as they drove. Each of them except Kevin had a gun either balanced on their lap or resting on the floor between their legs.

The people stationed in the intelligence cell in the desert fought back. They had their own stockpile of weapons. Their weapons were bigger and better than the revolutionaries' weapons. That's what you do when you're sequestered out in the middle of the desert—you get big guns; you get hand grenades; you ready yourself for an attack. The revolutionaries had only their makeshift assortment of armaments and Molotov cocktails. But the revolutionaries had the numbers. Thirty versus seven in the beginning.

The Intelligence Cell was the only visible building in the desert, surrounded by nothing but rocks and sand. They pulled up to it with five vehicles, quickly spreading out, driving across the hard-packed earth, surrounding the building. They stopped, like the five points of a star with the building in the middle. The SUV carrying Christopher, Evan, Addy, Dutty, Soledad, and Kevin faced the front of the building. Kevin stopped the vehicle, but he kept it running and in gear so that he could stay agile in case they had to move. He must have done something like this before, Christopher thought, watching him and wondering what type of job he had in the War that would make Dutty pick him to be his own driver, to be Christopher's driver. Once the car was idling, Kevin opened the sunroof. Christopher looked at the two other vehicles he could see, the ones that weren't blocked by the building. Somebody rose through the sunroof of one of the vehicles, holding his gun at the ready. Two people climbed out of the other vehicle with their guns, flanking each side of the van, which Christopher figured must not have a working sunroof. Dutty stood up out of their sunroof. First he placed his gun on the roof. Then he reached back down and picked up a battery-powered megaphone.

The seconds before the first order seemed to stretch on for an eternity. Christopher looked at the other people in the SUV, wondering what the hell all of them were doing here. This was insanity. Soledad and Kevin. He barely knew them. He knew that they had their reasons, though. They weren't merely there for him. Then his eyes fell on Evan. Evan had a gun in his hand, a gun that Christopher was sure Evan knew how to use; they'd practiced shooting together because Christopher made Evan practice with him. He had a sudden urge to tell Evan to go home. He didn't want to see Evan clutching an arrow sticking out of his neck. Even though he knew it was too late, Christopher almost said something to Evan. Before he could, the sky filled up with the screech from the megaphone and the single-word order: "Now!"

The opening gambit was just a series of gunshots meant to hit the side of the building. The shots came from all five of the vehicles, peppering the building's outer walls. At the same time that the shots went off, each of the drivers set his stopwatch. One hour. They had one hour before they would race off into the night. It's difficult to describe how long a single hour can be when every second lasts an eternity.

After the initial round of shots, Christopher heard the megaphone crackle again. "We're only here for the building and the contents of the building. No one needs to get hurt. This is not an idle threat. This is not a game. Christopher is leading us. And we are prepared to fight." None of them knew what type of answer they should have expected, but the answer they got caught them by surprise. Something shot out of the building, landing only a few feet from the van to Christopher's right. Then it exploded. Blood painted the side of the van as one of the two men flanking it collapsed in a heap. Christopher wasn't sure, but it didn't look like the person sitting on the driver's side of the van was moving either. The shrapnel ripped holes in the side of the van, but there was no way to tell how much damage was done to the people inside. Then the shots rang out. They weren't shooting to send a message. They were aiming for their targets.

Kevin immediately stepped on the gas as the sand next to their SUV sprang up with the machine-gun fire ripping through the ground next to them. Kevin wasn't running, though. He was driving toward the building. Dutty had dropped his megaphone and picked up his gun. He was still standing with his torso out of the sunroof, firing indiscriminately at the building as the SUV lurched toward it.

"We need to find out where they're firing from and where the grenade launcher is!" Soledad shouted with an eerie calmness. "And we're going to have to get out of the car! We're too big a target in here!" They quickly lost sight of the other five vehicles. They didn't even know if the one that nearly got hit by the grenade was still functional.

Dutty stopped firing and ducked his head back into the SUV. "When Kevin stops the SUV, we have to grab everything out of the back and move!" he yelled to them. The Molotov cocktails. Each vehicle had dozens of them. They seemed silly now when compared to a real fucking grenade launcher. Suddenly Kevin slammed on the brakes and the SUV came to a screeching halt. They opened the doors and ran out of the vehicle, keeping their heads down. Christopher could hear gunfire, but he couldn't tell where it was coming from. It felt like it was all around him. Soledad and Dutty ran to the back of the SUV, opened the doors and pulled out two milk crates full of Molotov cocktails. Once they got them out, Kevin hit the gas again and began driving away.

"Where the fuck is he going?" Christopher yelled to Dutty.

"We can't risk the vehicle," Dutty yelled back to him. "We've only got an hour. When that hour is up, we're going to need a ride out of here or we're all fucked." Dutty lit the cloth hanging out of one of the old whiskey bottles and hurled the bottle at the building. It exploded before it even hit the building, spraying gasoline all over the side of the building, and in seconds the whole side of the building was on fire. The first fire didn't last very long, but the Molotov cocktails didn't seem so silly anymore. Dutty handed one to Christopher and lit it. Christopher tossed it high into the air and it came crashing down on the roof of the building. The flames shot into the air.

Christopher heard more gunfire. He didn't hear just the crack of a gun firing; he also heard the thudding sound as the bullets hit the ground around him. He looked up in time to see a series of dust bursts making a beeline for Evan, who was standing over the other carton of Molotov cocktails with Addy and Soledad. Christopher looked up and, for a split second, saw the muzzle flash coming from the gun of a man standing in a high window of the Intelligence Cell. The man was squeezing the trigger of his automatic weapon as the bullets got closer and closer to Evan. Christopher instinctively raised his own gun and aimed for the muzzle flash. Then he fired. The shooting stopped. Evan didn't even look back toward Christopher. None of them—not Addy, not Soledad, not anybody—seemed to realize what had happened. Or maybe they all understood that they didn't have the time to care. Christopher took a deep breath, leaned down, and grabbed another gasoline-filled whiskey bottle.

It soon became clear that at least a few of the other vehicles were having success as well. It wasn't long before the whole building seemed to be burning. Then the main door at the front of the building opened and a man came running out. Christopher waited to see if the man was armed or if he was giving himself up. But the man was definitely running and there was something in his hand. He made it only about twenty steps before he was cut down. Christopher's eyes followed the line of the shot, afraid that he would see

Evan holding the smoking gun, but his eyes found Soledad instead, standing there next to Evan, her gun near her shoulder. She had pulled the trigger only a split second earlier. *So much for letting them run*, Christopher thought himself.

The main door was now open, and the five of them—Dutty, Christopher, Addy, Evan, and Soledad—carefully made their way toward it. They weren't even the first of the rebels to get inside. Members from one of the other cars had beaten them to it. They must have found another entrance because shortly after entering the building, Christopher saw the body of one of their own, lying lifeless on the ground, his chest stained with blood. It was becoming quieter. The explosions had stopped. Somebody must have taken out the grenade launcher.

It was hot inside the building. The fire was growing. Another round of gunfire cut through the air on the floor above them. "We should leave," Soledad whispered as they walked into the hell that they'd created. "This whole place is going to collapse and no one is going to be able to stop it."

"We've got ten minutes," Dutty responded. "Let's make sure that there's no one else here that we can pull out with us." So they kept walking.

They saw three more bodies—one of their own and two of the enemy's. The sounds had almost completely disappeared now. They heard only the popping and hissing of the fire slowly eating the building. "Dutty," Soledad said, reaching out and touching Dutty's shoulder, "it's time to go. Don't forget about our cargo." She motioned with her head toward Christopher.

They had no reason to believe that anyone in the building was still alive. But someone was. The last survivor was still there, hiding near one of the doors and waiting for reinforcements. He'd already killed four of the rebels himself, but he knew a fool's game when he saw one. It had been seven against thirty in the beginning, but now it was down to him against, he didn't know for sure, maybe nineteen or twenty. He was going to stay hidden. That was his plan, but he never expected to see what he saw next. A whole group of rebels was walking out of the building. He could have taken out the three of them in front before the rest of them even had a chance to respond. Or he could hide in the shadows, hope that the reinforcements arrived before the fire got to him, and try to survive. No one would blame him for that. He'd fought valiantly. He tried to protect the information. What did it matter anyway? All of the information in the Intelligence Cell was duplicated in another Intelligence Cell. It would take them only a few weeks to replicate it all using the information keys at the Intelligence Centers. As long as the Intelligence Centers were standing, they wouldn't lose anything except the pathetic lives of the guards. If they lost the Intelligence Centers, the information in the Intelligence Cell would be useless anyway. It would be like having a train schedule but having absolutely no way to find the train station.

He decided to stay hidden. It would have worked. He would have probably even survived if he hadn't seen something that caused him to back into the now smoldering wall and cry out in pain. What he saw was the Child. The Child was actually with them. He couldn't believe it. He'd seen pictures before, but he half believed them to be fakes. So he stepped backward, away from what had to be a hallucination. *I could shoot him*, he thought, but he knew that was suicide. So he took another step backward and his hand hit a chunk of metal that was hotter than the flames themselves. His skin sizzled and he gasped and they heard him. It was the woman, the one with the fire red hair that first aimed her gun at him. Everyone froze for a second. "It really is you," the man in the shadows said to Christopher.

"Yes," Christopher answered him and then Addy pulled the trigger.

What started as thirty versus seven ended when it hit twenty to none, although none of them ever knew for sure how many of their own side they lost, since their evacuation was sloppy and people randomly jumped into vehicles. All they knew was that their victory was not without its costs. When Dutty, Christopher, Evan, Addy, and Soledad stepped out of the building, Kevin was waiting for them in his SUV. He had picked up an additional passenger from the now disabled van that had been hit by the grenade. There wasn't time to evenly distribute the survivors. "We've got three minutes," Kevin yelled to them as they stepped outside. Christopher could see the fire reflected in the SUV's windshield and he counted six bullet holes in the vehicle's side.

They all piled into the SUV. Kevin slammed his foot on the gas pedal. All of Christopher's friends had survived this time. He supposed that was an improvement. He wasn't sure that they hadn't survived by pure luck. *Better to be lucky than dead*, he thought and made a miserable attempt at forcing out a chuckle. The additional passenger that they'd picked up was covered in the splatter of someone else's blood. He didn't say a word the whole trip back to L.A. He didn't look at Christopher like all the others had. Instead, he stared out the window in a daze.

Twenty-seven

They made it back to their base in Los Angeles before sunrise—
the ones who survived, that is. It was strange for Christopher,
Evan, and Addy, walking around the compound after returning
from the attack, because since they didn't know anyone anyway,
they had no idea who was missing. They didn't know where the
gaps were. They had no way of knowing who was mourning and
who was simply tired or in shock. Every death means more to
some than to others. They can't mean something to everyone.
There aren't enough tears or time for that.

Dutty showed the three of them where they were meant to
stay, noting as he did that they probably wouldn't be here for more
than another few days. He expected it to be a good few days.
Christopher had led them to their first victory, and the Web site
would be roiling with the news in a matter of hours. Dutty would
make sure of that. It wouldn't be long before people everywhere,
regardless of what side they were on, would know that the Uprising had begun.

Dutty had organized the building so that women slept on one
side and men slept on the other. He first showed Evan and Christopher to the room they would be sharing. It was at the far end of
the compound. Inside the room were two beds with a single night-

stand between them. Only one wall had a window, looking out across a desolate, dirt-strewn hill along the side of a highway. "You two need to rest," Dutty said to Christopher and Evan. "Don't let anyone bother you. I'll go back to the apartment and get your things. You'll have them before you wake up." Christopher took the bed by the windowless wall, giving Evan what little natural light came into the room. "We'll celebrate tonight," Dutty added. Then he led Addy down the hallway toward the room she would be sharing with Soledad and two other women that she'd never met.

Evan and Christopher didn't talk as they pulled back the sheets on their beds. Before climbing into the bed, Christopher, as was his habit, walked over to the window. "You mind?" he asked Evan before he passed Evan's bed.

"Go ahead," Evan said. He knew what Christopher was doing, knew that Christopher had to do it. Evan knew that Christopher couldn't go to bed without first looking out any windows to see if anyone was out there. "You know I used to think it was so weird when you did that," Evan said to Christopher. "It was like the toughest kid I ever met was checking under his bed for monsters before he went to sleep."

"And what do you think now?"

"I think I'd do it if you didn't. How's it look?" Evan asked as Christopher peered out into the slowly coming dawn.

"Like hell," Christopher answered. "It doesn't look like L.A. out there. It looks like a scene from a Mad Max movie."

"But no people?" Evan asked, not trying to hide the tinge of fear in his voice.

"No people," Christopher confirmed. He looked down at his friend. "You know you don't have to do this," he said to Evan. "You can go home."

"What about you?"

"You know I can't go back." Christopher stared at the wasteland outside and thought about the faces of his mother and father—his real mother and father, the ones who raised him. "Maybe this dump is all there is for me."

"I'm not going back if you're not going back," Evan said. The fear in his voice was gone. "So drop it, okay?"

"Okay," Christopher said. What Evan didn't tell Christopher was that he didn't want to go home. Not only because of Christopher but because of Addy too and for the sheer adventure of it all. His life was bigger now and he had always wanted it to be bigger. Besides, it was different here for Evan than for Christopher. No one looked at Evan funny. He was already becoming more accepted by these people than Christopher would ever, could ever, be. "I'm glad you're here," Christopher said.

Then, somehow, they slept.

Christopher could hear music when he woke up. It wasn't loud, but he could hear it drifting in from one of the building's other rooms. It was still light outside, but the shadows were growing long. Christopher checked the clock. He'd been in bed for almost twelve hours. The bed next to him was unmade but empty. Evan must have already gotten up.

Christopher sat up in bed. He put his feet on the floor and his hands on the bed next to him. He listened. Under the sound of the music, he could hear people talking. He could hear spots of laughter. He didn't want to go out there.

His bag, with what little in the world that he owned, was sitting at the end of his bed. Dutty must have dropped it off there while Christopher slept. Christopher slid down to the end of the bed and rifled through the bag. He found his jeans and a clean

T-shirt. He took his time getting dressed. The room had no mirror, so he just ran his fingers through his hair a few times to try to make sure that it wasn't too knotted or messy and that there was no soot or blood in it. Then, knowing that he was running out of reasons to delay the inevitable, he walked out of the room.

For a few seconds, Christopher was able to stand unnoticed and watch the others. Some of them had bottles of beer in their hands. The music was coming from a laptop computer somebody had set on a table outside the kitchen. Evan was standing in one corner of the room, drinking a beer and talking to two men that Christopher barely recognized from the night when everyone introduced themselves to him. He felt more than a little guilty for not remembering them all better, for not remembering each of their names.

Addy saw Christopher first. She was standing near the table with the computer on it. They made eye contact and after a moment's hesitation, Addy walked toward him. He was frozen, unsure of where to walk or who to talk to. He was relieved to see Addy coming toward him. He awkwardly pushed his hands into the pockets of his jeans. "I need to show you something," Addy said before leading him to the computer. When they got near the computer the music was loud enough that it drowned out the other sounds of the evening and all they could hear was the music and each other. "Look at this," Addy said, an unconquerable smile spreading across her face. She opened up a Web browser and pasted in the current URL for the Uprising's Web site. It loaded quickly, but Addy noticed with satisfaction that it loaded a little slower than normal because so many people were viewing it. Though Addy immediately recognized the colors, the bright yellow background and the dark green font, it was all new to Christopher.

"What are you showing me?" Christopher asked.

"Wait," she said. When the page finished loading, Addy scrolled down until the center of the screen was almost entirely filled with a picture. It was the first picture ever posted on the site. It was a picture taken at night but with enough light to see every detail. It was a picture of Christopher, holding a gun, aiming it at a man standing in the open window of a dark building on the edge of the desert. It was a picture of Christopher taken the moment before he shot the man who nearly shot Evan. The picture was somehow taken from over Christopher's shoulder so that you couldn't see much of the man in the window except for his gun and his silhouette. But you could see Christopher. Nearly half of the picture was taken up by the side of Christopher's face. You could see his pores. You could see the sweat dripping down his forehead. You could see the smudges of dirt already on his face. You could see in his face that he was about to pull the trigger.

"How the hell?" Christopher began to ask.

"Kevin took it from the car," Addy said. "He's got a really great zoom lens. It's great, isn't it?"

"Scroll down," Christopher ordered.

She scrolled down so that Christopher could see the caption Dutty had given the picture. The words below Christopher's picture read: BE YOU WOLF OR LAMB, *THE CHILD* SHALL LEAD US ALL. "Do you want to read what Dutty wrote?" Addy asked Christopher.

"No," Christopher answered, to her surprise. "Is this on the Internet? Aren't people going to see this? What's going to happen when people see this?"

Addy didn't understand Christopher's reaction. She thought he had come around. "That's why we're celebrating. We want people to see this. We're not celebrating what happened last night. We're celebrating the fact that everyone knows what happened last night and everyone knows that you were part of it. That was Dutty's plan. That's how it all starts."

"But what about regular people? What about my parents? What about the police?"

"You can't hide a revolution in the darkness. If you try, it'll die like a flame without oxygen." A deep voice spoke from behind Addy and Christopher. Christopher turned to see Dutty standing there. Dutty put his hand on Christopher's shoulder. "That's how they've kept us down for generations, for centuries—they've made us afraid, not only of each other but of the world too."

"And this helps somehow?" Christopher asked, looking at his own picture again on the screen. He barely recognized himself.

"People need a point of light to follow," Dutty said to Christopher. "You're that point of light. But they can't follow you if they can't see you."

"Yeah, but the people trying to kill me can't find me if they can't see me either."

"Have a beer," Dutty ordered Christopher. "Talk to your people. We can talk more about this some other time." Christopher was too confused to respond. So he walked into the kitchen and grabbed a beer. Then, beer in hand, he turned back toward the room. He thought about going to Evan, but Evan seemed to be fitting in so well, Christopher didn't want to ruin it. Instead, he began to walk through the building's rooms alone.

They still looked at him, all those people who merely wanted to touch him and introduce themselves to him. They still watched him without speaking to him. He walked from one room to the next. Each room was the same, the people in small groups trying their best to look happy and unafraid. A few of them smiled at Christopher as he walked by, but none of them talked to him. The faces of the people melted into each other. Christopher thought he recognized some of the faces from either the battlefield or the first night that he met Dutty, but he couldn't be sure. Then he spotted the one face that he was sure he remembered: the face of the old black man whose hand he shook on that first night. Suddenly, even though he couldn't remember the man's name, he remembered what the man had said to him.

Christopher walked up to the man. He was sitting alone in a chair in the corner of one of the rooms. The old man smiled at Christopher when Christopher got close to him. "You said to me that you knew my father," Christopher said.

The old man nodded. "I did say that and I did know your father."

"I forgot your name," Christopher confessed.

"You heard a lot of names that night," the older man said, excusing him. "Mine is Brian."

Christopher thought back to his father's journal, trying to remember all of the names his father had written in it. Christopher had read the whole thing cover to cover at least three times since it was first dropped into his hands. Then it dawned on him. "You were his intelligence contact."

Brian nodded and laughed easily. "Until they took him away from me. I liked your father. He tried to be a good person. He sure as hell wouldn't have wanted any of this for you."

"Yeah, well, I don't suppose he has much say in the matter."

"Do you want to know more about him?" Brian asked.

Christopher shook his head. "Not really," he answered. He wasn't in the mood to hear old stories about the War. "Not now."

"Then what do you want to know about?" Brian asked him.

Something in Brian's voice made Christopher think that this strange old man didn't really fit in with Dutty's people. He had an air of skepticism that set him apart from everyone else here. "What are you doing here?" Christopher asked him.

Brian leaned toward Christopher, who was still standing in front of him. He glanced around them before he spoke to make sure no one was listening to their conversation. "Reggie asked me to keep an eye on you."

Twenty-eight

They were putting a lot of faith on the signal runners. They had backups in case one of them got caught, but getting caught wasn't the only issue. The issue was also that no one had any idea what one of the signal runners would say if he did get caught. They were only kids—kids who didn't even have a stake in the outcome of the Uprising. No one could blame them if they got caught and leaked everything. All any of them got out of the deal was the promise of a safe place to stay for a few weeks and warm food to eat. Still, that promise was enough to make them more loyal than most adults. That's why the rebels needed to use them in the first place, because the radios and phones weren't safe anymore after Zé Carlos flipped. He told them everything he knew about the Uprising. Luckily, he didn't know as much as he thought he did. Sure, they had to start from scratch after he flipped. They had to make a whole new plan—a better plan—but Zé had no idea that they were coordinating with the others. He didn't know that Rio was only one city in a master plan to take down the whole world in one night. He didn't know that the Child was behind it all. If he had known all of this, he could have destroyed the Uprising. That's how fragile it was. Luckily, nobody ever trusted Zé that much to begin with. You can't buy loyalty with money. But with the street kids—the signal runners—you can buy loyalty with the offer of a warm bed and hot food and a few kind words. The kids want to be loyal. They've just never had anyone to be loyal to except each other.

Simone sat back in her little box of a home and stared out the open window. Anyone looking into her window could see Simone's face, but she kept her gun hidden from view. She wasn't afraid of being seen. She mixed well with the tens of thousands of other faces inhabiting the windows of the shantytown at any given moment. Simone's home was half-way up the hill, right in the heart of the shantytown. She was about as close to a literal version of a needle in a haystack as any human being could ever get. She'd paid real money for her shanty, but it was worth it. She was on the second floor of a four-story building, one made out of concrete instead of the corrugated metal and old wood used on the edges of the shantytown. Her building had running water on the first floor and a working toilet. A few of Simone's neighbors even had working electricity. Simone didn't, but she didn't need it. She was happy waiting in the darkness. At night she watched the hordes of people visible outside her window going about their lives. She often compared the War to the ongoing battles between the rival drug gangs in Rio. As far as Simone could tell, the only difference was that the warring drug gangs had a product.

Simone heard a knock at her door. "Who is it?" she called out. If the person knocking gave the wrong answer, she wouldn't be able to stop him from coming in, but she would have a second to jump out of her window and run. She wouldn't be able to get away, but at least she would die running.

"Han Solo," a boy's voice shouted from the other side of the door. He was supposed to yell "Boba Fett" as a signal to Simone if something was wrong. Simone had told the boy all about Star Wars. *She'd turned it into an epic bedtime story. She even promised to let him watch the movies if everything worked out. She could still hear the boy's excitement when he said the name "Han Solo." Simone thought that he might be more excited about the prospect of watching* Star Wars *than he was about the food. She didn't know if she was going to be able to keep her promise to him. Even if*

she survived, she had no idea what was going to happen to the shantytown after the Uprising, let alone what was going to happen to the shantytown's parentless children. Hiding an Intelligence Center in a shantytown seemed to Simone like a cruel joke. They must have known that destroying the Intelligence Center would mean destroying so much more. It gave her all the more reason to hate them.

She slipped her rifle under a tattered rug she kept near the window and walked to the door. When she opened it, Bené stood outside, alone. "Come in, quick," she said to him and ushered him through the door. Bené was smiling. He always seemed to be smiling. Simone had no way of knowing if he was really always smiling or if he only smiled when he was with her. "What have you got?" Bené reached under his shirt and pulled out the neck wallet that Simone had gotten for him. It was brown canvas, almost the same color as Bené's skin, and was impossible to see through his T-shirt. He fumbled inside it and pulled out a handwritten note. "Who's it from?" Simone asked as Bené handed her the note.

"Mr. Costa," Bené told her.

"Good," she said to Bené. "You did good." Simone heard the chop, chop sound of a helicopter flying by outside. It wasn't anything to be concerned about. The helicopters flew by rather frequently. They were meant to scare the drug lords into keeping their behavior in the shadows. They didn't care about the drug lords as long as the violence didn't seep out of the slums. Still, Simone wondered if those helicopters were going to pick sides when everything went down.

"What's it say?" Bené asked her as she unfolded the letter.

Simone smiled at him. "It says that Bené is the fastest boy in all of Brazil and that all the girls sigh when he runs by them." Bené blushed as Simone silently read what the letter actually said. The attack would begin at three a.m. that night. Simone looked at her watch. It was eight o'clock in the evening. She would have to wait only seven more hours. She would try to get a little sleep first.

Because of the increased surveillance since Zé betrayed them, the rebels were attacking from the north. The signal runners would help to coordinate the attack so that everyone moved in choreographed fashion. They'd learned that the extra surveillance was to the south and the east where the entrances to the Intelligence Center were. Since there were no doors to the north, there were no guards there either. So no guards but, since there were no doors, the rebels would have to use dynamite to blow holes in the wall. Simone was to stay in her location. From there, she was supposed to provide cover for the guys planting the dynamite and then for the ones running into the maelstrom through the newly exploded openings in the walls. If it even looked like anyone was trying to stop them, she was to shoot. Two other sharpshooters were providing cover from different angles, from different spots in the shantytown. Mr. Costa didn't add any details about whether her shots were supposed to be warning shots, shots to disarm, or shots to kill. He didn't have to. She knew. And she never missed.

Once all the others had made it inside the Intelligence Center, she was to leave her post and join them. They would need all the bodies inside they could get. Nobody knew what would happen after that. Nobody planned their escape. Government authorities would likely be called in after the attack. That's why they put the Intelligence Center in the shantytown to begin with—because of the additional security they got from the government out of it. There was more than a decent chance that the government would see the violence and use it as an excuse to tear the whole shantytown down. "What does it really say?" Bené asked.

"It says that there's going to be a raid tonight, that they're rounding up children," Simone lied to Bené. She wasn't even sure if raids ever actually happened, but she knew that the children talked about them, and feared them, like they were very real. "You need to get out. You can come back tomorrow, but tonight, you need to hide out somewhere else. Can you do that?"

Bené smiled. "I'm the fastest boy in all of Brazil," he said with confidence. "They'll never catch me."

"*Please, Bené, for me.*" Simone pleaded with the boy to leave the shantytown for one night.

"*Okay,*" Bené answered. "*For you.*"

"*Thank you, Bené,*" Simone said. She grabbed the boy and held him close to her chest and kissed him on the forehead. "*You've been a great help, Bené. You did so good.*"

"*Good enough for* Star Wars?" Bené asked her.

"*Good enough for* Star Wars," Simone answered. Then she kissed him on the forehead one more time and let him go.

Twenty-nine

"Maybe we should go outside to talk," Brian volunteered after his mention of Reggie left Christopher dumbfounded. Christopher didn't move. His head hurt. He was trying to process what Brian had told him, but the thick bass echoing out of the computer behind him kept pulsating in his brain, jumbling his thoughts.

"Maybe we should," Christopher finally agreed.

Brian slowly stood up from his chair. From force of habit, he looked around the room to see who might be watching them. He should have known who was watching them. Almost everyone was watching them. "Don't worry about them," Brian whispered to Christopher. "You're entitled to a little peace."

Brian led Christopher past Dutty as they headed for the door. "The kid wanted some quiet," Brian told Dutty as they walked by.

"Okay," Dutty answered, nodding to Christopher as he passed.

They walked together into the barren wasteland that Christopher had seen out his window. He could hear the cars speeding by on the highway atop the hill above the compound. The sun was sinking, turning the brown dirt beneath their feet to an almost golden color. "So, you must have some questions for me," Brian said to Christopher. They stood close enough together to talk quietly while still hearing each other over the roar of the traffic.

"Was it Addy?" Christopher asked.

"Was Addy what?" Brian responded.

"Was Addy the one that told Reggie I was here?"

"No," Brian said, shaking his head. "If Addy were still in touch with Reggie, why would he need me to keep an eye on you?"

"I guess that's true. But why did Reggie send someone to keep an eye on me anyway?"

"Because you're eighteen and you don't know what you're doing and these people aren't trying to help you."

"What are you talking about?" Christopher asked, glancing back at the compound. He could still barely hear the music. "These people worship me. Besides, Reggie just wants me to run away and I've decided that I don't want to die running."

"It's good to make decisions. So you've decided to lead a revolution?"

"I'm not leading anything," Christopher told him.

"I know. You aren't a true leader if everyone is following you but all you're doing is following somebody else." It was a practiced line. Brian had rehearsed it. Christopher could tell. Still, it hit Christopher hard.

"Why are you doing this? It's not like I was given a lot of choices here."

"I know," Brian said softly. "Run away or pretend you're somebody that you're not. It's more options than your father had, but I don't want to compare you to your father. Instead, what if I gave you another option?"

"Will it mean not running forever and not watching people die in my name?"

Brian shook his head. "No. People are going to die in your name no matter what you do. But I can give you an option where you get to stop running and you get to stop pretending to be somebody you're not."

Christopher looked back at the compound. They'd been gone for a long time already. He knew that they should get back soon so people didn't start getting suspicious. "And what do I have to do?"

"Simple. You come with me, back to see Reggie."

"And how does that help? I've already been there. Reggie wanted me to run."

Brian nodded. "Reggie knows what it's like to be a lost eighteen-year-old kid. When he was eighteen, somebody convinced him that running was the best thing that he could do. That's why he tried to get you to run. But if you don't want to run, he's got other ideas. He wants you to understand your own power."

"What's that?"

"People don't trust each other, but they'll trust you."

"How is that different from what Dutty is asking me to do?"

"We're not asking you to lead. We're not even asking you to pretend to lead. The leadership's already in place—real leaders with real power." Brian glanced dismissively at the compound. "All you have to do is help convince them to work together."

"Because they'll trust me," Christopher finished for Brian, not even trying to cover up his sarcasm.

"You don't understand how deep the hatred goes. It might seem frivolous to you, but it goes back generations. You don't have to decide now. Think about it. But try to make your decision before Dutty gets your head blown off." With that, Brian started walking back to the compound.

"What would my father have done?" Christopher called after Brian as he walked away.

"Beats the hell out of me," Brian answered. "And remember, you're not your father."

Thirty

Christopher was waiting for Addy. It was early in the morning. The air outside was still cool, the ground still wet. He had spent enough time with her to know about when she would wake up. No one else seemed to be awake yet. Even the highway running along the hill above the compound was quiet.

Addy nearly jumped when she stepped outside and saw Christopher. He was sitting on the ground in the dirt, his hands resting on the tops of his knees. She didn't expect anyone to be outside, not this early. She didn't like being surprised. In her experience, surprises were almost never good and they were far too often final. "Shit," Addy said after catching her breath. "You scared me. What are you doing here?"

"I thought I'd join you on your run," Christopher answered, "if that's okay." He knew she would be running. Every morning, like clockwork.

"Of course," Addy answered. What else could she say? Christopher had never asked to run with her before. She remembered that he'd run a few times with Max but never with her. She couldn't say no. Not to him. Not even if she wanted to. "Of course," she repeated without any added conviction.

"How far are you running?" Christopher asked.

"An hour."

"You go by time, not by distance?"

"Yeah. You go as far as you can in the time you're given. Some days you make it farther than others."

"Well, if I start slowing you down, feel free to go ahead without me."

"I'm sure you'll keep up," Addy told Christopher. Without any more discussion, they were running. They pushed each other, both running faster than they would have if they'd been running alone. They didn't say anything to each other for the first thirty minutes. They simply matched each other stride for stride. At the half-hour mark they turned around and began to run home. Their pace slowed considerably on the way back, so much so that they were nearly a full mile from the compound when the hour was up. They began to walk. It was the first time they'd been alone together since they found Dutty.

"Are you happy with how the raid went?" Christopher asked Addy as they walked. She started walking slower, wanting to give Christopher time to get whatever was bothering him off his chest.

"I'm glad we finally did something," Addy answered him.

"But do you think any good will come of it?"

Addy looked over at Christopher. "Why are you so unsure of yourself? After all of this, after how everyone's reacted to you, after they put their lives on the line for you, why do you still have doubts?"

"Because I'm not who you want me to be. I'm not the Chosen One. I'm not Harry Fucking Potter. I don't have any magic powers. Max knew that. I think you know it too, but you're afraid to admit it."

Addy shook her head. "No," she said. "The problem isn't that you're not who I want you to be. The problem is that you still think that this story is about you. You'll learn, though. This story is bigger than you. It started before you were born. I never thought that you had magic powers, Christopher. But I also don't think that you know what your role in this story is yet."

"Do you know my role?" Christopher asked, throwing it back at her.

Addy shook her head again. "I'm not sure. I only know that your role is important—that it's bigger than me and bigger than you. You and your parents mean too much to too many people for anything less."

"What am I supposed to do with that?"

"Just remember it," Addy told him. "Remember that it's not your story. It's their story. You're only a character in it. Take that knowledge and try to do your best and know that no matter what happens, we'll fight for you." The morning air was growing warm. A thick wind blew in from over the hills.

"Do you think you know what your role is?" Christopher asked Addy.

Addy shrugged. "I think that sometimes it's easier to figure out other people's roles than it is to figure out your own."

"Do you at least know what you would do if the War came to an end?"

"I have no idea," Addy said. "I've never thought that far ahead."

Christopher thought she might say more, but she didn't. "I'll race you the rest of the way back," he challenged. Addy smiled at him and, for the first time since that day when she saw Christopher walk into Reggie's compound, Christopher felt like she was actually looking at *him*. So much more had changed since then. They both knew it. Then Addy burst into a sprint toward the compound and Christopher chased after her.

Thirty-one

The authorities' attack on the rebels' base was eerily similar to the rebels' attack on the Intelligence Cell. They came in the dead of night and announced their presence with gunfire. But they were better armed and better trained. The rebels weren't ready to defend themselves.

The authorities had their orders. They weren't absolutely ordered to kill, but they were ordered to take zero risks. Zero. They all knew what that meant. It meant that no one would be facing repercussions for their actions. It meant that no one had to think before pulling the trigger.

"This is the purest battlefield you'll ever set foot on, gentlemen," the debriefing officer said. "They are all enemies. Enemies of the state. Enemies of the country. Enemies of human decency. I don't know what their politics are, and frankly I don't give a shit. They are criminals, murderers, and terrorists." The debriefing officer clicked a button on the mouse and a picture was projected onto the screen in front the men. It was an uninteresting picture of a two-story warehouse building on the edge of a desert. A small road ran in front of it. It was the before picture. The chief clicked another button and the serene but dull picture was replaced by a half-burned-out corpse of a building. You could see right into the building where the walls had disintegrated in the heat of the fire. You could see the bullet holes riddling the wall. They'd moved the bodies away before taking the picture. It didn't matter. They had pictures of the bodies too. "They killed seven innocent employees." *Click. Click. Click. Click. Click. Click. Click.* The debriefing officer left the last picture up on the screen. You could see where the bullet entered the man's head right above his left eye. Either somebody was a really good shot or the man was shot from close range.

"What was the building?" one of the officers asked.

"A corporate warehouse," the chief answered. "That's all you need to know. That's all anyone needs to know. We're not dealing with intelligent criminals here. We're dealing with a domestic terrorist group." The officer continued without moving the slide off the last picture of the dead man. "We've got some good information on them. We think we know all three of their locations in the greater Los Angeles area. We'll be splitting into three teams." Three of the lieutenants stood up and began dividing the officers and giving each of them his assignment. It looked a little bit chaotic, but there was a method to the madness. Each group had its own set of specialists: marksmen, pyrotechnicians, drivers, and grunts.

Donald was given his assignment. He'd be with the group hitting an abandoned building in a desolate section on the western edge of Los Angeles. It all seemed strange to him—the shoot-first, don't-ask-questions orders; the vague details about the terrorist group; the massive amount of resources being dedicated to this job; and, probably most curiously, the one-job-only alliance between LAPD and the FBI. "We'll break you up momentarily so that your team leader can go over the plans with your group," the chief said once everyone in the room had been given his assignment. "Off the record, I just wanted to give you all a word of warning. These are domestic terrorists. They're American citizens.

They're not going to look like what you expect them to look like when we throw around the word *terrorist*. They're going to look like any one of you. They're going to look like normal people. I'd like to give you more detail than that, but we've only got one picture." The chief clicked the mouse on his computer again, finally letting the last dead man rest in peace. A new picture came up on the screen. It was a picture taken at night, a close-up of a boy's face as he aimed a gun at a man standing in a window on the building's second floor. Even though it was dark outside, it was light enough to make out the details of the boy's face. It was also possible, if you squinted a little bit, to make out the figure in the window. All the officers knew what had happened to the man in the window. They all knew that there had been no survivors.

Donald knew something else too. He didn't realize it at first. He only knew that he recognized something in that picture. He looked at the building again, trying to remember if he'd seen it somewhere before, but it wasn't the building. Then he looked at the boy's face again. He'd seen the boy before. Well, he hadn't seen the boy himself before, but he had seen the boy's picture. Then Donald remembered where he'd seen the boy's picture and suddenly everything started to make sense. Donald tried to hide his epiphany. He tried to stay calm. He knew that he'd have a life to live after that night and that having people know that he was part of the War wasn't going to make that life any easier. At the same time, he tried to look around to see if he could spot anybody else who recognized the Child in the picture. He couldn't be the only one. Did the chief know? Was that what this was all about? Did the guys at the FBI know? How high up did this go? Donald knew that he'd probably never get answers to his questions. Still, here was his chance to be a hero.

Even though he didn't catch anyone else reacting to the picture of the Child, Donald was sure that he wasn't the only one in the room who recognized him. He knew that they would pull in as many people with a vested interest in this as they could. Donald didn't have anything against the kid. In fact, he kind of felt bad for him, but the kid had made his choice. They all make their choice. Even though he kind of felt bad for the kid, Donald knew that he'd be pissed if the kid wasn't at his target but was at one of the other two.

Christopher sought out Brian later on the same day that he'd gone on the morning run with Addy. He had made up his mind. Even if she didn't know it, Addy helped him. Brian, hoping all along that Christopher would come to see him, made sure that he wasn't difficult to find. "So, you figure out what you want to do?" he asked Christopher after the two of them were out of earshot from anyone else.

"Yeah," Christopher said, his voice nearly shaking. "I'm in. I'll go back to see Reggie, but I want Addy and Evan to come with me."

Brian looked at Christopher and then looked down at the floor. "What makes you think they would even want to come with you? Didn't Addy drag you here in the first place?"

"Addy didn't drag me here. I agreed to come here. And Addy and Evan will come with me if I ask them to. I know it."

Brian paused for a minute. He lifted his eyebrows and the wrinkles it caused on his forehead made his face look pained. "Well, it doesn't work that way, kid. They can't come. You've got to do this on your own."

"Why?"

"Because the whole point is to get people to trust you, and you don't get them to trust you by traveling with a fire-breathing rebel and an outsider." Brian put his hand on Christopher's shoulder. It was a brotherly touch. "You have to come alone, Christopher. That's just the way it is."

Donald had never actually ridden in a SWAT car before. He'd been on assignments where they'd been used, but he'd never been inside one. He felt like he was inside an army tank, though he'd never been inside one of those either. After the chief finished his debriefing, the officers split up into three different groups and walked outside. Nine SWAT cars were parked next to the station, waiting for them. Donald wondered what this felt like for his fellow officers—at least for the majority of his fellow officers who didn't know a thing about the War. He wondered how insane this must feel for them. Donald had never seen this much firepower before. No one had ever seen the LAPD gather this much firepower before. Maybe it made sense to them. Maybe it made sense that they'd be working together with the FBI to nab a bunch of kids who had murdered seven people and burned down a building. It's not like that type of violence happened every day—not even in Los Angeles—not that they knew about anyway. So they thought that everyone had been rounded up to go after some punk domestic terrorist kids, probably anarchists or environmental wackos. But Donald knew better. He was pretty sure that the chief was in on it too, and there must have been others. He reminded himself that when all this was over he needed to try to figure out which side of the War the chief was on. People above the chief must have been in on it too. It would take somebody pretty serious to bring all these resources together just to kill the Child. Well, to kill the Child and rip the hearts out of all those suckers clinging to the hope that one kid could do to two armies what neither of the armies could do to the other. Donald had never heard of them pulling in civilian resources to help on a matter related to the War before. He didn't like it.

They were packed into the back of the SWAT car. There were ten of them in this one car—the driver, the guy in the passenger seat, and eight in the back. The guys in the back sat on benches facing each other, four on each bench. Four of the guys in the back were LAPD and four were FBI. Donald sat in one of the middle two spots, shoulder to shoulder with somebody from the FBI and someone from the LAPD that he'd never met before. "How long until we get there?" one of the FBI agents yelled up to the driver. Donald could feel every bump in the road in his seat.

"You're not from L.A., are you?" the driver replied with a laugh.

The confused FBI agent looked to Donald for a translation. "L.A. traffic," Donald told him. "You can never tell how long it's going to take to get anywhere."

"Can't we put the sirens on?" another FBI agent asked.

"Not on this job," the guy in the passenger seat replied. "We were ordered to keep a low profile. We're not supposed to draw any attention to ourselves."

"That's why we're riding down the highway in an armored SWAT car," the cop sitting next to Donald said, and everybody laughed.

"What's your job?" one of the FBI agents asked Donald when the laughter died down.

"Firebombs," Donald answered and he began to think about how much more advanced his equipment was than the Molotov cocktails used by the rebels in their attack and, for a moment, he was really impressed. "You?" Donald asked the FBI agent.

"Sharpshooter," the FBI agent answered. There was no need for anyone else to say anything, no need to go around the car and have everyone else name their job. Everybody knew it. Everything that needed to be said about their mission had already been said. Firebombs. Sharpshooter. Flush 'em out. Take 'em out.

"You ever actually shoot anybody before?" Donald asked the FBI agent.

"Yeah," the man answered. "For this mission, they only picked the ones who have."

It was getting late when Christopher went looking for Addy. He knew that he was running out of time. He'd spent most of the day with Evan, though he'd never built up the courage to tell Evan that he was leaving. Instead they spent the day talking about . . . what did they talk about? Not about the future. They talked about the past. They reminisced about old times, about how much more those old times would make sense to them knowing what they know now. They reminisced about the days when they were ignorant. They tried not to pass judgment on which times were better. They took turns starting sentence after sentence with the word *remember*. *Remember* when. *Remember* that time. *Remember. Remember. Remember.* Remember the past because it is certain, unlike the future.

Christopher wasn't going to waste any more time telling Evan to walk away. He wasn't going to tell Evan to go home again. He knew that it would be pointless and he didn't want to spend his last day with his old friend arguing over things that neither of them had any control over. Evan wasn't going to leave the War now that he'd seen what he'd seen. He had spent his whole life training with Christopher for something like this. Abandoning it now, with nothing resolved, would seem like too much of a waste. Even so, Christopher would have liked to tell Evan that he was leaving. He would have liked to say good-bye like a true friend, but he didn't. Instead, he now had to go looking for Addy because he wanted to make sure that he told someone that he was leaving and he wanted to tell Addy to keep an eye on Evan. He had no idea what else he was going to say to her.

Addy was with Dutty when Christopher found them. They were talking, making plans for a future that would never occur. Brian would be picking Christopher up in twenty minutes. Christopher was supposed to wait for him on the side of the highway at the top of the hill. Then they'd start the long, lonely drive back across the country to Florida, where it all seemed to start anyway.

"Christopher," Dutty called out with joy in his voice when he saw Christopher walking toward them.

"I need to talk to Addy," Christopher said, cutting Dutty off before he could launch into details about the next raid that he was planning or the next message he was going to send to the masses. Christopher said the words with more confidence than any words he'd said to Dutty since they'd met and with more confidence than any words he'd said to Addy since she'd turned her hair the color of fire.

"Okay," Dutty said to Christopher, acquiescing not because he wanted to but because he knew that if Christopher was going to start making demands, he had to. "I'll leave you two alone." Then he walked out of the room.

Christopher didn't waste any time. He knew that any hesitation could lead to paralysis. "I'm leaving," he said to Addy.

"What?" That was the only word Addy could find to respond. It was like Christopher had sucker-punched her.

"I'm leaving," Christopher repeated, "tonight. I wanted you to know. I want you to take care of Evan."

"I don't understand," Addy said.

"I don't understand either, but you want me to be a leader so I need to start making my own decisions sometime, right?"

"So leaving is your own decision?" Addy asked, hinting that she understood more than she possibly could.

"I don't know," Christopher said. "I think it is—more than staying would be anyway."

Addy stood there, silently, swaying on her feet as if she might topple over. Christopher had never seen her like that before. He'd done more damage to her than if he had punched her in the stomach. She looked dazed. She looked at him, her eyes shiny with tears. "You can't go. You can't leave us. You can't leave me."

"Promise me that you'll take care of Evan."

Addy pursed her lips. She felt vulnerable, like a child. She thought that maybe if she didn't promise him, he wouldn't leave.

"Promise me, Addy," Christopher begged, though they both knew that he was asking for more than what his words implied. He was asking for her forgiveness too.

"You know that I'll watch over him," Addy said, finally promising. "Is that why you're leaving?"

"No." Christopher managed to force out a smile. "I'm happy for the two of you. I'm just sorry that I'm not the person you thought I was."

"You don't need to give up yet," Addy whispered, her voice cracking as she spoke. "None of us are who we will become."

Christopher wondered why Addy never asked him where he was going. He didn't understand that it was not something you asked people in Addy's world. Where you were going was never anyone's business but your own, even if you were the Child. "Please try to wait as long as you can before you tell anyone I've gone." That was Christopher's one last request of Addy. "You're the only one who knows." Then he turned and began walking away. When he'd made it all the way to the door leading outside, he took one look back at Addy. She hadn't moved. "I hope we will see each other again," he said to her. Addy only nodded in response, not believing that it was possible. Then he was gone.

It's possible that Brian and Christopher passed the SWAT cars on the road as their car raced away from the compound and the SWAT cars raced toward it. If they did, neither Brian nor Christopher noticed. They were already out of California when the first of the rebels hit the ground, struck down by a well-aimed bullet while trying to escape a burning building.

Donald and the others waited silently until they couldn't see any more movement inside the dilapidated old building. The place didn't look like much. It was one story, spread out over a barren stretch of brown dirt. Most the windows were still in place, but they were caked with mud. If Donald had known his assignment, he would have guessed that the building was just a way station for squatters. Hell, for all he knew, it was. For all he knew, the whole story about the domestic terrorists was one big lie meant to get them there, meant to give them cover to have the innocents help them find the Child as he hid himself among a bunch of L.A. street kids. Seeing the clearly defenseless, dirty building, Donald began to wonder what the other cops and agents were thinking, the ones who didn't know the real reason why they were there, the ones who saw the picture of the Child and figured he was some punk that needed to be taught a lesson. Donald wondered if he would be gullible enough to believe that they were amassing this much firepower to nab some punk kid if he were in their shoes.

They camped out on the other side of the highway until the building fell quiet, staking the place out with long-range binoculars, making sure that they were far enough away that nobody in the building would be able to see them through the darkness. It was late by the time things settled down. By the time they were given their orders to move, they'd already been waiting by the side of the road for more than two hours. The tension had been rising since they'd pulled off the highway, gotten out of their SWAT cars, and begun to check their weapons. Now they were chomping at the bit, ready to move, ready to attack. If any of them had had any hesitation before, it died a quiet death on the side of the high-way. "Time to roll, boys," the team leader said, motioning for the first wave to get in place.

Donald was in the first wave with the other two pyros. Four sharpshooters and two grunts accompanied them. Initially, the sharpshooters and the grunts were only there for cover. They had the place pretty well mapped out. They knew where the entry points and exit points were. They knew where three pyros needed to be to make their equipment count. The two grunts took the first spots in the line. They moved up quickly, like lead blockers, getting into position so that they could defend against any ground-based counterattacks. Then the sharpshooters moved into place, each one roughly equidistant from the next so that they could cover the entire front of the building. The pyros moved into place last, taking their positions between the sharpshooters and the grunts.

Donald took his spot on the far right-hand side. Once in position, he knelt down and removed four canisters from his backpack. One was already loaded into his launcher. Each of the pyros had five canisters. With that equipment, each one of them could have burned down the whole building by themselves. Together, they could have burned down half a town. It wasn't merely about burn-ing the place down, though. It was about speed. It was about gen-erating heat and fear and panic.

Donald rechecked the preloaded canister to make sure there were no issues. He would have to manually reload after each shot, but he could do that in under a minute. He was supposed to hit two rooms with two shots each. The fifth canister was in case he missed with one of the first four, but he never missed. If he landed the first two shots, he was supposed to shoot the fifth canister onto the roof. The canisters weren't meant to explode. They were meant to start fires. Shortly after being shot, they sprayed out a potent liquid in all directions, some mixture of diethyl ether and gasoline that was meant to catch fire easily and then burn hot and long. Once the canister sprayed out its contents, it would combust. The explosion wouldn't be enough to do any damage on its own. It was merely enough to ignite the fire, but once the fire started, it would be almost impossible to stop. Anything the liquid touched would burn to a cinder.

Donald aimed his weapon at the first window and waited for the signal.

Everyone but Addy was asleep. She was in bed, but she couldn't fall asleep. Her head was too full of questions. What were they going to do now that Christopher was gone? How would they keep everybody going? What would they say? What was she going to tell Evan? She lay still, forcing herself not to toss and turn. She didn't want to risk waking up the other women in the room. She didn't want to have to talk to them. So she kept her body still but her mind was running. She couldn't stop that. She saw Christopher's face over and over, all different versions of it—his face when Max first led him into Reggie's compound, his face when he first saw Addy walk out of the bathroom with her red hair, his face after Max was killed, his face right before he walked out the door. She wondered if she should have learned more from all those faces.

Addy was still awake when the window in their room shattered, spraying glass everywhere. The other three women were asleep when it happened. They woke up to the sounds of shattering glass and the feel of shards cutting their skin. Nobody, not even Addy, knew what it was that had broken the glass. Then the spray came.

The spray was clear and almost odorless, but they still all knew to try to avoid it. They moved quickly, ducking behind furniture or blocking the spray with blankets, but everything was happening so quickly. Not all of them moved fast enough. Addy held a blanket up and used it to keep the spray from reaching her. One of the other women managed to duck behind her bed. They didn't know what the spray was. They didn't know if it was acid or poison. It landed on two of them without having any immediate effect. One of the women, unable to block the entire spray with her pillow, merely got some of it on her pants leg. None of it hit her face or body. The fourth woman wasn't so lucky. The canister had landed closest to her and the spray hit her before she had time to move. For a second or two, it seemed like everything was going to be okay. The spray stopped and all of the women looked at Ruth. They could still see the dark marks on her clothes where the spray hit her. She reached a hand up to wipe some of the drops of liquid off her face. None of the others could smell anything, but she could. A few drops of the spray had landed right under her nostrils. She could make out a faint smell of eggs.

Addy was still staring at Ruth when the fire started. None of them had moved. They were still too surprised and shocked to realize what was happening. They heard noises from the other rooms, feet rustling and mumbled voices. Their room didn't ignite first. Addy heard it happen in one of the other rooms first. She heard the whooshing sound of air being sucked out of the room as the fire lit and began devouring the room's oxygen. That's when she realized what the liquid was. She watched as Ruth lifted up her hand to wipe a few more drops of the liquid away from her eyes. Everything appeared to be happening slowly. Then Addy saw the shimmering light of the four small flames that jumped from the canister. Then she felt the heat. Then she heard the whoosh in their room. Then she heard the screaming. Addy looked away from Ruth as Ruth clutched at her own skin, peeling away from her body. It was quick. It was far from painless, but it was quick. Once the screaming stopped, all that was left was the smell.

The woman who had gotten some of the spray on her pants had managed to get her pants off but not before her leg had been badly burned and when she pulled off her pants, some of the liquid got on her hands. Addy felt sick. She wanted to help but knew there was nothing she could do. Instead, she ran out of the room. The whole building was already quickly filling with smoke. When she got into the hallway, she dropped down to her hands and knees. Then she heard the first of the gunshots.

Donald watched as the flames grew. He'd gotten all four of his canisters into the building and landed his fifth on the roof. Another canister landed on the roof shortly after his. Then the third. All three of the pyros had been perfect. Twelve canisters had made it into the building. It was overkill. Donald knew it. He didn't worry about that, though. What he worried about was that the body of the Child would be unrecognizable if he got caught in the fire. He wondered if the leadership had thought about that, if they had the Child's dental records or something else they could identify his body with. He guessed it wasn't his problem, though. He knew that he was merely a tool. And rules were rules. And orders were orders. And he wasn't the type to rock the boat.

Donald was watching when the first of them tried to run out the door. The irony was that it was the fire that gave the sharpshooters the light they needed. Even those that escaped the flames couldn't escape the light. The first one came running out. He stood out, a black shadow against the brightness. He made it three steps before he was gunned down. The bullets came from all over, from at least three different directions. The first one was always that way. Everyone was so eager. A pattern would develop soon, though, with the sharpshooters taking turns so that no one escaped through the gaps. If someone did get through the gaps, that's what the grunts were for. They had guns too. Some carried handguns, some rifles, but their job was to catch the overflow. The second runner came and only two guns went off this time, cutting him down nearly on top of the first.

Donald put his equipment down and scurried back to the high-way. While he wasn't planning on doing any shooting, he did want to pick up a rifle so he could be useful if they needed him. Besides, he wondered what type of rewards could be in store for the man who shot the Child. The gunfire continued to echo around him as he scrambled back up the hill. It sounded eerily like a fireworks display, one with all the noise and none of the beauty.

The only thing Addy could think about when she hit the floor, dodging the billowing smoke, was finding Evan. She tried to tell herself that it was all because of the promise she'd made to Christopher. She tried to tell herself that her actions, ignoring the screaming and pandemonium around her to search for Evan, were still being done for the sake of the cause. She knew where Evan's room was and she made her way toward it, hoping that she would find more than a charred body. She was confused when she first heard the gunshots, but she had to crawl past the front door to get to Evan's room. People were already standing inside the door wait-ing. It quickly became clear to Addy what was going on. They were trying to time their runs out the door so that at least a few of them might escape the gunfire. Addy didn't know the odds of escaping, but she knew that they couldn't be good. She heard another volley of gunfire as she crawled down the hallway. She turned away from the front door and, with each sound of gunfire, knew that another one of her friends was being cut down. She wanted to care about each one of them. She *did* care about each one of them; she just didn't have time to care about them then.

When Addy finally found Evan, he was lying on the floor be-neath the smoke, calling out Christopher's name. Of course, no-body answered him because no one was there to answer. Christopher was gone. But only Addy knew that, and now wasn't the time to be telling secrets. Now was the time to run.

The building had three doors. Two faced the highway and one

was on the building's southern side. All three of the doors were covered. No one could get out of one of those doors without facing the gunfire of trained professionals. Donald found a spot high on the hill. He took out a pair of binoculars so that he could try to catch glimpses of the faces of the people as they ran out of the building. He checked every face, trying to spot the Child. The sharpshooters were working quickly and efficiently. Every single person that Donald saw run out a door was cut down before escaping the red glow of the building. Donald saw a lot of them, but he didn't see the one that he was looking for. The flames grew higher and soon the whole hillside was glowing orange except for the dark spaces that were filled with shadows. Donald remained diligent even though he didn't really expect to see Christopher. He didn't expect to have to be a hero. He didn't expect that he'd be the first one to spot the new plume of smoke pouring out one of the side windows.

Donald knew enough about fire to know what that meant. He knew that somebody had broken through the window. "The side," he shouted to the sharpshooters. "Watch the side." Those who were the closest peppered the wall near the window with gunfire, but their angle was poor and because of that, their accuracy was lacking. Donald began to run so that he could get a clear view of the window. One of the grunts followed him but was slow. The plans they had didn't show any windows on that side of the building, but there was a window and somebody had broken through it and Donald was the first one to spot them.

They threw something out of the window first. It was darker on this side of the building so Donald couldn't tell exactly what it was, but it looked like a small piece of furniture. The falling piece of furniture was met with another rip of gunfire, but the sharpshooters still didn't have the angle necessary to connect with their target. Donald lifted the binoculars in time to see a person with shoulder-length, unnaturally red hair jump out the window. A second later, another person jumped out. Donald got a good look at this one's face. It was a boy. It wasn't the Child, but it was a boy of about the same age. The two jumpers hit the ground. The first one pulled the second one to his feet and they stood up and ran.

Donald moved his binoculars back to the one with the red hair. Maybe if he could get a good look at the redhead's face, he could rule out the idea that the red hair was part of a disguise. Then, knowing that neither of the runners was the Child, Donald wouldn't have to chase them. He couldn't rule anything out, though. He never got a good enough look at the redhead's face to be certain that it wasn't Christopher in disguise. So Donald ran too, chasing after Addy and Evan.

Evan and Addy ran up the hill toward the highway, veering away from their attackers. Addy chose the direction. She knew that they would have been sitting ducks if they had run the other way. They would have been right in the snipers' sights, glowing beneath the light from the fire. Since they were going this way, the men with the guns would have to turn away from the burning building to see them. She tried to ignore the periodic snare drum of the gunfire. She only concentrated on running. None of the snipers shot at them, but they weren't in the clear yet. Addy spotted two men who had broken off from the rest—two men chasing them. One was far in front of the other. They both wore LAPD SWAT uniforms and the one in the front was quickly gaining on them.

Donald ran. He ran as fast as he could. He was gaining on them. He looked back to see that the grunt who had been following him was falling farther and farther behind. Donald could hardly blame him. The odds were that all the glory was back at the fire, not chasing these two kids into the night. But the possibility was still there. Donald knew that the possibility was there.

Donald looked up. He was close now. He might have been able to stop and aim his rifle, but he wasn't a trained sharpshooter. If he tried it and missed, they'd escape for sure. Besides, he hadn't come all this way to shoot a couple of random kids. He wanted to be sure first. So he kept running up the hill. The one with the dark hair was running in front. The redhead, the one that Donald really wanted, was trailing behind him. Donald knew that he had to reach them before they got to the top of the hill because once they crested the hill, they'd be able to disappear. Donald drew some air into his lungs, preparing to shout out, ordering them to stop. He didn't know if it would work. He didn't know if the sound of his voice would scare them enough to make them hesitate or if it would make them run faster. Whatever the consequences, Donald was prepared to try. Before he could, it happened. The redhead tripped on a dead root and fell to the ground right in front of him. That gave him the boost that he needed. He found it in himself to speed up and cleared the distance between him and the redhead in seconds.

When Donald neared his target, he lifted his rifle and aimed it at the red hair. He had no desire to play the action hero. He had no witty remarks planned. He wasn't about to trade safety for glory. Still, he had convinced himself that he was chasing the Child. He had become certain that beneath that red wig, he would see the face of the boy in the pictures. Donald didn't care what Christopher saw before he pulled the trigger. He didn't care about making an impression. He only wanted to confirm that this was the Child. He wanted to be sure that he should be proud of what he was doing before he pulled the trigger. Donald took one more step toward the fallen rebel, who had managed to get to one knee and was almost ready to stand. *Look at me*, Donald thought to himself, staring only at the red hair. Then, suddenly, Donald's gun was gone. His hands were empty. He looked up. The dark-haired boy had come back. He had pulled the gun out of Donald's hands and was now standing in front of him. A flickering hell of shadows danced across the boy's face, reflecting the giant fire that was burning higher and higher behind Donald. Donald got two swings in, first with his right hand and then with his left. The boy wasted no energy stepping out the way of each swing. Donald's hand barely missed the boy, never coming close to doing any damage. Then Donald was on the ground, as if pulled there. Then he felt pain. Then he saw darkness. Then nothing.

Addy didn't give Evan a moment to think about what he'd done. She didn't give him a moment to think about anything. Instead, she grabbed his wrist and pulled him. She pulled him away from the body of the policeman he had killed. She pulled him away from the fire. She pulled him away from the screaming and the gunshots. All the while, Evan thought about nothing and let himself be pulled wherever Addy was taking him.

Thirty-two

Christopher thought that Brian was taking him back to the compound in Florida. They'd been driving for a long time. Christopher began to feel like that was all his life had become. A series of long drives interspersed with moments of intense violence. Brian wasn't taking Christopher to the compound in Florida, though. Reggie had left the compound as soon as he got word that Christopher was coming to meet him.

"Where are we?" Christopher asked Brian as they sped across a long, straight road cutting through an endless sea of pine trees.

"New Jersey," Brian answered. Christopher knew that he hadn't been paying attention to where they were going, but he hadn't realized how far off course they'd veered from the destination in his head. He'd been distracted by thoughts about Addy and Evan. Even though he tried not to be, he'd been distracted by thoughts about how long it had been since he'd spoken to his parents. Then, even when he was able to stop thinking, images of the dead kept flashing through his head—the men who had come for him in the woods in Maine, Max and the others in Canada, the man he shot outside of Death Valley, the man Addy shot after he realized who Christopher was.

"This is New Jersey?" Christopher asked, staring out the window at the endless rows of trees. He felt like he should be surprised, but it was getting more and more difficult to surprise him.

"Yeah."

"It looks like Maine," Christopher said.

"Do you want to know where I'm taking you?" Brian asked.

The trees whizzed by them. "I think I know where we're going," Christopher said. Reggie was bringing him back to the place on the Jersey Shore where his father used to come when he was Christopher's age. "Isn't this dangerous? Won't they be looking for me here?"

"Everywhere is dangerous. Reggie had some business he needed to take care of nearby. We think you're as safe here as anywhere."

"That's not the most enthusiastic endorsement I've ever heard."

"Trust us, Christopher. We have no interest in making any more martyrs."

"I guess that's good. At least we've all got something in common." Christopher tried to laugh. "Did you leave the War because of what they did to my father?"

Brian didn't take his eyes off the road. "No. I left the War because I was pretty sure they were going to kill me."

"Why were they going to kill you?"

"They thought I was a spy."

"Were you?"

"No. I wasn't perfect, but I wasn't a spy. They've only got themselves to blame for turning me into what I am now."

"But you tried to help my father when he was on the run?"

Brian glanced quickly at Christopher and then returned his attention to the road. "Like I said, I wasn't perfect, but trying to help a friend isn't the same thing as being a spy."

"I might not even be here if it wasn't for you." Christopher said the words as much to himself as to Brian. "If they'd gotten to my father earlier, my mother never would have learned what she needed to get me back. My father would have died a loser instead of a hero. And I would be just one more kid in the War who didn't know any better than believing that he was good and the people he was fighting were evil. If it wasn't for you, nobody would care who I was."

"Would you like that better?" Brian asked Christopher

Christopher didn't know what he was supposed to say. He wondered if the question was some sort of test. "We almost there?" he asked instead of answering.

"About another hour and a half," Brian told him.

Christopher watched the trees buzz by, barely able to pick one out from the rest. "And Reggie will be waiting for us when we get there?"

"Yeah," Brian confirmed.

Reggie hung up the phone and stared out the window at the boats floating in the harbor. The wind was blowing across the harbor, causing the boats to rock back and forth as they bounced on the waves. This place had history. Reggie had been assured that meeting Christopher on this island would be safe. If he couldn't trust the people who gave him those assurances, then he and Christopher weren't going to make it very far anyway. It was a risk, but Reggie thought the history was important. He wanted Christopher to feel connected. Christopher's father used to come here with his friends, both the one that killed him and the one that died trying to find Christopher. This little island was the place where Christopher's father got it in his head that loyalty to the people who cared about him was more important than fealty to the rules. This little island was the place where Michael brought Christopher's mother and where Christopher's mother figured out what she needed to do if she was going to find Christopher and save him. Now this tiny island was the place where Reggie planned to enlist Christopher in a crazy scheme that would drag the two of them around the world, clinging to the hope that Christopher could do one thing that no one else could do.

It was beginning to get dark outside, but Reggie didn't bother turning on the lights. He took pleasure in the coming darkness. He found it soothing. He picked up the phone again and dialed. The crazy plan that they'd hatched wasn't Reggie's plan, not in the beginning anyway. He guessed it was his now. He owned it now, having purchased it with hundreds of phone calls and thousands of promises. He had to own it—completely, totally—if he was going to sell it to others. Reggie supposed that was how it always worked. He supposed that nobody ever did anything this big by themselves. Everybody was a cog in a machine, but if you pull out any one of the cogs the whole machine is not going to work anymore. After three rings, somebody answered the phone at the other end of the line. Reggie recognized the woman's voice.

"He's on his way," Reggie told the woman. "How is the schedule coming, Annie?"

"As well as can be expected," Annie replied. "Are you sure that you guys are going to be ready to leave tomorrow?"

"We better be," Reggie answered. "After all this, I don't see how any good is going to come from waiting any longer." *Not here anyway,* Reggie thought as he watched an old fishing boat pull into the harbor, barely beating nightfall. "Where are we going first?"

"Singapore," Annie said. "Only I don't know where you're going from there. They wouldn't tell me. They only told me that someone would be meeting you at the airport."

"That's it? I suppose they expect us to trust the first guy who comes to pick us up?" Reggie had them walking a tightrope over a sea full of sharks. Sometimes Reggie doubted his ability to manage it all.

"I'm still working on getting more details," Annie said apologetically.

"And our papers? How are we going to get our papers?"

"I'm working on that too. We're going to be sending a car to pick you guys up tomorrow. The driver should have your papers. If he doesn't, then they'll be at the airport."

"I feel like I could be walking the kid into a giant mess here, Annie."

"Just try to concentrate on Singapore. That's all we can do for now." Annie sounded as tired as Reggie felt. They'd already been working hard on the plan and it hadn't even started yet.

"You hear any more news about California?" Reggie asked. It was the last question Reggie'd been asking everybody ever since he heard the news. He knew that Christopher was still in the dark. Brian had made sure that Christopher didn't get any news about the raid and its casualties. He kept the car radio off and watched whenever Christopher checked his phone. Reggie wasn't going to tell Christopher anything either, not unless he was forced to. Reggie knew that he was going to have to get Christopher to abandon his phone. Nothing good would come of Christopher being connected to the world.

"Nothing new," Annie said. "It's hard to tell the difference between facts, rumors, and lies."

"It always is." Reggie had seen Evan's picture on the news like everybody else, but none of them really knew who Evan was or how important he was to Christopher. Reggie was just happy that someone survived the raid. He believed deep down that if anyone had survived the raid, Addy might have survived it too. Reggie had already lost Max. He had to believe that Addy was still alive. He was so tired of all of it. *One last hurrah*, he thought to himself. It wasn't only that he was tired, though. Reggie had given Addy a job. He didn't want to think that he gave such an important job to a ghost. If he was going to break a promise to the woman who had saved his life, the least he could do was tell her about his broken promise. Reggie tried to think about whether he had any more questions for Annie. "Thanks, Annie," Reggie said when he couldn't think of any. "Be careful out there."

"You too, Reggie. I'll e-mail you when I have more details."

Annie hung up and Reggie sat there, alone again, still staring out the window. He barely moved. He'd been sitting at the desk for almost three hours without getting up. He wondered who else he could call that might know something about California, but he worried about spreading himself too thin. Besides, he couldn't think of anybody who was more plugged in than Annie. Reggie had to make one more phone call before Christopher arrived. After that he could rest. He picked up the phone and dialed George's number.

George answered on the second ring. "George, it's Reggie. How are things?"

"Quiet," George answered. Reggie listened to see if he could hear the noises of the compound behind George, but it really was quiet. "What's going on?"

"Christopher's on his way," Reggie said.

"That's great," George said. "That's what we all were hoping for." Even though the words were true, they couldn't hide the fear in George's voice. George knew what the words meant.

"There's a letter in the top drawer of my desk," Reggie said. "When you find Addy, give it to her."

"And what if we don't find her?" George asked because he felt like he had to.

"It's only for Addy," Reggie said and let that subject die. A moment of silence passed, each of them waiting for the other to speak. "Are you guys ready?" Reggie finally asked when he was sure that George wasn't going to say anything.

"Are you sure you want us to do this?"

"Burn it down," Reggie ordered him. George knew the plan. Reggie knew that George still needed to hear the words. All of them knew that Reggie wanted the compound razed so they wouldn't have to worry about leaving behind clues about where they had hidden any of the hundreds of people that they had helped escape from the War. That wasn't the whole story, though. Reggie also wanted the compound razed because he didn't want to battle the temptation to go back. If Christopher was going to come to him, Reggie needed to be willing to go all in. He had to believe in the plan completely or it would be doomed to failure.

"You're sure?" George asked again.

Reggie understood George's hesitation. Once they burned the compound down, none of them would have anywhere else to go. That was part of the plan too. Nobody was allowed to be comfortable. Rebellion wasn't comfortable. "Can you handle this, George, or do I need to talk to Sam?"

"I can handle it," George told him.

"Good luck, George," Reggie said to his old friend and colleague. "I hope to see you when I get back." Reggie didn't wait for George to respond. He didn't want to hear George wish him luck too. Reggie had too many balls in the air for luck to do any good. Either he would figure out how to catch them all or they'd scatter to the ground. After hanging up the phone, Reggie finally stood up from the desk. He stretched the muscles in his shoulders and walked to the window. There, Reggie watched the darkening sky and waited for the sound of Brian's car.

Thirty-three

The first shots came before they even got off the boat. They hadn't expected that. At first they simply heard whistling noises and saw the rings in the water, as if it was beginning to rain. Then Sokhem got hit by a bullet and let out a scream before falling over the rail into the river. Sokhem had been sitting up at the front of the boat, hoping to be one of the first men off, hoping to be one of the first men to reach the Intelligence Center. He had dreamt of being a hero. He had dreamt of telling his grandchildren stories about his bravery, about how he led the charge that ended the War. The others had to jump over his floating body to get into the water and avoid the onslaught of bullets.

It was nearly one o'clock when they saw the first bullet hit the water. They were almost an hour and a half behind schedule. They hadn't expected to encounter any resistance until they were on the ground and approaching the Intelligence Center, but the people in the Intelligence Center were ready for them. Maybe it was because they were late. That would be better than the alternative—that there was a traitor among them. If they had a traitor among them, it would have all but guaranteed all of their deaths.

They were late because, despite the recent rains, the Sangker River was lower in spots than they'd expected. Twice, more than half of the twenty-three occupants of the boat had to jump into the water and swim beside the boat to keep it from running aground in the mud. Once, the men who'd jumped into the water had to pull the boat loose to get it moving again. It wasn't until they hit Tonle Sap Lake that the ride became easy. By then, they'd lost too much time to make up.

Sun Same had been the first man in the water when the boat hit the muddy bed of the Sangker River. The others laughed and cheered him on when he jumped in. Spirits were high. Sun Same worried that the others didn't realize what it might mean if they were late. Failure by any one of the groups could ruin everything. Sun Same didn't want Cambodia to fail. "Come on!" he shouted to the others. "We must free the boat! Jump with me!" Heng was the second man in the water. He left his gun on the bottom of the boat and jumped in. Tep followed him. Serey was the first of the nine women to jump into the water. Once she jumped, they kept coming until enough weight was off the boat for it to float again.

"Hurray for Sun, the hero!" Serey called out when the boat started drifting again. She flashed him a smile and he immediately forgave her for any intended sarcasm. Those in the water swam alongside the boat, lifting their feet to avoid kicking the mud as they swam. A group of boys, heading with a net to their favorite fishing spot, paddled past them. The youngest of the three boys, who could have been no more than five years old, pointed at the men and women swimming next to the boat and laughed. They were probably brothers—the three boys in their small boat. The boys had no way of knowing about the arsenal of weapons that the targets of their ridicule carried on their boat. They had no way of knowing that it was the weight of these weapons as much as the weight of the passengers that had caused the boat to run aground. If the boat had been carrying only the passengers, it would have cleared the muddy bottom with ease. It wasn't only the weight of the guns that got them stuck. It was the weight of the explosives too, explosives pieced together from new electronics and old land mines. The rebels knew how to account for the weight of the people. Nearly half of them had grown up on this river and the lake that it fed into. They were Cambodia's river people. Some of them had

learned to swim before they learned to walk. Three of them had never been in a car before, only boats and scooters. Yet the War still found them and wouldn't let them go—not without a fight anyway.

Sun Same swam through the river next to the boat. Narith, the boat's captain, moved it slowly through the shallow water, knowing that a fast beaching could take hours to undo. Sun watched their surroundings as they floated by: the green leaves from the trees, the smaller boats of blue, red, and brown, the floating houses, the houses built on bamboo stilts. Every child that they passed waved to them. Every old man and woman brought their hands together in front of their chest as if to pray and bowed their head. Sun and Narith had promised Apsara, who was coordinating the Asian attacks, that the boat trip would take less than six hours. They believed that they were being conservative. The trip would take only four hours during the height of the rainy season. Now, though, six hours no longer seemed to be enough time. Sun wondered what would happen if they were late. He wondered what would happen if all of the attacks weren't exactly coordinated. Then he tried to stop thinking about it. Turning back was not an option. They had their guns and their bombs and their hope, and that had to be enough.

Heng swam up next to Sun. "You are worried?" Heng asked Sun as they swam side by side.

"We should have given ourselves more time," Sun answered.

"No matter how much time you give yourself, old friend," Heng told him, "it's not enough." Heng and Sun had lived together in the monastery when they were boys. Heng had always been the wise one. Shortly after they turned eighteen, they found out that they were destined to be mortal enemies in a War that neither of them understood.

Sun thought about his friend's wisdom for a moment. "We should have given ourselves more time," he repeated. Christopher's plan required coordination. It needed the chain to be unbroken. When the water became deep enough again, everyone got back into the boat and Narith gunned the engine.

After Sokhem was hit with a bullet, most of them jumped into the water with their guns. They swam toward the land, holding their guns over their heads to keep them from getting wet. Holding their guns above them made them even bigger targets. Heng was cut down in the water. They shot his body a second time as it floated there to make sure that he was dead. A few of the rebels stayed on the boat, knowing that they needed to get the boat, and its bombs, onto the land for the plan to have any chance of working. The problem was that access to the beach had been effectively cut off by the gunfire from the Intelligence Cell, and the men and women in the water were being picked off one by one. Luckily, as things were beginning to look their bleakest, the helicopter arrived. Sun had radioed for it only moments earlier, before he leapt into the water. When the helicopter came, it came with wind and fire. Its wind blew the leaves on the trees and created great ripples in the water on the lake. Then its fire: the helicopter's first missile hit the Intelligence Center with a crack and then its machine guns flared, providing enough cover for Sun and the others to pull the boat onto the shore.

They were already down eleven men by the time they got the explosives off the boat, but at least there was hope.

Thirty-four

Reggie looked over at Christopher and saw that he seemed to have finally fallen asleep. They had adjacent aisle seats on the plane. The flight from JFK to Frankfurt was about eight hours, and then they would have another twelve-hour flight from Frankfurt to Singapore. Reggie hadn't known that Christopher had never been on a plane before. He did his best not to doubt his decision. He reminded himself that it had been Christopher's decision to fight, that he had given the boy every chance to run. Since Christopher had already decided to fight, Reggie was simply helping him to make sure that his fight wouldn't be wasted. That was what Reggie told himself anyway. He wasn't sure that Maria would agree.

"Why do you keep staring at me?" Christopher asked Reggie without opening his eyes.

"I thought you were asleep," Reggie answered.

"I can barely sleep in a bed," Christopher said. "How am I supposed to sleep in this chair?"

Reggie laughed. "When you get tired enough and bored enough, you'll sleep," he told Christopher. "You should try anyway. You need the rest. We're going to be busy when we get to Singapore and we have a few things to discuss during our layover."

"I was trying to sleep," Christopher told Reggie, "but it's hard with you staring at me."

"Point taken," Reggie said and closed his own eyes.

No matter how hard he tried, Christopher couldn't manage to drift off to sleep. It wasn't the chair that kept him awake. It was his inability to get his mind to settle in the present. His mind kept moving forward and backward in time, leaping over the present like a dancer leaping across a stage. He tried to imagine what it was going to be like when they landed in Singapore, but the images in his head were an abstract blur. Reggie had tried to explain everything to him, but eventually Christopher merely pretended to understand so that he wouldn't look dumb. When his mind got too jumbled by the enigma that was his own future, it jumped back into the past. His eyes felt heavy and he thought about the conversation he and Reggie had had in the house on the Jersey Shore.

"So I know why it is that you want me," Christopher had told Reggie when he got to the beach house. "I know that you guys think I'm the only person that everyone will trust since I'm the only person in this War without a side. But what's the plan? What chance do we really have of ending the War?"

Reggie still hadn't turned the lights on in the room. He and Christopher sat in the darkness. The boats still trolling the bay moved over the water like red and green fireflies. Reggie didn't want to turn the lights on. He didn't want to attract attention. He had thought that Christopher might ask him to turn the lights on, but Christopher never did. "There is a plan," Reggie said to Christopher.

"I hope so," Christopher answered. "I'd hate to think I abandoned my only two friends for nothing."

Reggie paused. It would have been an easy opening to tell Christopher what had happened to Evan, but Reggie let it pass.

"There's a reason why we need somebody that everyone will trust, and it's not because people from opposite sides of the War won't fight together or run together or work together. I don't know what Brian told you, but they will. Former rivals from the War have worked together in the Underground for generations. But no one has ever asked them to do what you're going to ask them to do."

The darkness outside the window seemed to close in on them. Christopher could feel his heart beating in his chest. He wondered what request could be so horrible that it would strike fear in the hearts of paranoid killers. What could be worse than the violence he'd already seen? Christopher thought about letting it go for now, but he didn't have the stamina for confusion. "What exactly am I going to ask them to do?"

"What do you know about how the two sides of the War are structured?"

Christopher shook his head. "I don't understand your question."

"Your mother must have said something in her journals about how the two sides of the War are structured. She must have said something about what she learned before she broke in to the Intelligence Cell in New York to find out where you were. What they did, breaking in to an intelligence cell like that and stealing information—people don't do that. She knew things. She must have written something about what she knew."

"I remember something. She had a conversation with that Dorothy woman. I don't remember the details. All I remember is that they had to risk their lives to find a piece of paper with my address on it. None of the other details meant anything to me."

Reggie pushed on. He wanted Christopher to find the answers on his own. He knew how much more powerful Christopher would be that way and how much more convincing. They were going to have to sell it as Christopher's plan anyway. That's the only way it would work. "That's not true, Christopher. Those details meant everything to you. You just didn't realize it at the time."

"Why are you talking in riddles, Reggie? I didn't leave my friends for fucking riddles. I came here because I thought you could give me answers."

"Do you remember in your mother's journal when Dorothy told her about the Intelligence Cells like the one that she and Michael raided?"

"Sure," Christopher said. He looked up at Reggie. Reggie's green eyes nearly glowed in the darkness.

"Back then, each side had about fifteen Intelligence Cells. They have even more now because of what your mother and Michael did. They added redundancy. You guys took out one of the Intelligence Cells the other day. It's not easy, but far from impossible. That's where all the information is. That information is what tells each side who their friends are, who to kill, and who to hate."

"So you're saying we did a good thing when we razed that building in the desert?"

"No," Reggie told him. "You didn't do anything. All of the information in there is backed up in other Intelligence Cells. There's triple, maybe quadruple redundancy. All you guys were, in the big picture, was a minor nuisance. You were a gnat buzzing in their ear. They'll have that Intelligence Cell rebuilt somewhere else in a week. And there's something like fifty of those all over the world."

"Okay," Christopher said, confused as to where this was going. "So why are you telling me all of this?"

"Because the key isn't destroying the information."

Christopher shook his head. When he read his parents' journals, he wasn't trying to solve the puzzle about how to end the War. He was trying to figure out who he was and why he was so afraid. Then a small spark came alive in Christopher's memory.

"There were other buildings, right? There were these central hubs where everything was mapped and organized?"

A smile crossed Reggie's face. "Right," Reggie said. "The information in the Intelligence Centers is the key to understanding how the information in the Intelligence Cells is organized. Without the information in the Intelligence Centers, the average person couldn't go into an Intelligence Cell and tell the difference between the paperwork of a friend and that of an enemy. A few of the old Historians might be able to piece together tiny bits of the big picture, but we're not too worried about them. The key isn't destroying the information—it's making sure that nobody can understand it. All this War is about is history. Take away the history, jumble it up into an incoherent mess, and nobody knows who to hate anymore."

"So all we have to do is destroy the Intelligence Centers and the War falls apart?"

"That's the theory."

"Didn't Dorothy tell my mother that the Intelligence Centers were basically impenetrable?"

"Yes." Reggie nodded slowly.

"How many of them are there?" Christopher asked.

"Seven."

"And you need me to go talk to people because—?"

"Because you're proof that people can survive without their history, that they can make their own history, that they are more than cogs in one side of a War."

"I'm proof of all that?" Christopher asked.

"You're here, aren't you? That's proof enough for now." Reggie left it at that, even though he knew that they would need more.

The plane hit an air pocket and ripped Christopher back into the present, lurching downward for what felt to him like at least fifty feet. His eyes shot open and he felt his stomach leap up to the top of his chest. He reached out and clutched the armrests of his seat. He looked around. The lights on the plane were out and everyone had the shades on their windows drawn. Most of the other passengers didn't budge, let alone wake up. Christopher tried to focus his mind on that moment. What the hell was he doing? This was silly. How were they supposed to end a War by destroying a bunch of pieces of paper?

Thirty-five

Evan waited until he was sure that Addy was asleep. He knew that he'd have to be really quiet because he knew how lightly she slept. The slightest sounds woke her up, and when Addy was awake she was wide awake. There was no transition out of sleep. Addy woke up ready to fight or ready to run, whichever option the moment called for. Ever since the second time that they made love, they'd slept close to each other, sometimes even touching. Even as he slipped away from her, Evan could feel her leg brushing against his. He moved his leg away from hers slowly, half convinced that the moment when their skin disconnected Addy would wake up. If she did, he would have to pretend to be merely tossing and turning in his sleep. As long as she didn't notice that his eyes were open, she would have nothing to be suspicious of.

Evan didn't like sneaking around on Addy like this. He didn't like planning his lies. He felt bad about what he was going to do, but he needed to do it. They'd been on the road for three days already. It had been three days since the compound in Los Angeles was raided, three days since they escaped, three days since Evan killed the policeman, and the only information he could get out of Addy was that his picture was out there and that they had to keep moving or somebody would find them. When he asked about

Christopher, Addy refused to say anything. She told him that there were no lists of the dead and no lists of the captured. There were only numbers—twenty-eight dead, even more captured— and even those were incomplete. Evan knew why she was doing this. He knew that she was trying to protect him. It's only that it's hard to accept being protected when you have no idea what you're being protected from. Evan needed to see what was on Addy's phone.

Three days, and Evan didn't even know where they were. He knew where they were going. He knew that Addy was trying to get him to Florida to meet up with someone named Reggie that Addy used to work with. She said he was one of the leaders in this thing called the Underground. There's a lot of space between Los Angeles and Florida, and hitchhiking wasn't the most direct way to travel. Evan tried to follow the road signs, but it wasn't easy when they jumped from one car to the next the way they had, barely caring what direction each car was taking them. Addy's theory was that as long as they weren't going backward, it was always better to be moving than standing still. Evan was pretty sure they were in Louisiana. It wasn't that Addy wasn't talking at all. She had told Evan so much in three days about her past, about the War and its history, and about what Christopher meant to the whole thing. Now, if she would just tell him what the fuck was going on today.

It was so dark. They were sleeping in an abandoned barn. That's where they lived now, in places that had been discarded by others. It was quiet outside. The only sound Evan could hear was the rhythm of the cicadas and crickets and frogs, keeping tempo like a mysterious heartbeat. He recognized the sound from his nights in Maine, but it was different here, thicker and slower. Evan slid his body away from Addy's. He felt the moment when the skin of his leg separated from the skin of hers. He felt the lack of warmth. He felt the air rush between them. Addy felt it too. Her body moved unconsciously back toward him. Evan quietly slipped farther away from her, trying to make sure their bodies stayed apart for the moment. Addy turned away from him in her sleep and then her body was still again.

Evan slid past Addy without standing up and reached for her phone. It was lying next to her head—close to her in case she needed to grab it and run. Evan had already learned that much from her. Be ready to run. Always be ready to run. Evan lifted up her phone and turned it on. It produced an eerie blue glow. That tiny bit of blue light lit up the entire barn. Everything around Evan filled with ghostly light and shadows. Evan took a deep breath, hoping that the light was weak enough that it wouldn't attract any attention from outside. Addy was adamant about the lack of light at night. She'd told him that she'd made that mistake in the past, but she wouldn't tell him the details. And Evan didn't ask for them. Some things you don't ask.

Addy's phone was password protected, but Evan had been watching her each time she checked it, which happened frequently. Most of the time she checked it when she didn't think Evan was watching, but Evan was always watching. He watched to see if he could read the password over her shoulder. He watched her fingers. Despite its total lack of meaning to him, he was fairly sure that he'd figured out her password. He typed what he believed to be the password into the phone: *canossa*. He hit Return. It was like he'd found the secret key. Evan now had access to everything.

Though he was tempted, he didn't open any of Addy's e-mails. He didn't check her personal files. He tried to leave her some semblance of privacy. All he wanted was access to the Internet. All he wanted was to know what everyone else in the world already knew.

He found his own picture in a matter of seconds. It was the picture from his driver's license—the one in the wallet that he'd left in the compound when he and Addy ran. The picture was everywhere. He didn't think he had time to read the articles. He could only scan them for words and ideas. *Killer. Dangerous. Terrorist.* At first it was disorienting, seeing pictures of himself everywhere, seeing his name in print, labeled as some sort of monster when all he'd done was save a girl. One article would have worried him. Ten would have scared him senseless. But thousands—seeing his picture and his name in thousands of articles was so absurd that he found it almost funny. He kept digging, his own situation becoming more ludicrous by the moment. He wondered what all the kids back in his hometown in Maine must be thinking about him. He wondered how many stories he'd seen in the news during the course of his life that were this tenuously tied to the truth. He now had to doubt everything. None of the Web sites he looked at contained any of the details that he was really searching for. He found an original article from the day after the raid on the compound. Addy had told him the truth. No names were released except for his and the name of the cop that he'd killed. Evan didn't read the cop's name. He didn't want to know it. Other than that, everything was written in numbers—this many dead, this many captured—almost like a code.

Evan kept searching. He wanted to find something—anything—about Christopher, but there was nothing to find. Nothing existed that mentioned Christopher by name. Evan wondered if it was possible that Christopher had been reduced to a number. After all the time that he and Christopher spent training while growing up and after all the adoration, bordering on worship, that Christopher had been showered with over the last few days, was it even possible that he'd been reduced to a number? And, if he was a number, was he one of the captured or one of the killed? Evan looked over at Addy. He watched her for a second to make sure she was still sleeping soundly. She lay there, dimly lit by the blue light from her phone. Her breathing was steady. Her face held the stern expression it always did when she slept. Her body didn't move. Evan listened to the night. He found the dissonance between his own surroundings and what he saw on Addy's phone to be the most disturbing thing of all. He knew that if he kept searching, Addy would eventually wake up and catch him, so he gave himself five more minutes.

Eight minutes later, he found a reference to Christopher in a piece that was dated after the raid. It didn't actually name Christopher. It merely showed his picture, the same picture that had been everywhere only a few days ago. It was the picture of Christopher with his face smudged with dirt, aiming a gun at a man standing in the window of a building. It was the only picture that seemed to matter to the world until Evan's picture had overtaken it. Now photos of Christopher had virtually disappeared, slipped from the collective consciousness like the lyrics of a pop song. Evan was able to find only one site that ran the picture with an update after Evan had replaced Christopher as the most reviled man in America. Even then, Christopher's picture wasn't alone.

Evan found an editorial where the picture from Evan's license was at the top of the page right next to the picture of Christopher aiming his gun. The editorial, which Evan didn't bother to read, was a preachy piece discussing violence and the state of youth in America. Evan didn't care about the article. It only took him fifteen minutes of searching on Addy's phone to stop caring about what everyone was saying. All Evan cared about was the pictures. He found something satisfying about seeing his and Christopher's pictures on the site together. There they were, brothers in arms. They were equals in notoriety, soldiers in a cause. Evan decided at that moment that whatever happened to Christopher, he would make it right. Whatever everyone else's cause was, that would be his cause. Not right now, though. He knew he couldn't do anything now. He knew that Addy was making all the right decisions now. She understood this world far better than he did. They needed to make it to Florida. They needed allies. Without Abby he would already be dead by now. She had saved him, was saving him. She was tougher than he had any right to believe he could ever be. But he also believed—had to believe—that when the time came, she would fight with him. Evan knew that Christopher meant almost as much to Addy as Christopher meant to him.

Evan took one more look at the pictures. He burned them into his memory. Then he clicked the phone off and everything went dark. He waited a moment for his eyes to adjust so that he could put the phone back exactly where Addy had left it. In the dark, the sounds coming from the night seemed louder. Evan was going to have to try to get some sleep. He and Addy were planning to shop for supplies at the convenience store down the road in the morning. They barely had any money left, but they would try to scrounge together enough to get something to eat. Addy had told Evan not to worry about the money, that things would work themselves out. He knew that she was merely trying to calm him down. So he didn't worry about the money. When he could see again, he put Addy's phone back. Then he lay back down next to her. He moved his leg so that it was touching hers again. When she felt his touch, she rolled onto her side without waking up and placed one hand on his chest.

Thirty-six

Reggie and Christopher never sat down in the Frankfurt airport. They had a two-hour layover, but Reggie wouldn't let them be still. He said it was safer to keep moving. So they walked. They walked past the tourists and the businessmen and the shops selling overpriced liquor and perfume and then they circled back and walked past them all again. "Why can't we sit and rest?" Christopher asked Reggie.

"I don't know this place," Reggie told him as they strode past a woman behind a counter selling coffee and doughnuts. "Everything about this plan is fragile. A lot of people are going to have to know about it before it's all said and done, but if the wrong person hears the wrong thing, we're finished. It's over." Reggie looked at Christopher without breaking his stride. "And if anything happens to you, then I've blown it for everyone."

Two hours later, they boarded another plane bound for Singapore. Then they landed again without incident.

They had made it through customs without any issues and stepped into the gigantic main concourse. Christopher had never seen anything like it before. He'd never even heard of anything like it before. They began walking. "Where are we going?" Christopher asked Reggie as they walked.

"We walk," Reggie told him. "They're supposed to find us."

Annie hadn't been able to give him any additional instructions. The people that Reggie and Christopher were coming to meet wanted it that way. Nobody trusted anyone.

The Singapore airport was spotless, crowded and almost distractingly quiet. Reggie was a man of ordinary height in New York, but here he towered over everyone that they walked past. He literally looked like a giant among men. "Well, finding us shouldn't be difficult," Christopher said to Reggie. "Well, finding *you* should be pretty easy anyway."

"Don't remind me," Reggie whispered under his breath. They turned down a long, crowded, quiet corridor. Christopher could tell that the people around them were of many different Asian nationalities, but he had no way of knowing who was from where. It was simply a hodgepodge of foreign faces. They passed a few other white people. Reggie was the only black person that he saw anywhere. An Asian man in a maroon suit with a name tag on the lapel walked up to them. He bowed slightly in their direction.

"Can I help you find something, sir?" the man asked.

Reggie became confused for a second, wondering if this was some sort of trick question or some sort of code. "I don't think so," he muttered when he recovered. "Can you?"

"If you are arriving, you can find transportation in that direction," the man said, pointing past the giant koi pond laid out in the middle of the airport and toward the airport's exits.

"Thanks," Reggie said to the man, realizing that he was merely an airport employee, nothing more. Still, they walked in the direction the airport employee had suggested if for no other reason than that they didn't want the man to grow suspicious. Besides, they didn't know where they were going anyway.

As they neared the koi pond, Christopher could see the giant orange-and-white fish swimming right below the water's surface. Tall plants, as tall as small trees, grew around the pond. A platform was built above the pond with benches on it and a small wooden bridge arched over a waterfall. They neared the pond and then they heard the voice. "Reggie?" it asked in little more than a whisper. It was coming from the bridge over the koi pond. A small man stood at the top of the curved bridge, gaining both height and vantage point in doing so. His skin was light brown and wrinkled around the sides of his eyes. He was wearing beige linen pants and a white button-down short-sleeved shirt. Reggie looked up at him. When the two men made eye contact, the Asian man nodded and beckoned them up onto the bridge.

"Reggie?" the man asked again. This time Reggie gave the man a nod of his head and stretched out his hand. The Asian man took it. Christopher watched the two men's hands fold together. Reggie was more than a full head taller than the Asian man, but their hands were of strikingly similar size.

"My name is Jin." Jin turned to Christopher. "And you must be him?" Jin didn't say it like the people in the compound had said it. His voice was full of curiosity and devoid of awe.

"I must be," Christopher answered without sarcasm.

"I've been waiting for you," Jin said to them.

"Good," Reggie said, "then we don't need to waste any more time." He looked around them. Reggie knew that people were looking at him, but everyone around them seemed to be an expert at looking without looking like they were looking. "I'm not sure it's safe here. You can take us to where we're supposed to go in Singapore?"

"You're right." Jin laughed. "It's not safe. But we're not staying in Singapore."

"Then where the hell are we going?" Reggie asked Jin.

"We're taking a ferry to Indonesia," Jin informed them. "Follow me. I'll get us there." Then, without any more fanfare or assurances, Jin started walking quickly through the quiet halls of the

Singapore airport, dodging groups of people as he went, and Reggie and Christopher followed behind him.

Christopher wished he could hide. He wished he could hide behind Jin, but Jin wasn't big enough to conceal him. He wished he could hide behind Reggie, but what good would that do? It would be like hiding behind the only tree in a desert.

They walked from the airport to the parking garage. Reggie and Christopher had their bags slung over their shoulders. Jin paused before stepping into the parking garage. He reached into his pocket and pulled out his car keys, gripping them like a weapon. His eyes scanned the rows of cars in front of them. It was the first time he'd stopped moving. Reggie and Christopher stopped behind him.

Reggie passed Christopher a look. "Is there something you want to tell us, Jin?" Reggie asked.

Jin smiled a conspiratorial smile without taking his eyes off the cars. "To know that you do not know is the best. To pretend to know when you do not know is a disease," Jin said to them through that smile.

"Okay," Reggie whispered to Jin through his teeth. "Is there something that you want to tell us that makes sense?"

"Come," Jin said in a single huffed breath and then, without warning, he ran. Having long before gone past the point of no return, Reggie and Christopher ran after him. Reggie waited for a moment before he ran, pushing Christopher in front of him so that Christopher would be between him and Jin.

"Go," Reggie whispered to Christopher before pushing him, and the word sounded to Christopher like an apology. Christopher ran, not knowing if anyone was chasing him, not knowing what he was running from. His feet pounded on the concrete. Jin ran silently in front of him, much faster than Christopher would have thought possible. Christopher could hear Reggie's feet pounding as

Reggie ran behind him, but other than Reggie's footsteps and his own echoing through the dark, covered garage, he heard nothing. Jin reached the car well before Christopher and Reggie. By the time Christopher got to the car, Jin was holding the back door open, motioning for him to get in. Christopher dove into the backseat. Jin jumped into the driver's seat at the same time and started the engine. He put the car in reverse and pulled skidding out of the parking space before coming to a screeching stop, the car now pointed toward the exit signs.

"Wait!" Christopher shouted and reached forward to try to grab Jin's hand to keep him from putting the car into drive. For a second, he thought Jin was going to kidnap him, but he missed Jin's hand as Jin reached over his own. Then Jin pushed the passenger-side door open.

"Get in," Jin shouted to Reggie.

Reggie leapt into the passenger seat and Jin stepped on the gas before Reggie could even close the door. The momentum itself slammed the door as the car lurched forward, and they sped toward the exit. Christopher looked out the window. He still hadn't seen anything. He still didn't know what had gotten into Jin. He turned his head and looked in front of them. He could see the light from outside the parking garage entrance. Then a man stepped out from between the cars to their left. He was another Asian man but was much bigger than Jin. He was probably almost as big as Reggie. The man stepped directly into their path and put his hand out as if ordering them to stop. Jin didn't even slow down. Already at nearly top speed, their car barreled through the man. The man's body hit the hood with a thump and flipped violently into the air. Christopher wasn't sure if the man's body flew backward or if the car simply sped under it, but the body bounced once off the top of the car and then toppled behind them. Christopher looked back in time to see the body hit the concrete behind the car. As it did, two more men came out from between the cars. One raced toward the broken body and one raced after the car.

"Behind us!" Christopher yelled to Jin before ducking down in the backseat. Jin cut the wheel hard to the left and the car careened around the corner, straightening out barely an instant before it would have rammed sideways into other parked cars. Christopher thought that Jin must be taking them to a different exit. He expected to hear gunshots, but the sound didn't come. Then Jin pulled another hard left. Then another. He kept turning until they'd circled back to the same stretch of garage, barreling back toward the broken body that Jin had already left in his wake. One of the other men was standing over the broken body, trying to help him. Everything was so loud—the screeching of the tires, the howl of the engine. Jin clipped the second man, having to turn sharply to avoid running over the body already sprawled on the pavement. Jin didn't care about the car, but he didn't want to risk pulling the man's body under the tires and hurting their chance of escape. The clipping was probably enough. The man's body flew across the garage and into one of the parked cars. Christopher looked for the third man, but he was nowhere to be seen. Jin didn't circle again. This time he pushed the car even faster and headed for the exit.

"What the fuck was that?" Reggie asked after the car raced into the light and pulled into traffic. Christopher's chest was heaving. His heart was pounding. Reggie looked to be in the same boat.

"Your trip here, unfortunately, failed to go unnoticed," Jin said calmly.

"Did you know that was going to happen? Do you know what's at stake here? Do you know how important he is?" Reggie yelled at Jin.

Jin nodded. "This is why we are not staying in Singapore," he said with some force as he made a sudden turn off the highway onto a side street.

"Where did they come from?" Christopher asked from the backseat.

Jin peeked at Christopher in the rearview mirror. Christopher was still lying low in the backseat, trying to avoid being seen from the outside. "From much closer than where you came from," Jin told him.

"No shit," Christopher replied, peeking out the window at the strange, giant, gray city surrounding them, full of huge buildings shaped like cruise ships and tall glass towers stretching into the sky.

Jin glanced at Christopher in the mirror again. "Have you been to Singapore?" Jin asked Christopher, all but ignoring Reggie.

"I haven't been anywhere before," Christopher told him. Jin laughed. He slowed the car down and was now meandering through Singapore's side streets.

"Are we going to be safe where you're taking us?" Reggie asked Jin.

"Whoever can see through all fear will always be safe," Jin answered him. Even in the backseat, Christopher could feel Reggie's frustration radiating off him like heat.

"Are you from Singapore?" Christopher asked Jin.

"Do I look like I'm from Singapore?" Jin asked him in return.

"I have no idea," Christopher answered him honestly.

Jin shook his head. "I'm Chinese," he said. "I used to come here on business when I was part of the War." Jin didn't elaborate about what his business entailed. He stopped at an intersection and looked in each direction before moving forward again. "When I decided to run from the War, it made sense to come here."

"How long have you been out of the War?" Christopher asked.

"Seven years," Jin answered.

"Why did you run?" Reggie asked.

"Because if you do not change direction, you may end up where you are heading," Jin answered.

"Are you going to talk to me like that the whole time we're here?" Reggie asked him.

"Have you ever been to Singapore?" Jin asked Reggie.

"No."

"Have you ever been to Indonesia?"

"No."

"Have you ever been to Asia?"

"No," Reggie admitted.

"That's what I was afraid of," Jin said to Reggie. "There's the ferry terminal." Jin pointed a few blocks in front of them. "We'll leave the car here. We should be safe now for a little while, but always be ready to run. Can you swim?" Jin asked Christopher.

Christopher nodded, though the implications of the question made him nervous. "Are you coming with us?" he asked.

"I'll get you on the ferry, but I won't be on it with you. I have another matter to attend to."

"More important than getting Christopher to the meeting safely?" Reggie asked him.

"Nothing is more important than getting Christopher to the meeting safely," Jin replied. "We should say farewell here. We won't want to make a scene inside the ferry terminal." Jin turned toward Reggie and reached out his hand. Reggie took it. Christopher watched them. Their difference in height seemed to have somehow shrunk between the airport and here. "When you get to Indonesia, a man will find you. His name is Galang. His English is spotty, but he'll take you where you need to go next."

"Where is that?" Reggie asked.

"You don't need to know until you get there," Jin answered.

Then Jin turned to Christopher. Christopher reached out his hand for Jin to shake. Jin refused. Instead he lowered himself down onto his knees in front of Christopher. Once on his knees, Jin splayed his hands out in front of him on the concrete sidewalk. Then he lowered his head between his arms until his forehead actually touched the ground. Christopher wanted him to stand up. Christopher was embarrassed. Instead of getting up off his knees, Jin bowed two more times, each time lowering his head until his forehead touched the ground. When he finally stood up, Christopher could see a mark on Jin's forehead from the concrete. Christopher was still standing awkwardly with his unshaken hand outstretched. Jin still did not take Christopher's hand. This time Jin stared at Christopher and said, "When armies are mobilized and issues are joined, the man who is sorry over the fact shall win."

For some reason the words made Christopher think about his father—not his father in Maine, but the man whose genes he shared, the man that Christopher had never met. "I don't know what you're talking about," Christopher replied.

Jin nodded. "You're young. In time, you'll know." Jin glanced up and down the streets around them. "Let's go," he said to them. They left the car parked on the side of the road in a spot that couldn't possibly have been legal. Christopher didn't ask questions, though. He didn't want another answer he couldn't understand.

The ferry terminal was on top of what was essentially a shopping mall that, other than a few bizarre food stands, didn't look much different from the shopping malls in Maine. Without saying much, Jin led Reggie and Christopher through the mall and up to the ferry terminal. He bought them their tickets and showed them where to go to catch the ferry, and then he disappeared as mysteriously as he'd come.

Reggie and Christopher didn't say anything about him until

they were on the ferry. It was a big commuter ferry, carrying hundreds of people from Singapore to Indonesia. Christopher hadn't even known that Indonesia was anywhere near Singapore, but the ferry ride was only about an hour long. The ferry had no outdoor space. Everybody jammed inside on seats that made the inside of the boat look like a bus. A kung fu movie was playing on the giant television at the front of the ferry. Reggie picked his and Christopher's seats, about two-thirds of the way back, against a window. Moments later, the boat pulled away from the dock and into the harbor. "What was up with the bowing?" Christopher whispered to Reggie as he watched Singapore disappear behind them like a forgotten sequence of a long dream.

"You don't like the bowing?" Reggie asked Christopher.

"No."

"Why not?"

"Because I haven't done anything to earn it," Christopher said.

"Well, accept it now," Reggie told him, "because you're going to have to earn it later. And when you do, there won't be enough bows to balance those scales." Reggie looked past Christopher and out the window. "I just wish I knew where the hell we're going."

Christopher looked out the window too and wondered if where they were going even mattered.

Thirty-seven

Evan sat up in bed. He was sweating. It was two o'clock in the morning on the East Coast of the United States. Evan could feel the drops of sweat running down the side of his face. The room wasn't hot. He'd woken up suddenly, escaping the dream he'd been having the only way his brain knew how, by ejecting. Evan tried to calm his breathing. His chest was heaving almost to his chin with each drawn-out breath. Addy woke up too when she felt the bed move. "What's wrong?" she asked Evan, seeing the distress on his face. They were sleeping in a bed together for the first time. They had some money now. Reggie had made sure to leave Addy some money so that she would have the resources to do the job that he had left her. Reggie didn't know that she wasn't going to be doing the job alone. Evan and Addy found a cheap motel that fell within their new budget, justifying the cost by telling themselves that they both needed the rest before they started searching for Maria.

"I was only dreaming," Evan said, half to himself, his voice relieved. "I keep having these dreams about fire."

"What happens?" Addy asked him, reaching up and trying to comfort him by running her fingers along his back.

"I'm not even sure," Evan told her. "Everything seems normal at first. At first, it's almost like a memory. I see me and Christopher and we're kids playing in the woods. I recognize the woods from back home. It's the woods that Christopher and I used to play in growing up. Christopher used to make up these crazy war games. We'd build these intricate camouflaged forts out of rocks and tree branches to hide in and then we'd run around diving over fallen trees and pretending we were fighting off an ambush. It's all so clear in my dream. It's like I'm there again, only I'm not living it this time. I'm watching it instead. Then, out of nowhere, everything bursts into flames—the trees, the ground, even the sky. The fire moves fast and it's so loud, like the sound of a giant wave that never stops breaking. Then I feel the heat. Then the fire gets to Christopher. Then the fire comes for me."

"That must be why you're sweating," Addy said. Evan nodded. "I think it's normal," Addy assured him. "After everything we've been through, that's got to be totally normal. After what happened to us in L.A. and then seeing the remnants of my old compound in Florida. After what we've seen, I sometimes start to feel like the whole world is on fire even when I'm awake. Maybe the world is purging itself with the flames. That would at least explain everything."

"I know. I know you're right, but the fire in my dreams seems different. It comes out of nowhere. My brain is never ready for it." Even the memory of the dream gave Evan the chills.

"What happens after the fire? In your dreams, what happens next?"

"There is no after the fire. When the fire gets to Christopher, I always wake up. I wake up right before—" Evan stopped in midsentence. He didn't want to finish what he was saying. "I'm sorry I woke you up," he said instead, looking back at Addy lying there in their bed. "I didn't mean to."

"It's no problem," Addy told him. "I was having trouble sleeping anyway."

"Are you having nightmares too?"

Addy sat up in bed. She pressed her chest against Evan's back and spread her arms around him, locking her hands in front of his chest. She kissed him once on the back of the neck for no other reason than because she had the sudden desire to see the hairs on his neck rise with her kiss. "No," Addy said. "I don't know how we're going to find her, that's all."

"We'll find her," Evan assured Addy. "Your friend Reggie gave us everything we need to get started. He told us where to go. He told us what she looks like and the name she goes by."

"Do you think that's enough?" Addy asked.

"I do. Besides I think I'll recognize her." Evan tried to picture Christopher's face on a thirty-five-year-old woman. "If she looks anything like Christopher, I'm sure I can spot her in a crowd."

"I still can't believe Maria's alive," Addy said. "Everyone thought she was dead. People said it like it was a fact, but all this time Reggie knew that she was alive. I don't know how he kept it a secret. I don't think I would have been able to. I wonder what she's like."

Evan wondered too, but for vastly different reasons. "What do you think Reggie wants from Christopher's mother anyway?" he asked Addy.

"I don't know," Addy answered. "I guess the only way to find out is to bring her to him."

Evan nodded. "We should sleep," he said. "We've got a long way to go tomorrow."

"We should," Addy replied, but then she kissed him on the neck again, longer and harder this time. After that it was some time before either one of them fell asleep again.

Thirty-eight

The sun was beginning to set as their boat neared its destination. The air was warm. The sensation of the boat rocking as it bounced over the waves nearly lulled Christopher to sleep, but he fought to stay awake. He was afraid of falling asleep. He was afraid of not knowing where he'd be when he woke up. Galang spoke better English than Jin had given him credit for. Galang found Reggie and Christopher in the ferry terminal with frightening ease. Hiding in crowds was an impossibility here. Reggie and Christopher had expected Galang to pick them up in a car. Instead, he led them away from the ferry terminal on foot. The three of them walked across the terminal's parking lot, through a gap in a chain-link fence, and down a long dirt road that ran parallel to the water. They walked for about a mile. Galang said nothing to them as they walked. He didn't tell them where they were going. He merely looked back at them every few hundred feet to make sure that they were still behind him and motioned them forward with his hands. They moved quickly. It was late in the afternoon. The sun was still hot and Reggie and Christopher were sweating as they walked. The heat didn't bother Galang. All he seemed to care about was the pace.

The farther they walked, the quieter everything became. Reggie kept glancing behind them, trying to make sure that they weren't being followed. Christopher only looked forward, doing everything he could to stay focused on what was in front of them. Eventually they came to a lone pier made of strung-together bamboo, jutting out into the South China Sea. A small boat was tied to the end of the pier, rising and falling as the waves lapped toward the shoreline. "My boat," Galang said to Reggie and Christopher with a smile that betrayed his relief that the boat was still there.

"Where are you taking us?" Reggie asked again and it began to sound to Christopher like the chorus to a song he'd already heard too many times.

"Someplace safe," Galang assured Reggie. Even though Christopher didn't believe the answer to be true, it made him feel better. "Come." Galang beckoned them toward the pier with another wave of his hand. Reggie and Christopher followed Galang down toward the water. The pier shook as the three of them stepped onto it, bending with their weight but never showing any signs of breaking. It was built for this, to bend with the tides but to last. They walked to the end of the pier. Galang helped Reggie into the boat. Then he turned to Christopher. Before helping Christopher into the boat, Galang bowed deeply. "My honor," he said to Christopher when he lifted his head from his bow. Then he helped Christopher climb aboard, untied the boat from the dock, and jumped aboard himself.

Galang's boat was long and thin. It didn't seem big, but it could have easily accommodated another ten passengers. The boat was the color of wood and was covered only with a single green tarp as a shade against the sun. Galang steered the boat into the busy sea and they quickly joined the flow of traffic as dozens of small wooden boats darted over the water, weaving between giant metal ships being loaded with hundreds of containers, each container the size of a truck. The little wooden boats were dwarfed by their larger cousins. Everything around Christopher seemed so foreign.

He couldn't imagine that it would be possible for him to be any farther from home. He watched as two men stood astride their rowboat amid the giant ships and prodded the sea with a long bamboo pool.

"What are they doing?" Christopher asked Galang, pointing toward the men.

"They are feeling for lost scrap metal," Galang told Christopher. "When they hit"—Galang mimicked holding the long pole with his hands—"they will dive for the metal."

"Where's their scuba gear?"

Galang shook his head. "No gear. They have hose for breathing." Christopher could see it, an ordinary garden hose coiled on the floor of their boat.

"That's insane," Christopher said. Galang smiled and nodded. Christopher was pretty sure that Galang didn't understand what he'd said. Christopher glanced up at Reggie, who was sitting near the bow of the boat with his back to the sea. Christopher still couldn't get used to the insanity, not yet. He wondered if he should trust Reggie. Max had, and it would be awfully lonely if Christopher decided not to.

"How are you feeling?" Reggie shouted back to Christopher when he noticed Christopher staring at him.

"Tired," Christopher answered. They were on Galang's boat for nearly two hours before they neared their destination. The farther they went, the fewer boats they saw. Eventually they saw nothing but tiny fishing boats hugging the shorelines of islands that they passed. Then, as the sun dipped below the far-off islands and the sky darkened to a bloodred color, they arrived. People were waiting for them on the pier; Reggie and Christopher could see their silhouettes standing there in the distance.

Galang had taken them to what looked from a distance to be a floating village connected by bamboo bridges to an otherwise deserted island. A few dozen huts stood on stilts above the water, connected to one another the same way they ultimately connected to the beach. Galang made a beeline for the biggest of the huts, the one with the dock jutting off its back. Four other boats were already moored to the dock and Christopher wondered how many people had already arrived, how many people were waiting for them. Galang circled once by the dock so that they all got a clear look at one another. Reggie assumed that this was planned, that Galang had been told to pull close and make sure that the right people were there. He was sure that Galang had been ordered to run if the right people weren't waiting. After veering close to the dock on the first loop, Galang pulled the boat around again and threw a line to one of the four people waiting for them on the dock.

Though all four of the people were Asian, Christopher could spot their dissimilarities. He remembered Jin asking him if he thought Jin looked like he was from Singapore. He still didn't know what it meant to look like you were from Singapore or China or Indonesia. The people on the dock were different in size and color, and their eyes had different shapes. It was three men and a woman. The woman was smaller than the men, but her eyes were lively and something in the way she stood reminded Christopher of a coiled snake.

Galang leapt from the boat, over the water and onto the dock. Two of the men pulled on the rope Galang had thrown them and maneuvered the boat close to the dock as the boat bobbed up and down in the water. Then the biggest of the men stepped forward and reached a hand out to help pull Reggie from the boat. Reggie turned to grab his bag. "Don't worry," the big man said in a deep voice, "we'll get your bags." So Reggie gave the man his hand and the man hoisted him onto the dock. Christopher went next. He almost withered under the man's grip. He could feel all the man's immense strength in his hand.

Once his passengers were safely off the boat, Galang jumped back in to get the bags. As he did so, the woman stepped forward and reached out a hand toward Reggie. "Good to finally meet you," she said with a smile that seemed dangerously genuine.

"The same to you," Reggie replied. "At times, it felt like it might never happen."

The woman glanced quickly at Christopher and then turned back to Reggie. "I trust your trip here was adequate?"

"We had a bit of an adventure in Singapore with your friend Jin. But we're here in one piece."

The women nodded. "Yes. We heard about Jin. He was supposed to join us here tomorrow. He'll be missed." Christopher tried not to flinch. He looked at Reggie, determined to react however Reggie reacted. Reggie's face showed no reaction.

"Christopher," Reggie said, putting his hand on Christopher's back and leading him toward the woman, "this is Sara."

"Sara?" Christopher said, shaking the woman's hand.

"Apsara," the woman responded, "but when working with Westerners, I go by Sara."

"I like Apsara better," Christopher said.

"If all goes well here, you can call me whatever you want," Apsara said to him.

"Who are your friends?" Reggie said to Apsara, turning to face the men. Apsara introduced them all to Reggie by name and by country. The big one was Chinese. The slight one, Katsu, was Japanese. The one who had helped Galang dock the boat was Indonesian. Apsara was Thai. They each shook Reggie's hand in turn. They each bowed to Christopher. Christopher tried to hold their names in his mind, but they slipped out almost as quickly as they entered. It was a handicap of growing up without friends. To Christopher, names were the least important things about people.

"Is this everyone?" Reggie asked. He was answered by a deep laugh from the big Chinese man.

"No," Apsara said to Reggie. "There are others. We wanted to welcome the Child first. We didn't want to overwhelm him."

"He's not a flower," Reggie told Apsara, ignoring how easily Christopher could have been overwhelmed at that moment.

Apsara nodded again, her face lacking any sort of remorse. "He will meet them all. You will both meet them all." Then she looked at Christopher. "You are ready to convince the people of this continent who have proven nothing to the world except that they abhor war to fight a war in your name?" This caught Christopher off guard. He didn't know how to respond. He looked toward Reggie, begging for a lifeline with his eyes.

"If only it were that simple," Reggie joked. Each of the men standing with them laughed. Only Apsara remained stoic.

"So what's the plan, Sara?" Reggie asked the woman.

"We'll show you to your hut. You've had a long trip. You can rest. We're having a celebration tonight on the beach in your honor. You can meet everybody then. I'm sure you'll both be ready."

The Indonesian man led Reggie and Christopher to their hut. Galang carried their bags. The bamboo bridges creaked and swayed under their feet. Reggie and Christopher could hear others inside their huts as they walked by. They spoke in unnecessary whispers. To Christopher, their languages, like their faces, were distinct but unrecognizable. With each whisper, all Christopher could think about was how deeply in over his head he was.

"Don't worry about Sara," Reggie said to Christopher as soon as they were alone in their hut with the door closed behind them. "She's with us."

"Then who should I worry about?"

"Everybody else. This isn't Dutty's land of misfit rebels where everybody is simply looking for a better excuse to die." Reggie stopped himself before he said any more, remembering that he still hadn't told Christopher about the raid and he still didn't know what had happened to Addy and Evan. "Don't get me wrong, Chris. They want to believe in you. That's why they're here. But you have to sell it. They need to see something in you that I can't give you."

"Apsara doesn't think I'm ready for this, does she?"

"Don't worry about what she thinks. She only met you ten minutes ago. Besides, she's got more riding on you than you can understand."

"What does that mean?"

"Let's just say that it's not easy for her to hide from the War after the career she had. People listen to her for a reason. No matter what you do, she's not going to think you're ready until the War's over."

"Do you think I'm ready?" Christopher asked Reggie.

"I may not know much about the parents that raised you, but I do know a little bit about the blood that runs in your veins. I know how strong and how brave that blood is. I've seen it firsthand. This is the job you were born to do, Christopher. I know it's a cliché, but it's also true."

"But do you think I'm ready?"

"Your mother taught me a lot of things in the short time that I knew her. One of the biggies was that the world doesn't wait for you to be ready. You're here. Here is better than ready."

Christopher tried to be satisfied with Reggie's answer. "What do you think happened to Jin?" he asked, changing the subject.

"I've learned not to ask questions that I don't think I want the answers to," Reggie said without hesitation. "Let's get some rest before we have to face whatever it is that's out there."

Thirty-nine

To welcome Christopher, they brought in someone to dance in the fire. Everybody walked to the beach for the celebration, where a great roaring fire was the only source of light. It glowed hot and seemed to stain the world and everything in it a bright orange color—the sand, the sea, their skin, the surrounding trees. Christopher looked out over the water. Eventually the orange gave way to blackness. In the daylight, he'd been able to see a few far-off islands across the sea but now, at night and without light, they were utterly alone. The only things that existed in the world were this fire and the stars over their heads. Then the first man, naked except for the long skirt tied around his waist, ran into the fire.

"There's usually chanting," Apsara said to Christopher. "There are usually fifty men or more chanting, creating music for the dance, but we obviously couldn't risk bringing fifty men here. Everyone here is risking their lives by being here. So secrecy is essential."

Christopher nodded in response. He looked at the faces of the people sitting across from him, on the other side of the fire. There were twenty-nine people in all, every one of them risking their life for this moment. They came from almost every nation in Asia, from every corner of the continent. Christopher had been introduced to each one of them. It wasn't like the worship he had experienced at Dutty's. Here, each one greeted him with defiant pride. Christopher remembered how the people at Dutty's had laid their hands on him, how Evan had said that Christopher was like a god to them. If he was a god in Asia too, then this island was full of agnostics and skeptics. Even the devout hid it from the others. He wondered how he was going to earn their trust, what he could do, what he could say. A few of them met his gaze. The shadows thrown off by the fire danced across their faces.

When the man ran into the fire, it exploded into a tower of orange and yellow cinders that jumped high into the sky like silent fireworks against the black night. The dancer huffed and stamped his feet in the sand like he was in a trance. "The dance is a form of exorcism to ward off evil spirits," Apsara told Christopher. "It's Balinese, even though this part of Indonesia is Muslim. It is usually preceded by another dance, an epic dance about Hanuman, the Monkey King, and his search for the beautiful kidnapped wife of a wise prince."

"What happens?" Christopher asked Apsara. "To the Monkey King?"

"He is captured after he finds the prince's wife and begins to destroy the city where they were keeping her captive. They catch the Monkey King and bind him up for burning." The dancer rushed into the fire again, kicking at the burning logs with his bare feet, running through cinders dancing in the air like falling stars. The dancer was sweating in the heat. Christopher could see his sweat glistening in the orange light of the fire. His feet became black with soot. Each time he ran through the fire, each time he pummeled the embers with his bare feet, another man took a long stick and rebuilt the fire, pushing the embers back together until the flames rose again into the night. As the man rebuilt the fire, the dancer huffed and pounded his feet into the sand as he readied himself for another run into the flames.

"Do they burn him?" Christopher asked Apsara.

"No, he uses magic and escapes."

"And then what happens?"

"Nothing. That's where the dance ends."

"That doesn't seem like much of an ending," Christopher complained.

"What would you have preferred?"

"Some sort of resolution. What happens to the prince and his wife?"

The fire was dwindling now. Each time the dancer ran through the fire, it became smaller and the night darker and the faces of the strangers more obscure. The twenty-nine included twenty men and nine women. Some were taking advantage of the darkness to stare at Christopher now. He could feel their eyes on him. It didn't matter that he was halfway across the world. Watching eyes always felt the same.

"You want closure?" Apsara asked Christopher.

"Doesn't everyone?" Christopher answered. Now that the fire had gone down, Christopher could hear the breathing of the dancer. The dance wasn't a trick. Christopher knew that. The dancer's only defense against the fire was to move through it quickly and to know that pain preceded the burning, even if by only a split second. Pain was a warning. "What happened to Jin?" Christopher asked Apsara quietly, now that the sounds from the fire had subsided.

"He tricked the people who were chasing you into following him. He led them away from the ferry terminal. Once he got them to chase him, there was no way for him to get away. Is that enough closure for you?"

The dance ended when there was nothing left of the fire, when the dancer had extinguished it with his bare feet and the sheer force of his will. The light from the fire gone, tiki torches were brought out and placed them along the beach so that everyone could still see. Once the dancer had mostly recovered, they escorted him to Christopher. The dancer spoke no English. He merely bowed to Christopher. Christopher couldn't take his eyes off the man's blackened but blister-free feet. This time Christopher bowed back.

"How did you like the dance?" the man from Indonesia asked Christopher after the dancer had walked away. Christopher gathered that this man was the owner of the island.

"It was inspiring," Christopher answered. The man smiled and, for the first time in a long time, Christopher felt like he'd said the right thing.

"Now," the Indonesian man said, "it's time for business." He looked over at Reggie, who had been doing his best to disappear, letting Christopher take center stage. "Shall we bring out chairs?" the Indonesian man asked Reggie.

"There's no need," Reggie answered. "We can talk without them."

So they sat in a large circle in the sand, thirty-one of them counting Christopher and Reggie, and all Christopher could think was *how do you end a war by destroying a bunch of paper?* Christopher wondered who would speak first. He thought that maybe it would be Reggie or Apsara, who acted the part of the leader. In the end it was the Indonesian man, the host. "Thank you all for coming," he said to the crowd in English. Christopher understood that he was speaking English solely for Christopher's and Reggie's benefit. "I hope you all feel safe here. We all know how dangerous it is to gather together like this, but we are all professional secret keepers and lie tellers, so I have faith that no one will find us. We are alone on this island. The nearest village is on another island, at least twenty minutes away by boat. We can talk freely here. I hope we will." When the man finished, he looked toward Christopher as if for approval. Christopher nodded to him in response, not knowing what customs might dictate and hoping that he wasn't supposed to talk.

The nod seemed to suffice. Apsara spoke next, as if the order were ritual. "Thank you, Bejo, for your hospitality." Then she addressed the rest of them. "We all know why we're here. Together, we represent the Underground in Asia. I reached out to each of you because I know the power that each of you wields. But we are not kings. We have no kingdoms. We are leaders, and leaders who don't lead are nothing. We all know that being here is dangerous. Let's make it worth our while." She didn't look at Christopher when she was finished. She looked at Reggie.

"We've all heard the rumors that the Child has a plan to end the War," somebody shouted. Someone else laughed. Christopher felt his cheeks burn. "Let's hear it." Murmurs of consent echoed through the air.

Reggie looked over at Christopher to see if Christopher would respond, but the look on Christopher's face told Reggie everything he needed to know. So Reggie spoke instead. "We have a plan. It's not all Christopher's plan, but it falls apart without him."

"Out with it," the giant Chinese man shouted.

"We all know how the two sides in the War have organized their histories and their intelligence," Reggie continued with admirable calm. "The structures are remarkably similar."

"Quite a coincidence," one of the men shouted. He was a Cambodian man, Christopher remembered, named Sun Same. Half the circle laughed. Christopher had never thought about what it meant that the two sides were built around the same essential structure. He wasn't sure if it meant anything, but many of the people there apparently thought it meant a lot.

"Intelligence Cells exist all over the world," Reggie continued, ignoring the heckling. "We don't know where they are. We don't care. They come and go. They change. Throughout history, we know, rebel groups have attacked individual cells." Reggie looked at Christopher again. "Even when successful, that achieves nothing. It's the equivalent of killing a single ant. It has no impact on the colony. It doesn't prove your power. It reinforces their power and demonstrates your overwhelming impotence. The only way to rid yourself of the ants is to kill the queen and make sure that no one takes her place."

"Parables are for monks and dreamers," a woman shouted.

Reggie nodded. "Intelligence Cells exist all over the world, but there are only seven Intelligence Centers. One side has three, the other four. We now know where these Intelligence Centers are: Costa Rica, Tokyo, Istanbul, Rio de Janeiro, Cambodia, Paris, and New York. These are the queens. These are the keys to the organization of the information on both sides of the War. Without the Intelligence Centers, the Intelligence Cells are feckless warehouses of pointless information."

"Feckless?" one of the men of the circle asked.

"Powerless," Reggie clarified. "As useless as a few random sentences from a history book."

"So we start taking out the Intelligence Centers?" someone asked.

"Yes," Reggie replied.

"It's been done before," said an older man sitting almost directly across the circle from Christopher. "It wasn't rebel groups. It was during the course of the War over a hundred years ago. They re-created it. They had all the information they needed in the other Intelligence Centers."

Reggie nodded. "That's why we need global coordination. That's why we need to hit all seven of them at exactly the same time." A hush fell over everyone.

"What if someone fails?" someone eventually asked, breaking the silence. A few people broke off into side conversations in other languages.

Reggie spoke more loudly, trying to get everyone to listen to him. "If someone fails, we all fail."

"How do we know that everyone can be trusted to do their part?" a man shouted.

"How do you know that everyone here can be trusted?" Apsara shot back at the man.

"I don't," the man replied.

"How do we know they won't rebuild from the information in the Intelligence Cells?" another woman interrupted. "It would be extremely difficult, but it's not impossible. Mistakes might be made, but over time it could be done."

The murmuring increased. "That's why we need the Child," Reggie shouted over the foreign whispers. It was the first time Christopher heard Reggie refer to him by his awful nickname. Everyone went silent. "We can trust everyone because everyone will believe that the plan can work. We can be sure that no one will rebuild the Intelligence Centers because no one will want to waste the effort because everyone will believe that the War is over. The War ends when everyone believes it's over."

"And they will believe all of that because of that *feckless* boy?" one of the men called out, holding the new word in his mouth for a moment. Everyone's eyes turned back to Christopher.

"They will believe it because they want to believe it. They will believe it because that's the only way to complete the legend. They will believe it because it's the only way to end the story and still have it mean something."

"They will believe it because the only way to get a fool to retry what he's already failed at repeatedly is by convincing him that this time something is different," said Katsu, the Japanese man who had greeted Christopher and Reggie on the dock earlier that day, without a hint of scorn or sarcasm in his voice.

"Who are the fools?" someone asked.

"We are all fools. Otherwise this War would have ended generations ago. The Child is what makes it different this time." Katsu spoke the words as if suddenly awakening to the idea.

"Then let him speak!" shouted the man who had called Christopher feckless. "Let the Child speak."

The words brought Christopher out of his daze. He looked at the man who had spoken. He was not a big man, though he looked strong and weathered. Christopher wished he could remember where the man was from. Was it Hong Kong? Mongolia? Korea? All Christopher could remember from when he'd been introduced to the man was that the man hadn't smiled. Christopher tried to think of what he could say to make them believe that he had the power to inspire belief in others, but he couldn't think of anything. So Christopher asked the man, "What do you want me to say?"

The man laughed dismissively and looked around at his colleagues to find others who believed this to be a giant joke.

"You called him powerless," Reggie said to the man, "but when was the last time all of you met together?"

Twenty-eight people began to look at each other. "This is the first time," Apsara said.

"Would any of you be here if Christopher wasn't?" Reggie asked.

They all looked at each other again, shaking their heads. "No. We would not," Sun Same, the Cambodian, called out.

"No," the giant Chinese man agreed, "but there is a difference between getting us here and getting others to believe that the War has ended because of him."

Reggie looked over at Christopher. Christopher could see the light from the torch flames flickering in Reggie's green eyes. It was time for Christopher to say something. He knew it. Everybody sitting in that circle knew it. The problem was that Christopher still didn't know what to say. He knew what he wanted to say. He wanted to tell everybody about his paranoia. He wanted to tell them that his paranoia was different from theirs because he wasn't complicit in his own paranoia. He wanted to tell them that they were all crazy and that he blamed every single one of them for everything. He blamed them for the fact that he had only one real friend in the whole world. He blamed them for the fact that he'd put that one friend's life in danger and the only way for him to make it right was to end the War. He wanted to blame them for the fact that he couldn't go home to his parents again until the War ended and, even then, he wasn't sure what he could do. He wanted to tell them that he hated the War and all of them with it. He blamed them all for needing him, but he couldn't say any of these things because he needed them too.

So instead Christopher thought about Dutty. He thought about Dutty's ability to inspire people with his words. But Christopher had no desire to be Dutty. Then he thought about Dutty's desert raid of the Intelligence Cell. Then he spoke. "I'm new to this. I've only known about this War for a few weeks now, but already I've seen the futility of symbolic violence," Christopher began. "Even while it's happening, it's clear to all but the ideologues and the desperate that symbolic violence does more to inspire your enemies than your allies." Then Christopher thought about Addy. He wondered what Addy and Evan were doing at that moment. He wondered if Addy was protecting Evan like she'd promised. He thought about the others too—the ones so thirsty for hope that they were thrilled with the chance merely to tell Christopher their names and to reach out and touch him. "I've also seen the hopelessness of a life spent running and hiding. That's no way to live your life." Finally, Christopher thought about Max—poor Max with an arrow sticking out of his neck. "And I know firsthand that a martyr's death makes no sense if there's no one around to be inspired by the martyrdom." Everyone in the circle was silent, staring at Christopher and awaiting his next words. Christopher wished he knew what else to say. Maybe it would have been better if he had stopped while he was ahead—but he didn't. "So someone needed to have a plan," he said and even before he finished, he could feel the weakness of his words. "I may not be a leader or a hero, but Reggie's plan is a good one and it's the only one we have." Before anyone even responded, Christopher could feel that he'd broken whatever spell he'd nearly cast over everyone. They wanted him to lead and instead he'd told them to settle.

"There are no good plans without good leaders," a woman to Christopher's right said. She was Indian. When they'd been introduced, she was eager and shook Christopher's hand with both of hers. Christopher looked toward Reggie, hoping for some sort of salvation. He thought that Reggie could lead them if they would just listen to him. But Reggie was busy staring bullets at the little man who had first questioned Christopher's role and caused all the problems. The man held Reggie's gaze and threw it back at him. The group broke up into a dozen side conversations now in at least eight different languages so that no one could be heard or understood.

"That's enough!" shouted Apsara over the din. She shot Christopher a look like an ice pick. "No one expected us to have all the answers tonight." It was a lie and everybody knew it, but no one argued. "Let's adjourn until tomorrow." With that, they stopped arguing and stopped talking and everyone began to walk over the long bamboo bridges leading from the beach to their huts. Soon the only sounds were footsteps on bamboo and water lapping beneath them.

Christopher walked alone. He looked back to see Reggie talking in whispers to Apsara. Then they parted and Reggie caught up to Christopher. "What was that all about?" Christopher asked Reggie.

"Damage control," Reggie said. He didn't look pleased. He didn't look angry either. Christopher decided that he should stay quiet for a while.

Forty

Despite his failure, Christopher slept. The island made him feel safe. For the first time that he could remember, he truly felt hidden from the prying eyes that had haunted him his whole life. They were miles away from anywhere else in the world. Plus, he had Reggie sleeping in the other bed, not far from his. The sea air blew through the windows of their hut and Christopher could hear the water lapping beneath them. Reggie didn't say much to him before they went to bed. All he said was, "We'll try again tomorrow. Try to have a little fun with it." Christopher didn't believe that trying again or having fun with it would help. He couldn't believe that anything would change in a day. So instead of thinking about it, he slept. He slept deeply and peacefully until he was shaken out of his slumber by a stranger in the middle of the night.

It was so dark inside the hut that Christopher barely remembered where he was. He could barely see, let alone recognize the faces of the men grabbing him. It wasn't until he heard their voices that he remembered. "We're taking you away," a voice said. "Don't resist." When he heard the accents, he remembered Asia. He remembered everything that had happened. He remembered what was said.

"Reggie," Christopher cried out before a hand clamped over his mouth.

"Reggie's gone," a voice whispered in Christopher's ear. "There's no reason to fight."

Christopher didn't answer. He knew how important it was to save his breath for the fight. So instead of talking, he kicked at the man trying to grab his feet. His kick was firm and direct. He could feel the man's muscles give way as his foot slammed into the man's kidney. Christopher heard the grunt of pain. Then he pulled his right hand as hard as he could, freeing it from the grip of the person holding it. Christopher swung his hand the same way that he'd swung his foot. It was too dark to see details, so he aimed for the largest shadow. His hand connected with something hard. He felt pain shoot up his hand, past his wrist and all the way to his elbow. Whatever he had hit barely moved. Christopher guessed that his fist had connected with the side or back of somebody's skull. A second later, someone grabbed his hand again and, this time, the grip was like a vise. In the darkness, Christopher couldn't even tell how many men he was fighting. Hands seemed to be grabbing him from everywhere.

The man that Christopher had kicked to the ground got back up and tried again to corral Christopher's feet, though Christopher continued to kick with all his might. At least two hands were holding his wrists and a third was clamped over his mouth. Then, instead of kicking, Christopher brought his knee up as hard as he could, catching one of his attackers in the chest. He could hear the wind leave the man's lungs. Then he took his chance. Using all of his remaining strength, he flipped his whole body over, throwing off the two attackers who had been struggling with his hands. With the flip, Christopher threw himself off the bed. For a moment, he felt no hands on him. He struggled to his feet, knowing that he had no more than a second or two to escape. He could see a little bit now. At least he could make out the outline of his hut's door. It was only a few steps away. He was half standing when one of the attackers came down on him again. Maybe Christopher could have withstood the man's weight if he hadn't already spent so much energy fighting, but the weight was too much for him and his body collapsed under the force of it.

Christopher tried to get up, but the weight on top of him was far too great. Then his attackers took out straps and tape. They got his feet first. Christopher felt them being cinched tightly together. He could still kick but without any power or accuracy and even then, even if he managed to kick all of his attackers away, he wouldn't be able to run. His hands were next. They pulled Christopher's hands behind his back one by one and then cinched them together too. Finally, they taped Christopher's mouth so he couldn't scream or yell for help.

It turned out that there were only three of them. Christopher saw them after they picked him up and carried him outside the hut and into the moonlight. He recognized two of the men from the events of that evening. They hadn't said anything, at least not to the group. They'd merely sat in the circle and watched as Christopher performed his seemingly inevitable flameout. He wasn't sure if he recognized the third man because he couldn't get a good look at his face. He tried screaming, but only a small, muffled sound made it through the tape. His eyes scanned the other huts, looking for someone—anyone—who might be able to save him, but the whole place was deserted. *Everyone*, he thought. *Everyone was in on it.* Then he wondered whether they'd gotten Reggie too or if Reggie had given up on him and agreed to let them take him.

Once outside, the three men hoisted Christopher onto their shoulders and carried him across the bridge. Christopher saw the water below him and stopped struggling, worried that if he kept it up, they might drop him in the water, where he would sink to the bottom with no way to swim. The three men carried him to the edge of the bridge, where a lone boat was tied up. There, they swung him off their shoulders and pitched his body into the boat. With his hands and feet tied, Christopher could do nothing to break his fall. The fall was short, but he landed hard on the boat's wooden bottom. Then he lay motionless, his face pressed into the soggy bottom of the boat as the three men climbed in, untied the ropes, started the engine, and began to steer the boat out of the harbor. Once they were underway, Christopher heard the crackling sound of a radio coming from the front of the boat. One of his captors spoke into the radio and somebody on the other end of the signal replied, though Christopher didn't even know what language they were speaking, let alone what was being said.

Meng, one of the three men assigned to get Christopher, radioed to Galang and Apsara to let them know that the deed was done. When Galang heard the message over the crackling radio, he was already pushing his boat as fast as it could possibly go, racing over the dark water. Galang knew his boat and knew its limits well. Apsara's boat raced along about a hundred feet to his left. The whitecaps from its wake were the only sign that anyone could see of Apsara's boat in the darkness. Galang worried that they had too much weight. He had seven men and one woman in his boat and the boat they were chasing had only one. Jung-Su, running from them all, was alone. Apsara's boat had seven passengers, one fewer than Galang, and three of them were women. Her boat was already beginning to pull away from Galang's. Galang had one advantage over everybody else, though. He knew these waters. That meant something, especially in the dark. This part of the sea was full of tiny islands and if you didn't know the waters, the channels running through the islands could quickly become a form of maze.

Galang picked up the radio again. "Stay on him," he said to Apsara through the radio. "I'm going to try to cut him off."

"Good luck," Apsara answered. With that, Galang turned the steering wheel of his boat hard left, cutting behind Apsara's. Galang didn't pull back on the boat's throttle as they hit the wake from Apsara's boat. Instead, he steered straight into it. His boat jumped the wake and bounced when it came down on the water, like a stone skipping over the surface. Galang was taking a risk. He couldn't be sure that Jung-Su would steer his boat into Galang's trap, but Galang knew where the islands would lead him if he was lost and alone and trying to escape. Galang had to believe that it was only a matter of beating Jung-Su to that spot.

Jung-Su pressed on the throttle again, trying to get his boat to go faster, but the throttle was maxed out. He was already pushing the boat as hard as it would go. He knew that he ran the risk of burning out the engine at that speed, or worse, crashing into a rock or running ashore in the darkness. He wasn't ignoring the risks. He knew that his pursuers were behind him. He made a choice not to slow down, to guess on the turns and to hope that he could make it out of their sight before daybreak. Jung-Su didn't see Galang's boat cut to the left. The two boats chasing after him were running without their lights and were too far back for him to make out clearly without losing sight of what was in front of him. If he'd seen Galang's boat turn, he would have done things differently. He would have veered right at every chance even if it risked driving him in a circle. Instead, Jung-Su pressed on as if his life depended on his escape, and Apsara's boat followed him.

Even with the extra weight, Apsara's boat was able to keep up with Jung-Su's and might even have been gaining on him. They got the extra speed by staying inside the smooth waters of Jung-Su's wake. Apsara wasn't behind the wheel of her boat. Instead, she stood near the bow with binoculars and tried to gauge the distance between her boat and Jung-Su's. She could barely make out the outline of his boat in the darkness. He couldn't be allowed to escape. Everyone knew what they had signed up for coming here. Escape wasn't an option for any of them.

Galang's boat was moving too slowly. He could feel it. It was riding low in the water from the weight. Even if Jung-Su took every turn as Galang predicted, none of it would matter if they didn't speed up. "We're too heavy," he called out to his passengers in English, not sure if there was another language that everyone in the boat would speak. "We need to get lighter."

The men behind him on the boat began to search the boat for excess supplies or gear, but the boat was already running stripped down since it was used primarily to transfer big groups of people to the island. "There's nothing to throw off," one of them called out. "We can't get any lighter."

Galang looked behind him at his passengers. Even in the darkness, he didn't fear the water in front of him. He knew when he would have to turn. "Life vests are under the seats," he said to his men. "There is only one Jung-Su. We only need three of us." They looked at each other, the boat still screaming over the jet-black water. Then they looked over the side of the boat. "I'll radio to make sure you're picked up." Nobody moved. "We have no time!" Galang shouted. "The heaviest five!" He didn't slow the boat down for them. He couldn't afford to. After Galang shouted, they moved. When they moved, they moved quickly. Nobody argued about who should go overboard and who should stay on the boat. Galang could feel the boat speed up even before he heard the splash of the bodies hitting the water, while the bodies were still in the air. Then the splashes came, one after the other, five in all. Galang picked up the radio and tried to explain to the voice on the other end where they'd dropped the men. He hoped that they'd all retained consciousness when they hit the water. The boat was moving fast and the water would be hard at that speed for the jumpers. If they didn't stay conscious, Galang hoped that the life vests would keep them afloat because he knew that nobody was likely to find them until daybreak. But the boat was moving now, cutting across the black water like a bullet. To Galang, to all of them, that mattered more than anything else. He picked up the radio again to see if Apsara could tell him where they were.

Jung-Su could see Apsara's boat. He knew it was catching up to him. He understood what was happening. They were riding his wake. Even with their heavier load, they were catching up because he was breaking new water and they were riding on his coattail. He had to do something about it or they were going to catch him. He began to weave back and forth, to snake this way and that way just enough to upset the line that Apsara's boat had been taking. Soon, Apsara's boat was bouncing in and out of Jung-Su's wake, and Jung-Su began to get farther and farther away again.

Jung-Su saw in front of him a small slit between two islands. He headed for it, believing that he could make it through and cause the boat chasing him to lose sight of him. Then he'd be in the clear. Sure, Apsara still had Jung-Su's cell phone. They'd confiscated all their weapons and cell phones as soon as everybody got to the island. The lack of a cell phone and contact list would be an annoyance, but if Jung-Su could get to the mainland by morning without being caught, he'd be able to get in touch with people. He'd be able to tell them all not to believe. He could warn them. The channel between the islands was thin and Jung-Su was closing in on it fast. The weaving had created some distance between him and his pursuer, but he straightened out now and headed straight for the gap. The weaving helped Jung-Su lose Apsara, but little did he know that it also gave Galang time to catch up.

Jung-Su was close to the islands now. Close enough to see the other side of the channel. All he could see through the channel was beautiful black water, and he aimed for that. For a moment, he truly believed that he was going to make it. He went straight into the channel and, only a few moments later, plunged out the other side. Jung-Su didn't even hear Galang's boat approaching. Galang's boat was light now and Galang, still at the helm, was not letting up on the throttle. He came around from the other side of one of the islands, his timing perfect. Galang was bearing down on Jung-Su's boat. It was dark, but Galang didn't waiver. He didn't hesitate. He aimed his boat through the darkness at Jung-Su's boat like a missile. A split second later, the two boats collided, both moving at top speed. Galang's boat tore into the back half of Jung-Su's boat, bounced off it, and ricocheted into the air, throwing its three passengers out before it capsized.

After the collision, Jung-Su was left standing at the front of his boat. He'd held on tightly to the steering wheel as his boat spun. Unlike Galang, Jung-Su was lucky enough to have his boat stay upright, and he was able to stay on his feet. When the world stopped spinning, Jung-Su looked back at his boat to assess the damage. The boat was more or less intact. The only problem was that Galang had managed to tear the boat's outboard motor clean off. Jung-Su was stranded, any dreams of escape sinking to the bottom of the South China Sea. He looked behind him again, just in time to see Apsara's boat headed straight for him.

Forty-one

Christopher managed to sit up in the back of the boat. It took a bit of squirming. His hands were still tied behind his back and his feet were still lashed together, so he'd had to use his chin and his shoulder for leverage against the side of the boat. The three men in the boat ignored his struggle. All three of them were standing near the front of the boat. One was holding a radio. He periodically spoke into it in a language Christopher didn't understand. The other two kept scanning the water around them, one with binoculars and one with his naked eyes. They'd been sitting in the same spot for what seemed like a long time, though Christopher didn't trust his current ability to judge how much time had passed. Nothing was making any sense. His kidnappers had driven the boat out to this spot in the middle of the sea and cut the engine, letting the boat drift silently over the water. Lying on the bottom of the boat, feeling every ripple of waves the boat jumped over reverberate through his body, Christopher didn't know where they were going, but he assumed that they were going somewhere. At first he had only managed to roll himself over so that he could look up at the stars in the sky over his head as the boat buzzed over the water. They were different stars than he was used to. He couldn't find a single star that he knew was out of place, but the whole sky looked different.

Once the boat stopped, Christopher began the struggle to get his body upright. He didn't know what he expected to see once he was able to sit up, but he wasn't expecting what he saw. What he saw, once he could see over the sides of the boat, was endless nothingness. They were nowhere. They had driven him off to a spot in the sea where not a single speck of land or a single light from a single other ship could be seen. The world was black water and black sky and somewhere, off in the distance, the water stopped and the sky began. Christopher wanted to scream at them. He wanted to ask them what they were going to do with him, but he couldn't even do that. The tape was still sealing his mouth shut.

After Christopher had been sitting up for a while, listening to the three men talk to each other, trying to will himself to understand the ununderstandable, one of the men noticed that he'd managed to crawl up from the bottom of the boat. "Should we take the tie off his wrists?" the man asked, obviously speaking English for Christopher's benefit.

The other two men looked toward Christopher now too. "We can't," one of them said. Their English embarrassed Christopher. "If we free his arms, he might get brave and jump in the water and try to swim for it."

"Where's he going to swim to?" the first man asked with a laugh, staring out over the miles and miles of black water.

"The little fucker has some fight in him," the third man said, swearing in English with the ease of an American, if not the accent.

"Reggie warned us about that," said the man who was worried that Christopher would swim for it, staring at him with a look of mild respect. The words stung. *So Reggie was in on it*, Christopher thought.

"Reggie says a lot of things," the first man said. "Should we take the tape off of his mouth?"

"What if he screams?" the Doubting Thomas said.

"Who is going to hear him?" the one with the talent for English curse words asked. "If we take the tape off of your mouth, are you going to scream?" he said to Christopher. He was the biggest of the three men. Christopher guessed that he was the one who had grabbed his hands so firmly.

Christopher shook his head. He couldn't see what good screaming would do. So the big one came back toward him and with one clean, fast tug, pulled the tape from Christopher's face. It stung as all the hair on his face was pulled off with the tape. Christopher thought about lunging for the man. He thought about biting him, about tearing off a chunk of the man's flesh with his teeth. But what good would that do? Hadn't somebody recently said something about the futility of symbolic violence? Instead of attacking, Christopher took a deep breath. He appreciated his ability to still breathe deeply.

"What are you going to do with me?" Christopher asked his captors.

"We don't know," the man with the radio said, holding it up for Christopher to see, showing Christopher that his fate was in the hands of someone who wasn't even with them.

"Who does know?" Christopher asked, fearing that he already knew the answer.

"What are we going to do with him?" Reggie asked Apsara as they pulled Jung-Su into their boat. Up to that point, Reggie had tried to stay out of the way. This wasn't his place. He merely wanted to be on a boat to make sure that the job was really done.

"I don't know," Apsara answered him. "It's not for me to decide. We'll have to bring him back to the island. We'll bring everybody back." They'd found Galang's body and the body of the women from his boat in the water. They'd pulled the third man from Galang's boat out of the water alive and conscious. Someone would have to try to find the people that Galang had left behind in the water. Then they could all go return to the island—at least what was left of them anyway.

Forty-two

"Do you think that's her?" Addy whispered to Evan. They had taken seats in a dark corner of the pub and from there were staring across the room at the diminutive dark-haired woman behind the bar. "Do you think that's Maria? She looks too old be Maria."

"It has to be her," Evan whispered. It wasn't any specific feature that convinced him that this was his best friend's mother, though some of her features did remind Evan of Christopher. It was more the way she carried herself, like she was trying to pretend that she wasn't walking on a tightrope over a bottomless pit. The small things gave it away, like the way she never relaxed her hands even when she thought no one was looking or the way her eyes darted around the room every few seconds to appraise her surroundings. Evan had seen those things in Christopher. Maria took out a rag and began to wipe down the bar. When someone came in that she recognized, she greeted the person with a bright smile but with dead eyes. Evan could see the pain in her eyes. The pain was the clincher. "That has to be Christopher's mother," he repeated, as much to himself as to Addy.

It had been five days since Addy and Evan left Florida. They stopped only the one time. Other than that, the only sleep either of them got was when they took turns napping in the car while the other person drove. They'd made it the nearly two thousand miles from Florida to Quebec City in a little more than two days. When they crossed the border into Canada, Evan hid in the trunk of the car under a blanket and their bags. They knew that he would never get across the border by showing his papers. He was a wanted man. He'd been labeled a terrorist after killing the cop in Los Angeles. His picture was still being blasted everywhere. They considered taking the safer route, having him hike across the border and meet up with Addy later, but they were afraid of how much time that would take. They hadn't been given a deadline, only Reggie's instructions to "find Maria and bring her to New York." But everything was happening so quickly now that they couldn't imagine wasting a full day minimum with Evan hiking through the woods, so instead, they hid him in the trunk. They purchased a black blanket. About five miles before the border, Addy pulled over and Evan climbed into the trunk. Addy covered him with the blanket and then replaced their bags. She managed to arrange the blanket and the bags so that even with the trunk wide open only the most discerning eye would have noticed the body hidden there.

As soon as Addy threw the thick black blanket over Evan, he stayed as still as he could. He knew that he was in no danger of being seen unless the car was stopped and somebody opened the trunk, which wasn't likely. They had no reason to believe that the car that Addy's old colleagues had given them along with Reggie's orders was anything but clean. Even so, Evan was afraid that if he moved, he would upset the mirage that Addy had created on top of him to hide him. He was only in the trunk for a half hour, but it felt like ten times that long. It was quiet and dark and he tried not to move a single muscle. Only the rumbling of the car over the highway reminded him that he was conscious. Then he felt the slowing of the car as it came to a gentle stop at the border so that the border patrol could question Addy. Those five minutes were as close to death as Evan had ever felt. He was sure of it. He'd stood in front of bullets and raced through fire, but those moments didn't make him think of death. They made him feel alive. The blank passivity, lying there, waiting—that was death. Luckily for Evan, Addy had all the right answers for the border patrol. Evan had known she would. Soon the car was moving again and Evan was alive again. Ten miles later, Addy pulled off to the side of the road and let Evan out of the trunk.

Addy and Evan's initial destination was never in doubt. Reggie had told them where to go first. He'd told them that he'd been sending Maria letters at a P.O. box in Quebec City for years. He addressed them to Sophie Escolla. Addy could barely believe any of it. Addy wanted to ask Reggie so many questions, but Reggie wasn't around to answer them. Reggie was with Christopher, somewhere, trying to raise an army. So Addy tabled her questions and she and Evan headed for Quebec City, looking for Sophie Escolla and hoping that Evan would recognize a woman that he'd never seen before.

"What should we do?" Addy asked, staring at the woman behind the bar and secretly hoping that this woman could be the hero for her that Christopher hadn't been. "How can we be sure it's her?"

Evan shifted in his seat, readying himself to stand up. "I'll go talk to her. She'll talk to me. I'll tell her that I know Christopher."

Addy put a hand on Evan's arm. "You can't go. She might recognize you from the TV reports. We might scare her away." Evan stopped. He wouldn't be able to live with himself if he scared her away. "I'll go," Addy said.

"What are you going to say?" Evan asked Addy before she stood up.

"I'm going to ask her if she wants to see her son again."

It hadn't been easy finding this woman that Evan and Addy thought might be Maria. Neither Evan nor Addy had ever been to Quebec City before. Neither had any idea what to expect. They definitely didn't expect what they found—a tiny walled city, sitting high on the cliffs above a raging river, looking to the young rebels more like a giant medieval castle than a city. They soon learned that the part of the city that looked like a castle was now a luxury hotel. The rest of the city was so quaint and perfect that it made Evan and Addy uncomfortable. Seven years earlier, it had had the exact same impact on Maria. Now she came to the city only once a month, to pick up her mail. Evan and Addy didn't know that, though. The city was their only lead, so they were going to stay until they had somewhere else to go.

It had taken Addy and Evan three days of wandering the city before they found another lead they could follow. After the initial excitement of arriving in the city wore off, Addy and Evan began to believe that their assignment wasn't possible. All they had to go on was a fake name and Reggie's description of what Maria looked like. They didn't give up, though. Youth is nothing if not a panacea for the impossible. They split up. Evan stayed near the post office. He watched the people come and go. He hid from view and studied the faces of strangers. At the same time, Addy hit the streets. She went to the hotels, the bars, and the restaurants and asked everyone—everyone except those who gave off the scent of being part of the War—if they knew someone named Sophie Escolla. Evan and Addy would meet for dinner each night and then they would continue to prowl the city by moonlight, listening to conversations and praying for clues. The person who finally answered their prayers didn't look like an angel. He was a burly biker sitting in one of the seedier bars Evan and Addy had found in the quaint city. He was drinking beer and complaining to the bartender. Most of his complaints were aimed at another bartender from some bar in some town in the middle of nowhere north of the city. "She's a little thing," the man said to the bartender, "but man, she's got an attitude."

"What happened?" the bartender asked, not really caring but knowing exactly when to pretend to care in order to maximize tips.

"I asked her what her name was. She says, 'Sophie.' I told her that I thought Sophie was a dog's name." The burly man laughed, shaking his head. "So she says to me, 'I've had other names. You should know that I picked this name myself. And I'm a lot of things, but I'm not a dog.' Then she walks to the end of the bar, lights a cigarette, and refuses to give me another drink. She sits there smoking her cigarette and not looking at me until I leave. She was a serious bitch."

Addy and Evan were sitting at the bar a few stools down from their new angel. "Did you catch her last name?" Evan leaned in and asked the man.

"I didn't catch anything after that." The man laughed again. "Bitch wouldn't say a word."

"Where is this bar?" Evan asked the man and Addy memorized everything else that came out of the man's mouth. The next morning Addy and Evan drove north through the country to the tiny town of Saint-Joachim.

All that searching led them to this moment. Addy stood up and started walking toward the bar. She eyed the woman standing behind it and tried to temper her excitement. She reminded herself what her excitement had cost her the last time. She remembered how giddy she had felt when she found out that the boy she saw walking through their compound was Christopher and what that had led to. This was different, though. Christopher was an aimless child. This was Maria. This was the woman who had already beaten the War once. It didn't matter how small or personal that victory might have been. It was a victory. Great things come from small victories.

Addy reached the bar and sat down on one of the stools. It was afternoon and still light outside. The place was mostly empty. An older man sat at the bar also, about three stools down from Addy, nursing a tall beer. Two men, both probably around thirty years old, sat in one of the booths telling stories to each other in French and laughing obnoxiously loudly. Addy watched the bartender as she approached her to take her order. As the bartender came closer, Addy began to wonder again if this really was Maria. Would she even be able to tell? Evan might have known Christopher longer than she had, but she had spent a lot of time with Christopher too. She'd even kissed him once. Hadn't she? Would she see Christopher in Maria's face?

"What can I get for you?" the bartender asked Addy in English, picking up their language preference from earlier, when Addy and Evan ordered their first drinks.

Addy lost her train of thought for a second. This woman didn't look like Christopher. She'd come over to Addy and Evan's booth to take their order when they first came in, but they had been too nervous to get a really clear look at her. Up close, Addy noticed how much smaller the bartender was than Christopher. She seemed almost frail in comparison to him. Christopher hadn't been everything that Addy had hoped for, but he had always seemed formidable, even when he was afraid—sometimes even more when he was afraid. Then Addy looked into the woman's eyes and she knew for certain that she had seen those eyes before. They were younger and some of the sadness was replaced by confusion, but she had seen them before. "We're still okay with our drinks," Addy said to the bartender, gesturing toward the two nearly full beers sitting in front of Evan and speaking quietly so the older man at the bar wouldn't be able to listen in on their conversation. "I was wondering if you could answer a question for me."

It was only a split second, but Addy could have sworn that she saw a look pass over the bartender's face, a look of annoyance mixed with fear. Before responding, the bartender took a long look at the face of every person in the bar, hanging for a few extra beats on Evan's face. A minute later, she turned back to Addy. "What's the question?"

"What's your name?" Addy asked in a tone that implied that depending on how the bartender answered this question, many other questions would follow. Maria was immediately suspicious. She hated questions.

"Sophie," the bartender answered.

"Sophie Escolla?"

Maria paused for a moment. Then she turned toward the cash register and picked up a pack of cigarettes. She was confused. They'd never been this direct before. They'd been following her without a break for six years, and this was the first time one of them had come up to her and started asking questions. Maria pulled a cigarette out of the pack. "Yes," she answered the young woman. Maria noted how much younger this one and her friend were than all the others. Her friend looked even younger than she did. He was probably about the same age as Christopher. Maria slipped the cigarette between her lips. "You're American, aren't you?"

"Yes," Addy replied.

"We don't see a lot of Americans up this far. What brings you here?"

Since she asked, Addy figured she should just lay down her cards. She spoke in a hushed voice. "Reggie sent us to find you, Maria. He sent us to bring you back."

Maria took the unlit cigarette out of her mouth. She felt like she'd been punched in the head. For a second, she could barely move, but then she collected herself. "I don't know what you're talking about," she said. This might be a trap or, even worse, the woman could be telling the truth. Either way, Maria didn't want anything to do with her. "So, do you want another drink or do you want to go back to your table?"

Addy should have been more ready for Maria's response than she was. For some reason, she had thought that all they would have to do was find Maria and their job would be done. They'd found Maria. Now what? Addy thought about going back to the table and letting Evan give it a try. That option was there, but Addy wasn't ready for it yet. Instead, she leaned in toward Maria—who had somehow turned from a small, meek woman into a force of nature—and said in her most earnest and honest voice, "You can trust us, Maria. We're on your side."

It wasn't the words that the young woman spoke that reached inside Maria and grabbed her. It was the desperation in her voice. Maria didn't know if there were more things in her life that she wanted to forget or more things that she would do anything to remember. The desperation in Addy's voice made Maria think of both. Suddenly she remembered standing in a dark alley with a knife pressed against her throat, trying to convince the man holding the knife that he could trust her. Maria was them once.

Addy watched as Maria scanned the room quickly again, checking to make sure that no one was watching her. Then she glanced out the window. Finally, she took a long, hard look at Evan. When she was done, Maria turned toward the cash register and grabbed her receipt book and a pen. She began to write something on the receipt book. Addy was certain that Maria was about to tally up their bill and send them on their way. Maria ripped off the top page and passed it to Addy. On the page, Maria had written the words "Who are you?" with the directness that Addy had initially feared.

Addy knew that this could be her only chance, so she took the pen from Maria and wrote under the question "Friends of Christopher."

Maria read the words. Then she lifted her head. She stared at Evan for a long time again. Then she stared for just as long at Addy. It took all of Addy's strength not to squirm beneath Maria's gaze. Maria began to write something else on the pad. As she did, she said loudly, "It's down the road a ways on the left. You can't miss it. It's the tallest building for miles." Addy looked down at what Maria was writing. The note on the pad said, "Can't talk here. Not safe. Come to my place after midnight tonight. Wait until all the lights are out. Come in through the back door, facing the woods. I'll leave it open. Go through the door opposite the back door, into the basement. Make sure you're not followed. Don't turn on the lights." She wrote her address at the bottom of the page. Then she tore the page from the pad and handed it to Addy as if she were passing her driving directions.

"Thank you," Addy said sincerely, taking the paper from Maria's hand. She was confused about how this tiny, nearly empty bar in the middle of nowhere could be dangerous. She wondered if everything that had happened to Maria had driven her mad. After all, Addy knew the legend. She knew that Maria had no genetic predisposition to paranoia. But Addy took the paper, walked back to Evan, and told him that they had to leave. Evan didn't ask questions. He left money on the table for the beer and then stood up and followed Addy out of the bar. On the way out, Evan turned back and looked at Maria one last time. Maria was watching them. She watched them walk out the door. She would watch them through the window once they were outside. She would watch them get into their car. She would watch them drive away and hope that the people who were following her—the people who had been following her for the past six years—didn't end up following the kids in that car too. Once Maria couldn't see those kids anymore, she grabbed her pack of cigarettes, thought about lighting one, and then remembered the advice an old friend had given her eighteen years ago about trying to hide when you smelled like cigarettes. It was advice that she was suddenly going to need again. So instead of lighting a cigarette, Maria took the whole pack and threw it in the garbage.

Forty-three

They left Jung-Su tied up in one of the huts while they decided what to do with him. From the window of the hut, he could see the moon hanging low over the sea. He could hear the waves lapping gently under the floor beneath him. He questioned himself, wondering if he should have waited. Should he have acted like everything was normal, gone back to Korea and then leaked the entire plan? If he'd done it that way, he wouldn't have been able to help them catch Christopher. The only way he could be sure to help them catch Christopher was to sneak out in the middle of the night and notify someone while Christopher was still on the island. So he tried and he failed. Now he was trying not to think about what the punishment for his failure would be.

"I want to talk to him," Christopher said while all those around him debated Jung-Su's fate. They had gathered in the largest of the huts, the one used for meals, to discuss what to do with Jung-Su. They were down to twenty-six people from twenty-nine. The subtracted three were Galang, the other casualty on Galang's boat, and, of course, Jung-Su. They had found the others, the ones that jumped off Galang's boat into the dark water. A few had symptoms of whiplash and they were all cold, but they were all accounted for. They had joined hands in a circle as they floated in the sea, waiting and hoping someone would come for them. "I want to see him and I want to talk to him," Christopher repeated even louder this time. Nobody had asked for Christopher's opinion. He almost felt like they'd forgotten that he was even there.

"I don't think that's a good idea," Reggie said softly to Christopher, as if he was hoping that no one else would hear.

Christopher glared at Reggie. "I think it's a better idea than having me kidnapped in the middle of the night to try to protect me," Christopher said loudly, hoping the opposite.

Reggie shrugged. "If you'd known what was happening, you would have demanded to come on one of the boats chasing after Jung-Su and we couldn't take that risk. We needed to get you off the island in case Jung-Su was able to contact someone. We can't afford to lose you, Christopher."

Now others began to pay attention to Reggie and Christopher's conversation. A few of them began nodding their heads. Even more of them stared blankly at Christopher as if trying to see in him what it was that Reggie saw. Reggie's words didn't soften Christopher's glare. "What good am I to you if you're going to treat me like a child? If you want me to inspire people, then you have to risk letting me do something inspirational."

The nods increased now. They wanted to believe, but Reggie had failed to give them anything to believe in. "What can it hurt to let them talk?" Apsara asked Reggie. "He should be allowed to face the man who betrayed him."

Slowly, the nods evolved into murmurs. Soon there was no way for Reggie to say no even though he wanted to. He was still afraid. He was afraid that, as loosely as Christopher already gripped the belief in what they were doing, any tiny shred of doubt would pry him free. "I suppose it's not my call to make," Reggie said out loud to the room. "You all believe that Christopher should go talk to him?" Reggie's question was met with a grumbling consent. "Okay, can we at least send two men in with him as bodyguards?"

The room seemed ready to concede to this demand until they were interrupted again by the Child. "No," Christopher said. "I want to talk to Jung-Su by myself." Christopher didn't really understand this urge. He wasn't even sure that he wasn't making demands out of spite. But there was something about Jung-Su that made Christopher want to talk to him. There was something about Jung-Su that Christopher admired. *At least Jung-Su had made a decision*, Christopher thought. *At least Jung-Su had acted without doubt.* "I'm not asking."

Christopher had believed he was going to die out on the water, watching the stars, merely waiting for these three men to determine the time and conditions of his demise. He was wrong. He didn't die. The three men were trying to protect him. How much more was he wrong about?

"Can we at least post someone at the door?" Reggie asked Christopher.

"You can all stand outside the door if you like," Christopher answered the room as much as Reggie, "so long as I go into that room alone and none of you listen to our conversation."

Three of the men led Christopher to the hut where they were keeping Jung-Su. They had put him in the hut jutting farthest out in the South China Sea. To escape any way other than by jumping into the water, Jung-Su would have had to walk past the congregation that was debating his fate. One of Christopher's escorts opened the door and motioned for Christopher to go inside. Once he had stepped into the hut, his escort stepped away and closed the door behind Christopher.

They had stripped the hut bare. Christopher wondered if it was always like this, if they had always kept a designated jail cell. Not a single piece of furniture remained. The only things in the hut were three windows, the door, and Jung-Su. He was sitting on the floor in a kneeling position. They had taken his pants and his shirt and left him in only his underwear. His legs were bound together and his hands were bound behind his back. The rope around his hands was then tied to a bolt sticking out of the wall. Christopher wondered if the hut that he and Reggie were staying in had a bolt too or if only this hut had one. He looked at Jung-Su's face. Jung-Su's eyes were cold. They'd tied a rag around his head as a gag to keep him from shouting. Christopher took a step toward him. He wanted to untie the rag, but he was worried that Jung-Su would try to bite him like some sort of unmuzzled rabid dog. "Can I ask you a few questions?" Christopher asked Jung-Su.

Jung-Su didn't move.

"You don't have to answer them if you don't want to," Christopher said, though he wondered what the point was of asking questions that wouldn't be answered.

Jung-Su bent his head down toward his chin. For a moment, Christopher thought he was either bowing or praying. Then he realized that Jung-Su was showing him the knot in the rag so that he could untie it. Christopher took one more step closer, wondering why he was afraid of this man who was shackled and incapacitated. Christopher stopped close enough that he would be able to reach forward and untie the knot holding the rag over Jung-Su's mouth. He didn't think that Jung-Su would be able to bite him from that far away, at least not anything but his hand anyway. Christopher tugged on the knot and it came loose. The rag fell away and Christopher quickly stepped backward, away from Jung-Su's mouth.

Christopher assumed that Jung-Su would say something then, but the man remained silent. He merely lifted his head and met Christopher's eyes. Christopher was amazed that Jung-Su, who was tied up and tethered to the wall of his enemies, appeared to be less afraid than he was. "Are you going to say anything?" Christopher asked.

Jung-Su didn't respond.

"Do you want me to put the rag back over your mouth?" Christopher asked, letting anger seep into his voice.

Jung-Su didn't respond.

Finally realizing that Jung-Su was merely taking Christopher up on his offer and not answering questions that he didn't want to, Christopher asked, "What do you think we should do with you?"

"I think you should let me go," Jung-Su told Christopher.

"But you betrayed your friends," Christopher said. "They all could have died if you'd made it out."

"My friends betrayed themselves," Jung-Su responded.

"How did they betray themselves?"

The look of disgust on Jung-Su's face was unmistakable. "They accepted lies for truths. They put their own interests ahead of their true destinies. I almost did the same, and all because of you."

"How is that my fault?" Christopher asked him.

"Because you are a false prophet," Jung-Su said.

Christopher shook his head. "I never claimed to be a prophet. I never claimed to be anything. I'm not the one who started all of this. All I want is for this War to end so that I can go home."

Jung-Su didn't say anything. He stared silently out the window toward the moonlight.

"You said that your friends put their own interests ahead of their true destinies. What are their true destinies?"

"The War," Jung-Su said.

"That's ridiculous. Nobody's true destiny is this stupid fucking War."

Jung-Su spit on the floor of the hut. The spit landed only a few inches from Christopher's feet. "Mine is," Jung-Su said. Then he looked up at Christopher again. "What is yours?"

"Like I said," Christopher muttered. "To go home."

"Then why don't you go home? Why are you here pretending to be something you are not?"

"If I had given a great speech, what would you have done? If I had convinced you that I was a prophet, would you have followed me?"

Jung-Su didn't look at him now and didn't answer him.

"You were willing to kill everyone on this island because why? Because you were hoping that I could guarantee you victory? Because you were hoping that I could do what? Wash away your sins?" Jung-Su still didn't look at him. Christopher was becoming frustrated. He tried one more question. "Two people died going after you tonight. Do you feel guilty about that? Would you have felt guilty if everyone on this island had died because of you?"

This question got Jung-Su's attention. He looked at Christopher again with only anger in his eyes. "Would you?" Jung-Su answered.

Christopher stood in the barren room staring at this insolent, nearly naked man tied to the wall like an animal. "I came in here to talk to you because I thought I admired you and hoped that I might be able to help you." Christopher licked his dry lips. "They're going to kill you. I thought you might tell me something that I could use to save your life."

Jung-Su looked away from Christopher and out the window toward the moon again. "I don't want your help."

Christopher had heard enough. He walked back to the door of the hut. The three men who had escorted him there were still standing outside. "Retie the gag," Christopher ordered them. They nodded, acknowledging his order, and stepped into the room as Christopher left.

Then Christopher walked back toward the dining hut. The walk felt long. The walk aged him. By the time he reached the dining hut, Christopher was far older than when he started. The minutes weren't measurable in seconds, only in moments, and the moments took forever. Christopher still didn't believe that he was a prophet, but he began to realize that he might never be able to get home if he kept denying it. Either way, he was now certain that he couldn't afford to suffer doubters.

They were still debating when Christopher walked back into the hall. No one looked up upon his return—not until he spoke. He spoke loudly and as clearly as he could through the lump in his throat. Everyone heard the two words he spoke: "Kill him." Then he walked over and sat down next to Reggie. He decided that he wasn't mad at Reggie anymore. He felt like he now knew what Reggie was trying to protect him from.

The room went silent. All the eyes followed Christopher as he sat down. "What did you say?" One of the men broke the silence.

Christopher stood up again. He addressed the room, the whole room, turning his head and making eye contact with everyone. "I said, 'Kill him.' You all know that you have to. You all know that it's inevitable. You can't carry him around like a pet. You have no prison for him. You sure as hell can't leave him here. Every option but one is too dangerous. You all know that you have to kill him, but you sit around here debating and pretending you have options because you all want to think that you're better than that now. The whole reason why you're here is to be better than that—to end the War—to stop killing—but you're not better than that. Not yet. So I'm giving you all an out. I'm giving you your option. You don't have to decide to kill him, because I already have. I'll carry this one. I'll take it. Kill him so we can move on and finish this thing."

The silence after Christopher spoke lasted a long time. Christopher didn't bother sitting down. He stayed on his feet, waiting for a response. "Who should do it?" somebody asked.

"It doesn't matter," Christopher said, "because whoever does it will be doing it with my hands, so make it quick and painless. We can at least be good enough for that." He looked around at the faces in the room. They were expressionless. "If no one else has anything to say, I'm going back to my hut," he said. He was suddenly incredibly tired. No one said anything else, so Christopher left.

An hour later, Reggie came into the hut. Christopher was lying on the bed, staring out the window, unable to sleep. He turned toward Reggie as Reggie walked through the door. Reggie had a bottle of liquor and two glasses in his hands. "Jung-Su is dead," he told Christopher. He walked over and set the two glasses on the table between the beds. Then he uncorked the bottle of liquor and poured out two full glasses. He handed one of the glasses to Christopher.

"What is it?" Christopher asked Reggie.

"It's called arak. It's Indonesian. They make it from palm trees. Apsara had some stashed away in the kitchen."

"Are we supposed to be celebrating?" Christopher asked.

"No," Reggie told him. Nothing in Reggie's voice made it sound like a celebration. "I'm hoping that the liquor might help you to get some sleep."

"I've killed people," Christopher said. "Jung-Su's not even my second." Christopher counted in his head. "He's my fifth."

"Yeah," Reggie said, sipping from his own glass, "but you've never had to think about it first. Thinking makes it different."

Christopher downed half the liquor in one gulp. It burned his throat. He was about to ask Reggie if he'd done the right thing, but he stopped himself. It didn't matter what Reggie thought. It was too late to change anything now anyway. "How did they do it?" Christopher asked instead.

"They bled him over the water."

"What does that mean?" Christopher asked.

"They hung his neck over the dock and slit his throat." Reggie saw the disgusted look on Christopher's face. "It's what Jung-Su wanted. They asked him. He said he wanted his blood to feed the sea."

"What's wrong with these people, Reggie?" Christopher finished his drink and held the glass out for Reggie to pour him another one.

"These are my people too," Reggie told him. "Maybe that's what we need you for—to tell us what's wrong with us." He forced a smile. "Let's try to get some sleep. The sun will be up in a couple hours and we're leaving here in the morning."

"Is everyone leaving?"

"No," Reggie said. "Just us. They'll need time to talk about us after we leave and to talk about whether or not they want in on the plan."

"And if they don't?"

Reggie's eyes told Christopher everything he needed to know. "These people represent a third of the world, Christopher," he said. "Let's try to get some sleep. We're leaving for Istanbul in five hours."

When the liquor finally hit Christopher, it hit him hard. It knocked him out cold. Reggie wasn't so lucky. He stayed awake, worrying that someone else would betray them, worrying about what he was doing to Maria's son.

Reggie let Christopher sleep for as long as he could the next day. By the time he woke Christopher, he'd been sleeping for more than four hours. Their bags were already packed and loaded on the boat. Reggie had left out one outfit for Christopher to change into. When it was time to go, Reggie gently shook Christopher awake. "It's time, Christopher," he said, placing a hand on the boy's shoulder. "We've got a long way to go."

Christopher opened his eyes to the brightness of the morning. Everything around him glowed golden in the sunlight. Even Reggie was golden. "I fell asleep," Christopher said to Reggie as he tried to shake off the sleep.

"Yeah," Reggie said, "that was kind of the point. The boat's ready now. We have to go."

Christopher sat up in bed and looked around. "It seems a shame to come this far and not see anything," he mumbled, only half kidding.

"Well, you can always come back when this is all over," Reggie said to him. "You've got clothes on the dresser. I need you outside in ten minutes."

Christopher waited until Reggie had closed the door behind him before he climbed out of bed. He walked over to the window and looked outside. The water was a pristine blue. Slowly, he began pulling apart in his mind what had actually happened the previous night and what he had dreamt. But it was all real. The dream was the blank, empty space between the madness. He walked over to the dresser and found his clothes. He dressed slowly, still trying to make sense of everything he'd seen and everything he'd heard and everything he'd said and everything he'd done.

They were waiting for Christopher when he stepped outside into brightness that the view from his windows had only hinted at. The light came from all directions, sparkling off the water almost as brightly as it came down from the sky. They were lined up along the bamboo bridges leading from Christopher's hut to the dock where the boat was. All of them were there—all the survivors anyway. Christopher had to squint through the sun to see them all. He began to walk, passing a person every few steps. They said nothing to him as he walked past them. Instead, they simply placed their hands together in front of their chests and bowed as he passed. Christopher was unsure what it all meant. He was unsure if he should thank them or say good-bye to them. All he was sure of was that he shouldn't bow back.

All in all, Christopher passed twenty-two different people who bowed silently to him. The only ones that hadn't lined up were Reggie, Apsara, and the person that had been selected to replace Galang and drive them back. Christopher had walked slowly, trying to at least honor their bows by being present for them. Still, he was relieved when he finally saw the boat with Reggie already in it. Apsara was standing beside it. Bejo, the island's owner, sat behind the wheel of the boat and a pang of guilt ran through Christopher, remembering first Galang, and then Jin and then Max. Then he remembered Jung-Su and waited to feel guilty about that too, but the guilt never came.

Christopher walked up to Apsara and, to Christopher's relief, instead of bowing she reached out her hand for him to shake. "Good luck in Istanbul, Christopher," she said.

"Thank you," Christopher answered.

"We're counting on you to convince them to follow you, the way that you convinced us."

Christopher stood there silently, feeling a pang of joy in his chest that he wasn't sure was warranted. He was worried that he'd heard her wrong. He hadn't. Apsara smiled and nodded. "They decided last night," she said. "Subject to the rest of the world agreeing, we will fight." Christopher looked over Apsara's head at Reggie. He didn't smile or even acknowledge that Christopher was looking at him, but Christopher could tell that Reggie had already heard the news. "Stay safe, Christopher," Apsara said, sending him off.

"You too," Christopher replied. "All of you." Then he stepped into the boat and they pulled away from the dock and were off.

Forty-four

The plan in Paris was to collapse the Intelligence Center into the earth and then blow it to smithereens. The rebels had thought that the Intelligence Center was impenetrable, but then they realized that it was built over an old, forgotten section of the catacombs. Since they couldn't figure out how to get into the building, they had to figure out a way to bring the building down to them. It was a demolition job, strategically planting bombs in the various dark corners of the underground tunnels running beneath the city so that when the time came, the bombs would all go off and the Intelligence Center would come tumbling down. They would destroy the pillars holding up the Intelligence Center and it would collapse into the tunnels under its own weight. Then the second set of bombs would go off, ensuring that everything that fell into the earth was utterly destroyed. Only then would the rebels move in to clean up anything that was left.

"Are you sure you know what you're doing?" Anouk asked Xavier as he descended deeper into the darkness of the tunnel with fifty pounds of explosives strapped to his back. She shined the red light from her flashlight after him, hoping to keep him from tripping or bumping into something. Anouk was pretty sure that a collision involving the explosives wouldn't end well for either of them.

"You know they asked me to do this for a reason," Xavier fired back at

her. He walked in front of her, glowing red like a devil in the beam of her infrared flashlight.

"Yeah," Anouk answered, "you and five other guys."

Xavier stopped walking and looked back at Anouk. "Just pay attention and make sure nobody sneaks up on us and shoots me, okay?" he said, motioning toward Anouk's hand that wasn't holding the flashlight, the one that was holding the gun.

"Don't worry about that," Anouk said. "You know they gave me this job for a reason, right?"

"I know," Xavier said, suddenly not joking. He remembered how excited he'd been to have Anouk assigned as his guide through the tunnels. She was the best they had. He'd heard stories about her before he'd ever met her. She had brought more people into the Underground than anyone else in France. Not only that, but she often pulled them out when their situations appeared the most dire. She was the one who knew about the lost tunnels. She had hidden people in them before. The list of people who owed Anouk their lives was long. Xavier hoped not to join that list, but he knew there were plenty of worse lists to be on. Xavier was no slouch either—not when it came to blowing shit up, and that's what they were there to do.

Six pairs of them were roaming the darkness of the tunnels. Each pair was assigned a different section, each section lying directly below one of the Intelligence Center's key support points. Xavier had been one of the people consulted when the tunnels were divided into sections for the plan. It wasn't possible to pick the exact spot where to place the bombs from the maps of the tunnels that they had, though. The maps were too old to be trusted. The team had to be inside the tunnels for that. So that's what they were doing. Setting the bombs and then getting the hell out of there before the whole thing blew up. Everything was strictly timed. They had two hours.

"Do you think what we're doing is a bit extreme?" Anouk asked Xavier as she closed the distance between the two of them so that she could talk to him quietly enough to avoid an echo.

"What do you mean?" Xavier asked, his face now shining in her light.

"I mean, we're taking out a whole city block in a historic district of Paris to try to end a War that most people don't even know exists."

Xavier shrugged. "Well, they'll know now, I suppose. Maybe it's long past the time when they should have known. It's too late for doubt now anyway. We all had our time for doubt and all it did was make us all look like fools."

At that moment, they heard a noise coming from behind them in the tunnels. In one quick motion, Anouk pushed Xavier into a dark corner, flicked off the flashlight, and aimed her gun at the noise. The red light was meant to help their eyes adjust to the darkness faster, but no eyes could adjust where they were, in the middle of the complete absence of light. Neither Anouk nor Xavier moved a muscle. They froze and waited for another sound. Then they heard something again, not far from them, down one of the tunnels. Xavier didn't dare make a sound, but he wanted to whisper to Anouk that they were losing time and that they probably didn't want to be in the tunnels when the others started detonating their explosives.

Anouk did what she could. She stepped away from Xavier so that if they saw her, they still wouldn't see him. She turned on her flashlight for a split second, then turned it off again. For that split second, the tunnel flared the eerie red color of the flashlight and the image of the tunnel during that tiny piece of a moment burned itself into Xavier's brain. The image was of an empty tunnel. Then the tunnel lit up again, still for only a fraction of a second, with Anouk farther away from Xavier now. Then there was blackness again. The noise grew louder. Then the light came a third time, beating back the darkness for a moment like a red flashbulb of a camera. Then a fourth time and a fifth, until it was like Xavier was watching Anouk in a flip-book coated in blood. The advantage that Anouk had created for herself over anyone that was following them was that only Anouk knew when she would turn the light on. But after the *seventh time, she stopped. Then she made her way back to Xavier in the darkness.*

"Only rats," Anouk whispered to Xavier when she got close to him.

"Are you sure?" Xavier asked.

"Now's not the time for doubt," Anouk said. Xavier began growing fond of Anouk's ability to throw a person's words back at him.

"Let's plant these bombs," Xavier said, "and bury this War forever."

So they made their way through the tunnels, feeling their way along the walls, using the light less frequently now even though they seemed to be being followed only by rodents. They turned the light on when Xavier thought he found a good place to plant a piece of the explosives. The trigger for each of the bombs was on a timer, all of them set to go off at exactly the same instant. They had talked about using a radio signal but worried that it wouldn't penetrate deep enough into the abandoned stone mines. So, with each planted bomb, their time to get out grew shorter, but they kept going, knowing that failure to topple the entire Intelligence Center would mean failure of the entire Uprising.

The tunnels were wet, cool, quiet, and dark. By the time Xavier had planted the last of his fifty pounds of explosive, he and Anouk had only fifteen minutes to find their way out of the catacombs. They'd come so far without the light, made so many turns based on feel and sound, that backtracking was difficult. Twice, it became evident to both of them that they had walked in a full circle, returning to where they'd started after wasting precious minutes. The red light was on now ceaselessly, the tunnels glowing like veins in a body. Lost, Xavier and Anouk tried not to panic as their chance of escape grew more and more remote.

They took one more turn, took one more chance moving down a tunnel that they only maybe recognized. Then, without speaking a word to each other, they started to run.

The bombs weren't perfectly coordinated. They were close but not exact. So Xavier and Anouk heard the echoes of the first bombs wailing their way through the tunnels before they saw the light and felt the walls around them shake. Whether it was because the timing of the bombs was close or because one explosion kept igniting the others, once the first bomb went off, the rest began to follow in a chain reaction. Even as they ran, Xavier listened to the sound of the explosions. Whether they were going to make it out of the tunnels or not, he wanted to know if it had worked. He wanted to know if the Intelligence Center was going to come crashing down like they planned. What he heard in between the sounds of the explosions was the creaking of stone sliding against stone and the cracking sound of crumbling rock. Those were the sounds that he wanted to hear. Those were the first sounds of the fall. Those were the sounds that meant that they'd done it.

Then the walls around them began to shake. Then the red light from Anouk's flashlight was eaten by the white light from nearby explosions. The destruction reached out toward Xavier and Anouk, but it didn't catch them yet, so they ran even faster.

Forty-five

Maria couldn't remember the last time she'd climbed into bed without locking all of her doors first. That night, she left the back door unlocked. She did everything else the same as she did on any other night. She got home from her work at the bar, not early but not late by bartending standards. She went into the kitchen, opened up a can of soup, and poured it into a pot on the stove. She turned the television on as she stirred her soup and then she sat down at the kitchen table and watched TV while she ate out of the pot. When she was done, she went up to her room and changed into a pair of dark gray sweatpants and a matching hooded sweatshirt. Then she went around the house, the same way she did every night, and checked every door and every window to make sure that they were all locked. Only this time, when she got to the back door, the one facing the woods, she only pretended to check. Instead, she flipped the lock so that the latch locking the door in place came free. Then she looked out the window into the dark woods, for only a second. She didn't see anything. She hoped that nobody had noticed.

When her routine was finished, Maria climbed the stairs leading to her bedroom, turning off the lights as she went. She got to her bedroom and pulled the covers off the bed. She consciously

did every single thing that she'd done unconsciously for years, trying to make sure that nothing about her awareness leaked into her movements. The last light that she turned off was her bedroom light. Then she climbed into bed.

Addy and Evan waited outside in the woods. They'd parked the car a few miles away as instructed and had made their way through the woods on foot. Addy was certain they hadn't been followed. She knew what it felt like to be followed. She knew what it took not to be followed. When they'd left the bar that afternoon, they had driven clear out of town. Evan drove north for over an hour while Addy studied the map, divining a way back that took them across back roads and over old bridges. The hour-and-a-half drive north took them three hours on the way back. The whole time, Addy watched the road behind them, waiting to see any evidence that someone was following them. No one was behind them. If anyone was going to get to them, it wouldn't be because someone was following them. It would be because someone was waiting for them.

Maria's lights were still on when Addy and Evan made it far enough through the woods to see Maria's house. They knew their instructions. *Wait until the lights are off.* So they hunkered down in the woods, making sure that they couldn't be seen. Then they waited. They were close enough that they could barely make out movement inside the house. They watched as, one by one, the lights in the house began to go out. First it was downstairs, one light after another going black. Then the single light upstairs went out and the entire house was dark. Even then, Addy and Evan didn't move. They waited, thinking that now that the lights were out, something would finally happen. Nothing did. Everything was quiet.

"Should we go?" Evan whispered over the pulsating rhythm of the forest around them.

"Not yet," Addy replied, remembering the look on Maria's face from earlier that day. "I think we should wait a little longer." She wanted to believe that there was more to Maria than rank paranoia. So they waited another thirty minutes. They still didn't see or hear anything suspicious.

"Let's go," Evan said after it was clear to him that nothing was being accomplished by their waiting.

"Okay," Addy conceded, growing worried now that maybe everything that had happened to Maria had broken her. The two of them got to their feet and walked toward Maria's house. They were still careful. They were still afraid. Maybe they weren't afraid of someone being out there anymore, but they were still afraid of Maria, of what she might think or what she might do. They moved in silence. The house in front of them was completely still. The woods nearly butted up against the back of the house. They saw the door—the one that Maria had promised them would be unlocked. It was all about trust now. They could see the door to the basement through the window of the back door. It hung open, only slightly.

"I'll go first," Evan told Addy. Then he stepped out of the cover of the forest and took the two steps toward the back door. It swung open, as promised, with only the slightest squeak. Evan stepped inside. Before going through the door to the basement, he looked back at Addy and waved her forward. When she started coming toward him, he slipped through the basement door and began to descend the dark steps.

The basement was even darker than the woods. It had no windows to draw in even a single sliver of moonlight. Only the open door at the top of the stairwell gave off any light, and that light got swallowed by the darkness after only a few feet from the top step. It was dark enough that when Evan made it to the bottom of the stairs he froze, unsure of what to do. Then Addy came through the door at the top of the steps and closed it behind her and the blackness was complete. Addy made her way down the stairs by holding on to the handrail. When she reached the bottom of the stairs, she felt Evan's hand reach out to her. She knew by touch that it was Evan's hand, but that gave her only the slightest bit of comfort.

"Evan?" Addy said out loud, wanting to be further comforted by the sound of his voice.

But another voice answered Addy before Evan could. "You're sure you weren't followed?" A woman's voice came from the darkness. It was only a few feet from them.

"Yes," Addy answered, "we're sure." Addy heard a clicking sound and then a light flared on.

It took a few minutes for Addy's and Evan's eyes to adjust to the light. They'd been in the darkness for that long. When they could finally see, they saw Maria sitting alone at a plain wooden table, a bare lightbulb hanging above her head.

The light in the room was now stark, bright and clear. Evan got a good look at Maria for the first time. To him, the resemblance was undeniable. "You're Christopher's mother," he half mumbled through the shock of seeing so much of his best friend in this middle-aged woman in front of him.

Maria looked Evan up and down. He was no more than a boy. "Let's assume that's true," Maria said, not giving anything away. "What's it to the two of you?"

"Reggie sent us here to get you," Addy repeated the words that she had said to Maria that afternoon. Maria shot Addy a look in response, a look that could have turned water to poison. Addy didn't know what the look meant, but it froze her throat. She began trying to think of what else she could say.

Before Addy could think of anything, Evan spoke. "He's my best friend," Evan told Maria. "He's been my best friend since we were little kids. I see him in you." Evan paused, trying to compose himself. "I just want him to be safe," he finished.

Maria stared at Evan, but not with the same icy stare that she'd given Addy. Maria's look for Evan was deeper and gentler. "How long have you known my son?" she asked Evan, vulnerability slipping into her voice for the first time.

Evan shrugged. "As long as I can remember."

"What's he like?" Maria asked. Even if Addy couldn't have understood the words that Maria spoke, Maria's tone alone would have made her want to cry.

Evan didn't know what to say. Christopher was the most complicated person that Evan had ever met. He didn't think that they had time for him to give Maria the answer that Christopher deserved. He settled on a single word to describe Christopher. He muttered, "Different" barely above his breath. Maria didn't say anything in response. She simply kept on staring at Evan. "Different than everybody else," Evan clarified under the weight of Maria's stare.

Maria seemed to accept this. "Is he happy?" she asked Evan.

Evan thought hard before answering Maria's question this time. He tried to think of a way to qualify or soften his answer. The similarities between them made Evan feel almost as protective of Maria as he felt of Christopher. He couldn't lie to her either, though. "No," Evan answered. "I wouldn't call him happy."

Maria's eyes began to shine in the light. "And you—" Maria turned back toward the fiery redhead. She could see that the color was fake and remembered a time when she had disguised herself too. "How do you know my son?"

Addy felt her throat constrict again, but she fought it. "I tried to help him run away from the War after *they* found him," she said, "but running didn't work."

Maria stood up now. She began to pace, still keeping the table between her and Evan and Addy. "When did they find him?" she asked the two of them.

"They went after him the day he turned eighteen," Addy told Maria.

"But he felt them following him long before that, for as long as I can remember," Evan finished on Addy's behalf.

Maria paced faster now. Evan almost thought that she was going to break into a run. "All of this for nothing," Maria whispered to herself. Then she stopped pacing and looked at them again. "Where is he now?" she asked. "Where is my son now?"

"He's with Reggie," Addy answered. "That's why Reggie sent us to get you."

"With Reggie?" Maria repeated, as if she didn't believe it. "What is he doing with Reggie?"

"They're going to start an uprising," Addy said. "They're trying to end the War."

With that, Maria fell back into her chair. Her eyes transformed from merely shining to becoming the source of matching rivers of tears. She looked like all the strength had been sucked out of her. "Where are you supposed to take me?" she asked.

"Back to New York," Addy told her. "Will you come with us?"

"I want to," Maria said. "You have no idea how badly I want to. But I can't."

"Why not?" Evan asked. He wanted to do this for Christopher. "You have to do this. Christopher needs you."

Evan could see that the words stung Maria, maybe even more than he wanted them to, but they definitely hit their mark. "I can't because I'm being watched," Maria told them. "I've been being watched almost every day since I was let out of jail five years ago. They started following me the day I left prison. That's why I never went back to get Christopher. I thought that they were watching, hoping that they could use me to find him, that I would lead them to him." Maria shook her head. "But you're telling me that they knew where he was the whole time?" Evan nodded. "So why were they following me?"

It was a rhetorical question, but Addy chose to answer it anyway. "Because they were afraid of you," Addy said. "They were afraid of what you could teach him." The silence after Addy spoke went on for several minutes, until Addy finally broke it. "You can still teach him, you know?"

Maria shook her head. "They'll follow me. I would lead them right to him. It's true now, even if it wasn't before. The day that Christopher turned eighteen, I didn't see anyone following me, but they were back again the very next day."

"We can take care of them," Evan promised out of the blue. "We can take care of them, and Addy can make sure that no one else follows us."

"Can you do that?" Maria asked Addy.

Addy nodded. "I can."

"How do you know?" Maria asked.

"Because Reggie taught me how to run, and he learned from the best."

"So where are these people that are following you now?" Evan asked, eager to move forward and see his friend again.

"Right now," Maria answered him, "they're outside, watching the house."

Forty-six

Reggie and Christopher were on a flight from Kuala Lumpur to Istanbul. After what had happened to Jin, they didn't want to risk flying through the Singapore airport again. Instead, they took a boat from Indonesia into Malaysia. Then they caught a ride for the three-and-a-half-hour drive from the coast to Kuala Lumpur. The man who drove them had already heard about what had happened in Indonesia. He'd already heard that the heads of the Underground had decided to follow Christopher. He was excited. This was what he'd been waiting for his whole life, he said. Christopher felt like warning the man about what happened to people who got too excited about working with him. But then Christopher reminded himself that the excitement was important. The plan needed it.

They made it to the airport and into the air without any problems. Once they were in the air, Christopher tried to sleep. Reggie was still trying to figure out how Christopher had pulled it off, how he'd gotten them to believe in him. *One down, two to go*, he thought to himself. *Then the hard part*. "Why are you staring at me again, Reggie?" Christopher asked, looking at Reggie through half-closed eyes.

"Can I ask you a question?"

"Sure," Christopher answered, "if you promise to stop staring at me and let me get some sleep."

"How come you never ask questions about the War?"

"Like what?"

"Like what it's all about or how it started."

Christopher didn't move. He didn't even open his eyes. "Why should I care? What does any of that have to do with me?"

"Don't you want to know why they killed your father and took you away from your mother?"

Christopher shook his head. "No matter what anybody tells me, I'll never believe that whatever this War's about or how it got started has anything to do with my mother or my father or me. I don't see how it has anything to do with you either, Reggie. It's not like you had a say in any of it. I don't see why anybody cares. I'm worried about how we're going to end the War, not about how the goddamn thing started. Why do you care?"

"I never thought I had the option not to," Reggie said.

"Well, I do," Christopher said. "Now can I get some sleep?"

Forty-seven

"We didn't see anybody outside," Addy told Maria.

"That doesn't mean they're not out there," Maria answered quickly.

"How do you know?" Evan asked.

"Because they're always out there," Maria told him. "I killed the first two. I didn't think I had a choice. I thought that it was the only way that I'd get away, but they just kept coming. I moved to Kansas after I got out of prison—literally the middle of nowhere. I thought I could get my act together there and then go find Christopher. I wasn't going to tell him who I was. I only wanted to see him. Then they showed up and started following me everywhere."

"So you killed them?" Evan asked.

"It was easier than I remembered," Maria answered. "I thought it was the only way that I could see Christopher. It only took two days for the second unit to show up. I didn't fight them this time. They never approached me. They're just always there." Maria looked over at Addy. "Have you ever been to Kansas?"

"No," Addy said, trying to determine if she believed that people were really out there or that Maria was crazy.

"It's a godforsaken place. The strangest part is how flat it is, how you can stand there and look out at the horizon and see forever. Then there's the wind. Without anything to stop it, the wind blows across the plains, gaining speed and power like a freight train. When it hits you, it's like someone is trying to push you over."

"That's how you get tornadoes, right?" Evan said, pulling out the only thing he knew about Kansas.

"That's the thing, Evan." Maria spoke to him in the motherly tone she'd been practicing in front of mirror after mirror for over a decade. "As long as you can feel the wind, you don't need to be afraid of the tornado. It's when the wind stops that you need to be afraid."

"Okay," Addy chimed in. "Assuming there are people outside, what do you suggest we do?"

"The only way to get away is to get rid of them before they know something is up, before they have time to call for backup," Maria answered.

"What do you mean, 'Get rid of them'?" Evan asked.

Maria shot a glance at Addy and then looked back at Evan. "In the world we live in, getting rid of someone only means one thing. You weren't born part of the War, were you?"

Evan shook his head. "No. I'm just trying to help Christopher."

"I wasn't born into the War either," Maria said. "Eventually that doesn't matter anymore."

"Couldn't we do something else with them? Do we have to kill them?" Evan asked.

"What else can we do?" Addy replied.

"I don't know. Convert them. Maybe they hate the War as much as you guys do. Maybe they'll want to join the Uprising." Even Evan didn't have faith in his idea.

"If that's true, they could have left the War by now. Others did. Eventually it has to be too late," Addy said in a rush, as if trying to bury the idea as quickly as possible.

"We can't take that chance," Maria said to Evan, somewhat more sympathetically. "So are you guys in?"

Evan and Addy shot glances at each other. Neither of them had any trouble reading the other's thoughts. "Yes," Addy confirmed for Maria, "we are. What's the plan?"

"They switch shifts now. Ever since Christopher's birthday, they've been splitting the day into two shifts. Two of them are on every shift. There's two tonight. There will be two tomorrow. I imagine they're getting a little complacent. I mean they've been following me for five years and it's been well over four years since anything's happened. If they didn't see you come inside, you should stay inside. Leaving tonight is an unnecessary risk. You guys can stay down here. I'll sneak back upstairs. In the morning I'll act like everything is normal. I have tomorrow off and I'm overdue for a trip to Quebec City to pick up some mail. They'll follow me when I leave. They don't worry about me not seeing them. Sometimes I think they want me to see them, just to scare me. Do you guys have a phone?"

"I do," Addy responded.

"I'll send you a message when it's safe to leave. I won't go straight to Quebec City. I'll go out for breakfast first. I'll eat slow. I'll make them wait. That will give you guys a chance to get a head start. About halfway between here and Quebec City there's a little gas station. I know the guy who works there. He works alone. He sells soda and candy out of his store. I'll go inside to get a soda and he'll come with me so that I can pay him. I want one of you to be in the store waiting for us. Whoever it is will force him into the bathroom, trap him in there, and act like you're kidnapping me. That way, when this story gets out, both sides of the War will think the other side finally lost its patience and got me."

"What about the two people following you?" Addy asked.

Maria looked down at the floor, shadows covering her face.

"I've stopped at this gas station before. They know it too. They'll pull up right behind me. I told you before, sometimes I think they want me to know that they're following me. Whoever isn't inside the store . . . It has to be quick. They can't know what hit them. We can't give them any chance to call for help." It was clear to Evan and Addy that this wasn't the first time that this plan had jumped into Maria's head.

Addy and Evan slept on the floor of the basement in the dark, their fingers intertwined.

Maria woke up the next morning and kept up her act that everything was normal even though it'd been nearly twenty years since anything was normal. She woke up, got out of bed, brushed her teeth, showered, and got dressed. She tried not to think about how whatever clothes she picked might be the clothes she would be wearing when she saw her son for the first time in more than seventeen years. She tried not to do anything too quickly. She struggled not to do anything too slowly. She tried not to think about the two kids asleep in her basement. She tried to forget that Evan had told her that Christopher wasn't happy. All Maria wanted, all she wanted in the world, was for Christopher to be happy. Nothing else.

Maria walked out of the house, consciously thinking about every step that she took. She got in her car, started the engine, and drove. Less than a minute later, a car pulled out from the side of the road. It had been parked in a spot that was almost impossible to see. It turned in the direction Maria had driven and followed her.

Addy had set her phone to vibrate. She and Evan were both awake when they heard it buzz on the floor between them. Addy picked up the phone and looked at the message. It read, "it's safe.

go now." Addy didn't know that Maria had typed it while lying in bed last night, readying it so that all she had to do was hit Send when the time was right.

"Let's go," Addy said to Evan. They didn't waste any time. They climbed out of the basement. They left Maria's house through the back door. They followed the path through the woods that they'd walked the night before. They got to their car and climbed in. Maria had given them directions to the gas station the night before. They knew where they had to go. They barely spoke. The road they took twisted back and forth, hugging the St. Lawrence River. On the other side of the road were trees, old gnarled trees sprouting young, vibrant green leaves.

As promised, Maria ate slowly. She sat alone at the restaurant. She ordered pancakes with real maple syrup. It was one of the few joys she allowed herself. The men shadowing her didn't come inside while she ate. Sometimes they did, but not that day. Instead, they waited outside in their car for her to leave. Maria was eager to get going, but she knew that she had to give Evan and Addy enough time. She knew that they wouldn't be able to find the gas station as easily as she could. The waiting gave Maria time for things that she didn't want, like thinking. So she concentrated on the sound her silverware made as it scraped against her plate and tried not to think about Reggie and the promises Reggie had made to her that he broke. She tried not to think about Christopher or Michael or Joseph. She tried not to think about a seventeen-year-old, curly-haired girl named Maria and all her hopes and dreams. She tried not to think of how lost the last seventeen years seemed. She tried really hard.

When nothing was left on her plate but crumbs and drops of unused syrup, Maria asked for the check. She paid, leaving the type of tip that someone leaves at a place when they're never coming back. Then she walked out to the parking lot. She could see the men sitting in their car waiting for her. They'd parked across the street. She tried to avoid making eye contact with them—just like on every other day. She'd spent four years trying to pretend, to herself at least, that she didn't know that they were always watching her. She got back into her car, pulled back onto the road and headed south, her shadow following behind her.

Addy and Evan had no trouble finding the gas station. It was a single-pump job off to the side of the road. It looked more like a 1950s movie set than a real place. Behind the pump was the small store where the proprietor sold soda and candy. Next to that was a two-car garage with various tools hung along the walls. All the metal was slightly rusted. Even though they saw it immediately, Evan and Addy drove past it. They kept going for another mile before pulling off to the side of the road.

"You go inside," Addy said to Evan once the car was stopped. It was the first thing either of them had said to each other since they left Maria's house. "I'll stay outside."

Evan knew what that meant. They both knew what that meant. Addy would be the killer. "Okay," Evan said, relieved that all he had to do was threaten and lock up an innocent man.

"How are you going to get inside the store?" Addy asked Evan.

Evan knew that it was merely a test. Addy wanted to make sure Evan had thought about it. "I'll wait in the garage," he told her. "When the old man goes out to help Maria pump her gas, I'll slip inside."

"That should work," Addy said.

"What are you going to do?" Evan asked Addy. He wasn't testing her.

"It doesn't really matter," Addy answered him, "as long as I do it quickly. Pop the trunk."

Evan leaned forward and pulled the lever that automatically opened the trunk. He and Addy both got out of the car. Addy reached into the trunk and pulled out the shotgun that she and Evan had taken from the convenience store in Louisiana. Evan reached into the trunk and grabbed one of the handguns that Sam and George had given them before they left Florida. "You good?" Addy asked Evan.

Evan looked at the gun in his hand and how his hand held it. "I've never been worse," he said to Addy and smiled. "But I'll be okay."

"Let's go," Addy said. "We don't want to fuck this up by standing around for too long talking."

They walked the mile back to the gas station together, ready to hide in the woods if any other cars drove by. They didn't split up until they were only a few hundred feet from it. At that point, Evan made his way toward the garage while Addy kept walking past the gas station.

Maria never sped. She never had any reason to rush anywhere. She didn't speed that day either, trying her best to conform everything she did to the way the woman she had been yesterday morning would have done it. She wanted to stomp on the gas pedal because she no longer was the woman that she had been yesterday morning. Maria didn't see Addy or Evan when she pulled up to the gas station. She could feel them, though. They were there.

Maria pulled up to the single gas pump and got out of her car. The gray-haired, round gas station owner hustled out from behind the counter in the store when he saw Maria so that he could offer to pump her gas for her. Normally, Maria would have already started filling up her car by the time he reached her. This time she waited, giving the old man a job to do while Evan slipped into the store from the garage where he'd been hiding. Maria only caught a glimpse of Evan. She didn't see Addy at all. Addy was too good for that.

Once Maria was sure that Evan was in place, she told the old man that she wanted a soda. "Of course," he said and led her back toward the store. Two minutes after Maria had pulled into the gas station, her shadow's car pulled up right behind hers.

The old man didn't notice Evan hiding in plain sight in the corner. He spoke French to Maria, so Evan didn't know what he was saying to her. His voice was full of excitement, though. Evan figured it was either because female customers were infrequent or because he had a thing for Maria. Evan held his gun down near his waist and readied himself. He wanted this to go smoothly. He didn't want to have to pull the trigger. He had already internalized the *us* and *them* distinction between people in the War and the innocents.

"Coke," Maria said to the man in response to the question he had asked her. The old man then turned toward the standing refrigerator full of bottled sodas. He started to reach out to open the refrigerator door. Then he stopped. He froze completely. He finally saw Evan standing in the corner, holding a gun.

For a moment, Evan worried about the potential language barrier. For a moment, he worried that the man wouldn't understand what Evan was saying to him. Then Evan remembered the gun. The gun needed no translation.

"Get into the bathroom!" Evan shouted, lifting the gun and pointing it at the man's chest. The man's eyes were full of fear. Evan was beginning to get used to people being afraid of him, but this was different. This time the fear wasn't based on a news report with Evan's picture on it. It wasn't based on an artificial label calling Evan a monster. This time, the old man's fear was justified. The old man glanced at Maria. "Get into the bathroom!" Evan shouted again, and this time he motioned toward the bathroom with the hand holding the gun. The old man didn't move. He glanced at Maria again. For a second, Evan worried that the old man was going to try to be a hero. What would Evan do then?

The old man took a small step toward Maria, putting his body between Maria and Evan. He was scared but brave. Evan saw this and it made him want to have to shoot the old man even less. *"Allez!"* Maria begged the man, faking fear so authentically that even Evan believed it. Or maybe she was afraid. Maybe she was afraid she was going to get the old man killed. *"Je vais être bien."* The old man looked at Maria with warm, sad eyes when she said those words, and it was clear that he wasn't going to let Evan have Maria without a fight. Then they heard the first shotgun blast and that changed everything.

The men following Maria didn't get out of their car after pulling up to the gas station. Addy saw them. They were exactly like Maria described them. They were real. Addy guessed that they had filled their car with gas before their shift even began so it wasn't necessary now. They simply pulled up about ten feet behind Maria's car and waited. Addy wondered what it would have been like to live like that for so many years: to live knowing that people were right behind you all the time, following you, without knowing what they might do at any moment. She wondered this, and then she stepped out of the woods holding the shotgun up near her shoulder.

They never saw Addy. That's how it was supposed to be. They never knew that it was a young fire-haired woman who ended them. They heard the glass shatter and then felt the burn as the shotgun blast and broken glass entered the backs of their heads. Addy stood behind the car and fired once, aiming the shot at the man in the passenger seat. She assumed that he would have quicker access to a phone to call for help, so she wanted to take care of him first. After the first shot, she pumped the shotgun, aimed it at the back of the driver's head, and shot again.

Evan, Maria, and the old man heard four shotgun blasts in all—all within about ten seconds. They didn't see Addy take two shots through the back window of the men's car and then quickly run to the passenger-side door, open it, and take two more shots at the men inside the car at point-blank range to make sure they were dead. Evan, Maria, and the old man merely heard the shots. They didn't see anything. The shots were loud and they were scary and they did the job on the old man that Evan couldn't do alone. The old man heard the shotgun blasts, took one more sad look at Maria as if to apologize, and then, without any more prodding from Evan, walked into the bathroom.

Evan didn't waste any time. He gave a quick sigh of relief and then slammed the bathroom door behind the old man. Then he took the desk that the old man used as a check-out counter and pushed it in front of the bathroom door. It wouldn't keep the old man in there forever, but it would keep him in there long enough. The plan was to call 911 as they drove away and report hearing gunshots and seeing a woman dragged into a car whose description didn't match the description of the car they were driving.

Inside the bathroom, the old man sat down on the toilet without lifting the lid. His shoulders slumped and he stared down at his shaking hands in the dark. He could have turned on the light, but he didn't bother to. He didn't want to see any better than he already could. He didn't want to be able to see himself in the mirror. He wouldn't even try to push the door open. He did nothing but sit there in the darkness until the authorities came and let him out.

Almost as soon as Evan had pushed the desk in front of the bathroom door, Addy opened the door to the store. She was still holding the shotgun and Evan could see a tiny bit of blood splattered on her shirt. "Come on! Let's go!" she whispered excitedly to Evan and Maria. The three of them left together. Maria and Evan saw the wreckage of the men's car as they ran past it, the back window shattered and the passenger-side door still hanging open.

They saw the two bodies lying slumped in the front seat. They kept running, Maria trying her best not to let the images stir buried memories in her mind. All that was left was for them to run to Addy and Evan's car. They made their way up the road. No cars drove by them. They got to Addy and Evan's car without incident.

Once they were inside the car and back on the road, Maria dialed 911 on her phone. She told the dispatcher exactly what they'd rehearsed: They were driving down the road and heard gunshots. Then they saw a woman being dragged into a gray, four-door sedan, which took off driving north. Once Maria had given the operator all the details, she hung up and threw her phone out the window.

Then they drove—south, with no one following them. Maria looked out the back window at the empty road behind them and took a deep breath, one that she hadn't felt like she'd been able to take in years. She was going to see her son, wherever he was.

Forty-eight

Whereas Asia felt to Christopher like another planet, Istanbul felt like a whole other universe. He felt like he'd stepped onto the set of a science fiction movie about faraway galaxies. It was mostly the smell, he thought—that lush, spicy odor that permeated every corner of the city—but it was also the call to prayer. Christopher jumped the first time he heard it echoing out over the loudspeakers posted everywhere around the city. He thought it was some sort of emergency warning system that he couldn't understand. The sound was so foreign. Christopher had never heard anything like it before in his life. Reggie laughed at Christopher when he saw the fear in Christopher's face. "You'll get used to it," Reggie said. "It happens five times a day."

The two of them stepped out on the balcony of the hotel where they were staying. From there, Christopher could see the spot where the Sea of Marmara, the Golden Horn, and the Bosporus all came together. Huge shipping boats were floating in the Sea of Marmara and, as Christopher watched one of them, he saw a dolphin leap out of the water next to it. He let his eyes drift toward the city and the giant pillared mosques that dotted it. The city was shining with colors from the flowers and the buildings and the cars.

"Let's get something to eat before our first meeting," Reggie said to Christopher, looking at his watch. "We're supposed to meet Umut in two hours." Unlike in Asia, Reggie and Christopher knew who they were going to meet here. They knew when and they knew where. They had gained credibility. People were beginning to believe that the Uprising could be real.

"Okay," Christopher said. "I'm starving."

They ate in a rooftop restaurant high above the city. It was only late afternoon, but the restaurant was already bustling. The servers carried around giant metal trays full of meats and other food, and Reggie and Christopher ordered by pointing to what they wanted. They ate lamb and fish and stuffed peppers. Everything tasted like they were living in a dream. Everything smelled like a dream. Everything sounded like a dream too—the language the people spoke so quickly to each other, the call to prayer echoing out over the city again in the afternoon. "How come they don't all go to pray when they hear the call to prayer?" Christopher asked Reggie.

"A lot do," Reggie answered. From their vantage point high above the city, Christopher could see men shuffling in and out of the mosques.

"But not all of them," Christopher said for confirmation.

Reggie shook his head. "It's not that kind of city," he told Christopher. "There are the believers and there are plenty of non-believers."

Christopher and Reggie met Umut later that evening in Umut's apartment which was deep in the heart of the city, miles from the tourist attractions—the Blue Mosque, the Hagia Sophia, the Top-kapi Palace—surrounding Christopher and Reggie's hotel. They traveled unchaperoned this time, hailing a cab at random, thinking that this was the safest way to go. Reggie passed the cabbie his cell phone so that Umut could give the cabbie directions in Turkish. Then they left, driving up a steep hill and into the mass of endless civilization that is Istanbul. "They say that there's over twenty million people in this city," Reggie told Christopher after he caught Christopher staring out the window with his mouth wide open. The buildings grew shorter as they went farther from the central city until they passed what appeared to be shantytowns with makeshift houses layered one on top of the other. "If you cross the river, you go from Europe to Asia, but you're still in Istanbul," Reggie told Christopher. Christopher kept staring out the window as they drove and Reggie kept staring at the cabdriver. Eventually the cabbie pulled up in front of a small, unassuming apartment building.

Umut was waiting outside when they got there. He was an average-sized man with dark hair and bushy eyebrows. He was dressed like an American, in slacks and a button-down shirt. He shook Reggie's hand as Reggie stepped out of the cab. Umut paid the cabdriver. Then he turned to Christopher. Christopher feared that Umut was going to bow to him, but Umut didn't bow. He simply reached out his hand for Christopher to shake and Christopher shook it. "I'm glad you made it," Umut said in nearly perfect English. "Come inside. I have tea."

The three of them went into the apartment. It was sparsely decorated. A small table sat on a beautiful rug in the middle of the main room. The rug seemed to change color as you walked around it. Umut led Christopher and Reggie in and asked them to sit down. Then he set a glass of hot tea before each of them.

"I heard the Far East was quite an adventure," Umut said to Reggie with a half smile.

"The adventure is what convinced them to join us," Reggie confided to Umut. "It gave the kid here a way to prove his mettle." Reggie motioned toward Christopher. "They wouldn't have agreed to the plan if it weren't for that."

Umut stared at Christopher. "I guess only prophets can tell the difference between good and bad fortune before all the cards are laid on the table."

"I'm not a prophet," Christopher said, remembering what Jung-Su had said to him before Christopher had ordered that he be killed.

"Thank Allah for that," Umut said with a loud belly laugh. Then he stood up and slapped Christopher on the back, making Christopher choke on his tea. Once Umut laughed, Reggie laughed with him. Christopher merely coughed, trying to clear his throat.

"What are we up against here?" Reggie asked Umut.

"History," Umut answered.

"What does that mean?" Christopher asked, having recovered.

"We go in front of a tribunal tomorrow to argue our case," Umut said.

"Who is *we*?" Christopher asked.

"The three of us," Umut told him. "I'm already in. It's the others we need to convince."

"How hard are they going to be to convince?" Reggie asked.

"What I've heard is that after what happened in Asia, they have faith in Christopher's ability but they're unsure of whether or not they believe in the plan."

"What is my ability?" Christopher asked Umut, still trying to figure it out for himself.

"Depends who you ask," Umut told Christopher. "And that's an ability all by itself. Just don't show them any leaks and they'll believe that the dam will hold."

"But they don't believe the plan will work?" Reggie asked.

Umut shook his head. "They're not even worried about what happens if the plan doesn't work. They're past that. They're worried about what happens if it does work."

After three hours of preparation, Umut sent Reggie and Christopher on their way into the night. They were supposed to meet again the next day near the Süleymaniye Mosque, by the university, where the three of them would talk one last time before going before the tribunal in the afternoon.

Christopher didn't ask Reggie what would happen if they couldn't convince the tribunal to join them. He knew the stakes. With a plan like this, every stone is a cornerstone. They took a cab back to their hotel. Christopher thought that the city was even more beautiful at night. He couldn't get over the sight of the mosques lit up like giant moons that had landed on Earth. They went into their hotel and took the elevator up to their floor. Reggie checked the room before he let Christopher go inside. It wasn't late, but Reggie suggested that they get some sleep. They'd talked enough for one night. Christopher agreed even though he wasn't ready to sleep. Instead, he waited for Reggie to fall asleep. Then he got out of bed and snuck out into the city because, sometimes, that's what a teenage boy needs to do.

When Christopher stepped outside the door, he realized that it was the first time he'd been alone since he met Max, the morning after his eighteenth birthday. The city was quieter this late at night, but no less alive. Christopher walked quickly away from his hotel past streets lined with youth hostels and cheap restaurants buzzing with young travelers. He didn't know where he was going and didn't care. He wanted to be alone and to walk and to forget. He didn't even know what he wanted to forget. Everything, he supposed. For a few minutes he wanted to forget everything.

Even though it was nearing the middle of the night, the city wasn't dark. Christopher doubted that the city, or at least this part of it, ever went dark. He walked past more tourists. He walked past an outdoor restaurant where Whirling Dervishes were dancing inside for the customers. The men in long white skirts and tall hats danced to strange-sounding music, spinning in circles and letting the white cloth from their skirts balloon around them. Christopher thought about how dark it would be at home at this hour. He remembered the nights in Maine. He remembered chasing fireflies like they were tiny, flying stars and catching them in his hands. Sometimes the fireflies were the brightest thing in the night. He remembered competing with Evan to see who could catch more. It was the one thing that Evan could regularly beat him at.

There were no fireflies in Istanbul. They would have gotten lost in all the light anyway. The light seemed to come from everywhere. Lights were draped in trees. Buildings with restaurants and bars on their roofs shined light down onto the streets. But mostly the light came from the giant mosques. All of that light didn't mean that there wasn't any darkness. It was merely confined to the corners and the shadows. The corners and shadows were even darker because of the light. Christopher ignored the darkness, at least for now, and kept on walking. He wasn't ready to see what was inside the darkness, even if it was following him.

Christopher walked down two more streets, turning randomly, reveling in the moments of freedom. *What if I keep going?* he thought to himself as he stared down the empty street in front of him. *If there really are twenty million people in this city, what if I keep walking? Would they be able to find me? Would it even matter?* For a few moments, it all seemed possible. It all seemed very real. Christopher was going to walk away and disappear. If he had only looked forward, he might have done it. If he had only kept his eyes in the light, he might have left everything—but he couldn't not look into the darkness. So before he walked away forever, Christopher looked into the shadows behind him. The shadows were dark, but they weren't empty.

Everything that Christopher had been trying to forget came back to him in a flash. He remembered every skill he had ever taught himself. He remembered every lesson he had ever taken. He remembered why he'd learned all of that in the first place. They were always watching him. Christopher began walking faster, trying to pretend he hadn't noticed the man in the shadows, but the man followed him. The man in the shadows wasn't tall, but he was broad, with dark skin, dark hair, and dark eyes. Christopher turned a corner, looking back only then to try and get a better look at the man following him. The man was young, but he looked young only in age, not experience. Christopher thought back to the men in the woods and Maine and wondered if the man following him was armed. Christopher tried to look at the man's hands, but they were still shrouded in darkness. After turning the corner, Christopher sped up even more.

Christopher cursed himself as he opened up his stride to a near jog. He thought that maybe he could turn another corner before the man saw where he'd gone. How could he have been so stupid? He wondered if Reggie was still asleep, if he was still lying in bed oblivious to how quickly Christopher had ruined everything. Hadn't there been other sounds? Hadn't the city only moments ago been full of music and noise? Now, the only sounds that Christopher could hear were the sounds of his own feet on the cobblestones, followed beat for beat by the sounds of footsteps of the man chasing him. There were other sounds, Christopher knew. He simply couldn't hear them anymore.

It was a race to the corners now. The two men were racing to see who could turn the next corner first. If Christopher won, he might be able to lose the man chasing him. If the man won, the chase would continue. The streets seemed darker to Christopher now too. All of the sound and light faded away and now everything was merely footsteps chasing footsteps down dark and shadowy streets in this strange city. The man won race after race, turning the corners more quickly than Christopher and closing the gap between them. Christopher couldn't lose him down an alley now. Christopher thought that maybe he would be safe if he ran toward the street with the hostels or the Whirling Dervishes or the giant mosques, but no turn seemed to lead him there.

Christopher looked back again and saw both of the man's hands. The man had a short, thick knife sticking out of one of his fists. It lit up in the shadows like a source of light. Christopher was breathing heavily now. He wasn't tired. His body was taking in extra oxygen, preparing for a fight. Suddenly Christopher was in the woods in Maine, on his eighteenth birthday, running, and he knew what he had to do. He had to stop. He had to fight. But first he had to hide and wait for the man to come to him.

Christopher turned down another dark and empty street. He knew it would be the last turn before the man was upon him. The only light that he could see was a sliver of the top of the Blue Mosque over a high rock wall lining one side of the street. Across from the wall were a series of shuttered and locked buildings. Christopher had to disappear into that emptiness.

The man with the knife turned the corner. He brandished his weapon, holding it high so that it would be seen and so that he could strike quickly. The man with the knife knew these streets. He knew them better than the person he was chasing and he knew that he knew them better. He didn't have to worry about witnesses here, not if he was fast enough. So he turned the corner and lifted his knife, expecting to be on his victim in a flash. He gritted his teeth in anticipation. But the street that he turned down was empty. The man knew that this street had only one outlet, so he sped up, not wanting his prey to get away from him.

Christopher listened to the footsteps and waited. He needed to time this right or all was lost. When the man with the knife was only a few feet from him, Christopher jumped. He had climbed halfway up the rock wall, as high as he could go without falling.

He was barely noticeable in the shadows before he jumped. When he jumped, he came out of the darkness like the devil himself.

Christopher landed on top of the man with the knife. He led with his elbows, jamming his left elbow into the crook of the man's neck. He felt the flesh give way and heard the man grunt in pain before he fell to the ground. The man still had the knife in his hand as he lay on the cobblestones, but Christopher took care of that quickly too. He stomped on the man's hand, breaking at least one finger and probably more. The knife came loose and Christopher picked it up. Christopher was surprised at how easy this all was. He'd thought that he was supposed to be fighting against professionals. Max had told him not to expect them to underestimate him ever again.

Christopher held the knife in one hand and reached down and grabbed the man by the scruff of his neck with the other. He lifted the man to his feet and pushed him against the rock wall. He held the knife against the man's neck. The man began to cry, quickly and without hesitation. First came the tears and then the smell. Christopher looked down and saw that the man had pissed himself.

"Tell me what you know," Christopher ordered the man as he touched the man's skin with the knife blade. Something wasn't right.

"I know nothing," the man whimpered in broken English in between fearful sobs. "Please don't hurt me."

"If you don't know anything, why were you chasing me?" Christopher pressed the knife farther into the man's skin. He could see the skin on the man's neck compress under the blade of the knife, but it didn't break. Not yet.

"I don't know anything," the man repeated, and Christopher saw confusion in the man's eyes. "I'm sorry."

"WHY WERE YOU CHASING ME?" Christopher yelled at

the whimpering man now. He seemed so much smaller than he had before.

"Money," the man said. "I want your money. You are American, no? I'm sorry. I'm sorry."

"You're a thief," Christopher said with disdain, spitting the words out of his mouth. "That's it? You came after me because I'm white, not because you know who I am?"

"I know nothing," the man pleaded for the third time.

Christopher stepped away from the man. The man immediately hunched down on the ground into a protective ball of piss and tears. "How can I be sure?" Christopher asked himself out loud. He touched the blade of the knife with his thumb. It was sharp. "Guess my name," Christopher ordered the ball of a man in front of him.

"I don't know!" the man cried.

"Guess," Christopher said, aiming the knife at the man again.

The man looked at Christopher and then he looked up at the sky. "George," the man guessed, and it wasn't a bluff. The man was clearly unsure if it was better to guess wrong or right.

"Fuck," Christopher muttered to himself. This man was no one. He was nothing. He was meaningless, to Christopher anyway. Christopher wasn't home in Maine. He was a world away from home. He was as far away as anyone could possibly ever get. He threw the knife back on the ground near the whimpering man. "Don't follow me," he ordered the man and began to walk away, backward at first, watching the man. The man made no attempt to even get up, let alone follow him. Then Christopher turned around and moved more quickly. It took a few blocks for him to get his bearings again. He used the river and the Blue Mosque as visual guideposts. Once Christopher knew where he was, he didn't waste any more time. He headed straight back to the hotel. This time he kept his head down and tried to walk in the shadows as much as possible.

Reggie was awake when Christopher got home. "Where have you been?" he demanded, sounding more like a father than a friend.

"I wanted to go for a walk to think," Christopher answered.

"How did that go?"

"Fine," Christopher replied.

"I'd prefer it if you didn't do it again," Reggie said, trying to find the right balance of respect and authority with his words.

"Don't worry," Christopher promised him. "I got it out of my system. I'm not going for another walk alone until this War is over."

"Good," Reggie said. He didn't ask for any more details. "I know that I'm putting too much on you, that you're too young for this," he said, as if apologizing.

"The world doesn't wait for you to be ready," Christopher replied. Then he turned the lights off and climbed back into his bed.

Forty-nine

Jared walked down the halls of his New York office building carrying a folder full of papers that he needed to get approved. *Action Items*, they were called, but Jared thought nothing could be less worthy of the moniker. Jared wore the clothes that he always wore to the office—khaki pants, dark brown shoes, and a dark blue shirt with a white collar. He used to wear a suit, but by now, at forty-four years old, he'd given up on the idea that that might help him get anywhere. Now, when he went downstairs into Grand Central Station or walked up Park Avenue for lunch, no one could differentiate him from any of the other human worker bees trudging in and out of offices. Even Jared's hair, which had turned gray years ago, was beginning to thin out in the back, and his once startling physique now sagged around the middle. He still believed that his mind was as sharp as it had ever been, though. The problem was that nobody seemed to notice or care.

The man with one of the corner offices was on the phone when Jared arrived, even though Jared showed up right at the scheduled time. The man's door was closed, but Jared could see him through the window next to the door of the man's office. He held up a single finger to tell Jared to wait outside because he would only be one more minute. Jared knew that the man was never only one more minute. Jared considered himself lucky whenever he was forced to stand outside the man's office for less than five minutes. He'd waited longer than that in the past. Ten minutes. Fifteen minutes. Every time, Jared wanted to walk away, but he knew that the repercussions would be too great. He would get the lecture again, the talk about learning to be a team player. The decisions that Jared had once made in his life had real repercussions—life-and-death repercussions—but now the thing he feared most in the world was getting that dull, condescending lecture. It wasn't so much the lecture itself that he feared. It was the way the lecture reminded him of what his life had become. So Jared waited in the hallway as the man, a man who was actually at least seven years younger than Jared, finished talking to whoever it was that he was talking to on the phone. Then the man hung up the phone and waved Jared in.

Jared opened the door and walked inside. "Jared," the man said, "sorry about that. That was the wife." The man smiled and his smile made Jared wonder if the man had ever managed a single genuine smile. Jared wondered if the man even knew how. "You know how wives can be, right?" the man asked with a laugh, even though he knew that Jared wasn't married.

"Sure." Jared laughed back while nodding his head.

"Anyway, what have you got for me there?"

"We wanted to get your sign-off on these Action Items," Jared said, handing the folder over to the man behind the desk. Jared said *we* even though he didn't give a shit about the Action Items, but the guy with the corner office on the other side of the building didn't walk folders around for signature himself.

"Let's see here," the man behind the desk said, opening the folder and flipping the pages. He propped his feet up on his desk as he read. He lifted a pen to his lips and began to suck air through the pen's cap, making a horrible whistling sound. Then he started to shake his head. Jared always knew it was bad when he shook his head. "No, no, no," the man said. He sat back up in his chair again and wrote on one of the documents with his pen. "This doesn't look right to me at all. This isn't what we agreed on." Jared watched as the man crossed out whole sections of the paper with his pen and then began scribbling notes in the margins. "I think you guys are going to have to keep working on this," the man said, handing the single piece of paper back to Jared.

"What about the others?" Jared asked, looking at the other seven pages in the folder that the man hadn't bothered to look at.

"Let's get this one right first," the man said. "Then I'll look at the others. Okay?"

"Sure," Jared said to the man. Then the man handed the entire folder back to Jared.

"Thanks, Jared. You can close the door behind you when you leave," the man said before Jared began to walk away.

"Sure," Jared said. Then he left, closing the door behind him, as requested. He probably should have taken the marked-up page across the floor to the other corner office. He probably should have worked with everyone to iron out their differences and get his documents finalized. But what was the point? He'd be walking back and forth through the halls from one corner of the building to the other all day. Week? Month? Year? Even if Jared got the documents finalized and signed off on, he knew that he would have new documents on his desk tomorrow. So he tucked the papers under his arm and walked back to his office, glancing out the windows of the building as he went. The office was up on the thirty-seventh floor of the MetLife Building. The view could make an atheist believe in God. Every window opened up on to another swath of New York City so that if you did one lap around the office, you'd see the whole damn thing. The offices used to be on lower floors but, as other tenants left, they slowly moved up in the world. They had five floors, and the thirty-seventh floor was the highest one they had. They still had a ways to go before they reached the top. Jared had begun to think that maybe that was what their real goal was. Fuck winning the War. What was really important was the view.

Jared's office wasn't on a corner. Jared's office wasn't even along an outer wall. Jared had a small, inner office with a window that looked into the hallway. If he craned his neck, he could look through his window, into the office of the woman across the hall from him, and out her window, where he could see a small sliver of sky. Jared dropped the folder on his desk and closed his office door behind him. At least he had a door that he could close. He was grateful that he hadn't screwed things up so badly that they refused to give him a door.

Jared sat down at his desk. He stared at his blank computer screen and wondered, as he had countless times before, where the last eighteen years had gone. They had forgiven him for Joseph. What Joseph had done didn't hurt Jared. In fact, the way Jared had handled his best friend's betrayal even looked for a little while like it was going to help his career. Sure, it wasn't great to be associated with someone who causes such a giant mess, but when you're the one who cleans up the mess, such associations are forgiven. If Joseph had been the only mess that Jared had been involved in, he would have come out of everything with the luster still on his rising star. After all, anyone can get caught up in one mess. The first mess is a coincidence. The second mess is a stain. Jared knew that he had only himself to blame. He knew that he never should have given Michael the information that led Maria to Christopher. If he hadn't given Michael that information, then maybe Michael would still be alive and Jared would be somebody—somebody who made decisions that mattered—and not the shell of a man that he'd become. And the Child? Joseph's child? Christopher? Jared truly believed that he would have been better off being part of the War instead of a poster child for misplaced hope. But what Jared believed and what he wished he had done didn't matter anymore.

Jared's phone rang.

Jared let it ring twice before picking up. He knew that people could hear the phone ring through his office's thin walls. He didn't want to seem too eager. "Hello," he said when he finally answered.

"Are we still on for this evening?" asked the voice on the other end of the connection.

"Yeah," Jared said. Then he looked at the folder of Action Items on his desk. "But I can meet earlier than that if you still want to."

"How early?" the voice asked.

Jared looked at his watch. "Give me an hour."

"You want to meet at the same place as last time?"

"Sure," Jared said. "That should still work."

"Okay. I'll see you in an hour then."

"In an hour," Jared echoed before hanging up the phone. He looked out the small window of his office to see if anyone was watching him. He strummed his fingers on his desk for a moment nervously. Then he stood up. If he was going to make it to Battery Park in an hour, he didn't have much time to waste. It took eighteen years, but Jared finally decided that even misplaced hope beat the living hell out of no hope at all.

Fifty

Umut waited until the midday call to prayer before he walked up to Christopher and Reggie. He used the call to prayer as cover. Christopher and Reggie were standing in the large courtyard next to the Süleymaniye Mosque, surrounded by streetside cafés and passing students. As the call to prayer echoed over the city, Umut casually walked up to Reggie, appearing out of nowhere, and whispered something in Reggie's ear. The sounds of the prayer made it impossible for anyone but Reggie to hear what Umut whispered. Reggie gave Umut a quick nod to let him know that he understood. Then Reggie motioned to Christopher to come closer to him. "Follow Umut," Reggie said to Christopher. "He'll take you to the tribunal."

"What about you?" Christopher asked, fearing that he already knew the answer to his question.

Reggie shook his head. "They want to meet you alone."

"We can say no," Christopher said. "We can make demands too."

The call to prayer ended. For a moment, the city of twenty million people was silent. Their cover gone, Reggie shook his head solemnly and start walking away. Christopher turned his gaze back to the thick-browed Umut. Umut gave Christopher a quick nod that was meant to convey a million words. It was meant to give Christopher comfort. It didn't. Christopher followed Umut anyway.

They walked along the steep, narrow streets leading away from the Süleymaniye Mosque. Umut took turn after turn and Christopher began to feel like he was walking through a maze. "Where are you taking me?" he eventually asked Umut.

"You can't be too careful," Umut replied to Christopher and kept making turns, walking without a pattern to keep them from being followed.

They walked for nearly forty minutes before stopping in front of a nondescript building on a street that looked the same, to Christopher, as every other street that they had walked down. For all Christopher knew, they had been walking in circles. Umut rang the building's buzzer. A tall man with dark, weathered skin opened the door. The tall man looked at Umut and then at Christopher and then stood aside so that the two of them could enter. Once they were inside, the tall man closed the door but not before taking a few extra glances up and down the street.

Once the door was closed, The tall man turned toward Umut. "Everyone is upstairs," he said in English in a deep, gravelly voice.

"How many people came?" Umut asked the man.

"As many as we allowed. Fifteen are here. We had to turn away about thirty others. We didn't want to overwhelm the Child," the tall man said, glancing at Christopher.

He led them down a long hallway to a wooden door that opened into an ancient elevator. The three of them stepped inside with barely enough room to breathe. "How did you decide who got to come?" Christopher asked the tall man as the elevator slowly pulled the three of them up to the building's third floor.

"They separated everybody by region and then had each region draw straws."

"And you drew a winning straw?" Christopher asked.

The tall man smiled. "I didn't have to. No one else was from my region."

"Where are you from?"

"Afghanistan," Tor Baz answered Christopher.

"You're Tor Baz?" Umut said to the tall man, smiling.

"I am," Tor Baz answered, smiling back, excited to be known. The elevator stopped moving. The door opened onto a white-walled room that covered the entire floor. Tor Baz held the door so that Umut and Christopher could step inside the room.

Christopher counted the people in the room. True to Tor Baz's word, there were fourteen. Tor Baz made it an even fifteen. About half of them had dark skin, a few with skin even darker than Tor Baz's. The other half had light skin. *Europe*, Christopher thought as he scanned the faces of the people in the room. *Africa. The Middle East.* The people in the room—nine men, six women—stared back at him.

"C'est l'Enfant," a man in the back whispered to himself. "It's the Child," Xavier then said in English when he realized that everyone could hear his whisper over the almost overbearing silence.

"Welcome," a woman said, stepping forward to greet Christopher. Her accent was lush and her voice husky. It sounded to him the way Istanbul smelled.

"This is your house?" Christopher asked the women.

"Yes," she answered.

"It's lovely," he told her.

"Thank you," the woman said to Christopher. Then she turned to Umut. "Umut, shall we begin?"

Umut seemed to think that there would be more formality first, perhaps even introductions. Christopher could see it on Umut's face. Yet Umut knew that anything he said would reflect on Christopher. So he turned back to the woman. "If you're ready," he said.

Christopher had been so busy looking at the faces that he hadn't noticed the chairs. Sixteen tall leather chairs were set up in the middle of the room. Fifteen of them had been arranged in a semicircle, facing inward. The sixteenth was placed at what would have been the center of the circle, alone, facing the rest.

Christopher knew which of the chairs was his. He knew what was at stake, and he was afraid. The running and the fighting and the killing and the hiding all scared him, but not like this. So Christopher did what he always did when he was afraid. Without waiting for an invitation, Christopher walked toward the sixteenth chair, the one in the middle, and sat down. "Let's get this started," he said to no one in particular. Christopher didn't catch the smiles on Umut's, Tor Baz's, and Xavier's faces at his act of brazenness, because after Christopher sat down he only stared at the fifteen empty chairs. And soon all of the chairs were occupied.

The chairs filled up quickly. Everyone knew where to sit. The seats had been assigned ahead of time. Umut was left without a chair, a mere spectator. He stood near the elevator door. Tor Baz was stuck on one end of the semicircle. The host sat in the middle. Xavier sat two chairs to her left. The twelve others filled in the remaining seats. "We've been impressed by what we've heard about your trip to the Far East," the woman began, "and we've all heard about the plan." She looked around at the others, all of them staring at Christopher. "But we have questions."

"I would hope so," Christopher said coolly, trying to remember everything that Umut had told him and Reggie the night before so that he would maybe, possibly have satisfactory answers. *They believe in Christopher's ability but they're unsure of whether or not they believe in the plan,* Umut had told them. Christopher wished that Reggie was with him to help him describe the plan or that Addy was there with him to help him be brave or that Evan was there with him to be a true ally. Christopher was alone, but he didn't let anyone see his fear. "Fire away," he said, scanning the faces of his interrogators.

The questions started out easy enough. In the beginning, Christopher had answers. They were answers to questions that he and Reggie had already discussed.

"How will the planning for the destruction of each Intelligence Center be done?"

"We'll leave it up to the local people to plan. They'll know better than anyone else what will work. Nobody can micromanage something this big." Christopher wasn't sure he believed that answer. He hadn't been sure he believed it when Reggie first said it to him. Reggie had explained to him why it had to be done that way though. It was as much political as practical. Reggie knew that they wouldn't get people to agree to be subjects in their own homes. Not these people anyway. After all, everyone in that room was already a rebel.

"How do we know that the people in other cities can be trusted to do the jobs?"

"Everybody knows the ramifications of what we're doing here. They all know what it would mean if we failed. And we're not picking people off the streets for this. These are people who have already proven themselves. They're leaders in the Underground."

"What order will the cities go in?"

"It all has to be simultaneous. We can't give them any time to warn each other. We can't give them a chance to bolster their defenses. We're outgunned and outnumbered. Surprise is the only real weapon we have."

"And then the War is just supposed to end?"

"No," Christopher told them. "It doesn't just end. The War ends because we give people a reason to believe that it's over.

That's what most people want. We're giving them the excuse they've been waiting for. How can people keep fighting a War when they don't know who their enemy is? What do you do when you no longer know who it is you're supposed to hate? Strangers can become strangers again. The paranoia can finally come to an end. That's what people want to believe, and we think we can make them believe it."

"Won't some people remember who their enemies are?"

"On the fringes, sure, but the numbers will be small. A few people will remember a few enemies. Some will even keep fighting, but how long can they keep fighting when they have no support and no hope of ever winning?"

"But what do we get to keep?"'

Christopher looked at the man who had asked him the question. He was a stocky white man with an accent that sounded Eastern European. For the first time in nearly two hours of questions, Christopher didn't know how to respond. It had been going so well. "I don't understand what you're asking," Christopher said.

"After we destroy the Intelligence Centers," the man clarified, "what do we get to keep?"

"Nothing," Christopher told him, still confused. The room went dead silent. "Everything has to be destroyed."

"We can't destroy everything," one of the women gasped.

"Why not?" Christopher turned toward her and asked.

"That's our history," one of the black men chimed in. "We can't simply destroy it all."

"Your *history*," Christopher said the word as if he wanted to spit, "is what's feeding the War. That's how we end the War. We starve it. You can't keep your history and still end the War. That's the whole point."

"You're a book burner!" shouted a shocked voice. Christopher didn't even see who shouted it.

Christopher stared at them all. "What is it that you think you'll find in that history? What do you believe is in there that's worth keeping?" The room went silent. Nobody wanted to say anything. Then Christopher remembered his conversation with Reggie on their plane ride from Malaysia to Istanbul. Reggie had asked Christopher why he never asked about how the War started. Reggie had hit on Christopher's blind spot. Now Christopher looked at the people sitting in front of him. They all knew what they hoped they would find in those histories, but nobody wanted to say it out loud. "You think you'll find absolution in there," Christopher said to the row of silent faces after it hit him. "Even you, a room full of rebels who claim to hate the War, you still think that you'll find something in the past that will justify the things that you did before you left the War, the things that your friends did, the things that your family did. You want history to wash away your sins.

"Don't you all understand by now that it doesn't work that way?" If Christopher couldn't get them to understand, then the whole plan was hopeless. "None of it matters. You think it matters, that it makes some sort of difference, but it doesn't. It doesn't matter who started the War. It doesn't matter why the War started. All of you still think that something in that history will prove that you have always been the good guys. But knowing how the War started or who started it wouldn't change anything. It wouldn't change what you've done or what you watched be done in your name or what you allowed to be done while doing nothing to stop it. Nothing that happened in the past can absolve you of sins you've already committed. All that matters is what we do now."

"So we'll never know the truth?" someone asked.

"You'll become the truth," Christopher said, needing to give them something. The faces of the men and women in the room were expressionless—utterly blank. "We'll all become the truth," Christopher finished.

The late-afternoon sun dipped in the sky and began to shine directly through the windows into the room. The room began to heat up. No one spoke for what seemed like a very long time. Christopher could feel sweat rising on his skin. He wanted to say something, but he had nothing more to say. Then the heavyset Eastern European man huffed, "He's a kid. What does he know anyway?" Christopher thought the man's comment would be met by nodding heads and murmurs of agreement, but it was met by even more silence. For the longest time after that, nobody even moved. It was almost like everyone in the room was in a state of shock.

"Are we done here?" Umut eventually asked, walking up and placing a comforting hand on Christopher's shoulder.

"I think so," the woman who owned the house said.

So Christopher stood up. He turned toward the others, readying to say good-bye, to tell them that he hoped they would make the right decision. As he turned, Umut squeezed his shoulder with a grip like none Christopher had ever felt before. He held Christopher in place, keeping him from facing the tribunal again. "Don't say more," Umut whispered to him. "You've said enough." Steering with the hand that was gripping Christopher's shoulder, Umut maneuvered Christopher toward the elevator. Neither of them looked back. They waited for the doors to open. Then they stepped into the elevator. A moment later the doors closed behind them and they once more descended towards the city.

Fifty-one

Evan, Addy, and Maria were staying in a motel outside of Albany, waiting for word that they should head into New York. The motel reminded Maria of the places where she and Joseph used to stay when she was pregnant with Christopher and they were on the run—cheap, nameless hotels sitting precipitously close to the edge of existence. The motel's walls were painted concrete. The water never got hotter than lukewarm. The three of them agreed to keep the blinds drawn so no one could see inside, even though there was no evidence that anyone had picked up their trail. They made it across the border without incident, hiding Evan in the trunk again.

The three of them shared the room. It had two beds. Addy and Evan slept in one bed and Maria slept in the other. Evan and Addy made Maria feel old. She had to fight to keep herself from questioning them about whether or not they were too young to be sharing a bed. She had an urge to suggest that she and Addy sleep in one bed and Evan sleep in the other, but she bit her tongue. She kept reminding herself that she had been younger than Addy when she and Joseph were on the run together. The two of them were so much like her and Joseph. They were young and in love. Theirs was that crazy, youth-against-the-world kind of love. It was the Romeo and Juliet kind of love, the kind that never led to anything good. It was the same sort of love that Maria had shared with Joseph, though her romance with Joseph seemed like a very long time ago, almost like it took place in another life. She worried that Evan and Addy's romance, like her romance with Joseph, was destined for trouble.

Maria tried her best not to talk much when the three of them were all together. She didn't want to intrude on what Evan and Addy had. She talked only when one of them was out of the room, when one of them was in the shower or running an errand. She didn't have much to say anyway. She only had questions and she really only wanted the answer to one of those questions. So Maria waited until Addy had gone out to buy food, so that she knew Addy would be gone for a good chunk of time, to ask Evan that one question. "Tell me about my son," she said to Evan once Addy had left.

"What do you want to know?" Evan asked in return.

Everything, Maria thought, but she knew that was too much. She knew she had to guide Evan. He was so young. "What was his mother like?" she began.

Evan smiled. "His parents are really nice. They're great. They love him." He answered in the present tense, as if Christopher could go back to them. Maria knew better.

"And Christopher?"

Evan nodded. "He loves them too. He's trying to protect them from all of this."

"They deserve to know where he is," Maria said, thinking about her own parents, both gone now. "Tell me more."

"What else?"

"Did he know that they weren't his biological parents?"

"Yeah," Evan told her. "They told him when he was little. I think he would have known anyway."

"Did he wonder about me? Did he think about me? Was he mad at me?"

Evan nodded. "I think he did wonder about you, but there was so much going on that he didn't understand. I don't think he was mad at you. He was too busy trying to make sense of everything."

"Do you think he'll be happy to meet me?"

"Yes," Evan said without hesitating. "I think he will."

Maria had to fight back tears. She didn't know if Evan was telling her the truth. She hoped that he was, but she was grateful even if he wasn't. "Thank you," she said to him.

Evan saw the tears build up in Maria's eyes. "You can ask me more," he said to her. "You can ask me anything about him."

Maria smiled now. Her smiles were so rare that she felt the muscles in her face tire almost immediately. "What does he like? What's his favorite thing?" And on and on it went like that for an hour, until Addy returned. Then Maria became quiet again, trying to once again disappear into the background.

Fifty-two

Brian was sitting on a bench in Battery Park, staring out over the Hudson River. Jared saw him from a full two blocks away. Even from that distance, Jared recognized the gray hair, the wrinkled eyes. Jared wondered how Brian had survived this long. Brian was probably only about fifty years old, but that was ancient in his line of work. It was hard enough getting old when you were a part of the War. Usually, the only ones who survived past the age of forty were the ones that retired, settled down, and had kids. The breeders. Rebels didn't get to retire. Only a handful of them made it past the age of thirty-five, let alone fifty. Jared liked meeting with Brian. Brian was one of the few people that Jared talked to that made him feel young. Jared also remembered what Brian had done for Joseph. Without Brian's help, Joseph might have been killed eighteen years ago, before Jared was able to protect him. Without Brian's help, someone else would have killed Joseph. Joseph deserved better than that. Jared had never wanted Joseph to go out like an ordinary punk. He wanted Joseph to go out like a hero. If Jared had to kill Joseph to make that happen, he was willing to make that sacrifice, even if nobody else understood it. What Jared had failed to antici-pate was the blowback. If it had been only Joseph, Jared could have come out of it a star, and he and Joseph would both have gotten what Jared wanted for both of them. Both of them would have been heroes—heroes to different causes, but heroes all the same. But Jared had neglected to think about Michael. That was his mistake. Because of that mistake, only one of them got to become a hero. People had mostly forgotten Michael by now, and the only people who remembered Jared hated him.

Jared walked up and sat down on the bench next to Brian. They didn't look at each other. They didn't shake hands. "Thanks for coming," Brian said.

"No problem," Jared answered. "What's this meeting about?"

"You offered to help us," Brian said. "We think that we're finally ready to accept your help."

"I guess you didn't get any better offers?" Jared joked.

Brain answered him with a glare. "Does your offer still stand or not?"

"I told you that I was willing to help but that I have no desire to become an ordinary spy. If you want me to help you, you better have something big planned. I've seen what being a spy does to you guys."

Brian knew that Jared was referring to him and his gray hair and his wrinkled eyes. "I was never a spy," Brian said to Jared. "I was only looking out for a friend."

Jared laughed. "Whatever you say. So are you guys working on something big or not?"

Brian nodded. "Do you remember the plan that I told you about last time?"

Jared stared out over the water. "I do. I didn't think you were serious, but I remember."

"We are serious. This is as serious as it gets. Asia is in," Brian said, speaking softly. "I received word this morning that Europe, Africa, and the Middle East have all agreed to join the plan too. They made the decision last night after meeting with Christopher.

With all of them in, the Americas are a foregone conclusion. Christopher will still have to meet with them, but it's only a formality."

"The kid must be a firebrand," Jared said, thinking back to the baby he'd taken away from his best friend eighteen years ago.

"They tell me that he's growing into the job."

"Can I meet him?" Jared asked.

The request caught Brian by surprise. "I don't know if that's a good idea."

"Why not?" Jared asked, wondering which of the million possible excuses Brian would use.

"We don't know how Christopher would react to meeting you. Besides, we're not even sure that we can trust you yet."

"Fair enough," Jared said, willing to abandon the request for now—at least until he had more leverage. "Then what is it you want me to do?"

"We want your help devising a plan to destroy the New York Intelligence Center."

"My office?" Jared laughed again. "You think you'll beat the War by destroying my office? The people in that office are bureaucrats. They're not warriors."

"You know as well as anyone that one bureaucrat can do the damage of hundreds of soldiers. Besides, we don't care about taking out the bureaucrats. All we care about is destroying the information inside. So, are you interested in helping us?"

Jared looked around him. He looked past the river and past Brian. For the first time, he noticed a woman sitting on the grass to his right, pretending to read a magazine. Then he looked to his left and saw a man sitting on another bench reading a book. Both of them glanced up every few seconds to stare at him and Brian. "Do I have a choice?" Jared asked. He was armed—he had a small gun in his pocket. The problem was that he'd been pushing pencils for years. He'd known even before he came down here that the only thing the gun would do for him was make sure he took one man out with him if they double-crossed him. His days of winning fights where he was outnumbered three to one were long gone.

"You always have a choice," Brian said. "There's just no guarantee that you're going to like all your options."

"If I help you with this, what's the rest of the plan?"

Brian shook his head. "You don't need to know the rest of the plan."

"If you guys don't trust me, then why are you asking me for help?"

"Because you have the knowledge and the grudge that we look for in informers. Putting your personal history aside, you don't merely fit the profile of an informer. You *are* the profile."

Jared knew that Brian was right. They were asking him for the same reasons that Jared was considering saying yes. "I'll help," Jared said.

"Good," Brian replied. "Now go back to work. Make sure no one gets suspicious. I'll contact you again soon so that we can begin working on the details."

Jared stood up to go. "You don't like me, do you, Brian?" he said before walking away.

Brian didn't look at him. "I can't think of anyone in the world that I like less," he answered.

"Well, this is going to be fun," Jared said, letting the sarcasm poison every word that he spoke. Then he turned to his right and walked away. He winked at the woman sitting in the grass as he walked past her. She didn't respond. *She was probably hoping she'd get to kill me,* Jared thought to himself as he walked toward the street to hail a cab.

Fifty-three

They were told that it was too risky to meet Christopher at the airport. It would be too much of a scene to meet in public. Instead Addy was given the address of a warehouse in Brooklyn. They were told to go to the warehouse and wait. They had no idea how long they would have to wait. They didn't know who was going to meet them at the warehouse. No one would even promise them that Christopher was coming. And still Maria, Evan, and Addy were brimming with excitement as they climbed into the car to leave the motel. Each of them was excited for a different reason, but that didn't mean they weren't unified by their excitement. They all wanted to find Christopher. None of them could predict where things would go from there.

Christopher and Reggie once again found themselves on a plane together, flying halfway around the world. But this time they were going home. They were on a direct flight from Istanbul to New York. "You're making me nervous," Christopher said to Reggie when they were well over the Atlantic Ocean. He'd been riding an almost supernatural high since he'd found out that the trip to Istanbul had been a success.

"Why's that?" Reggie asked.

"Because you're not staring at me. You're always staring at me on planes when I'm trying to sleep. Why aren't you staring at me?"

"I figured that you'd done enough. I thought I'd give you a rest," Reggie lied. The truth was that Reggie felt too guilty to even look at Christopher. Reggie could hardly reel off all of the half-truths and secrets he'd been keeping from Christopher. He was counting on Maria. She was Reggie's gift to Christopher that was supposed to make Christopher forgive the fact that Reggie hadn't told him about the attack on Addy and Evan's compound in California. Her sudden appearance was supposed to make up for the fact that Reggie had never even told Christopher that Maria was still alive. Finally, and maybe most importantly, Maria's existence was supposed to distract Christopher from the fact that they'd enlisted Jared's help to bring down the New York Intelligence Center. "Go to sleep," Reggie ordered Christopher. "We still have a lot of work to do in New York."

"Aye, aye, Captain," Christopher said. Then he closed his eyes.

When they first got to the warehouse in Brooklyn, Addy, Evan, and Maria thought they must be in the wrong place. The warehouse sat in an industrial dead zone near the Gowanus Canal. It was like a ghost town. The street was lined with buildings, but all of them were covered in graffiti and appeared to have fallen out of use. The sidewalks were empty. No cars drove by. Addy, Evan, and Maria felt like they'd been sent to the one barren space left in all of New York City.

"This can't be right," Evan said, looking at the utter lifelessness around them. Back in Maine, the absence of people meant trees and animals. This was concrete as far as the eye could see.

"This is the address they gave me," Addy said. She looked out the car window at the building they were parked in front of. It was a two-story warehouse. The only windows were small, grime-covered windows near the very top of the building. She couldn't see any movement inside.

"I'll go check to see if we're in the right place," Maria said. She opened her car door and stepped out onto the sidewalk. When her foot hit the sidewalk, her memories of New York, of Brooklyn, flooded back to her like she'd been struck by a wave. Eighteen years had passed since she'd watched a man with a gun chase Reggie over the Brooklyn Bridge to somewhere not far from where she was standing. Eighteen years had passed since she rode a subway with Michael to Coney Island to meet with the spy who would unlock the doors to help her and Michael find Christopher. She remembered riding the subway to meet with the spy, looking out the windows of the elevated train, staring at the seeming endlessness that was Brooklyn, and thinking that surely, if that much humanity existed, Christopher could escape inside all of it. Eighteen years, gone as if it had all happened in a single flash of light. Now she was back; Christopher hadn't escaped; and the endlessness that was Brooklyn turned out to be another casualty of the War. She rang the bell next to the door of the warehouse.

Nobody answered. She didn't hear any sounds coming from inside. *Could that crazy girl have screwed this up?* Maria thought to herself about Addy. She turned back to the car, ready to take control and try to figure out where they were really supposed to be. As she turned away, the massive loading dock door behind her began to open.

Maria watched the door as it finished opening. Two men were standing inside. "You Maria?" one of the men called out to her.

"I am," Maria called back to the man. "I guess we're in the right place."

The man who called out to her laughed. "Tell Addy to pull the car inside. We've been waiting for you guys to get here."

"Is *he* here?" Maria asked tentatively.

"Who? Christopher?"

Maria nodded. He was the only one anybody cared about.

"Not yet. They're not scheduled to arrive for another few hours. Let's get everybody inside for now. We don't want to draw attention to ourselves."

So Maria walked back to the car, opened the rear door, and said to Addy, "We're here. They want us to go inside." Addy drove the car through the open loading dock door. Once they were inside, the two men who'd beckoned them in shut and locked the door behind them.

It didn't take long after the door was closed for Addy, Evan, and Maria to be surrounded by dozens of people. Reggie and Christopher weren't inside the warehouse, but everyone else seemed to be. The warehouse had been retrofitted into some sort of hybrid office building and dormitory. Makeshift rooms had been arranged throughout the space. Some were turned into bedrooms, others into conference rooms. Men and women from at least eleven different countries were there—people from South America, Latin America, the Caribbean, and Canada. They began coming up to Maria, Evan, and Addy and introducing themselves. They spoke to Maria differently than they did to Evan and Addy, with a bit more reverence and awe.

"You're smaller than I thought you would be," a woman from South America who had introduced herself as Simone said to Maria.

"Why is that?" Maria asked her, confused by all the special attention.

"I don't know," Simone told her. "I guess it's that the stories about you are so big. You know?"

"No." Maria shook her head. "I don't know what you're talking about."

Simone was caught for a second, not knowing what to say next. At that moment Addy intercepted Simone and walked her away, whispering something in her ear as they went. Brian waited until the very end to go up to Maria. Until Brian, Maria had generally been handling the reverence and awe with sarcasm and scorn. "It's nice to meet you, Maria," Brian said to her. "You might not know it, but we've got some history together."

Maria's head was spinning from all of the attention. She only wanted to see her son. She hadn't bargained for the rest of this. "Do I know you?" she asked.

"I was Joseph's handler until he met you. After he met you, they didn't trust that I could handle him anymore." Brian offered Maria a smile. "I'm quite certain that they were right."

"You warned us once that we were in danger." Maria remembered that night in Charleston when they ran away after finding a bloodied body on the side of the road.

"I considered Joseph a friend," Brian said to her. "I hope we can be friends too."

"I'm fifty/fifty when it comes to Joe's old friends," Maria told Brian, thinking about Michael and Jared. "I'm not sure that I want to press my luck."

"I'm also friends with Reggie," Brian said, "and about two weeks ago I drove your son from California to New Jersey."

"Okay," Maria said to Brian. "Let's talk."

Jared sat down at the desk in his sparsely furnished, tiny two-room apartment in New Jersey. He'd taken the bus to work that morning the same way he did every morning, the same way he would have if nothing had changed. Jared went about his daily routine the same way he went about his daily routine every day, the same way he would have if he hadn't decided to abandon everything he'd ever worked toward. He got to the office. He waited in line in the kitchen for coffee. He sat at his desk, staring at his computer. For Jared, it was like stepping outside of his life and seeing for the first time how depressingly monotonous it had become. But that day he didn't feel like he was drowning in the monotony. That day, the monotony was merely cover. Nine hours of monotony acting as cover for those twenty other minutes spent slipping into rooms he wasn't supposed to be in and flipping through files he wasn't supposed to see. Jared's life had once again become something it hadn't been in over a decade. It had become something meaningful.

When the day was over, Jared took the bus back to his apartment in New Jersey. Only that day, Jared didn't leave the office empty-handed. He had papers with him, plans and schedules. In twenty minutes, he had gathered most of what he hoped he would need. Jared remembered fondly a time in his life when he had a reputation built on his ability to devise a plan. Michael was the party. Joseph had the heart. Jared made the plans. The heart and the party were long gone. Jared figured he had one last chance to do the one thing that he was born to do.

Jared looked out the window of his apartment. He stared over the tops of the trees outside his window and looked across the river at the lights on the tops of the tallest buildings in Manhattan. One of them was the building that his office was in. It was his job to figure out how to snuff out that light like a candle. Jared opened his briefcase. He slid his fingers over the top of the briefcase's felt liner until he found the fold. He pinched the fold with two fingers and pulled, tearing the liner away from the briefcase where Jared had glued it in place earlier that day. Behind the liner were the papers he had stolen. He took them out and laid them on the desk in front of him.

Jared knew before he even started that merely hitting the building wasn't going to be enough. They would need to do more. The papers confirmed that. The papers confirmed what Jared had always heard as a rumor, that an attack on the Intelligence Center would lead to a citywide response. The response wouldn't be limited to members of the War. The response would come from civilian forces too, forces that wouldn't know the real reason they were being called in. They had put the citywide response in place when the Underground started getting out of hand. The theory was that since the Underground wasn't part of the War, there was no need to follow the War's rules when fighting against them. Nobody sane talks about animal rights when swatting at flies. They had enough people inside the police department to make it happen. Jared knew that the rebels didn't have the numbers or the time to weather that type of response—not unless they created a diversion first. If the police were already busy somewhere else, their response to an attack on the Intelligence Center could be cut by as much as three-quarters. Jared's brain began to hum with the possibilities. They couldn't just attack the Intelligence Center. They needed to attack all of New York City. They needed to rock the whole city to its foundation.

Nobody came to meet Christopher and Reggie at the airport. Christopher knew that it was silly to expect anyone there and he didn't care when no one showed. They were home. He could feel it, even though he'd never been to New York before. Christopher and Reggie could once again walk through the airport without standing out like creatures from another planet. Reggie was no longer a head taller than everyone they walked past. Christopher's skin was no longer two shades paler than every person around them. They were normal again, even if only on the surface. JFK Airport was busy, and Reggie and Christopher made their way through the crowds quickly and with purpose. Reggie walked in front. Christopher followed a step or two behind him. At the taxi stand outside the concourse, they got into a cab. "Brooklyn," Reggie told the cabdriver. "Eighth Street and Second Avenue."

The cabdriver turned around in his seat and looked at Reggie. "Are you sure you have the right address?" the cabbie asked with a thick Pakistani accent that Christopher actually recognized. "I can take you, but I must warn you. There's nothing there—just warehouses and empty buildings. Maybe you want Eighth Avenue and Second Street, on the park? No?"

Reggie waved a hand at the cabbie, motioning for him to turn around and start driving. "No, it's Eighth Street and Second Avenue. We know where we're going. You don't have to worry. I'm from here."

"Okay," the cabbie said before putting the cab in gear.

They rode in silence at first. Christopher stared out the window. Nothing Christopher had seen had looked like this—not Singapore, not Istanbul—nowhere else looked like New York. Reggie sat fidgeting in the seat next to him. "Are you okay, Reggie?" Christopher asked. Reggie's face looked ashen and long.

"I'm okay," Reggie answered him. "It's just that we're finally coming to the end."

"One way or the other, right?" Christopher laughed sardonically.

"One way or the other," Reggie agreed softly.

It took them forty minutes to get from JFK to the low area around the Gowanus Canal. When they drove over the Pulaski Skyway, Christopher got his first unadulterated view of the Manhattan skyline. It didn't look real to him. It looked more like a comic book or the set of a science fiction movie. Christopher wanted to tell the cabbie to pull over, to stop right there on the bridge, traffic be damned, so that Christopher could stare at the view longer, at the tall buildings and the bridges. His eyes darted from skyscraper to skyscraper. Until that moment, Christopher had never thought about what the word *skyscraper* literally meant, but now, as he stared at the true leviathans reaching into the air, he understood. Those buildings really did scrape the sky. He didn't know it then, but it was going to be his job to blow one of those buildings out of the sky. Christopher didn't actually ask the cabbie to stop. He rode and stared and didn't think for a second about what was going to happen when the cab ride ended. But it did end.

"You sure this is where you want me to drop you?" the cabbie asked again as he pulled up in front of a graffiti-covered warehouse.

Reggie took a hundred-dollar bill out of his pocket. "This is good," he said, handing the bill to the cabbie. "Now, forget that you dropped anybody here." They got out of the cab, stood on the empty sidewalk and watched the cab drive away. When it disappeared from view, Reggie turned toward the building and waved. Only then did the building's loading dock door begin to open.

After Indonesia and Istanbul, Christopher had believed that he had outgrown the ability to be surprised. It had only taken him a couple of weeks to come to that conclusion, but that's what happens when every day begins as if you're peering over the edge of a roller-coaster car. So Christopher wasn't surprised when the loading dock door opened to reveal an interior that looked nothing like an abandoned warehouse. He wasn't surprised to see Brian standing behind the doors, waiting for them. "Welcome back," Brian said to Christopher and Reggie, greeting them with a salesman's smile. Brian approached Christopher first. He stretched out his hand for Christopher to shake. "We've heard amazing things," Brian said to Christopher. "You've done so well, Christopher. Your father would be proud." Christopher shook Brian's hand without saying anything. "I hope you now believe that you did the right thing coming with me."

"I do," Christopher finally conceded. "Have you heard anything about Evan and Addy?" He had avoided asking Reggie the question, knowing that there was nothing he could do about them when he was halfway across the world, but now he was back.

Brian put his hand on Christopher's shoulder. "Heard about them? They're here," Brian said, to Christopher's relief. "They're excited to see you." Brian squeezed Christopher's shoulder and gently guided him into the building. Once Christopher was over the threshold, Brian turned to Reggie. He shook Reggie's hand too, leaning in toward him and whispering something in his ear. Seeing Reggie and Brian together for the first time, Christopher thought about how everything seemed to be tightening around him. He had once read somewhere that the difference between fear and paranoia was that fear was rational. He'd always wondered what good that was when the world was fucking crazy. Reggie nodded to Brian and whispered a reply in Brian's ear.

"Secrets?" Christopher said out loud, admonishing Brian and Reggie.

"Nothing you won't hear about soon enough," Reggie promised him. Christopher wondered if Brian and Reggie would even know each other if it wasn't for him and his birth parents.

Christopher stepped into the building and wasn't surprised to see the silent faces of two dozen people staring at him. Alejandro was there from Costa Rica. So was Simone from Rio de Janeiro. So were so many others. Yet even as Christopher's world expanded, it seemed to be shrinking. His past was becoming part of his present, and his present seemed merely to be becoming a foil for whatever was in store for him in his future.

"Brian's going to take you to see Evan and Addy," Reggie said to Christopher. "I have some things I need to take care of."

"Okay," Christopher said, too eager to see his old friends to argue. He followed Brian up a flight of stairs and into a small, windowless room. The room was a stark white color, with a white conference table and white chairs.

"Wait here," Brian said to Christopher. Christopher nodded and Brian walked back out of the room. Christopher sat down in one of the chairs. He didn't know why, but his heart was pounding in his chest. He felt like he could hear the sound of it beating as it echoed around the room. Of all the things to be nervous about, Christopher couldn't understand why he was so nervous about seeing his friends again. They were alive. Brian had told Christopher that they were excited to see him. Christopher knew that, if what Brian said was true, Evan and Addy must have forgiven him for leaving them the way he did. None of the rationalizing Christopher was doing in his head had any impact on the beating of his heart. Reggie had been acting so strange. Something else was up, something that would test Christopher's newfound immunity to surprises. The thing was, Christopher was pretty sure that he didn't want to be surprised anymore.

Fifty-four

Maria stood alone on the roof of the warehouse, waiting for Reggie. Brian had brought her there. He told her that Reggie wanted to talk to her first. The roof was the only place Reggie knew that they could be alone. The roof wasn't very high, but Maria was surprised by how much she could see from that vantage point. Everything in this part of the city was low. A warm wind blew around her, and she could hear the distant sounds of the city on the breeze. She walked over to the edge of the roof, looked down at the empty streets below her, and waited.

Maria remembered the first letter she'd gotten in prison from Reggie. It was the first letter she got, period. The whole time she was in prison, eight years all told, nobody except Reggie wrote to her. Maria was nervous when she received that first letter. She was nervous that it would be from her father, nervous that her father might have found out what had become of her. But she never heard from her father. Her father never found out, and by the time Maria got out of prison, she didn't have to worry about her father finding out anymore. He died in the middle of her prison sentence.

Reggie didn't put any details in that first letter. Maria didn't even realize it was from him until she saw the name "Reggie," with quotes around it, at the bottom of the page. At first she didn't know how she felt about getting a letter from Reggie. After she had saved Christopher, she wanted to disassociate herself from the War. But she was so glad to find out that Reggie was alive and okay and so happy to have a connection to somebody. So she wrote Reggie back. They didn't talk about much in their letters, either while Maria was in prison or after. They rarely mentioned the War or Christopher. They wrote to each other, from the vantage points of two people living idyllic, ordinary lives. It was a game, a pleasant distraction, a way for both of them to make the world seem bearable.

The letters were almost entirely fictional, but sometimes some truth leaked through. Eventually Maria surmised from some of the hidden details in Reggie's letters that Reggie was working with the Underground. So for one letter, Maria stopped playing the game. For one letter, she wrote as herself, as Christopher's mother and as the woman who once saved Reggie's life. She made one request of Reggie, a request that Reggie agreed to without hesitation. One request that Maria had been relying on ever since she made it.

Maria heard the door on the roof open behind her. It was an old door with rust on its hinges and it squeaked as it swung open. She didn't turn at first. She wanted to say something before she faced Reggie and lost her resolve. She heard Reggie take a few steps toward her. "You promised me that you'd protect him," Maria said to Reggie without turning to face him. "You promised me that you'd keep him out of the War."

"I know," Reggie said, and she remembered his voice. "I never should have made that promise. I had no right to make promises that I couldn't keep. At the time I didn't have any idea what Christopher would become, what either of you would become."

Maria turned to face Reggie now. She was shocked by how old he looked. She had half expected to turn around and see a teenage boy standing behind her. What she saw instead was a man, a strong but weathered man. "Christopher didn't *become* anything," Maria said to him. "He's just a boy, Reggie."

Reggie shook his head. "That's where you're wrong, Maria. Christopher is a boy, but he's not *just* a boy. He's so much more."

"You're going to break him, Reggie. You're all going to break him."

"I tried to keep him out of all this, Maria. You have to know that I tried." Reggie stepped closer to Maria. They stood facing each other.

"What do you mean you tried? You flew him around the world to convince people to join some sort of revolution. How is that *trying* to protect him? You used him, Reggie."

"Yeah," Reggie admitted, "but at least it was me using him and not somebody else. I'm not going to waste him like other people would have. We're actually going to do this, Maria. We're actually going to end the War."

"And what if you don't? What happens then?"

"I gave him a chance to run, Maria. I put my best people on it. It didn't take." Reggie decided not to tell Maria about Max and about how Max died protecting Christopher. He couldn't see what good it would do. He was using Christopher. He wasn't going to win the argument that way. "Did you ever imagine that your son would get to see the sunrise in Indonesia or eat dinner on a rooftop in Istanbul?"

"No," Maria admitted. "Do you think that's worth it?"

"You'll have to ask Christopher that."

"But do *you* think it's worth it?" Maria pressed.

"No," Reggie answered her, "but it's something."

Maria thought about it for a second. "Do you still need him? Hasn't he already played his part? Can't you finish the rest without him?"

Reggie nodded. "We can. Christopher already did his part. He did it miraculously. He needs to meet with people here tomorrow, but it's only a formality. They've come from all over the Americas to see him—to see the legend with their own eyes. After that, if you can convince him to stop, he can stop." Reggie paused for a moment. "But you're not going to be able to convince him. I tried already. He wants to see this thing through."

"And if you can't convince him, what chance do I have?" Maria said with only a tinge of sarcasm.

Reggie shrugged off the sarcasm. "He's stubborn," Reggie said. "Like his mother."

"Where is he now?" Maria asked.

"He's downstairs, in a room, waiting. We wanted you and Addy and Evan to go in to see him together. We think it might help alleviate the shock."

"The shock?" Maria flinched. "Does he know about me? Does he even know that I'm alive?" Her voice suddenly got weak.

"No," Reggie said. "I managed to keep some of my promises."

Fifty-five

Christopher waited in the white room for what felt like hours, though it was actually little more than forty minutes. Then, without warning, the door swung open and Evan walked into the room. Christopher looked at Evan. Evan looked healthy but older, older than he should have looked. Christopher took a small step toward Evan. Before he could make it any farther, Evan reached out and pulled Christopher into a massive hug. They didn't say anything to each other. As the force of their hug subsided, Christopher looked up at the two other people who had walked through the door after Evan. He had expected to see Addy and Brian. Addy was there, her hair fading back toward its natural color but still with hints of the dark flame hue. But the person behind Addy wasn't Brian. The person behind Addy was a ghost. Apparently, the ability to be surprised is not something that you can outgrow, not if the next surprise is bigger than the last one.

Christopher couldn't say how he recognized the woman standing behind Addy. He couldn't remember ever seeing her before. Maybe it was because he had memories stored away that he didn't know existed. Maybe these memories were so powerful that they could bring back the dead. Christopher let go of Evan and Evan moved aside. Addy walked up to Christopher next. Christopher stood there, frozen in shock. Addy didn't try to break the spell. She simply stood on the tips of her toes and whispered to him, "We're glad to have you back," then gave him a gentle kiss on his cheek. Then she too stepped aside.

Maria watched Christopher's face. From the moment she'd entered the room, she couldn't take her eyes off his face. She'd waited for this moment for a long time and then spent an even longer time trying, and failing, to make peace with the fact that this moment was never going to happen. Now the moment was here and Maria was so worried about what it might do to Christopher that she couldn't enjoy it. All she really knew about her own son was what Evan had told her over the past two days. He looked so much like his father and still so much like his own person that it almost frightened Maria. And he looked so much like a man, so unlike the child that Maria had pictured in her head for all these years. When Christopher looked up at her, he didn't look angry, and she was grateful for that, but she readied herself for the anger that she thought would come once the confusion wore off. She remembered what it had felt like holding him for the first time after she'd found him in California when he was only one year old. She remembered how he'd struggled and cried out for someone else. To say she remembered it wasn't even really true because that implied that she'd stopped thinking about it. She'd never stopped thinking about it, but now she didn't merely remember it, she felt it again—that same ache in her heart. Only this time, she wasn't saving him. Addy stepped aside and Christopher's eyes fell on Maria. "This is wrong," Maria mumbled to Christopher. "I shouldn't be doing this to you again." Then she turned and headed for the door. A hand gripped her arm before she could reach the door handle. She knew it was Christopher. She could feel his father in his grip.

Until Maria spoke, Christopher couldn't move. He froze. He was staring at a ghost—both in his memory and in real life. Maria was dead. Max had told him that she was dead. Everyone knew that she was dead. Christopher didn't even want to think about what it would mean if she was alive, if she'd been alive the whole time. He stared at her, and she stared back at him, and he didn't know what to do or to say or to think. All he knew was that when he heard her voice, he didn't want her to go. He needed her to stay. That part of Christopher's memory that he hadn't known existed exploded when he heard Maria's voice. So when she turned toward the door, Christopher went after her. He reached for her and grabbed her arm before she could leave him again. His skin touched her skin. Unable to go forward, Maria turned back toward her son.

Christopher wanted to be angry, but he'd run out of anger. He already had too many people to be angry with. When Maria turned back toward him, she saw what was left of his anger on his face. When someone is all out of anger, all that's left is despair. Christopher no longer looked like a man to her. He looked like the child that she had once held in her arms. When Maria saw that child, her child, she had no choice but to go to him and spread her arms to him and try to comfort him.

When Maria put her arms around Christopher, he collapsed into them. He didn't want to be so vulnerable, but he didn't have the will to stop himself. He was supposed to be a leader now. He was supposed to be a warrior. At least, that was what everyone else wanted him to be. That was the mask that they made him wear. But deep down, he didn't believe that he was those things. Deep down, he had no idea who he was. At that moment, though, he was still a frightened child in the arms of a mother. It didn't matter in that moment that this wasn't his only mother. His body remembered what it felt like to be held by this woman, and it collapsed. And he wept like a child.

"It's okay. It's okay," Maria whispered to Christopher as she stroked his back.

"They told me you were dead," Christopher said between sobs.

"I know," Maria said, still gently rubbing his back, trying to soothe him. "I told them to. I'm sorry. I was trying to protect you. I never wanted to hurt you." She would have cried too if she hadn't realized that in that moment she needed to stay strong for her son. "You have your own family. Whether I'm alive or dead shouldn't mean that much to you."

"But it does," Christopher said, burying his teary eyes in the crook of Maria's neck. "It does."

"I know," Maria said again. She held his head against her so that she could absorb his tears. "I'm alive and I'm here with you now and I'm never going to leave you again."

"Promise?" Christopher said, sounding very much like a little boy who'd gotten separated from his mother in a department store.

"I promise," Maria said, stroking Christopher's hair. Then she held him away from her and looked into his face. "We've probably got a lot to talk about. Evan? Addy? Can you give us some time alone?"

"Of course," Addy said. Addy and Evan began to walk out of the room, but before they left, Addy turned back to Christopher. "Are you okay, Christopher?" she asked, sounding almost as maternal as Maria.

"Yeah," an embarrassed Christopher assured her. "I'm okay." So Evan and Addy continued out the door. "Guys," Christopher called out to them as they walked away. Both Addy and Evan turned toward him. "I'm happy to see you guys again. I'm happy you're safe. We'll talk when I'm done here, right?"

"Of course," Evan replied. "We're good, Chris. Don't worry about us." Evan's words meant everything to Christopher and Evan meant everything when he said them. Then Evan and Addy slipped out of the room, leaving Maria and Christopher alone, for the first time in more than seventeen years.

"The last time I saw you," Maria told Christopher, "you were still in diapers." She remembered what Addy had told her that night in her basement in Quebec. Addy had said that there were still things Maria could teach Christopher. Whatever it was that she could teach him, she would.

"Why?" Christopher asked, not knowing where to start. He could have been asking a million different questions, so Maria went with the one response that she knew could answer every one of them.

"Because I loved you so much. Because I wanted you to be happy and I didn't care how much it had to hurt me to help you be happy."

"Did you know my parents?" Christopher asked Maria.

"Yes," Maria told him. "I knew them when I was young. I knew that they would love you and that they would be wonderful to you. And I hoped that by giving you to them I was giving you a fresh start."

"There's no such thing as a fresh start," Christopher told his long-lost mother.

"You don't know that," Maria said. "You only know that we haven't found it yet."

"I have so many questions," Christopher said. "Tell me about my father. Tell me about you. Tell me why you never came to find me. Tell me about the couple that I lived with in California. Tell me about everything."

"I don't know what you've heard, good or bad. Your father was a decent man, trying to become a good man, and I loved him. And he loved you. Those are the things that really matter."

"Can I tell you a secret?" Christopher asked Maria. Though she'd had a chance to answer only one of his questions, he already felt that he could tell her things he couldn't tell anyone else.

"Of course."

"I hate everyone. I hate everyone involved in this stupid War. I even hate the people who are fighting against it. I hate them all."

"No, you don't," Maria told him. "You want to, but you don't. I was the same way. I wanted to hate all of them except your father. Then I met Michael. Then I met Dorothy and Reggie. Pretty soon, you only hate the ones that you don't know, and that means that you don't really hate any of them at all."

"So, after everything you've been through, you don't hate any of them?" Christopher asked.

"Only one," she said. "But now's not the time to talk about him." *I want to talk about you*, Maria thought. *I want to talk about you being done with all of this. Fighting the War is just another part of the War.* But now wasn't the time for that either. She needed to gain his trust first. She needed to be patient. She knew that she wasn't to Christopher what he was to her. The problem was that she didn't have a lot of time. So she had to make the most of the time she had. "You must have other questions for me," she said. "You can ask me anything." So Maria answered all of Christopher's questions as best she could. Evan and Addy didn't get to see him again for another five hours.

Fifty-six

Dave had never been up this high on the Brooklyn Bridge before. He'd crossed the bridge countless times, of course, and as a kid, he'd even snuck up onto the cables a couple of times, but he ran up only a few feet before getting scared and climbing down again. He'd never dreamt that one day he would be sitting on the top of one of the towers, strapping explosives to its side.

He wasn't the only one. They were all over the city that night, scrambling up its bridges and towers. The George Washington Bridge. The Manhattan Bridge. The Williamsburg Bridge. The Verrazano-Narrows Bridge. The top of the Flatiron Building. The top of the Chrysler Building. The top of the Empire State Building. Even the top of the arch in Washington Square Park.

Dave looked down at the black water flowing far below him. He watched the reflection from the city's lights glisten off the waves. It looked like there were stars twinkling deep beneath the water. Then Dave lifted his head and looked at the real thing, staring out over the city. To Dave, the city looked magical at night. He'd always felt that way. The utter impossibility of it all amazed him. He wasn't going to pass up the one chance he'd probably ever have to see the city from his perch high above the East River. He felt like Spider-Man, for Christ's sake.

"Dave?" Dave suddenly heard a shouted whisper drift up from beneath him. "*Are you ready or what?*" Hector called up from about twenty feet below Dave. Hector was sitting on one of the cables, strapped into a piece of nylon rope with a carabiner on its end. A forty-pound box of explosives dangled in the air beneath him.

"*Yeah. Hook it up,*" Dave called to Hector before throwing down one end of about thirty feet of rope. Hector held on to the cable he was sitting on with one hand and reached out into the dark, empty space with his other, catching the end of the rope. Cars drove over the bridge below them. Hector and Dave could hear their engines and see their lights. A few late-night couples and tourists—the true romantics—were still walking across the bridge. All of them were blissfully unaware of what was going on over their heads. Hector took the end of the rope that Dave had thrown down to him and tied it to the box of explosives.

"*Here it goes,*" Hector shouted up to Dave. Dave nodded and braced himself. Then Hector let go of the box. The box swung through the empty night air. Dave waited until it stopped swinging, until it hung loose below him, and then he started pulling on the rope. It took five minutes for him to pull the box out of the darkness and onto the ledge where he was sitting. By the time he had pulled the box to the top, Hector had managed to climb to the top as well. Dave and Hector had climbed up almost the entire way in these fits and starts, pulling the box of explosives behind them. They started out on the footpath, carrying the box up from Brooklyn. Then they waited for a moment free of strangers. It was late, well past midnight, so the foot traffic on the bridge was intermittent. Once they found the right moment, Dave jumped onto the base of one of the thick cables and, as quickly as he could, scrambled up high enough that nobody on the bridge would think he was anything other than a strangely shaped shadow. Then he dropped the rope for Hector to attach to the explosives and they were on their way. It took them more than an hour to get all the way to the top of the tower. They might have been able to go faster, but once they'd disappeared into the shadows, they'd taken their time. Neither of them was in a rush to finish their job.

"If I'd known it was this easy to get up here, I would have tagged the shit out of this thing when I was a kid," Hector said to Dave as he sat down next to him. They dangled their legs over the tower's edge and looked at the city together. They could see everything from their secret perch. Without saying anything, both of them began taking a mental inventory of the targets, imagining that the people assigned to each of the other targets were doing the same thing at that moment. They were close enough to the Manhattan Bridge that they thought they might be able to see their counterparts climbing through its cables. The Williamsburg Bridge wasn't too far north of that. The East River was going to be a disaster area. The Verrazano-Narrows Bridge stood small in the distance to the south, but they could still see its lights towering over the water. They could even almost see the George Washington Bridge all the way on the other side of Manhattan. And then there was Manhattan, riddled with buildings being targeted. "You know P. T. Barnum once marched twenty-one elephants across this bridge just to prove that it wouldn't collapse," Hector said to Dave as they sat dangling their feet in the empty air.

"Yeah?" Dave answered.

"That was like a hundred years ago."

"I guess it didn't collapse?"

"Nope."

"A hundred years is a long time," Dave said to Hector.

"Do you think what we're doing is crazy?" Hector asked Dave as he stared at the hundreds of thousands of lights on in the windows of tens of thousands of buildings.

"Yeah," Dave said to Hector, "but sometimes you've got to fight crazy with crazy. You ready to hook this shit up?" Dave motioned towards the black box.

"Let's do it," Hector said.

The contents of the box had been prearranged. All Hector and Dave had to do was line it up properly and tie it down so that it wouldn't shift in the wind. It was set to detonate via remote control. Somewhere in the city, somebody had a button. Dave looked out over the city one last time when they were almost done. "You think that there's one button that sets everything off at once?"

Hector tightened the last knot holding the box in place. "That would be one serious fucking button," he said, looking over their handiwork. "Let's get out of here."

The two of them climbed back down the bridge's cables. When they were close to the bottom they pulled the hoods of their sweatshirts back up over their heads. Then they waited for a moment when no one was looking and they slipped off the cables and back into the flow of people walking over the bridge.

Fifty-seven

Brian and Jared didn't meet in Battery Park this time. They had too much to discuss to do it out in the open. Brian wasn't about to invite Jared back to the compound either, not with Christopher and Maria there. Brian and Reggie were all too aware of the powder keg they were building. It wasn't only that, though. Reggie still wasn't confident that they could trust Jared. They were doing their best to have people shadow Jared, to watch him. The problem was that none of those people had the access that Jared had. He was the only one who could get them where they needed to be. The people watching Jared did have their orders, though—to take him out at the first sign of anything suspicious. Jared had survived this far. So, instead of at Battery Park, Brian and Jared met at an out-of-the-way bar in Red Hook where they could be reasonably sure that no one was watching them.

"Does it have to be so messy?" Brian asked after Jared relayed the whole plan to him. Brian looked down at the papers that Jared had prepared. Jared had been careful not to give Brian anything too detailed. He had to make sure that they still needed him. If they wanted the plan, they were going to have to take him with it.

Jared took a swig from his beer. He wiped the foam off his lips with the back of his hand. "Did you guys really think that you were going to be able to end the War without getting your hands dirty?"

"But this is all over the city. These are innocent people." Brian looked at the map Jared had given him with each of the targets marked.

Jared laughed. "You're supposed to be rebels. You're not bound by the rules. If you were, Christopher wouldn't be a hero. He'd be shunned."

"It's not about the rules," Brian said, shaking his head. "It's about innocent people getting hurt."

Jared's frustration began to come through in his voice. "I think you and I have different definitions of what *innocent* means. You know as well as I do that the willful blindness of these 'innocent people' is the whole reason why the War has lasted as long as it has." Jared waited for Brian to say something. When he didn't, Jared lost his patience. "Fine," he said in answer to Brian's silence. "You guys can do what you want. But this plan"—Jared poked the papers on the table—"is the only way to be sure that this is going to work. If we don't distract them with chaos, if we don't light this city up, then all those innocent people that you're worried about protecting are going to come down on us and they're going to come down hard. Do you know what that means?" Jared asked Brian, rolling now like he hadn't in years.

"What?" Brian deadpanned, knowing full well that he was being used as the straight man.

"It means that we don't destroy the Intelligence Center because we don't have time. It means that the War limps on and all the work that you guys have done will have been for nothing. Worse, after your little rebellion ends, the War will get stronger. If you fail this time, no one is going to follow you again because they'll have lost faith in what Christopher represents and there's never going to be another Christopher. The War won't allow it. And all that to save a few people whose only saving grace is that they were born of parents lucky enough to not be part of the War. Is that what you want?"

Brian leaned back in his chair. He took a sip of his beer. It was dark and bitter. "No," Brian answered.

"Who's making the call here?" Jared asked, pulling the papers back from Brian, unwilling to let him keep even the generic stuff.

"Reggie," Brian answered.

"What about the kid? What about Christopher?"

"He's already done enough."

Jared laughed. "Are you telling me that the kid doesn't have any say in his own revolution?"

"He's still just a kid."

Jared paused, not sure if now was the right time to make his demand. He thought maybe he should wait for Brian to take the plan back to Reggie. Maybe then Jared would have more leverage. But he decided not to wait. He picked up his beer and knocked back the third of a glass that was left in two gulps. Then he set the glass on the table and stared at Brian. "Did you know that I was the one that fired you when you used to handle Joseph?"

"I had my suspicions," Brian answered.

"I thought you were a bad influence on him. I thought you were making him soft."

"I wasn't making him anything."

"Yeah, I know." Jared motioned to the waitress for another beer. "It was Maria, but I didn't know that then. And then the kid came along."

"Where are you going with all of this, Jared?" Brian asked, beginning to lose his own patience. He didn't have the type of time that Jared had.

Jared stared down at the table. "I want to meet Christopher," he said.

"No way." Brian shook his head.

"You don't even have to tell him it's me," Jared bargained. "I just want to see what all the fuss is about."

"Why would we let you anywhere near Christopher with your history? We're not even sure if we can trust you yet."

"You can trust me, Brian. Because you're trying to erase history, and nobody has more reason to want history erased than I do."

"I'll talk to Reggie, but I wouldn't get your hopes up." Brian stood up. "I'll be in touch," he said. Then he walked away.

Jared remained in the booth. He finished his beer. When he was done, he ordered another one.

Fifty-eight

Everything was going fine until the lights went out. Christopher was talking to Alejandro when the room went dark. Alejandro reacted quickly to the darkness, pushing Christopher into a corner and putting his body in front of Christopher's to shield him from whatever it was that might be attacking them. Christopher moved without knowing what was happening. He couldn't see anything. His body hit the wall after Alejandro pushed him and he turned around. When he turned around, the only thing that he could make out in the darkness was Alejandro's back.

It wasn't supposed to be this way. This was supposed to be the easy one. "No inquisition this time," Reggie had promised Christopher. The Americas was supposed to be a foregone conclusion. Reggie set up a room in the back of the warehouse that was large enough to fit everybody. It was dangerous putting everyone in a single room in the middle of Brooklyn, but sometimes you have to balance risk and reward. The risks were high, but the way Reggie saw it, the rewards would be worth it. It was a show of confidence. If this night went well, the whole world would be united.

Christopher walked into the already full makeshift banquet room with Addy on his arm. She'd found him half an hour earlier, still getting ready for the evening. Reggie had asked Christopher to dress for the event—no tie, but a shirt with a collar and a sports coat. The only other time Christopher could remember wearing a sports coat was when he'd had to go to the funeral of a great-aunt. She died in her home at the age of eighty-two. At the time, Christopher didn't even know people could live that long. Christopher put the jacket on and stared at himself in the mirror. The jacket was a little bit broad in the shoulders but was otherwise a good fit. Brian had had it delivered earlier that morning. He had estimated Christopher's size. Christopher was still staring at himself in the mirror when he heard a knock near the entrance to the room he was given. Christopher thought it would be Reggie or Brian or maybe Evan or Maria. "Come in," Christopher called out, staring at the reflection of the entrance to his room in the mirror.

Addy walked in. Christopher saw her in the mirror. Their eyes met in the reflection. She saw that Christopher was still getting ready. "Is it okay if I come in?" she asked.

"Of course," Christopher answered. He and Addy hadn't exchanged more than a few words since he'd gotten back. She'd deferred to Evan and Maria, knowing her small role in Christopher's life.

"Big night," Addy said as she stepped closer to Christopher.

"How so?" Christopher asked, watching her reflection move toward him, looking to see if she got his joke.

"This is it," Addy said. "After tonight, everything is official."

"Then I guess it is a big night," Christopher agreed as he turned to face the real Addy.

"You look good," Addy said, looking Christopher up and down. She stepped in front of him and reached out to fix the crease on one of his lapels.

Christopher was glad Addy had come to see him. He wanted to get something off his chest. "Listen, Addy," Christopher started, "I wanted to tell you how sorry I was for leaving you and Evan the way I did. I didn't know about the raid. Reggie didn't even tell me about it until yesterday. He promised me that he didn't know about it beforehand. He promised me that my leaving that night was purely a coincidence."

"Promises," Addy echoed with a playful lift of her eyebrows.

"Well, at least I didn't know," Christopher said. "I wouldn't have left you guys if I'd known."

"And then none of us would be here." Addy laughed. "You don't need to apologize to me and Evan. We're on your side no matter what."

Addy's words were a relief to Christopher. "So, you and Evan, huh?"

"Yeah," Addy said, adding coyly, "but you knew that before you left."

"I did, but I didn't know it was going to last."

"I was the opposite." Addy smiled. "I didn't know it was going to happen, but as soon as it happened, I knew it was going to last." Christopher caught a slight blush on her cheeks. "We didn't mean anything by it, Christopher. If that's why you left, I mean."

"You and Evan don't need to apologize to me. I'm happy for the two of you. I didn't leave because of you."

"Then why did you leave?"

"I don't know. I got scared. I saw how all those people looked at me. I saw how you looked at me, and I knew that I couldn't be the person that you all saw."

"But look at you now," Addy said, barely able to hide the thrill in her voice.

"It's not what you think," Christopher said. Addy hadn't been in Indonesia or in Istanbul. She didn't know that all Christopher did was tell the truth to people who'd been waiting for a long time to hear it. He wasn't a hero. He didn't do anything. By a fluke of circumstances, he was the only person that they would all listen to. He was still only a cog in the machine. But he didn't want to debate that. He didn't want to talk about himself at all. It wasn't only because he still didn't feel like a hero or a prophet or a leader. It was also because he didn't want to be any of those things. After everything that had happened to him, after being paranoid his entire life only to have that paranoia justified, Christopher still hadn't figured out what he wanted—other than for all of this to be over so that he could have the simple life that other people had. So he changed the subject. "So what's next after all of this for you and Evan?"

"I don't know. What do you think? Maybe you and me and Evan should move to an island somewhere where nobody remembers your and Evan's faces." Christopher had almost forgotten that he wasn't merely the War's most wanted man. He was a fugitive in the real world now too—he and Evan. Christopher had heard what Evan did for Addy and how it had made the rounds on the news. "Maybe we can find you a nice local girl there so you don't have to be our third wheel forever," Addy teased.

"That sounds nice," Christopher said, smiling at the thought. "Your hair—the red is growing out. Are you going to dye it again?"

Addy reached up and pulled a few strands of her hair in front of her face to look at the color. "I haven't decided yet. Evan likes the natural color." She paused, looking down at her watch. "So, are you ready for this?" she asked, motioning toward the door.

"Yeah," Christopher answered. He'd never felt so ready for anything in his life. He was ready for the beginning of the end.

Reggie had done what he could to formalize the event. They had drinks in the back of the room—nothing fancy, merely beer in coolers, but even that was something. The room was almost full by the time Christopher and Addy walked in. People had already cracked open the beer. Addy and Christopher didn't pause at the door, so it took a few moments before anyone noticed that they had arrived. As soon as someone finally saw them, the applause began. It was sparse at first, but grew as each set of eyes in the room found Christopher. When about half the room had caught on, Addy slipped away from Christopher's side so that he was standing alone. Then she began to clap too. Before long, it was almost everyone. Christopher's eyes scanned the room. They met Reggie's and Brian's. He saw Evan, standing near the back of the room. For a moment, Christopher let himself forget that they hadn't actually accomplished anything yet. Only one person in the room wasn't clapping. Maria was standing in a corner, her eyes wet with tears, her arms crossed over her chest.

Reggie took a fork and banged on a beer bottle to draw everyone's attention. Christopher's eyes moved from his mother to Reggie. The room became silent. "I wanted to welcome our guest of honor," Reggie said, his eyes falling on Christopher. "I'm sure he will take the time to speak to each of you if you like. But before we start the mingling, I should note that I have been informed that the Americas have officially joined us and the rest of the world in this one chance to end the War." Reggie's words were met with more applause, this time even louder than before. Reggie lifted his beer in the air, "To the end of paranoia," he said. Everyone in the room raised a glass to Reggie's toast. Christopher looked over at Maria. This time, even she lifted her glass and smiled.

The mingling began after the toast. People flocked around Christopher. He was the candle to their moths. They came to him with stories to tell about their own youth and their own parents and their own revolts against the War. When the stories were over, they came to him with questions. They asked him for advice about their own plans, their hometown plans to rid the world of the Intelligence Centers. He heard stories about armed boats riding along the coast of Costa Rica, beaching themselves and letting off gunmen like in a miniature Normandy. He heard stories about a frontal assault on a building in the shantytowns of Rio. Then he heard whispers about New York, about explosions, citywide mayhem, and mass hysteria but no specifics. Reggie hadn't told Christopher anything about New York yet. Christopher heard everything thirdhand. He wanted to know more. He wanted to know what was being done in his name. He'd known that Reggie was hiding something from him. When he met Maria, Christopher thought that might be it, but there was more. Christopher now knew that there was more.

Out of the blue, another beer bottle was being raised and tapped like a bell. Christopher was shocked to see that this time it was Evan who had drawn the attention of the room to himself. He got the attention, apparently more quickly than he had anticipated, since for a few seconds, he stood frozen as everyone stared at him. "Speak," Addy yelled from the back of the room. That seemed to break Evan's trance. He cleared his throat and said, "I just wanted to say that Christopher has always been like a brother to me. Neither of us had our own brothers. We only had each other." Evan's eyes searched out Christopher in the throng of people. When his eyes connected with Christopher's, he finished, "No matter what happens, Christopher will always be a brother to me. I am willing to share my brother with all of you in order to get this done. Then, when it's over, I want my brother back."

The cheers for Evan's speech were more muted and less confident than the cheers for Reggie's had been.

Alejandro was the first person to reach Christopher after Evan spoke. Christopher shook Alejandro's hand and Alejandro told Christopher where he was from. "Costa Rica," Christopher echoed, remembering what he'd been told earlier that evening. "Will you be on the boat?"

"No," Alejandro said with pride, "I will meet the boat on the beach," and Christopher couldn't help but be proud too. Then, without warning, the lights went out and the room went dark.

Panic looks different when you're in a room full of people who've been taught since they were young never to panic. It's not loud and chaotic. It's silent and it's swift. Everyone in the room moved through the darkness like they were part of a rehearsed, silent ballet. In seconds, each of them either found cover—in a corner or behind a piece of furniture—or crouched down, making as small a target as possible. Those who had weapons, which were most of them, drew them. Alejandro pulled a knife from his pocket. Christopher saw the shine of the metal. Alejandro's body blocked everything else. Alejandro was using his own body as a shield, placing it in front of Christopher, putting Christopher's life ahead of his own. Christopher hated it. With everyone in place with weapons drawn, the room froze and waited. They all knew that there was nowhere to go. They'd stand there, fight there, and win or die there.

A voice cut through the darkness. It was an unexpected whisper. "Everyone stay quiet," the voice said. "There are people outside the building. We don't know what they're doing here, but we're watching them. Hang tight." Then the voice was gone and the room was silent again. A few people took the moment to reposition themselves so that they were facing the door, ready to pounce if necessary.

"You don't have to protect me," Christopher whispered to Alejandro's back.

Alejandro lifted his hand, motioning for Christopher to stay quiet. Evan was in the back of the room, not far from where he'd given his toast, squatting down near the floor. Addy was closer to the door, muscles tense, ready to rush the door if it came to that. Maria was across the room from Christopher, her eyes not moving from the spot where she knew her son to be, not ready to lose him again. The silence and the darkness lasted for another twenty minutes. For twenty minutes, nobody moved and nobody made a sound. Then as quickly and unexpectedly as they'd gone off, the lights came back on. Christopher could see the room now, like a statue garden, everyone but him in fighting position.

"False alarm," the whisperer returned, obviously now a member of Reggie's security team. "It was just a couple of kids painting graffiti on the building next door. They're gone now."

"You sure?" Reggie called out to him, still speaking in his own elevated whisper.

"Yes," the guard answered. "They're gone. It was nothing."

"Okay," Reggie called out to the room in a normal voice now. "Perhaps that should be our sign to call it a night. I think most of us can hold off on any more adventure until we're the ones causing it." Reggie's declaration was met by murmurs of consent. Without any more fanfare, people started moving toward the door.

Alejandro began walking silently toward the door too. Christopher caught up to him and put a hand on his shoulder, stopping him. "You didn't have to do that," Christopher repeated to Alejandro.

Alejandro turned back toward Christopher. "Yes, I did," he said. He said nothing more and then turned and headed for the door.

Christopher stayed. He watched the room empty slowly. He waited until almost everyone was gone except for Reggie and a few stragglers, but he kept his eyes on Reggie and not the others. Christopher walked up to Reggie. He didn't waste any time on formalities. "I want to know what the plan is for New York," he said.

"I already told you. We'll find a part for you, something real but safe."

"I don't want you to find a part for me. I want to know the details. I want to have a say. I don't want another person to die in my name while I stand on the edges doing nothing but talking."

"I can't," Reggie replied. "You've done everything already, Christopher. You should be proud of what you've done for us. I'll give you something, but I need you to be safe. I've gone back on enough promises about you already." Reggie turned away from Christopher and started to walk away.

"What promises?" Christopher called, confused. He was sick of being confused. "What else are you hiding from me?"

"Promises he made to me," said a voice behind him. It was Maria. "Years ago I made Reggie promise me that he would protect you from becoming involved in the War. But here you are anyway."

"Is that why you pushed me to run first?" Christopher asked Reggie.

Reggie nodded. "But then you ended up with Dutty. So I figured that if you were going to choose to fight anyway, I should at least try to give you a gambler's chance of winning."

Maria jumped into the conversation again. "But a promise is a promise. So Reggie owed me one promise, and with it I made him promise me that he would keep you out of danger from now on. You've done enough already, Christopher. You shouldn't have to do any more. Let them finish it. It's their War, not ours."

"Maybe it's not your War," Christopher said to Maria, "but it is mine—at least until it's over. It's always been inside of me. I've spent my life trying to get it out. Nobody is going to be able to do that for me." Christopher turned back to Reggie. "I need to know the plan. I'm sick of people making my decisions for me. Besides, you're hiding something from me, Reggie. I can tell."

"There are parts of the plan that you're not going to like," Reggie answered.

"Those are the parts that I want to know about the most." Christopher's voice trembled. Reggie looked at Maria, waiting for a sign from her that it was okay to speak, but she was like a stone. "Don't look at her," Christopher said to Reggie. "She has no say in this."

"But I'm your mother, Christopher," Maria said.

The three of them stood in the middle of the empty room. Christopher shot Maria a look. He was too kind to respond to her with anything more. The look was enough. The look tore at Maria's heart. "Tell me what I'm not going to like about the plan," Christopher demanded of Reggie.

Reggie looked to Maria again, wanting to do right by her, pleading with her with his eyes. "Tell me!" Christopher demanded when Maria refused to respond to Reggie's stare.

"To be sure that the plan will work, a lot of innocent people are going to get hurt and a lot will probably die," Reggie said to Christopher. "We're planting bombs around the city as a diversion. Without the diversion we don't have a chance."

"And this is your plan?" Christopher asked. It didn't seem like a plan that Reggie would devise.

"No," Reggie admitted. "We have a source on the inside that we're working with." Reggie hoped the questioning would die with that.

It almost worked. Christopher didn't think any more of it. His thoughts were on the plan, but Maria's thoughts were on the source. "Who is it?" Maria asked, even though, deep down, she already knew.

"We didn't do it on purpose," Reggie said, apologizing to both Maria and Christopher now, before they could even be sure what he was apologizing for. "We couldn't afford to take any shortcuts. Of all the people who could help us, he's the best by far. He knows everything and no one is more bitter than him."

"Who are we talking about?" Christopher asked, still not filling in the gaps but feeling nervous all the same.

"Our man inside—," Reggie started.

"Who is it?" Christopher demanded.

"It's Jared," Reggie said. Maria physically flinched when she heard the name.

"The man who killed my father?"

"The man who stole you from me," Maria said.

"He's a spy?" Christopher asked, dumbfounded.

"He is now."

Christopher was in shock. He reacted like a cornered animal, flailing at the greatest threat first. "I want to meet him," he said, expanding on his demands. Now he wanted everything, every goddamn thing. "I want to meet Jared and I want him to explain the plan to me."

Reggie looked at Christopher, with deep, sad eyes. "If he's going to meet Jared, I'm going with him," Maria announced. She wasn't about to let him face that demon alone.

"This isn't negotiable, Reggie," Christopher said. What had Addy once told him? Nobody gets what they want, and those that do want something else as soon as they get it. But what if all you wanted was for things to make sense?

Fifty-nine

Jared was surprised when Brian called him to arrange the meeting. He thought that his request to meet Christopher was nothing more than a shot in the dark, but there he was, standing in a small apartment on 130th Street on Manhattan's West Side, waiting. A man named George had patted him down before letting him into the apartment. Jared didn't complain. He couldn't blame them, all things considered. "Are you going to pat them down too?" Jared asked, handing George the gun he was carrying before George had a chance to feel it in his belt.

"No," George answered flatly. So Jared was going to be the only person hated by everyone else in that room and he was also likely going to be the only person in the room who was unarmed. George opened the apartment door and Jared walked inside.

Jared wondered what he was going to say to them. He hadn't really thought this through. Some things you just can't plan. Brian had told him that Maria was coming too. Jared didn't know who else would be there. For all he knew, this might be a setup. For all Jared knew, he wasn't going to walk out of this apartment alive. He'd made peace with that. He was an old man by soldier standards. *If this is supposed to be the end,* Jared thought to himself, *at least there'll be some drama to it.*

Jared paced up and down inside the apartment, waiting for the others, unable to sit for more than a few seconds. He was trying to burn nervous energy. He'd been pacing for more than twenty minutes when he finally heard a sound outside the door. He saw the doorknob begin to turn. Only then did he sit down. He picked a seat facing the door. He watched as the doorknob finished turning. He watched the door begin to open. The next thing he knew, he was pulled back in time.

When the door swung open, Jared saw his old friend Joseph standing in front of him, but the strangest part was, it wasn't the Joseph from the last time Jared had seen him alive. It was the Joseph from when they were both boys growing up. It was the Joseph from high school in New Jersey. Jared almost said something to his old friend and then the two people standing behind Joseph broke his trance. Then it wasn't Joseph anymore. It was a boy. The similarities were still there, but there were differences too. The boy was smaller than Joseph and he had an intensity about him that Jared never remembered seeing in Joseph—not until that last time they met anyway.

"You must be Christopher," Jared said to the boy as he stepped into the room. Maria was right behind him. She was so much older than Jared remembered. Time had hardened her. Behind Maria was a tall black man. Jared recognized Reggie too, but only because he'd seen his picture at work. Reggie was one of the War's most wanted rebels.

"You're Jared?" Christopher asked, staring at the old man sitting in front of him. He was thin, almost frail. His hair was thinning and his skin was peppered with age spots. The man in the chair didn't match the powerful image of Jared that Christopher had in his head.

"I am," Jared said to Christopher. Then he turned to Reggie. "And you must be the infamous Reggie."

"Well, I guess we got the introductions out of the way," Reggie said.

"Not all of them," Maria said, stepping forward and staring at Jared. "Do you remember me?"

"Of course," Jared responded. "How could I forget the woman who turned my two best friends against me?"

"Enough of that," Reggie broke in. "That's not what we're here for. We don't have time for the past here."

"Fair enough," Jared said. "Then what are we here for?"

"Christopher wanted to know about the plan," Reggie told him.

"So you brought him here so that I could tell him what you were afraid to?"

"I've told him. He wanted to hear it from you," Reggie said. "We told him it was your plan."

"You told him all the details?" Jared asked Reggie with a smile.

"No," Reggie admitted. "Not all the details."

"Okay," Jared said. "Have a seat." Jared motioned to the chair across from him. Christopher moved slowly toward the chair. "Don't worry, Christopher," Jared said. "They patted me down before I came in here. You're safe. So you want to know about the plan?"

"Yeah," Christopher responded.

"That's why you're here?" Jared asked him.

"Yes," Christopher answered.

"You're not here because you want an apology?" Jared looked at Maria. "She's not here because she wants an apology? You just want to know the plan?"

"Yes," Christopher repeated.

"Okay," Jared said. "That's good. Because I'm not going to apologize to you or to her."

"Okay," Christopher said with a raised chin.

"The way I figure it, there's only one person who I might owe an apology to and it's not you and it's not her." Jared pointed at Maria.

"I told you, I'm not asking for an apology. I only want to talk about the plan. I only want this all to be over."

"Me too," Jared said. That was enough of a thread to pull them together. Jared began to tell Christopher about the plan. He told Christopher about the targets, about the buildings, about the bridges, and about the bombs. Christopher imagined explosions and screams coming from all over the city, all a mere diversion so that no one would pay attention to the real target. Christopher assumed that they'd use bombs there too. They could take out all four floors in one blow.

"That's insane," Christopher said. "Why do we need to hurt all these innocent people?"

"Innocent?" Jared spoke to Christopher as if he were the only other person in the room. He didn't care about Maria or Reggie. He only cared about the Child, about his best friend's son.

"They're innocent," Christopher repeated. "They've got nothing to do with this War."

"Just because they're not part of our War doesn't mean they're innocent," Jared said. "Everybody hates somebody. Most people just don't keep a list. You tell me who's more innocent: the ten-year-old who was born into the War but hasn't been told about it yet or the thirty-year-old who's spent the better part of his life ignoring the evidence that the War exists. Who is more innocent? Tell me."

"I don't do riddles," Christopher said.

"Well, you should," Jared told Christopher, "because solving riddles is the only way you're ever going to get answers to any questions around here."

"There has to be a better way," Christopher said.

"There's not. We can cut corners to save the lives of some strangers, but every corner we cut makes it less likely that the plan is going to work. We're only going to get one chance at this. Brian and Reggie have already agreed." Jared looked up at Reggie. "I heard that they're the ones in charge. What makes you think you have a say in this anyway? How long have you been a part of this War? Four weeks?" Jared shook his head. "What do you know, really? Your father understood how little he knew and he'd been knee-deep in the War for years before he died."

"Before you killed him?" Christopher said before Maria could.

"Before I killed him," Jared confirmed.

The anger began to rise within Christopher. "It doesn't matter what I know. I get a say because this is my revolution," Christopher told Jared, clenching his fists. "This is my Uprising. It's mine and Addy's and Evan's. It's not yours. You had your chance. You all had your chance. You wasted it. You could have had your own revolution, but you chose to kill your best friend instead. So don't tell me how little I know."

"Your Uprising?" Jared asked with a smile. He liked the kid's fire. He appreciated the fire.

"Yes," Christopher said through clenched teeth. Christopher finally realized what he wanted. He felt it in him. He didn't want power or glory. He didn't want fame. He wanted this all to end, sure, but before that happened he wanted something else. "After everything I've been through," Christopher said, glancing at Reggie and Maria, "I want some control over my own life. I know you guys did what you did to protect me, and I appreciate it, but that's over."

Jared laughed. "You want control?"

"Yes," Christopher answered.

"Take it from somebody who knows, control is an illusion, kid," Jared replied.

"Don't listen to him, Christopher," Maria said, nearly shouting. "You can control your life. You can." She ran up to Christopher, grabbed his hand, and stared into his eyes. "That's all I ever wanted for you. That's all your father wanted for you. He never had it. Neither did I. But you can, and if this is what you need to do to get it, then don't listen to him," Maria said, shooting daggers at Jared with her eyes.

Christopher looked up at Reggie and Reggie said, "I know I've been walking a thin line, trying to use you to start this Uprising but trying to protect you at the same time. I thought that was what would be best for you, but this is your Uprising. It doesn't exist without you. Remember, whatever you decide to do impacts a lot more people than the four of us."

Christopher didn't say anything. He took in what Maria and Reggie said to him, the gifts that they'd bestowed on him, and then he turned back to Jared.

"Well, then," Jared said, "if this is your Uprising, let me give you some advice. *They're* not going to care about collateral damage or hurting innocent people when they see you coming. They're going to do whatever it takes to destroy *your* Uprising. They have rules for when they fight each other but not for when they fight you. They know full well what they have—what you're trying to take from them. It's not just history. It's a history stripped bare of pleasantries. It's a history of hate and fear. Whoever controls that part of history has all the power." Jared leaned forward, closer to Christopher. "I've seen what they do to dissidents. I've been there. They showed me. They wanted me to learn in case I was thinking of following in my friends' footsteps. I've heard the screams. I've seen the blood and the torn flesh. You're a kid. You don't know the wrath of what you're about to go up against. I do. I know what will happen to all of us if you fail. So, if this is your Uprising, then I suggest you drop the sentimentality and do whatever it takes to win it."

Sixty

The start of the Uprising was only twelve hours away and everywhere was quiet. It was quiet in Tokyo. It was quiet in Cambodia and in Istanbul and in Paris. It was quiet in Rio and in Costa Rica. It was even quiet in New York. The quiet wasn't going to last. It had been a week since Christopher met with Jared that first night. At first, Christopher didn't think one week was enough time. Then Reggie explained to him that each of the plans was almost complete, that all that was left, for the most part, were minor details and logistics. "The most dangerous part now is the waiting," Reggie told Christopher. "The longer we wait, the more likely it is that somebody who knows something leaks information or gets caught. If someone gets caught, there's a good chance they might give something away. Even the best people crack under certain extreme pressures."

"Are you sure that's enough time?"

"People have been waiting for almost as long as you've been alive. It's enough time."

"Okay," Christopher said to Reggie, his heart pounding. "Tell everyone to get ready."

So Reggie and Brian sent the word out. Everyone scattered back to their home bases to prepare. They had seven days and now those seven days had dwindled to twelve hours. It was nearing noon in New York. The explosives had been planted throughout the city the night before. No matter how the night ended, the quiet wasn't going to last.

Evan was walking through the makeshift halls of the warehouse in Brooklyn, looking for Christopher. He'd heard that Christopher wanted to talk to him. The place seemed empty now that most people had gone back to their homes in South America or Central America or wherever else they were headed to prepare for their part in the Uprising. Only ten of them remained: Christopher, Evan, Addy, Reggie, Brian, Maria, and four others who had nowhere else to go. Evan had been with Addy. They wanted to be alone together one more time, in case it was the last time. Every time Evan entered Addy, the two of them were blissfully tightening the knots in the ropes that would bind them together forever. This last time, they were slow and patient, trying to pretend that it never had to end. Then it ended.

The halls were quiet. The loudest sound that Evan could hear was the sound of his own footsteps on the concrete floors. He walked slowly toward the back of the building where Christopher slept and stayed when he wanted to be alone. "Chris," Evan called out, turning another corner. "Are you there?"

"I'm over here." Evan heard a voice coming from his right, from the makeshift office. It really wasn't much more than a cheap desk and three chairs, but it served its purpose.

Evan peeked through the doorway. "I heard you were looking for me," Evan said to Christopher. Christopher was sitting behind the desk, staring at a bunch of papers that he'd laid out. He felt overwhelmed and inadequate, but at least he was doing something. At least he had that.

"I was," Christopher said. "I wanted to talk to you about tonight, about the plan. I talked to Reggie. There's something that we want you to do."

"I told you that I want to go in with you," Evan said. "I don't want to be stuck on the sidelines. I'm only here because of you. We should be in this together."

"You've got other reasons to be here now," Christopher said to Evan. Evan knew that Christopher was talking about Addy. "But I told you that I would find something for you," Christopher said. "I promised."

"So what is it?" Evan asked. "And don't you dare give me some bullshit job so you can say that you kept your promise."

"It's not a bullshit job," Christopher said. "I need to explain the plan to you first, though." Christopher looked at the papers on the desk in front of him. "There's a little more to it than what I think you probably know."

"I'm listening."

"Tell me what you know first."

"I know about the bombs," Evan said. "I know that they're meant to be a distraction to keep civilians away from the Intelligence Center. I know that once those bombs go off, a team is going to attack the Intelligence Center. I heard that the plan was to blow that up too."

"That's all you know?" Christopher asked.

"I haven't really been kept in the loop."

"I know," Christopher said. "I wanted to protect you. Just because I had no choice to become a part of this doesn't mean you had to too. Then I realized that I need you, so here we are."

"You need me?" Evan repeated it to make sure he'd heard Christopher correctly.

"Yes," Christopher said.

"What for?" Evan asked.

"We're afraid to use bombs in the Intelligence Center," Christopher told Evan. "It's too risky. Even if we brought the whole building down, some of the information might survive. We have to make sure we destroy all of it. There are no moral victories."

"Then what are you going to do? You can't exactly shred it all."

"No. Instead of bombs, we're going to use this flammable gas that Jared told us about. He said he'd heard about it being used in the past but on a smaller scale. It's highly flammable. It catches easily. It burns extremely hot and burns out fast."

"What has it been used for in the past?" Evan asked. Even he didn't trust Jared.

"I didn't ask. I didn't want to know but Brian knew about it too. Brian confirmed that the gas would work," Christopher said. "The Intelligence Center covers five stories. Each story requires about one tank of gas. Six of us are going to go in—each one of us with a tank of gas. That gives us one extra tank in case one of us doesn't make it. Once inside, we're going to seal the place up so that the gas can't leak out. We'll seal the doors and the windows. We'll make sure that all of the inner drawers and doors are open. Then we'll release the gas. It will only take a few minutes for the rooms to fill up. We figure fifteen minutes at most. Then, all it will take is one small spark and the whole place will burn in seconds. Everything in it will turn to dust. Once we've let all the gas out, we'll get the hell out of there."

"So what do you need me for?"

"You're the spark. Once we're out, we'll need someone to light the fire. Remember, it only takes one spark. We want you to be on top of the building across the street. We've got a rifle for you. All you need to do is take one shot into the building. You don't even have to hit anything. One shot and everything will burn."

"Why do you need me for that, Chris? Anybody could do that."

"Yeah, Reggie had given the job to somebody else. I asked him to let you do it."

"Why?"

"Because whoever is on that roof is also going to have a radio. Whoever is on that roof is going to be our eyes on the world. You're going to tell us what's happening outside."

"I still don't get why you need me."

Christopher looked at Evan. "I want it to be your voice that I hear on the radio because you're still the only real friend I have." Christopher hesitated before saying anything else, but then decided to go on. "I want it to be your voice on the radio because I'm afraid." There was a tremor in Christopher's voice. "I think that hearing your voice will make me less afraid."

"What are we going to do when the War is over, Chris?" Evan asked. "It's not like we can go home. We're not just a couple of loser kids in Maine anymore. We're fugitives now. Tonight isn't going to change that. In a lot of ways, we fit in better inside the War than out of it. In here, we're revolutionaries. Out there, we're nothing but a couple of criminals."

"It'll be different when the War ends," Christopher promised Evan, trying to convince himself that the words were true even as he said them. "Addy said we should all move to an island where no one would recognize us."

"That sounds nice," Evan said, though he couldn't picture it in his head.

"So, do you want to be the guy who fires the shot that ends the War?"

The start of the Uprising was only twelve hours away and Jared was sitting in his office trying to pretend that everything was normal. He was getting ready to go to lunch when he received a call from one of the secretaries. He was being summoned to one of the corner offices. They didn't tell him why.

Jared hung up the phone. He took a second to compose himself. Lying wasn't an issue for him. He did that every day—to himself, to others. He wasn't nervous about the lying, but he had hoped to escape the day without any bullshit. On most days the bullshit was a mere annoyance, but today it could be trouble. Jared had a schedule to keep and things that he needed to do, though nothing he had to do was as important as making everything appear normal. He knew that. So he composed himself, stood up, and made his way toward the office as he'd been ordered to do.

The door to the office was half open. Jared knocked anyway before sticking his head inside. "I was about to go grab some lunch, but I heard that you wanted to see me," Jared said to the man sitting behind the desk. The man was another wunderkind, another boy ten years Jared's junior who was making decisions that Jared would never be given the authority to make.

"Jared," the man said when he saw Jared leaning through the doorway. "Yeah, come in. I wanted to talk to you." Jared took a few steps into the office. "Close the door behind you."

Jared did as he was told, closing the door and cutting them off from the rest of the office. "Sit down," the man behind the desk ordered Jared, motioning to one of the plush leather chairs on the other side of his desk.

"This can't wait?" Jared protested. "Can't we talk after lunch?"

"No. This can't wait," the man said, deadly serious. "Sit down."

"All right." Jared sat. "What's going on, Peter?"

Peter tapped his fingers on the desk. "Have you heard anything about Christopher recently?" he asked Jared. Jared should have been more ready for the question than he was, but he'd seen no evidence that anyone was suspicious of anything.

"Not since we lost him in Singapore," Jared lied. "Since then, it's been radio silence."

"I got a report this morning that claims that he was spotted in Istanbul over a week ago and that the last anyone saw of him, he was boarding a flight to New York. You don't know anything about that?"

Jared shrugged. "We hear rumors all the time. People see the kid everywhere. He's like Elvis or Bigfoot. I haven't heard anything that could be substantiated. What makes you think this rumor is real?"

"It's not a rumor. They've got airport surveillance photos. I've seen them. How could you not hear about this?"

"They don't show me things that they don't show you first," Jared told Peter, deciding on flattery as his first defense. "What does it mean anyway? Even if it's true, you said that it was over a week ago. He'd be long gone by now."

"Yeah," Peter began to agree, "or he could still be in New York, planning something."

"Planning something?" Jared laughed. "He's a kid. He's worse than a kid. He's a kid with no experience. How could he plan anything? Are you really afraid of this kid?"

"He's survived this long. Nobody expected that," Peter said, staring at Jared.

"Luck," Jared said, not liking where this conversation was going.

"Maybe," Peter conceded. "Or maybe he's working with people." Peter leaned in toward Jared. "Maybe he's got people on the inside who want to help him."

"You think we have spies?" Jared feigned surprise.

"I don't know. What do you think? You've been around here longer than anybody."

That was why Jared had been called in—because he was old. "I think he's a kid. I think everybody's getting all worked up over an ordinary kid. The luck will run out and everybody's going to feel stupid for caring so much. And I'm not just talking about us. I'm talking about the rebels too. These things, they come and go." Jared waved his hand in front of him as if he were shooing away a fly.

"You're probably right," Peter said, to Jared's relief. "This place is a fucking vault anyway. Nobody can get in here—not alive. Remember the last group that tried? How far did they get, the front door? It was like a war zone in here and they never even got the door open."

Jared remembered. He nodded to Peter. The last group that tried weren't rebels. They were from the other side. Normally, when the other side discovers one of your locations, you move it. Not this time. This time, they kept it as a sign of strength. It was a message. *We don't care that you know we're here because you can't get in anyway.* But those guys didn't know what Jared knew. They didn't know the holes in the system. They didn't have the right plan.

Peter kept talking. "Do you remember what you did to that one guy to make him talk?" Jared nodded again. He remembered. "I've never seen someone beg for mercy so fast."

"I don't play games," Jared said to Peter. "Speaking of which, can I go? Are you satisfied that we don't have anything to worry about?"

"You can go," Peter said, waving Jared away with his hand. Jared stood up and started to walk toward the door. "I'm still going to double the security, though," Peter said. "Just in case." Jared stopped. If they doubled the security, his plan wouldn't work. Jared knew it. If they doubled the security, no plan would work. They would fail and everyone would fail with them.

Jared turned back toward Peter. He could still save this. "Okay, you want me to send out the orders? We can probably bulk up the security by tomorrow night." *All we need is tonight*, Jared thought.

"No," Peter told him. "I'll tell everybody. No offense to you, but if I tell them they'll get the extra security in place now. We won't have to wait until tomorrow night. When I tell them to jump, they don't ask how high. They just fucking jump."

Jared tried to think about his options. He tried to think about what card to play here. "You want to put it in place now? I'm telling you, Peter, you're going overboard. You're going to scare people."

"Scaring people doesn't bother me," Peter said. "People work harder when they're scared."

Jared needed another tack, another plan. "You know, now that you mention spies, I do have something I might want to show you. It didn't really register with me until now, but it might be interesting."

Peter gave Jared a skeptical look. "What is it?" he asked.

"It's in my office," Jared told Peter. "Do you want me to go get it and show it to you?"

"You tell me you have something about spies and then you ask me if I want to see it? What do you think? Stop wasting my time. Go get it and bring it back here."

"I'll be right back," Jared said. Then he turned and opened Peter's office door. He glanced at the desks surrounding Peter's office. They were all empty. Almost everyone was at lunch. "Give me two minutes," Jared called back to Peter. Jared rushed back to his cramped little office. People would be coming back from lunch soon. There was paper on Jared's desk. It was blank. And a metal pen. Jared grabbed them both. He felt quick on his feet again, like he used to feel when he was young. He jotted something down on one of the pieces of paper and then put them all under his arm. He put the pen in his pocket. Then he walked back toward Peter's corner office. Jared thought for a second about what exactly he should tell Peter. The truth was, if the rebels were going to fail, Jared would be far better off if he had nothing to do with them.

Back at Peter's office Jared knocked on the door and again waited for permission to enter. "Come in, damn it," Peter, ten-years-Jared's-junior, yelled at Jared.

Jared held up the blank paper in his hand, only the top sheet having any writing on it. "We should do this in private," Jared told Peter. "Can I close your blinds?"

"This better be real," Peter said, nodding in consent to Jared's request. Jared walked from window to window and closed the blinds. Then he closed the office door. It was like they were in a cave now.

A small, dark wood table sat in the corner of the office opposite Peter's desk. It had three chairs huddled around it, perfect for small meetings. Jared walked over to the table and put the papers on it. "Do you want to come over here so I can show you what it is I think you need to see?" Jared asked Peter, trying to hide the hatred in his voice.

"Fine," Peter said. He stood up from his desk and began walking over. Peter didn't suspect anything. He was incapable of it. He'd seen what Jared was capable of, but it was all at Peter's or someone else's request. To Peter, Jared was merely a tool, as unlikely to turn on him as a hammer or a gun lying on a table. Peter only wondered what information Jared had. Spies. If Peter could find spies, he would surely take another step toward the top.

Jared stood next to the table. He pulled a chair out for Peter to sit in. He spread the blank papers over the table and turned the one piece of paper with writing on it toward Peter's chair. He put his one hand in his pocket and gripped the pen. Nobody would be doubling security today. Jared wasn't sure if the plan he'd given Christopher and Reggie was going to work. Others had tried in the past and failed. The only thing that Jared was sure of was that he wasn't going to let Peter be the one to stop it. "You're going to want to sit down for this," Jared said to Peter. Then he waited for Peter to sit down.

Peter was beginning to get excited. *Maybe the old-timer really knew something. Maybe somebody had confided in him because of his ties to the kid.* Peter took another step toward the chair Jared was standing next to and sat down. When he sat, Jared pushed the chair in closer to the table with a single thrust and Peter was suddenly surprised at how strong the old man seemed.

Jared listened for any sounds coming from outside of Peter's office. He was trying to determine if anyone was out there and, if they were, if they would be able to hear what was happening inside. He didn't hear anything. Either nobody was out there or the walls muffled the sounds. Either way, nobody would hear.

"Okay, what do you have for me?" Peter said without looking down at the papers on the table.

"Read," Jared said, giving orders to the man who usually gave orders to him. It felt good.

Peter looked down at the papers. At first he was confused. Most of the papers spread out over the table were blank. Then his eyes found the one closest to him, the one with writing on it. The words were handwritten, like words on a note passed in confidence. He read the words scrawled hurriedly in ink, in all capital letters. STRUGGLING WILL ONLY MAKE IT WORSE. Peter looked up at Jared, who was hovering over him now. "What is this supposed to mean?" he said, his voice angry. He hadn't yet realized that he should be afraid.

Jared pulled the pen out of his pocket. He placed his free hand on Peter's shoulder, holding him firmly in place. "It means what it says," Jared whispered into Peter's ear. Peter heard the tone of Jared's voice and finally knew to be scared.

Peter looked up at Jared, confused. It still didn't make sense to him that this could be happening. "Why?" he asked.

"Because I'm sick of all the bullshit," Jared said. Then Jared took the pen he was holding in his fist and jammed it deep into Peter's neck. He made sure to aim the wound away from him so that he wouldn't get any blood on his clothes. As much as he could, he aimed the blood toward the paper on the table. Some of it got on the floor, but it wasn't excessive. Jared moved his free hand up and covered Peter's mouth with it so that he couldn't make any sound, though it would have been hard for him anyway with the hole in his throat. Then, leaving one hand over Peter's mouth, Jared pulled the pen out of Peter's throat and thrust it into his chest. After that, it was only a matter of letting Peter bleed out.

Jared held Peter's body over the paper until the bleeding stopped. The life stopped well before the bleeding did.

When Jared left Peter's office, he locked the door behind him from the inside. The office appeared to be empty. The only signs that anything had happened were the body in the closet, the blood-covered papers in the trash can under the desk, and the small stains of blood on the carpet near the table. Jared walked up to the woman who sat outside Peter's office. "Peter had to leave on important business," Jared said to the woman. "He wanted me to finish up something in there, but other than that, he told me to tell you that no one is to go inside. He'll be back tomorrow."

The woman looked up at Jared. "Okay," she said with a shrug and a nod. Then Jared went back to his tiny office to sit for another four hours, once again trying to act like everything was normal before leaving for the day a few minutes early.

Sixty-one

It was six hours before the start of the Uprising when Addy and Evan's car pulled up in front of the warehouse in Brooklyn. Maria was driving. She had two passengers in the car with her, one in the front and one in the back. "This is it," she said. "He's inside." The woman in the backseat nodded. She seemed unconcerned by the location. The woman in the passenger seat looked like she was on the verge of tears, but she'd looked that way for pretty much the whole ride anyway. Maria guessed that she'd looked like that for quite some time now.

Inside the warehouse, Evan woke up with a start. He'd been napping, trying to get as much rest as he could before nightfall. He didn't know how late the plan would go. He didn't know what time it would be when he would be called on to fire a bullet into the Intelligence Center and start a fire that would erase hundreds of years of history. So he tried to rest now so he would be sure to be at the top of his game then. He didn't have any qualms about destroying the history. It wasn't a good history. It was a history of absurd violence, a history that bred nothing but hate. And it wasn't his history anyway. Even so, Evan's sleep was full of nightmares. When he finally woke, he was covered in sweat and he could feel his heartbeat in his fingers and toes. He pulled himself up in his cot.

"The nightmare again?" Addy asked him. She was sitting across the makeshift room from him on her own cot. The longer they stayed there, the more Evan thought the whole warehouse began to look like some weird fallout shelter.

"Yeah," Evan answered. "I thought they would stop when we found Christopher."

Addy shook her head. "After tonight they'll stop. After tonight it'll all be over."

"Do you believe that?" Evan asked Addy. Everyone but Evan seemed to be putting a lot of faith in tonight's outcome. Addy chose not to answer him.

"I'm coming with you tonight," Addy informed Evan.

"What do you mean?"

"I'm coming with you. I'll be with you when you make the shot. I don't think it is safe for you to go alone. While you watch Christopher, I'll watch you." Evan almost asked Addy who was going to watch her, but he knew the answer to that. Addy didn't need anyone to watch her.

"You sure that's okay?" Evan knew how intricately the plan had been laid out.

"I already asked Reggie and he's okay with it."

"You asked Reggie or you told Reggie?" Evan smiled at Addy. The red was almost gone from her hair now. Her natural dirty blond color was coming through. Evan liked the natural color better. It looked more real. He found it strange that in all this madness he'd found Addy, the best thing in his life.

Addy smiled back at him. "I talked to Reggie," she said. "Let's try to get some more rest." Then she lay back down on her cot, stared up at the ceiling, and pretended that there was some way she'd be able to fall asleep.

Jared didn't go home after work. He didn't see any point in heading back to New Jersey when all the action was happening in the city. Instead of going home, he went to a bar in midtown about ten blocks from his office. He got there around five o'clock and started drinking. He was already five drinks deep by seven o'clock. He'd taken everything worth keeping from his office, knowing that if everything went according to plan, anything left behind would be incinerated. Everything Jared had that was worth keeping didn't amount to much. He had a couple old pictures—no frames or anything, just pictures on paper, frayed at their edges. One was a picture of an old girlfriend. The relationship never amounted to much, but it was the closest Jared ever came to something serious. The second picture was a picture of him at the beach when he was about twenty years old. He was young and tan. He was shirtless, standing with his arms wrapped around his two best friends, Joseph and Michael. They were all smiling. It was the only picture all three of them had ever taken together. They weren't supposed to take pictures like that. They were told it was too risky, that it would endanger the other two if any one of them ever got caught. Jared laughed at that now. He remembered when they'd had the picture taken. It was Jared's camera. That's how he ended up with the photo. He normally used the camera to help him case the homes of his targets. That day, though, there were a bunch of cute girls on the beach. It was Michael's idea. The picture was his ruse to break the ice with the girls. "Just ask one of them to take our picture," Michael begged Jared. "Then they'll have to talk to us."

"No way," Jared had said. "We're not supposed to take pictures together."

"Yeah, but we're not supposed to be hanging out off the clock together either," Joseph had chimed in.

"Come on," Michael prodded Jared. "You should want to do this. It's the perfect plan. Not only will they have to talk to us, but they'll have to look at us through that camera. It'll look like a moment and everyone wants to be part of a moment. Look, after we meet the girls and you get the film developed, you can throw the picture out." Jared finally relented. Michael asked the prettiest girl of the bunch to take the picture. The plan worked. Michael and the girl who took the picture spent the night together. Jared never threw the photo out. At the time, he wasn't sure why he'd kept it. At the time, he never would have guessed that the photo would outlive two of its subjects, Jared's two best friends, by nearly two decades.

"Another scotch," Jared said, motioning to the bartender.

"Maybe you should think about pacing yourself," the bartender replied.

"I think it's a little late for that," Jared answered.

Counting Addy, twenty-five of them had active roles in the plan. Addy and Evan were the ultimate trigger men. Ten of them were stationed at various spots throughout the city, near where the explosives had been planted. It was their job to be the eyes and ears on the ground. They were supposed to report back what they saw and heard to Evan and Addy. They were supposed to make sure that no order emerged in the chaos. They were supposed to make sure that no one was called away from the chaos to go back to defend the Intelligence Center. If people were being called away to defend the Intelligence Center, they were supposed to do whatever they had to do in order to stop them. Brian was the thirteenth man. He was the one that was going to set the explosives off. They were set to detonate via cell phone. A single number was supposed to set off all of the explosions. A single number was supposed to light up the night skies of New York like they had never been lit before. Brian would be on a rooftop in Gramercy Park. From there, he could dial in the number and see to it that everything worked. If any of the explosions failed to go off when Brian dialed the number, it was the job of one of the ten men on the ground to make the failed explosion happen.

That left twelve men. Six of the twelve would be stationed as security around Grand Central Station. The whole building was to be evacuated at around eleven thirty that night. Jared had told them about the building's evacuation procedures. He'd told them the easiest way to trip the alarm. Jared had also warned them that just because everyone was supposed to evacuate the building when the alarm went off, that didn't mean that everybody would. A trained security team would stay behind in the Intelligence Center. They would stay even if their mission was a suicide mission. They were the most dangerous people of all. The six men on the ground didn't have to worry about them, though. Their only job was to make sure that once everyone else left the building, nobody went back in.

The final six were the six people, five men and one woman, who were carrying the gas canisters into the building. Reggie and Christopher were among them. Christopher laid the guns he'd been given for the mission out on the cot in front of him. Every one of the six of them would be carrying an automatic rifle and a handgun. They'd need them to get inside. They could slip into the building while everyone else was rushing out, but after that they would need the guns. They had backpacks big enough to hold everything they were taking with them on their mission: most importantly their rifles, their gas masks, and their canisters of flammable gas, which were the size of small scuba tanks. Christopher opened up his backpack. The tank of gas was already inside. He picked up the rifle, unscrewed the barrel, and put that into the backpack too. Then he grabbed his gas mask. He slipped it back onto his head one more time to make sure it was adjusted properly.

When he put on the mask, he felt like he was stepping back out of the world, like reality was nothing more than a movie or a video game. The mask was adjusted perfectly. He took it off and dropped it into his backpack too. Then he reached down to lift the backpack, to test its weight. It was heavy. They'd have to carry the backpacks up more than thirty-five flights of stairs. Christopher took solace in the fact that the backpacks would be much lighter on the way back down.

As Christopher placed his backpack on the floor, he heard a voice behind him. "Christopher?" the voice said weakly.

Christopher turned. It was Maria. "Hey," Christopher said. "I was looking for you before. They told me that you'd gone out."

"Yeah," Maria told him. "There was something I needed to do. Something I needed to get." She paused. "For you," she finished.

"You didn't need to get me anything," Christopher said. "You've done enough for me already. I know I might have sounded ungrateful—"

"I needed to get you this." Maria cut him off. "Whether it's something you want or not."

"I don't understand."

"You will if you come with me," Maria told her son. And he was her son. She may not have been his mother, but he was her son. That was immutable. He was her son and somehow she loved him more now than when he was born and she got to hold him in her arms. She loved him more now than when she'd fought the world to find him, only to sacrifice her happiness for a long-shot bet that he could escape the War. Her love for him had caused all the greatest pains in her life, but she cherished that love and the pain that went with it. And the pain wasn't over. She knew that. "Will you come with me?" she asked Christopher.

"Sure," Christopher told her, "but we don't have a lot of time. I have to get ready."

"I know," Maria said. "I know you think you have to do this, and I'm not going to try to stop you anymore. I promise you that we have time for this."

"Okay," Christopher said, and followed Maria down the hall.

Brian shook Reggie's hand. They were standing near the door to the warehouse. Brian was about to leave, to go get in position, to make sure that he could see all of the explosions at once. "I'll see you back here in the morning," he said to Reggie.

"See you back here in the morning," Reggie echoed back to Brian. The plan was to reconvene at the warehouse in the morning to assess the Uprising's success so they could determine the next steps. If everything went well, they would simply disperse and wait to see if all of their destruction actually did the job.

"It's been quite a ride," Brian said to Reggie, thinking back to when he used to work with Joseph, before Christopher, before Maria, before Reggie, before everything. He felt old. In the world they lived in, he was old. He once wondered what it all meant—the War, the rules, everything—but that was a long time ago. He'd seen enough. Now he only wanted to see it end.

"Don't judge the ride until it's over," Reggie answered. Brian nodded. Then he turned and walked out the warehouse door and into the coming night.

Sixty-two

After Brian left the warehouse, the rest of the rebels split up into pairs, each pair leaving the warehouse together. Everyone had their assignments. Some of the pairs would split up later, when they got closer to their ultimate objectives. Addy and Evan would stay together through the night, as would the three pairs tasked with surrounding the Intelligence Center and the three pairs tasked with going inside. They left the warehouse in shifts to avoid a noticeable mass exodus. Once outside, each pair headed toward their ultimate destinations through their own specific means. Addy and Evan left early. Their plan was to walk over the Manhattan Bridge and then catch a cab uptown. They had keycards and everything else they needed to get to the roof of the building where they were supposed to spend the night in silence. Christopher hugged Addy and Evan before they left. The three of them didn't say anything to each other. None of them had anything left to say. Reggie and Addy hugged too, both of them knowing that they had inadvertently teamed up to make this Uprising happen, that they had teamed up to turn Christopher into the person he had become. "For Max," Addy whispered into Reggie's ear as they embraced.

"For Max and all the others," Reggie whispered back.

Christopher and Reggie were the last pair to leave. Reggie

wanted to see everyone else off first. When everyone else was gone, Christopher and Reggie slung their backpacks on their shoulders and started walking toward the subway. With all the other pairs already gone, the warehouse was quieter than if it had been empty. It wasn't empty, though. Three people were still inside, silently watching Christopher and Reggie. Those three would barely speak another word until morning. They would silently wait for the return of their son. Each of them was used to waiting.

The backpacks that Christopher and Reggie carried were heavy. Christopher could feel the straps of his digging into his shoulders. He walked behind Reggie when they left, letting Reggie lead him through the dark Brooklyn streets. Christopher looked at Reggie's backpack, trying to see if it was possible to guess at the backpack's heft. Christopher couldn't see it. They were walking through the streets with their guns and their gas canisters hidden from the world by an eighth of an inch of canvas. Nobody looking at them would suspect anything out of the ordinary. No one would know the kind of destruction that they were planning. "You think the backpacks will look suspicious on the subway?" Christopher called up to Reggie.

Reggie turned back to him and smiled. "It takes a hell of a lot more than a couple of big backpacks to look suspicious on the subway."

"It must seem right to you," Christopher said, speeding up so that he was within whispering distance of Reggie, "to end it here, since you grew up here. It's like coming full circle."

"It's seems right to end it," Reggie said, "circle or no circle."

"I guess if it was a true circle, it wouldn't end."

"Let's worry about the philosophy later, Chris. We've got shit to blow up."

They turned another corner and came to a stairwell leading

down to the subway. Reggie stopped and let Christopher go first, doing one last scan of the surrounding streets before following Christopher underground. The subway station was mostly empty. Only a handful of people were waiting on the platform. They glanced up as Reggie and Christopher descended the stairs but then looked away again, back down at their books or their feet or whatever it was that they were looking at before Christopher and Reggie arrived. Christopher followed Reggie toward an empty part of the platform.

"I've never ridden on a subway before," Christopher confided to Reggie as they waited for the rush of air that would herald the train.

"You've got a lot of firsts left in your life, Christopher," Reggie answered, but the last part of his sentence was drowned out by the sound of an oncoming train. They got on the train and found seats. Christopher mimicked everything Reggie did, taking his backpack off and resting it on the floor in front of him between his knees. Then he leaned back in his seat, feeling the ground rumble beneath him and wondering how the hell he'd gotten to where he was. That's when he remembered that he'd neglected to ask for the first woman's name.

Christopher had recognized the woman. He must have recognized her. Strangers' faces made him nervous. Hers didn't. Her face made him feel safe. She had soft, wrinkled skin and curly gray hair. "Who are you?" he had asked her, like an asshole, when Maria led him into the little room. The woman didn't speak at first. She only stood there, staring at Christopher like she didn't remember how to talk.

"She was your mother once too," Maria told Christopher, standing behind him to make sure no one stood between Christopher and the woman, "before I took you away from her."

Now it was Christopher's turn to lose the ability to speak. The woman nodded her head. "It's true," she said. "I was with you when you spoke your first words." Her voice trembled. "You used to call me Mama."

Christopher didn't have a clue what to do or say. He turned back toward Maria, hoping she would guide him, hoping she would tell him how he was supposed to react to this, hoping she would tell him why she was doing this. "Do you remember her?" Maria asked Christopher.

Christopher didn't know how to answer Maria's question. He didn't remember her, but whatever it was that he felt, it was deeper than memory. It was the same way he'd felt when he first collapsed into Maria's arms. It was the feeling that he belonged to the world. Christopher turned back toward the woman, back toward his second mother. "How did you get here?" he asked her.

The woman motioned to Maria. "Maria found me," she said. "She brought me here."

"She was easy to find," Maria said. "She's been part of the Underground for over ten years now." Christopher looked at the woman. She didn't look like a rebel.

"Why?" Christopher asked the woman. "After everything that happened?" And everyone in the room knew what Christopher meant. After Maria killed her husband and stole her child, why would this woman join the people that helped Maria do it?

The woman stepped toward Christopher. She extended her hand, slowly, toward Christopher's shoulder as if silently asking him if it was okay for her to touch him. Christopher inched forward, stepping into her hand so that her hand was resting on his shoulder. He could feel the woman's muscles relax when they touched. "It was the only way that I could think of to get closer to you." She stepped closer to him now, bending her arm, wrapping her hand around his neck. "I heard all the rumors. I heard them calling you the Child. I heard them using your name—your real name, not the one I gave you. Nobody knew who I was. Nobody knew that for the most wonderful eight months of my life, I had been your mother. I wanted to be close to you again. I wasn't mad at anyone for what Maria did when she took you from me." She shook her head. "I was mad at first, but then I realized that what she did was right." Her voice got even softer. "I should have realized it sooner. I was going to let them turn you into a monster, like the rest of them. I wanted to make that up to you. I thought that by joining the Underground, I might be able, in some small way, to keep you safe."

"Safe was never really an option for me."

The woman's eyes welled up with tears at Christopher's words. "I remember how much you loved music when you were a baby. You used to clap your hands when I played certain songs, and you'd laugh. I remember thinking that maybe, if things were different, you could grow up to be a composer or a musician. I used to daydream about seeing you all grown up and playing in an orchestra or at a jazz club." She paused, lost in thought. "Do you still love music?"

Christopher searched his brain for any memory, any inkling he might have to show that the child this woman was describing was still part of him. Did he still love music? Did he love anything? "I will," Christopher said to the woman, making a promise to her and to himself. "I'm sorry if knowing me ruined your life," he finally said to this woman who raised him for eight months seventeen years ago and who lost her husband and spent the rest of her life on the run because of it.

The woman pulled Christopher into her arms. "You didn't ruin anything. My life didn't even start until I met you." Then she looked past Christopher. "Thank you so much for giving me this, Maria."

They rode the subway for a while. Christopher stopped counting the stops at ten. "This is us," Reggie said when they reached Forty-second Street, breaking Christopher's trance. Reggie stood up and swung the backpack over his shoulder. Christopher mimicked Reggie's movements. Once they stepped out of the train, Christopher looked down at his watch. It was almost an hour before midnight. "You ready?" Reggie asked Christopher before they climbed back up onto the streets of the city.

"I'm ready," Christopher affirmed and the two of them walked up the stairs.

Brian stood on the roof of his designated building and stared out over the city. He took the cell phone out of his pocket. It was a prepaid phone, impossible to trace to any person. The lights of the city shimmered around him. They went on for miles in every direction. To the south and the east, the lights stopped only when they hit the black ocean, and even then he could see the lights of the boats floating offshore. To the west and the north, the lights never stopped.

Brian checked his watch. He counted the targets again. There were ten in all. The Brooklyn Bridge, the George Washington Bridge, the Manhattan Bridge, the Williamsburg Bridge, the Verrazano-Narrows Bridge, the Flatiron Building, the Chrysler Building, the Empire State Building, the Arch in Washington Square Park, and Yankee Stadium in the Bronx. Brian could actually see most of the targets from where he was standing. Even if he couldn't see the targets themselves, he knew that he'd be able to see the explosions. He looked at his watch again. Eighty-four seconds had passed. The city was quiet and beautiful. In less than ten minutes, Brian would have to dial the code.

Christopher and Reggie headed east on Forty-second Street. They were aboveground for only a single block. Reggie pointed up into the sky at one of the skyscrapers towering over them. "That's it," he said. "That's the building."

Christopher looked up, almost getting dizzy from the height of it. He tried to count floors, starting from the bottom and counting up. He wanted to see if he could figure out which five floors they were going to burn. He lost count at around twenty.

They didn't go straight to the target building. The plan was to enter the building underground, traveling through a service tunnel leading from one of the buildings adjacent to their target. Jared assured them that the adjacent building's delivery entrance would be open and unguarded. He'd pulled the necessary strings to make that happen. When Christopher and Reggie reached the delivery entrance to the second building, Reggie pulled the pistol out of his backpack, holding it low to conceal it from view. It wasn't that Reggie didn't trust Jared. At moments like this, Reggie didn't trust anyone. Reggie burst through the delivery entrance, leading with his gun, but the room on the other side of the door was empty. He surveyed the room, spotting the staircase in the corner heading downward. "There," Reggie said to Christopher, pointing to the stairs.

"Should we arm ourselves first?" Christopher asked. His heart was already pounding. He tried to calm it by slowing his breathing. He knew that he needed to save energy for the trek up the stairs. Reggie nodded. The two of them swung their backpacks off their shoulders and placed them on the floor in front of them. Christopher unzipped his and pulled out his handgun and the pieces to the automatic rifle he was carrying. He began to assemble the rifle. He could do it quickly now. He'd been practicing over and over for the past few days. He was even faster than Reggie. When he finished, he shouldered the backpack again. The backpack was lighter now. The only material of any weight left in it was the gas canister. Christopher put the handgun in the holster he had attached to his thigh. Then he lifted the rifle into the air. For a moment, he felt powerful, but he fought the feeling. He didn't want to feel powerful. He'd settle for brave and would have to hope that would be enough to pull him through the night.

A moment after Christopher was done Reggie stepped up next to him, identically outfitted. "Let's move," Reggie said. The two of them headed for the stairs, ready for anything.

The service tunnel running between the buildings was dimly lit. Half the tunnel's lights seemed to be turned off, leaving the tunnel a pallid gray color. The floor was concrete and the walls and ceiling were a dusty white tile. As far as Reggie and Christopher could tell, the tunnel was empty. They couldn't see anything but footprints in the dust on the floor and torn pieces of paper littering the ground. They moved through the tunnel fast, knowing that there was no cover—no place to hide—until they made it to the other end. They could hear their own footsteps echoing through the tunnel as they went. It was impossible to walk lightly while carrying that much weight. Christopher's heart was thumping in pace with his footsteps. It didn't matter that they were in a tunnel underneath New York City; for a few seconds, those footsteps were the only sound in the world. They needed to get to the security control room beneath their target building. From there, they'd be able to trip an alarm requiring every floor of the building to evacuate. Then, while almost everyone else in the building was headed down the stairs, Reggie, Christopher, and the others would head up. The only other people left in the building were the psychopaths left to guard the Intelligence Center during the emergency.

At the end of the tunnel, Christopher and Reggie came to another door. Through that door was the building that housed the

Intelligence Center. They would be there in moments, only thirty-seven floors below their target. They paused outside the other door again, not sure what they were going to face on the other side.

"We go through fast and quiet," Reggie said to Christopher. Christopher could see the sweat glistening on Reggie's forehead. He had never seen Reggie sweat before. "I'll go first. If you don't hear anything, wait five seconds and then come after me. If you hear something"—Christopher knew that by *something* Reggie meant gunshots—"wait until I open the door and let you in."

"And what if you don't open the door?" Christopher asked.

Reggie shrugged. "Then you're on your own. You'll have to find your own way in." Reggie didn't wait for a follow-up question. He stepped toward the door, opened it, and without a sound slipped to the other side.

Christopher counted five seconds in his head like he was a kid playing hide-and-seek, all the while praying for silence. One one-thousand. Two one-thousand. Three one-thousand. Four one-thousand. Five one-thousand. He didn't hear anything, so he stepped toward the door and pushed it open.

Reggie was already on the other side of the room, his back pressed up against the wall. He had his rifle slung on its strap over his back and was holding his handgun. Past Reggie was another hallway. Reggie put his finger to his lips so Christopher knew to be quiet. Then he waved Christopher over to him. Christopher sped across the room, trying to move silently the way he'd seen Addy and Max move. Seconds later, he was standing next to Reggie. Each step brought them closer to the security control room.

"I saw someone moving down there," Reggie whispered to Christopher. "We can't afford to fire any shots unless we have to. Surprise is our best weapon. We don't want to lose that." Christopher nodded. "We'll go together, move down opposite sides of the hallway. If you have to attack, try to use your hands first and gun only as a last resort." Christopher nodded again. It was all he could think to do. Then they started moving.

As they started down the hallway, Christopher saw what Reggie had seen. It wasn't a person, only moving shadows. They were about two-thirds of the way down the hall when the shadows suddenly got larger and two armed men turned into the hallway. Christopher lifted his gun, knowing full well what it would mean to shoot but being ready to shoot anyway, but also ready to charge like a bull toward a fluttering cape. Reggie moved quickly forward, toward the two men. Christopher followed him—step after step after step—both of them with their guns raised. The men at the other end of the hall saw them coming and raised their guns too. Everybody aimed, but no one seemed to want to fire. Then everybody stopped.

"Reggie," one of the other men called out in a loud whisper.

"Hector," Reggie answered with relief. It was Hector and Dave, two more of the six rebels assigned to climb up the building. Now the four of them were together. "You guys seen the others?" Two more and the team would be assembled.

Hector nodded silently and pointed around the corner in the direction of the security control room was. Reggie looked at his watch. They still had fifteen minutes until the explosions started in New York and everywhere else. Everything was right on schedule.

The four men and one woman cleared a path for Reggie so that he could make his way to the door of the security control room. He walked up to the door and put his ear to it to see if he could hear anything going on inside. He couldn't hear a thing. The door was thick and virtually soundproof. They would have heard gunfire inside but not much else. Reggie turned back to his team. "You all know the drill," he said. "There's five of them inside. There's six of us. They have guns. We have bigger guns. One of them is part of the War, but there's no way for us to know which one. The others are innocents. If one of them tries to be a hero, we all agree on the assumptions we need to make, right?" Everyone nodded, even Christopher. "Otherwise, we should be able to do this without too much bloodshed."

"Fast and ready," Hector said to the group. Everyone nodded again. They lifted their weapons in unison. Then Reggie went for the door.

Only two of them could fit through the door at a time. Once Reggie pulled open the door, Dave and Hector would go in first. They'd fire shots, aimed away from the people and away from all of the security equipment. The last thing they needed was to accidentally break the alarm trigger. The shots were only meant as a distraction, meant to make the five security guards inside flinch long enough for the others to get through the door. Linda and Mike went in second. Reggie and Christopher would go in last. The earlier you went, the more dangerous it was, but nobody argued about the order.

Reggie opened the door and Dave and Hector ran through it. Christopher heard the shots fired—three in rapid succession and then two others, spaced out more deliberately. Linda and Mike ran through next. Christopher didn't hear any more gunfire but he could hear shouting. First a voice he didn't recognize saying words he couldn't understand, and then Dave shouting, "EVERYBODY ON YOUR FEET, HANDS IN THE AIR."

Then it was Reggie and Christopher's turn. They went in shoulder to shoulder, guns aimed in front of them. By the time they were through the door, everything seemed to be under control. Christopher saw the five security guards first. They were already lined up against one wall with their backs to the room and their hands above their heads. Their hands were pressing up against the wall. Christopher couldn't see their faces. Then he looked at their equipment. The wall in front of him was lined with television sets showing color pictures of dozens of entranceways and stairwells. Below that was a table full of buttons and levers. Christopher looked at the televisions. All of the stairwells were empty. The screens showing the various entranceways were mostly motionless, only a random person walking across one of the screens every few minutes. It was almost midnight. The images on the screens were serene, like abstract art about the tedium of normal life.

"Okay, where are the buttons?" Reggie said, stepping toward the control panel. Linda went with him. She'd been assigned to study the plans that Jared had stolen for them, the plans that told them what buttons they needed to press.

"Over here," Linda said, motioning to the right side of the control panel. "Each one of these red buttons triggers the alarm for one of the floors."

"And if we want the alarm to go off on all of them at once?" Reggie asked.

"You flip that switch there," Linda pointed, "and then you hit the top button."

Reggie looked at his watch again. They still had eight minutes. "Okay, and where is the evacuation announcement button?"

"Over by the microphone," Linda said, pointing to another part of the desk. "You don't have to say anything. You just hit that top yellow button on the right."

"And then the people leave?"

"And then they leave," Linda confirmed. Seven minutes.

Christopher was still standing in the back of the room. Hector, Dave, and Mike remained standing with their rifles pointed at the security guards. "Get the restraints," Hector said to Christopher. Christopher walked behind Hector and unzipped his backpack. Christopher saw Hector's gas canister but he looked past it, to the bottom of the backpack. Christopher reached inside and moved Hector's gas mask out of the way. Beneath the gas mask were a few dozen plastic wrist ties. Beneath those were three rolls of duct tape. Christopher took the wrist ties and the duct tape out of the bag. He left the gas mask and the canister inside. "Give me those," Hector said, taking everything from Christopher. This was as planned. Christopher wasn't supposed to get too close to the security guards. "Take my place," Hector said to Christopher before stepping toward the first man with his hands splayed against the wall. Christopher moved to the spot where Hector had been standing, next to Dave and Mike, and aimed his gun at the backs of the security guards.

"We don't have all day, Hector," Reggie called out, glancing down at his watch again. Reggie had stationed himself near the alarm switch while Linda stood near the button that would play the full evacuation message.

Hector walked up to the first of the guards. "Give me your hands," he ordered him. The guard took his hands off the wall and moved them behind his back. Hector grabbed them quickly and cinched them together with one of the plastic rings. "Now turn around and sit on the floor," Hector ordered. The man did as he was told. Hector helped him get down on the floor. Then Hector cinched his ankles together. Finally, Hector took the duct tape and wrapped it over the guard's mouth.

"What are you going to do to us?" the third security guard in line asked nervously as he watched Hector wrap the tape around his colleague's mouth.

"Nothing," Hector answered. Then he moved to the second guard and started the procedure over again.

"What do you mean, *nothing*?" the third guard asked as Hector cinched the second guard's feet together, the panic in his voice escalating.

"I mean nothing if you shut up," Hector said. "Our business is upstairs. We're simply going to empty the building and leave you guys here so that someone can find you tomorrow." Hector finished wrapping the tape around the second guard's head.

"Tomorrow?" the third guard asked as Hector approached him with the plastic handcuffs in his hand.

What happened next happened so fast that Christopher didn't even see what was going on until it was over. He saw the flash and then he heard the bang and saw the blood splattered against the wall, but none of it registered for a few seconds. The fourth guard slumped to the floor, blood seeping down the front of his face, a hole where his forehead used to be. Dave's gun was still smoking. The fourth guard had a gun in his hand. He'd turned all the way around and was facing us by time Dave shot him. God knows what he thought he was going to accomplish. At best, he would have taken one of the rebels out before they stopped him. Maybe he thought that would have been enough for him to be able to go out proud. Instead, he was dead and hadn't accomplished anything. "There's the inside man," Dave said quietly, staring at the man's body over his smoking gun. Everyone agreed because that's what they'd all promised themselves they'd believe. Whether it was true or not didn't matter. Hector moved quickly now to restrain the third guard. The guard began screaming. Not words, merely sounds. The sounds stopped only when Hector got the tape wrapped around the guard's head. They had only two minutes left when Hector finished with the fifth guard. They left the four of them, bound and gagged and sitting against the wall beside their dead colleague. They would move the four of them out into the hall when they were done to make sure that none of them could get to the control board. "Let's go," Hector said when he finished tying up the guards. "Hit the alarm."

"Not yet," Christopher said, looking at Reggie. "We can't be early. This all has to happen at exactly the same time."

Reggie looked down at his watch and nodded to Christopher. "Eighty seconds," he said, putting his hand near the button that he would press to trigger the alarm.

The six of them wouldn't hear the sounds outside when the Uprising finally began. They were too far removed from it, too far below the city. They wouldn't hear the explosions as they detonated all over the city. They wouldn't hear a television or a radio as they began to report unconfirmed stories about explosions and violence erupting, seemingly simultaneously, all over the world. They would watch the feeds from the security cameras as everyone but a handful of dedicated, hard-core soldiers ran out of the building. Then Christopher, Reggie, and the others would begin their climb up the stairs.

Christopher took the earpiece out of his backpack and put it in his ear. He knew he wouldn't be able to hear anything yet. They were too far underground, but he wanted to be ready. Once he'd climbed two flights of stairs, he wanted to hear Evan's voice informing him about everything that was going on.

Sixty-three

The bartender strolled down to where Jared was sitting, slumped over at the bar. "It's eleven fifty-five," he informed Jared.

"What's that?" Jared asked, squinting at the bartender, trying to get his eyes to focus. He hadn't stopped drinking since he got to the bar at five o'clock. He'd barely even slowed down.

"You told me to tell you when it was eleven fifty-five."

"That's right," Jared said, finally remembering through the alcohol-filled haze. "It's time."

"Time for what?" the bartender asked, skeptical that this drunk actually had an appointment that he had to keep.

"Time to watch the chaos start," Jared said, smiling at the bartender. He dropped two hundred-dollar bills on the bar. "Keep the change," he said, slipping off his barstool. It took him a moment to find his footing and stand up straight. Then he began to walk ever so gracelessly toward the door. When Jared opened the door and stepped out onto the sidewalk, the sky was quiet.

Brian looked at his watch. It was time. He was standing on the roof of a building near the East River. He did a visual scan of the targets one more time. He had already dialed the number into his phone. All he had to do now was hit Send and it would begin. Brian ran his thumb over the button. He looked out over the city, dark but alive. Then Brian pressed down on the Send button with his thumb.

Jared was standing on the sidewalk staring up at the sky when he heard the first rumble. The fresh air had sobered him up enough that he could look up without keeling over. The first rumble came from somewhere in the distance. Jared couldn't even determine from which direction the sound was coming as it echoed down to him through the streets. The George Washington Bridge? The Verrazano-Narrows Bridge? Jared waited, listening, wondering what he would hear next. He wondered if he would hear the screaming first or the sirens or maybe another explosion.

The next explosion was closer, not more than a few dozen blocks from Jared. It came like a series of bellowing thunderclaps, one after the other. The whole city must have heard it. Behind Jared, the patrons in the bar ran to the window to see what was happening, but no one actually stepped outside. Jared kept looking up, wondering if he would see the explosions at the top of the Empire State Building and the Chrysler Building when they blew, wondering how the rest of the world would react to entering into the chaos that he'd already lived his entire life in. Then the sky lit up with color.

Purple was first, flashing against the gray night clouds. Then green, an unnatural green that looked almost chemical. Then Jared heard another rumble—closer than the first but farther away than the second—and another and another as the whole city began to fill with thundering noise in every direction. It was here. The beginning of the end was here, but the colors—Jared couldn't figure out the colors. It wasn't long before he heard the first siren, added to the cacophony. The sirens were mixed in with the still-cascading sounds of explosions. The sky turned red, then orange, then blue. Confused, Jared shuffled as best he could to the corner to see if he could get a clearer view of the explosions.

When Jared turned the corner, he looked up and fell to his knees. He finally saw what the buildings in front of him had been blocking. *That idealistic son of a bitch*, Jared said to himself as he watched a burst of yellow fall through the sky like dozens of tiny, twinkling stars. Looking down the avenue, Jared could see tiers of color lighting up the night sky as they sprang from the buildings that he himself had designated for destruction. He could also see people—so many people—standing on the sidewalks, staring up into the sky. Another rocket launched from one of the buildings, whistling as it rose and then exploding into a giant circle of hundreds of tiny red flares. Fireworks. Christopher had taken Jared's plan and replaced the explosives with fucking fireworks. They were exploding in the sky all over the city, off the city's bridges and the city's tallest buildings, in an unprecedented display of light, color, and sound. Jared had been in this city for celebrations, for Fourth of July displays, and nothing he had ever seen came close to lighting up the sky like this. And this time no one had been expecting it. More sirens roared across the city, barely audible amid the sounds of bursting fireworks, rushing God knows where to do God knows what, likely rushing merely for the sake of doing something in response to this act of— Act of what exactly? Not violence. Wonder?

Still on his knees, staring up the sky, Jared whispered the words again, "That idealistic son of a bitch" and then he started laughing. Despite the impact of the fireworks, he knew that his plan was ruined. After all he'd told Christopher—after all he'd tried to teach Christopher—Christopher had still ruined it. This would lead to chaos but not enough chaos. The chaos from real explosions and the damage and death that followed would have lasted for hours. How long after the last rocket exploded would the chaos from this last? One hour while the masses tried to figure out what they had witnessed? One hour while the authorities rushed to each site to make sure that there truly was nothing there but fireworks? "I hope you've given yourself enough time, kid," Jared whispered, not to himself this time but to Christopher, wherever Christopher was. When the chaos ended, everyone would immediately remember the Intelligence Center. Jared knew that.

Jared stayed on his knees until the fireworks ended, watching the sky light up over and over again. It looked to him like the sky was liquid. Each new burst of color spread out from its center like a raindrop landing in the sea, which meant that Jared, and the rest of the world with him, was underwater. When it was over, almost twenty minutes after it had begun, Jared pulled himself up to his feet again. Christopher was risking everything. "He's your kid, Joe," Jared whispered, talking to ghosts now, not bothering to remind himself that he'd killed Joe eighteen years ago. "I hope you're proud of him."

Addy and Evan watched the fireworks too. While Jared was kneeling on the sidewalk, staring up into the sky, Addy and Evan were watching from the top of the building across from the Intelligence Center. They didn't know. Christopher hadn't told either of them that he'd changed the plan. Barely anyone knew. Not even Brian knew, and he was the one who had to pull the trigger on the whole thing. Christopher told only the people that he thought he had to: Reggie and a few of the others who helped him to arrange the boxes of fireworks. Reggie fought him at first, but Christopher had made up his mind. One thing. Christopher demanded that he get to make this one decision, threatening to derail the whole Uprising if Reggie didn't agree. Reggie didn't need to be threatened, though. All he needed was to see how much Christopher cared. Reggie wanted to help save Christopher, not destroy him. So he gave in.

For Addy and Evan, the fireworks weren't merely loud and colorful displays in the sky. From where they were standing, the fireworks were enormous. Addy and Evan watched each burst as it filled the sky right in front of their eyes. Soon they couldn't see any part of the city except through the haze created by the endless bursts of color. "There are no explosions," Evan said to Addy, looking through each burst of color for a real explosion emanating from a real bomb. "There's only this." Evan worried that it wouldn't be enough.

Addy stepped up next to Evan near the edge of the roof. They stood side by side watching what Christopher had created, the colors from the fireworks reflecting off their skin. Addy slipped her hand into Evan's. "Yeah, but *this* is beautiful," she told him as they watched the sky change color over and over again. Far below them, in the streets and from apartment windows all over the city, people looked up into the sky to see this parade of bursting light. They'd been frightened at first by the sounds, but when they saw what was happening, the fear was replaced by awe. Millions of people watched every burst lift into the heavens, sparkling and then falling or fading into nothing, only to be replaced by the next burst and the one after that. Everyone had seen fireworks before, but never a display like this. This was unexpected. And it was everywhere: above them, beside them, in front of them, behind them, like magic. Millions of people looked up at the sky and saw what Addy and Evan saw. Still, Addy and Evan stood on the roof, hands intertwined, alone together, and watched the spectacle as if it had been created only for them.

Sixty-four

They were running, all six of them, up the stairs. It was hot in the stairwell and their bags felt heavy. Christopher could feel his backpack pulling him down even as he pushed himself up one step at a time. It was an internal stairwell without any windows. The six of them couldn't see what was going on outside as they ran. They concentrated on step after step, flight after flight. Soon they were cresting the second flight and had only thirty-five more floors to go. Above Christopher, Dave and Mike swung their backpacks off their shoulders and began to dig through them, reaching inside for the tiny explosive they were going to use to blow open the doors when they got upstairs. Once they found the explosives they held them in their hands and reshouldered their backpacks. In all of that movement, neither of them stopped running. They all knew how little time they had. They all knew that the diversions they'd created, both inside and outside the building, wouldn't last forever. They knew that those diversions were the only thing making their impossible job possible. Instead of fighting thirty armed men, they would have to fight only five, but that would hold only as long as the diversions lasted and as long as their colleagues on the ground could keep reinforcements from entering the building. So they ran and even as they ran, only Reggie and Christopher knew about the fireworks.

Only they knew that the diversions outside the building wouldn't last as long as everyone else expected. Reggie, the oldest one of the group by at least a decade, sped up so that he was the first one in the line, leading the charge, pulling everyone else up with him.

Christopher clutched his rifle with both hands. He'd put his handgun back in its holster. He swung his rifle back and forth as he ran, using it for balance. He looked down at the stairs, concentrating on each step, trying to find a rhythm, trying not to slip, trying not to think about the chaos waiting for them when they reached the top of the stairs or the chaos waiting for him after that. He stayed close on Linda's heels. He didn't look up. He refused to look up. He tried to clear his mind of everything but step, step, step. Soon it was like a trance, and Christopher's mind drifted again—back to the warehouse, back to Maria, back to her second gift for him.

After Maria had taken Christopher to meet the woman who had been his mother for nearly a year and then given up her entire life for him, Maria took him to another room. "I don't have time," Christopher protested. The time for the Uprising was getting closer. He had to get ready. But his protest wasn't really about the time. He simply wasn't sure what else Maria had in store for him. He wasn't sure if he could take any more surprises. He feared any more distractions. He was still trying to wrap his head around the first one.

"You still have time for this," Maria promised him again, and the way she said it, Christopher didn't believe he had a choice. So he followed Maria around corners and through doors until they came to another door to another room, one that Christopher had never been to before. "Go inside," Maria said gently. Christopher opened the door and stepped through it.

Christopher looked across the room. He turned back to Maria. "What is she doing here?" he asked, his voice confused and angry.

There was no answer, so he asked the question again, more loudly this time. "Maria, what is she doing here?" His voice was trembling. "She can't be here. She shouldn't be here. It's not safe."

Maria stepped up behind him and put a hand on his shoulder but didn't say anything, unsure of what to say. She didn't have to say anything, though; the woman on the other side of the room knew what to say. The woman on the other side of the room had a lot more practice than Maria. "It's okay, Chris." The woman stepped closer to them. "I'm here. Maria told me everything. I know everything. Don't worry about me. I don't care about being safe. I only want to be here for you."

"But—," Christopher began.

The woman shook her head, cutting him off. "No 'buts,' Christopher. Nothing you can say will make me leave you. My heart wouldn't be able to take it."

"I'm sorry, Mom," Christopher said, now on the verge of tears, feeling not like the inspiration for a revolution but like a helpless little boy. It felt wonderful. Christopher didn't want the feeling to go away.

"Come here, Christopher. Come to me." The woman opened her arms for Christopher and he ran into them. Christopher's mother held him like she hadn't held him in years.

"What about Dad?" Christopher asked while still clutching his mother's shirt.

"He doesn't know anything. I wasn't allowed to tell him anything," Christopher's mother said, lifting her eyes to Maria.

"Men," Maria said out loud, responding to her gaze. "They're too dangerous. I risked enough bringing your two mothers here."

"You've met the others?" Christopher asked his mother, ashamed, like he'd been cheating on her.

Christopher's mother nodded. "I knew Maria when she was a young girl. The three of us drove here together." There was only a trace of weakness, a slight vulnerability in Christopher's mother's voice.

"Don't worry, Mom. You are my only mother." Christopher didn't think about how the words he said might affect Maria, but his mother did. She glanced up at Maria and saw in her face the pain the words caused her.

"It looks to me like you could use more than one mother right now," Christopher's mother said to him. "Maria was kind enough to share. I can do the same." She gave a pained, sad laugh. "It's not many men who get to have three mothers." She looked down and took her son's face in her hands. "You are so loved, Christopher."

Maria stepped forward toward Christopher. "That's why I brought them here, Christopher," she told him. "I wanted you to see how much more there is to you than the War. You don't have to limit yourself to what they want you to be."

Christopher let go of the mother who raised him and looked at the mother who gave birth to him. "But I do," he said to both of them. "Until this is over, they won't let me be anything else. That's why I need to do this tonight. That's what you have to understand. I'm not doing it for them."

Christopher's mother answered him. "I remember when your nightmares started when you were a little boy. I remember blaming myself for them. I thought that I must have done something wrong. I thought you were having the nightmares because of me."

"Well, now you know." Christopher reassured his mother. "Now you know that it wasn't your fault."

"But it was my fault because I couldn't stop them. That's why Maria gave you to me—so that I could stop them. I couldn't stop them then and I still can't stop them now." The tears that she had been holding back began to flow from her eyes. "I'm so sorry, Christopher."

Christopher reached for his mother and put his arms around

her. The two of them stood there, rocking back and forth together. He wanted to say something to her to make her less sad. He wanted words to come into his head so that he could tell her how grateful he was that she and his father had tried so hard to give him a normal life. But those words didn't come. He had images, images of riding on his father's shoulders through the county fairgrounds, images of drinking hot chocolate his mother made for him after he played in the snow with Evan, images of the three of them playing board games in front of the fireplace on autumn evenings. His head was full of images, but no words. In the end, Christopher was still a boy, so all he could think to say was, "Don't cry, Mom. Please don't cry. It will all be over soon" as they held each other the way only a mother can hold her son and as only a son can be held.

There was a sudden crackling sound in Christopher's ear. Then a voice. Christopher looked down to see the steps that he was still running up. "Chris? Are you there, Chris?" the voice in his ear echoed. It was Evan's voice. It was the earpiece. They'd made it high enough in the stairwell for Evan's radio to get through to him. Christopher kept moving, had never stopped moving—step, step, step.

"I'm here, Evan. We're on our way up," Christopher said between huffed breaths. "What's it like out there?" he asked, believing that he could hear the sounds of explosions behind Evan's voice.

"Crazy," Evan said to Christopher, looking out over the vast expanse of colors still exploding all around them. Christopher liked to believe that he could hear the smile in Evan's voice. "It's a madhouse. There are sirens and flashing lights everywhere and thousands of people milling around on the streets and no one seems to know what to do."

"So we have time?"

"Yeah," Evan said, "but I don't know how much. It's just fireworks, Chris."

"I know," Christopher huffed. If he'd had more breath, Christopher would have said more, he would have explained to Evan why it had to be fireworks, but he could barely breathe, let alone talk. It would have to wait. "Watch the building. Let me know if we're in danger."

"Will do," Evan promised. Evan stopped talking so Christopher could save his breath for the climb to the top of the building. Evan could hear the sound of Christopher's breathing over his radio as they climbed—fifteen stories and counting—and the fireworks kept exploding around him.

Far away, while Reggie and Christopher and the others climbed those stairs, the explosions began under the streets of Paris and in the slums of Rio de Janeiro. In Tokyo, people marched through the streets firing machine guns and flamethrowers. In Istanbul, a small army of disguised rebels pulled guns from beneath their burkas and trudged slowly up a hill toward their target. In Costa Rica a boat full of armed men stormed an otherwise peaceful, empty beach and ran like madmen into the jungle. Only Cambodia was behind schedule. None of the six of the people climbing the steps knew any of that. They wouldn't know anything for hours. All they knew was step, step, step.

At twenty floors up, Christopher began to go over the plan again in his head. He glanced up quickly, looking to see if he could spot the cameras in the staircase. "Of course they'll know you're coming," Jared had told them. "They'll be watching you on the security cameras as you run up the stairs. They'll be preparing for you."

"Is there anything we can do to keep them from knowing?" Christopher asked.

"No," Jared said, "but there are only five of them, for Christ's sake. That's the whole point of the plan. They'll know you're coming, but they won't be able to stop you—not on their own. They'll call for help. That's why you don't have a lot of time. That's why we need the distraction and the others on the streets to keep the reinforcements at bay until you can get the job done. But as long as it's the five of them versus you, you have two distinct advantages."

"What're those?" Reggie asked.

Jared lifted his fist and extended one finger at them. "You've got them outnumbered six to five." Then he extended his second finger. "They're highly trained. They know the optimum way to react to anything we can throw at them. It's been programmed into them."

"How is that an advantage?" Christopher asked.

"Because I'm the one that programmed them," Jared bragged. "I can tell you exactly what they're going to do in reaction to your attack. I can tell you exactly where they're going to be." Jared paused, thinking back on his entire life, unable to avoid taking at least some perverse pleasure in the irony. "I've learned that sometimes having a plan can be your greatest weakness—no matter how good a plan it is. It took me a long time to realize that."

"So what do we do when we get to the Intelligence Center?" Reggie asked.

"Simple," Jared told him. "You use explosives to blow open the back doors on the top and bottom floors."

"And then?" Reggie prodded.

"And then, while they're busy guarding the doors you blew open, you take this"—Jared held an electronic keycard in front of them—"and you walk right in the front door."

"This will work?" Reggie asked, taking the keycard from Jared, not trying to hide his skepticism.

"The keys are supposed to be disabled when the evacuation alarm goes off, but I've taken care of that."

"It seems too easy," Reggie said. Christopher wondered what part of blowing up half of New York City to create a diversion, breaking in to the security offices of a skyscraper to pull the evacuation alarm, running up thirty-seven flights of stairs, and then disarming five trained armed guards was easy.

"Don't complain about easy," Jared told him. "Everything feels easy when it works. It's only when things fall apart that they begin to seem hard. Follow my plan and things are unlikely to fall apart."

When the six of them finally made it to the bottom floor of the Intelligence Center's five floors, they split up. David, Hector, and Linda stayed on the bottom floor. David and Mike had the explosive they would need to blow open the doors. Mike went up the last five floors with Reggie and Christopher. After they blew the doors open, they were supposed to meet again in front of the main doors on the middle floor. Christopher felt strange running like this, knowing that every move they made was being watched by their enemies. Even as he tried to keep his head down, Christopher wondered if the people watching them would recognize him like everyone else in the War seemed to. If they did recognize him, Christopher wondered if they were chomping at the bit to get to him, like a prize or a trophy.

Reggie, Christopher, and Mike made it to the door they were meant to blow up. It was a metal slab right off the entrance to the staircase. If Jared hadn't given them the plans to the offices, none of them would have guessed that it led inside. It had no handle, no way to open it from the outside, not without explosives anyway. "We ready?" Reggie asked Mike when they reached the door. Christopher could see the sweat on their faces. All three of them were breathing heavily. They didn't have the time to catch their breath, though. Mike had the explosives in his hand. He'd been holding them since halfway up the stairs. That was part of the point, to let the people watching them see the explosives.

"Ready," Mike said. Christopher nodded. Then Mike went over to the door and attached the explosives to its base, near where Jared had told them the primary lock was. They had seemingly relied on Jared for everything, for every detail of the plan. They put all their faith in the man who had killed his own best friend in the name of the War. But that was a long time ago. For Christopher, it was an entire lifetime ago.

The three of them backed away from the door but not too far. They wanted to get far enough away from the explosion to be safe, but they also wanted to stay close enough to the door to still show up in the security camera's picture. The plan was to wait a few seconds after the explosion opened the door and then to disappear in the smoke. Christopher jumped when he heard the sound of the explosion. It was somehow quicker and louder than he had expected it to be, like the crack of a whip. It was all over in a flash of smoke. "Let's go," Christopher said as the smoke rose around them, eager to get away from where he knew their watchers were headed.

"Wait," Mike said, holding up his hand. Christopher and Reggie followed his gaze to the door. The door hadn't opened. The door was supposed to come loose with the explosion. They needed the door to open. The misdirection wouldn't work without it.

"Fuck," Reggie muttered under his breath. They were supposed to meet the other three two stories beneath them in about thirty seconds. So Mike did the only thing any of them could think to do in that moment. He took three steps forward and kicked the door as hard as he could. Christopher heard a sound when Mike's foot hit the door, a horrible crunching sound. Mike took one step backward, testing his weight on his foot. Almost miraculously, the door swung open. It swung slowly toward them, revealing the empty space behind it, space that would be empty for only another moment or two before it was filled with angry bullets.

"Now, let's go," Reggie said and he and Christopher turned back toward the stairs. Mike didn't turn with them.

"My foot," Mike said, staring at the now broken appendage that had carried him up more than thirty-five flights of stairs but that he knew would no longer get him down even two. "Go without me. I'll face them here. It'll make distraction more believable." There was no question in his voice.

"We might need you," Reggie said, knowing that each person carried only enough gas to cover one floor, "if one of the others doesn't make it."

Mike shook his head. "You don't need me. You need this." He took his backpack off his shoulders and handed it to Christopher. Mike had already taken the explosives and the guns out of his backpack. All that was left was the gas. Mike ordered Christopher and Reggie away with a simple word. "Go." So they went, leaving Mike behind.

Reggie and Christopher got as far as the stairwell before they heard the first shots being fired behind them. They could still hear the gunfire as they made their way down the two flights to the main entrance, though it got quieter in the distance as they ran. As long as they could hear the sounds of a gunfight above them, Reggie and Christopher knew two things—that, for now, Mike was still alive and that he was putting up a hell of a fight. Hector, Linda, and Dave were waiting for them when they arrived. Nobody asked where Mike was. They all knew enough not to ask questions they didn't want the answers to. Without any words, Reggie took out the keycard that Jared had given him. He walked up to the door and slid the keycard in the slot beside it. The light above the slot went from red to green. "We're in," Reggie said, and with the swiftness and eagerness of newly freed prisoners, the others stormed through the now unlocked door.

Jared's sleight of hand didn't eliminate the problem of the guards; it merely shifted the upper hand. The guards still had to be dealt with. Everyone knew what that meant. They all knew that these guards were willing to lay down their lives for their cause. These guards were, after all, the ones left behind in an otherwise evacuated building. Everyone knew that the fight between them and the guards would end only in death. And all the while the clock kept ticking.

The inside of the Intelligence Center didn't look like a war room or a bunker. It looked eerily like a normal office. The five of them stood on bland, dark green carpeting, staring at the empty reception area in front of them. In the middle of the reception area, a leather couch and a few leather chairs surrounded a dark wood coffee table adorned with magazines. The desk where the receptionist would normally sit was empty, the receptionist's computers still. To their right, a giant window stretched from the floor to the ceiling, looking out over the tops of the buildings in the center of Manhattan. To their left, a few hallways led from the reception area to the maze of offices and filing cabinets.

It was quiet inside—quiet and bright. The gunfire from upstairs had either stopped or was too far away to be heard anymore. Reggie and Christopher hoped for the latter. They hoped that the gunfire was too far away to hear but knew that the the gunfight was likely over already. They knew that Mike was probably dead and they knew that people were going to be coming for them next. All the office's lights were on. Christopher looked toward the giant window. It was so bright inside the office that it was almost impossible to see into the darkness outside.

"Remember," Reggie told the rest of them as they each stared down the empty hallways, "no gas until we're sure that we've gotten rid of all the guards. First, we secure the place. Then we let the gas out. Then we get out of here. If somebody fires a gun after we've let even a little bit of the gas out, this whole place will ignite with us in it." Everybody nodded. They'd all heard this speech before.

"So who's going upstairs and who's going downstairs?" Dave asked, needing to ask because Mike's absence required them to update the plan.

"Linda and I will go upstairs," Reggie said to Dave with everyone else listening too. "You and Hector go down." To Christopher, Reggie said, "You stay here to make sure that any guards that break loose don't get very far."

Christopher nodded. He knew what Reggie was doing. Reggie was trying to keep him out of the fight. Christopher didn't argue because he knew that it would be the last time anyone ever tried to protect him. It would be the last time that he was special. Soon he would be normal—or at least as close as he could get to it. "Okay," Christopher conceded and the others split into their two groups and ran off down the empty hallways.

Alone at the literal epicenter of miles of chaos, Christopher turned and walked toward the window. He could see more as he got closer to it. The fireworks had ended. Christopher missed them. He missed the colors and the light and the sounds. He could still see the haze they caused, floating over the city, the smoky remnants of the glorious spectacle that he had created. The smoke was only now beginning to settle into the shadows between the thousands of buildings across New York. The smoky haze went on as far as Christopher could see, like a mist or a shroud. He stepped closer to the window and looked down through the haze at the street. He could barely make out the people still standing down there, crowding the street, staring up at the sky, wondering what they might see next. For the first time Christopher could remember, he was proud of something he'd done.

"Chris," Christopher suddenly heard a voice say. He had almost forgotten where he was. He turned quickly to face whoever it was that was talking to him. No one was there. "Chris, it's me," the voice said. Christopher recognized the voice this time, but that only confused him more. He spun around again.

"Evan?" Christopher asked. Only then did he remember the earpiece. "Holy shit. You scared me. I forgot about the radio for a second."

"What are you doing, Chris?" Evan asked.

"What do you mean?" Christopher answered.

"I can see you, Chris. I can see you standing in the window. You're not doing anything. You don't have time to waste, Chris."

Christopher looked up. He hadn't realized that he was facing Evan and Addy's building. They were watching him through binoculars. They could see him standing in front of the window, looking out. Christopher lifted a hand, waving to his two friends. "Why?" Christopher asked, emerging from his fog as he waved. "What's going on?"

"We can hear gunshots, Chris, from all over the city. That means that they're coming for you guys. That means that our people are trying to stop them, but they'll only be able to hold them off for so long. The fireworks worked, Chris. They just didn't work for as long as we wanted them to. So you can't stand there. You have to do something. They're coming."

"There's nothing I can do," Christopher told Evan. "I have to wait here until the others have killed off the guards. I can't even start letting the gas out until we're sure the shooting is over or I'd risk blowing us all up."

"There's got to be something you can do," Evan pleaded.

Christopher looked around him and tried to think. It seemed

so strange to him that this mundane place was the key to ending the War. Jared had warned them about that. Jared told them that the Intelligence Center wouldn't look like much but that there was information hidden everywhere. What did Jared tell them that they had to do? "Open every closet door," Jared had told them. "Open every drawer. Make sure the gas gets everywhere. Make sure everything burns."

"I can open doors and drawers," Christopher said, half to Evan and half to himself. Then he went to the first drawer he saw and pulled it open. There were papers inside—nothing but papers in green hanging folders. Christopher reached in and pulled out a handful of paper. He looked at them. Each page was full of color-coded lists of names and corresponding series of numbers. The first number was ten digits long. The other numbers seemed completely random. Each name was printed in either red or blue. Christopher couldn't divine any meaning from any of it. He ran to another desk and pulled another drawer open. He reached in and grabbed a handful of papers from that drawer. They looked the same—a list of color-coded names and seemingly random numbers. Each page had dozens of names. All told, there had to be thousands of pages or more on those five floors.

"Ask him what he sees," Addy said to Evan as the two of them watched Christopher go from desk to desk, pulling open the drawers and rummaging through the papers inside.

"Addy wants to know what's in the drawers," Evan said to Christopher.

Christopher looked out the window in the direction of his friends. "Nothing," he said, sensing how disappointed Addy would be. "It's only names. Everything else is in code." Evan looked at Addy and didn't say anything. Evan didn't need to give Addy the details. He simply shook his head.

The gunfire was getting closer. Evan and Addy could hear it

down on the streets, closing in on them from all directions. Evan searched the other windows of the office to see if he could spot Reggie or the others, to see if they'd finished off the guards yet, to see if it was safe to tell Christopher to go forward. He saw them— all of them—running back toward Christopher. "They're done, Chris. Reggie and the others are finished. They're coming back to you."

A moment later all four of them burst into the room where Christopher had been waiting. "We're finished with the guards," Reggie announced. "We can start releasing the gas." Christopher looked at the four of them. David had blood pouring out of his shoulder. The rest of them looked like they'd come out unscathed. "Everybody take their floor," Reggie ordered. "We'll meet back here when we're done."

"No," Christopher said, stopping everyone before they left. "There's no time to regroup. The diversion didn't last. They're coming for us. Once each of us has prepped our floor and let out our gas tanks, we need to run."

David, Reggie, Hector, and Linda understood. They all nodded in response. Then they reached into their backpacks and pulled out their gas masks. "Let's go," Reggie said. Each of them slid their gas mask over their face. With their gas masks on and their guns at the ready, Christopher thought they looked like the monsters from a science fiction movie.

Before slipping his own gas mask over his face, Christopher whispered, "This is it, Evan. I'll still be able to hear you, but I won't be able to talk." Behind the gas mask, Christopher felt the world close in on him. Everything suddenly appeared two-dimensional. The depth was gone.

Everyone knew their assignments. Since David was the original backup, he took Mike's floor. Despite the work that he'd already done on the middle floor, Christopher was assigned to the top floor. He ran for the stairs. "They're getting closer," Evan told Christopher as he headed up the two flights. "Be quick." Christopher heard Evan and ran faster. He knew why Reggie had assigned him the top floor. It was because it should have been the last one that anyone from the outside could reach. Anyone from the outside should have had to climb up through the lower floors first.

Christopher reached the top of the stairs and slid both the backpacks—his and Mike's—off his back. He reached inside them and pulled out the gas canisters. They were heavy with gas. Christopher never understood how that worked. Now wasn't the time. He moved away from the stairs, toward the middle of the floor. He left everything but the gas canisters behind, not wanting anything to slow him down. He left his guns behind. What use would they be to him anyway? He couldn't fire them once the gas was released. Then, free of everything but his gas mask, Christopher began his search. There was a file room in the middle of the floor. Jared had told them that they should prop the file room's doors open and let the gas out in there. Christopher opened doors, searching for the file room, leaving every door that he opened open, propping open the ones that swung closed automatically. He could hear his own breathing in the gas mask. With the fifth door, he struck gold.

Christopher stepped into the file room. This room alone had to contain thousands upon thousands of names. He placed the gas canisters in the middle of the room and turned the nozzles on each so that the gas began to leak out. Then he began opening the drawers to all of the file cabinets. This time he didn't bother to look at the papers inside. He knew what they would say anyway. He could still hear the gas hissing out of the canisters when he left the file room to begin opening doors and drawers all over the top floor. He was making progress now, real progress, attacking cabinets and closets in every office and every room. He was about halfway done when Evan first warned him. "Chris," Evan said, "they've got a helicopter. They're heading for the roof. I'll try to hold them off, but I'm not going to be able to stop them." Christopher glanced up at the closest window. He could see the lights from the helicopter flash by as it swooped down toward the building. They were going to come down from the roof. Reggie's plan to protect Christopher by assigning him to the top floor had backfired. The last will be first, and the first will be last. Christopher sped up, rushing into offices and overturning desks and pulling open doors like a man possessed.

Addy and Evan hadn't thought that they'd have any need for more than one rifle. The plan required them to take only one shot. Even so, Evan took his gun and aimed it at the helicopter. He remembered for a second those days that he and Christopher spent in the woods, each shooting his rifle at rocks that the other threw as high into the air as he could. Christopher was always the better shot, but Evan hadn't been far behind him. Before pulling the trigger, Evan looked down over the edge of the building toward the street, trying to estimate how much damage he would do if he took the whole helicopter down. The street was still flooded with people staring into the sky, waiting for something else to amaze them. Evan aimed the gun at the helicopter again and pulled the trigger.

At first, Evan had aimed his rifle at the helicopter pilot. He could make that shot. It wouldn't even be hard with the scope he had on his rifle. One shot, he thought, and he could bring the helicopter crashing down. But then he had seen all those people down in the street. So instead of taking out the pilot, Evan aimed in front of the helicopter, firing a warning shot. He hoped that they would be sensible. He hoped that they were regular people, people smart enough to react to fear. He hoped that they weren't people who had grown up with paranoia. "Fly away," he whispered to himself, and at first the helicopter turned up and away from the roof as if it would go. Before it was too far off, though, the helicopter turned back to make another pass at landing on the roof.

"Chris!" Evan shouted into his radio. "You've got to get out of there, Chris. You've done enough." Christopher didn't answer him, but then he couldn't answer him, not with the gas mask on. Evan shot a panicked glance at Addy, unwilling to take his eyes off the helicopter for more than a split second. "Can you see what Christopher is doing? Tell me what he's doing. Is he running?"

Addy lifted the binoculars and scanned the windows, looking for Christopher. Then she spotted him, still moving through the building. The hose from his gas mask hung down in front of him like an alien appendage. He didn't look human, and still, Addy could tell from the way that he moved that it was Christopher. "No," she said to Evan. "He's not running."

Christopher heard Evan telling him to run. Evan's wasn't the only voice Christopher heard, though. He also kept hearing Jared's. "Open every drawer. Make sure the gas gets everywhere. Make sure everything burns." Christopher couldn't leave this job half done. He couldn't risk waking up tomorrow in an unchanged world. *Every drawer. Every closet. Every door. Make sure everything burns.* He only had a few offices left anyway. Then he would be done. Then he could run.

The helicopter swooped down for a second pass and Evan fired again, another warning shot. This time the helicopter did not heed his warning. Instead, it pulled its nose up, aiming the landing skids at the roof. In that position, the helicopter looked to Evan like a cornered animal, rearing up its head before a strike. Evan fired again—no warning shot this time—but from the new angle, all Evan could hit was the helicopter's white underside. He saw the bullet puncture the metal, creating a tiny hole in the bottom of the helicopter but the hole did nothing to stop its landing. Evan wanted to shout at Christopher again, but he didn't. Evan knew that Christopher would leave when he was ready to leave, and Evan didn't want to waste any more time distracting him. The helicopter came down now, the skids bouncing only slightly on the roof of the building before the machine settled. Evan aimed and fired again. This time he had a clear shot. The pilot's head jerked back and he was gone, but it was too late. The others were already stepping out of the helicopter onto the roof. Evan tried to get his sights on another one of them. He felt no remorse for killing the pilot. He felt nothing. He wouldn't feel any remorse if he shot another one too. He would be too numb to feel until he had shot them all, and then all he would feel was relief.

Evan's next shot missed. Five people ran out of the helicopter. They were hard to hit. They ran on the roof in zigzag patterns, like people trained to run from bullets while searching for cover. He missed only once. His next shot hit one of them in the leg. The man fell to the ground. Evan moved the gun imperceptibly higher and fired again, ending the man's life with a bullet to his chest.

"I can't get them all," Evan said, realizing the truth.

"I think he's only got one office left," Addy reported, following Christopher as he moved quickly but methodically across the office floor. "There in the corner." She didn't take her eyes off Christopher. "Just hold them off for another minute or two."

Evan fired another shot. This time he missed, but the bullet still served its purpose. One of the men had lurched out from his hiding spot on the roof, squatting behind an exhaust fan, and the shot scared him back into his hiding place. They were all hunkered down now, trying to avoid Evan's bullets. Evan knew he could manage another minute or two.

Christopher ran into the last office. It was a large corner office with a big desk on one side, a small table in one corner, and a closet with the door closed in a third corner. All the blinds were down.

This was the first office Christopher had entered where the blinds were down. In case it was meant to hide something, Christopher violently ripped each set of blinds down, exposing the office to the world. He was so close to being finished. He went to the desk first. He pulled open each drawer. The bottom drawer was locked, but he broke the lock with a single hard tug. Jared had been right. The papers were everywhere. Name after color-coded name, but they were out now. They were open. They would burn and every horrible thing linked to those names would be forgotten. Christopher stepped toward the closet door. He opened it, expecting to see more papers. Then he froze.

"What's he doing?" Evan asked after three minutes and then four minutes went by and Addy still didn't say that Christopher was running.

"I don't know," Addy answered. "He's just standing there."

Christopher stood, staring into the closet, trying to make sense of what he saw. In trying to make sense of it, Christopher forgot where he was. He forgot what he was doing. He lost his ability to move. *Why*, he wondered, *is a bloody, dead body in the closet, a pen still sticking out of the body's neck?* Even in a place where so little made sense, this really didn't make any sense. Who was he? How did he get there? Christopher grabbed the stiff body by the wrists and slid it out of the closet, stretching it out on the floor.

The men from the helicopter up on the roof finally came out of their hiding places all at once, all running for the door that would lead them downstairs. They finally thought to coordinate, to work together, to sacrifice a few for the larger cause. Evan began aiming and firing—shot after shot. He hit two of them quickly, but the other two made it all the way to the door. They stood in a single-file line, one in front of the other, the first blocking Evan's view of the second. The one in front pulled the door open. Evan fired again, hitting the second man in the back, between his shoulder blades. Then he planned on shooting the man in front. The man Evan shot bent backward and fell to his knees. When he fell, no one was in front of him. The door was open. One man had made it inside. "Chris! They're inside! Please!" Evan shouted.

Inside the building, Christopher was still in a strange trance. He wanted to get one clear look at the dead man, so he reached up and pulled the gas mask off his face. He could smell the gas spreading everywhere around him, but only vaguely. You weren't supposed to be able to smell it at all, but that didn't mean it wasn't everywhere. Christopher breathed, pulling the gas into him, into his lungs and his body. It made him feel the slightest bit giddy. He would put the gas mask back on in a moment, but first he needed to look at the dead man's face. He thought that the dead man deserved it before his body and all the evidence around it were incinerated.

Christopher looked at the body. The man had been ugly, but it was hard to tell if it was his life or his death that had made him ugly. Seeing his face was enough for now. Christopher lifted up his gas mask, intending to pull it back over his face. Then, slowly emerging from his trance, Christopher finally heard Evan shouting something into his earpiece. The sound of Evan's voice was followed by a small sound coming from behind Christopher. So instead of pulling his gas mask on, Christopher slowly turned around to face whatever it was that was behind him that Evan had been trying to warn him about.

Addy and Evan had seen the man from the roof as he ran past the office windows. After he had reached Christopher's floor, Evan aimed his rifle, ready to shoot the man through the window, until Addy yelled, "Stop!"

"Why?" Evan asked.

"Because your bullet will make a spark and the whole place will burst into flames with Christopher still inside." So Evan couldn't shoot. They could only watch, impotent to help.

"He's coming for you," Evan said into his radio, hoping Christopher could still hear him. This time Christopher did hear him, but it was already too late.

The man had a gun—a handgun—that he was pointing at Christopher's back before Christopher turned around. "Don't shoot," Christopher said to the man. "If you shoot, we'll both die and everything that you're trying to protect will burn."

"What do you mean?" the man asked Christopher, confused by this tactic.

"Can you smell the gas?" Christopher asked the man.

"I don't smell anything," the man said, almost certain that Christopher was bluffing.

"It's all around you," Christopher warned the man, "and there's nothing you can do about it."

In response to the dire warning, the man lifted up his gun and aimed it at Christopher's head. The man had to shoot. He had orders to clear everyone out of the offices, to protect the information at all costs. He didn't smell anything anyway. The man hesitated for only a second as Christopher spoke, seemingly into the air, as if he were praying. "I'm sorry I didn't run soon enough," Christopher said out loud.

"That's okay." Evan forgave him, speaking loud enough so that Christopher would hear.

Christopher looked into the eyes of the man who was pointing a gun at him but Christopher kept speaking to Evan. "I want you to shoot him before he shoots me," Christopher said to Evan. His voice was calm. "I want you to be the one to end the War."

End the War, as if that was all Evan was going to have to do. Evan trained his rifle on the man who was pointing a gun at Christopher. Evan watched the man's trigger finger. He wasn't going to shoot unless he saw that trigger finger twitch. He wasn't going to shoot unless he had no other choice. Neither Evan nor Addy bothered looking for any of the others. They didn't have the chance to see that two of them had already made it out and were heading down the stairs. They didn't see how close the woman was to getting out. They didn't see Reggie, still inside, as he headed up the stairs to try to make sure that Christopher was safe. Reggie was still trying to make good on the promise that he'd made to Maria all those years ago.

The man started to pull the trigger. Evan was faster. Evan pulled the trigger on his rifle and then . . . fire. The fire was everywhere, instantly. All five floors were bathed in flames, hot, bright flames that ate everything. Then a moment later, the fire went out and everything was gone. The papers were all gone. The color-coded names were gone. The dead body from the closet was gone. The man with the gun was gone. Reggie was gone. Christopher was gone. Everything was gone in the flash of fire, and Evan and Addy were witnesses to it.

Evan and Addy stood on the roof together, dumb with shock. It would take them hours to finally accept what had happened. They used those hours to decide what they needed to do next. It couldn't just be over. Not for them. Not like that.

Sixty-five

The next day, as the sun slowly rose throughout the world, the children of paranoia woke up to a new reality. At first they didn't know what had changed. Some of them found out in weeks. Some in months. They saw the stories on the news about the terrorist attacks in different cities and countries all over the world, but they had no way of immediately knowing what these attacks had accomplished. It took time. They knew for sure that the War had ended only when time went by and no one tried to kill them. They knew for sure that the War had ended only when time went by and they weren't given new orders about who to kill. From that night forward, all over the world, thousands upon thousands of people no longer knew who it was that they were supposed to hate.

The War was over. No more sons and no more daughters would die in this War. No more blood would be spilled. It ended in flames and bombs and bullets and blood, but the War ended all the same. The children of paranoia were finally free.

Sixty-six

"Wait," the young girl said, holding up her hand, stopping the old woman before she could say another word. "That doesn't make any sense. I thought you promised to tell me how the War started."

The old woman smiled at the young girl. "The story's not over yet," she said. "There's still a little bit more to tell."

Sixty-seven

The day after the Uprising all of the survivors met, as they had agreed, at the warehouse in Brooklyn. Only twelve of the twenty-five made it back. As they arrived, each of them was met by three grieving mothers. The mothers knew to grieve even before anyone told them what had happened. One uninvited guest would make his way to the warehouse as well.

Brian was the first one to arrive at the warehouse. He had waited on the rooftop of his assigned building until the fireworks ended. Then he stayed longer, holding his breath until he saw the flash of light coming from the Intelligence Center. The flash was over ever so quickly, especially when compared to the fireworks, which had seemed to go on forever and ever. It was little more than a second of bright light and then darkness. Everything was quiet after that and Brian made his way down off the roof. He was careful to make sure he wasn't being followed as he weaved his way back to Brooklyn.

It was Brian's job to find out if the others had been successful too. He had an office set up in the back corner of the warehouse where he could work the phones and e-mail simultaneously. The news came in slowly. Confirmation came in from Paris and Costa Rica first. Then the news came in from Tokyo, Rio, and Istanbul.

Brian had to wait the longest for the news from Cambodia. The sun was coming up by the time he received word that the mission in Cambodia was a success. Nobody talked about casualties or costs. Nobody talked about what was lost. People only talked about success over failure. When Brian finally received the news about Cambodia, the early light from the morning had begun to leak in through the boarded-up window next to him. Brian hung up the phone. He walked over to the window and pulled away the wooden plank covering it, revealing the sun. Then he sat down again and stared out the window, waiting for some sort of emotion to come to him.

The trickle of survivors came in throughout the night. Brian wasn't planning on facing any of them until he had gotten news from everywhere. Instead, Maria and Christopher's two other mothers greeted each of them. The three mothers tended to the wounded, both physically and, when they could, emotionally. The three mothers didn't ask questions, not even the one question that the three of them were dying to ask: *do you know what happened to my son?* They knew that they would get their answer soon enough, and each one of them knew enough to fear it. Even without the prodding from the three mothers, the survivors, once they had gathered, began to talk.

The three mothers brought each of the survivors into the grand room where they'd all gathered only a few days earlier to celebrate the world's decision to rebel. The room, with so many fewer people occupying it, seemed larger and colder than before. The survivors' injuries weren't severe. The ones who had been really hurt didn't make it back. The three mothers treated a couple of bullet wounds to extremities, a few scraps from shattered glass, and a burn to the side of one woman's face. The mothers didn't know where each of the survivors had been. They didn't know if any of the survivors had been with their son.

"What was up with the fireworks? Did any of you know that we were planting fireworks?" one of the men asked as Maria put antiseptic on the bullet hole in his thigh. "I thought it was supposed to be bombs." Nobody answered him. None of the survivors had known that Christopher changed the plans.

"It's better this way," someone finally chimed in. "Less people got hurt this way."

"Sure," the man with the bullet in his leg agreed, "but we could have at least gotten a warning. Maybe more of *us* would have made it back if we'd gotten a warning."

"Maybe the whole thing would have been a failure if we'd all known about the fireworks," the woman with the burned face said.

"Do you even know if it worked?" somebody asked the woman.

"Yes," Linda answered him, holding an ice pack on her face. She looked over at Hector, neither of them feeling as proud as they wanted to. "We did it." They were the only two to make it back from the Intelligence Center. Dave had been shot as the three of them were retreating from the building.

"How do you know?" someone else asked.

"Because I was there," Linda answered. "I felt the fire that burned the place to the ground." Then she showed them all the blisters on her face and when the people saw her blisters, they cheered.

As the cheering went on, the small older woman who had given Linda the towel and the ice for her face came back to her. "Were you with Christopher?" the old woman asked Linda. Linda had no idea who the old woman was or what she was doing there. Linda didn't know that the old woman had raised Christopher until he was a few days past his first birthday.

"I was," Linda told the old woman.

"Do you know what happened to him?" The old woman whispered her question as if the question itself was a secret.

Linda shook her head. "No," she whispered back, holding back her tears, knowing how much it would hurt her wounds if she began to cry.

Brian showed himself before Addy and Evan returned. They were the only two survivors who hadn't made it back yet by the time he stepped into the makeshift infirmary to deliver the good news. Brian would have waited for them if he'd known they were alive, but no one knew. No one could know. Each person knew only about the casualties that he or she had witnessed firsthand. Until Addy and Evan walked into that room, everyone assumed that they hadn't survived the night.

When Brian entered the room, everything went quiet. Without Reggie there, Brian was the closest thing that any of them had to a leader. They waited for him to speak. "We've won," he said softly, but loud enough that everyone in the room could hear. "I've gotten confirmation on each of the targets. They're all gone."

"So the War is over?" someone shouted.

"If people want the War to be over," Brian answered him, "it is." There was cheering again, but this time it was more subdued as people became more and more aware of the absences in the room. As they began to realize with more and more certainty that all of the people who were absent were unlikely to come back.

Linda waved the old woman back to her. "He had time to get out," Linda assured the old woman. "I know he had enough time." The old woman nodded, but the desperation in Linda's voice only made Christopher's mother more nervous.

Without Reggie or Christopher there to lead them, no one knew what to do. No one knew how long they should stay before giving up hope that any more survivors would return. Then, as the resignation began to spread from one survivor to the other, the door opened and in stepped Addy and Evan. They walked in with purpose. It hadn't been fear that they were being followed that had kept them from returning earlier, even though, unbeknownst to them, they were being followed. It had taken them so long to make it back to the warehouse because they weren't sure how to respond to what had happened. They had spent the night walking through empty parts of the city, talking about what they should do, what they needed to do now that Christopher was gone. They didn't head back to the warehouse until after they'd made their decision.

The hope in the room was revived for a moment when Addy and Evan walked in. If Addy and Evan were still alive, then maybe other people were alive too, maybe Reggie was still alive, maybe *he* was still alive. Nobody said the words, but everyone knew that it had suddenly become important to everyone that *he* was still alive. What good would ending the War be if they had to sacrifice the one innocent among them to do it?

The hope didn't last long, though. Evan smashed it into a million little pieces in seconds. "Christopher is dead," he announced without prodding or questioning. "They killed him." Evan's voice was not sad. It was angry. It was angrier than it had ever been before.

"What? No!" one of the mothers wailed.

"How do you know?" someone else asked. Unlike Linda, Evan had no scars to prove himself—none that could be seen anyway.

"We saw it happen." Evan motioned toward Addy, and she nodded in confirmation. "He burned to death along with all of your precious information." Evan didn't tell everyone that he had been the one who fired the bullet that lit the spark that started the fire that killed Christopher. Addy didn't say anything either. They had agreed that it didn't change anything that mattered. If Evan hadn't pulled the trigger, someone else would have and the building would have burned with Christopher in it anyway.

As Evan spoke, the man who had spent much of the night following Addy and Evan around the city slipped into the room. In all the commotion caused by Evan's words, he was unnoticed by anyone but Maria. Jared had mostly sobered up by then. He had seen Addy and Evan walk past him earlier the night before. He recognized Evan from surveillance pictures he had seen of Christopher years ago. Jared never forgot Evan's face because Evan was the best friend and Jared never forgot the importance of the best friend. Jared began following Addy and Evan, hoping to get one last glimpse of the War's end before disappearing forever into obscurity.

When Maria saw Jared, she rushed toward him. She gathered her strength. She had already lost a son that night. Whatever it was that Jared was planning, Maria was determined to stop it. This wasn't the time or the place for any more of Jared's cruelty. Maria remembered watching Jared kill Joseph. If Jared could do that to his own best friend, she couldn't fathom what he had planned for the people in that room. She wasn't going to freeze this time. Nothing could stop her. She wasn't going to fail again. Maria was so focused on Jared that she didn't even hear the words that Evan spoke as she rushed toward her old nemesis. If she couldn't protect her own son, the least she could do was try to protect Addy and Evan.

"What are you doing here?" Maria asked Jared, stepping between him and Addy and Evan.

Maria didn't trust the way Jared was staring at Evan. Evan was standing in the middle of the room, surrounded by the other survivors. When Maria spoke, Jared's eyes moved from Evan to Maria, and Maria saw something in those eyes that she had never expected to see. She saw regret. For the first time, she saw regret in Jared's eyes. "What is he doing?" Jared asked Maria, his voice weak. He didn't even care who he was asking. He motioned toward Evan. "Stop him," Jared begged Maria.

Eighteen years ago, on the eve of losing Joseph and her son in one fell swoop, it had been the cold hate and the anger in Jared's eyes that had frightened Maria. The look in his eyes on that morning was worse. The regret and the compassion in Jared's eyes frightened Maria more than she had ever been frightened before. She turned back toward Evan, not knowing what to expect. She half expected to see violence. She'd been trained to expect violence. When all was said and done, she would have preferred to have turned around and seen violence. Instead, Maria saw the crowd standing around Evan and Addy. Then she finally stopped to listen to what Evan was saying. Evan was nearly shouting, his clenched fist raised above his head. "We can't let them get away with what they did to Christopher," he yelled. "He didn't deserve to die like that. Somebody's got to pay for his death."

The room went silent for a moment—but only a moment.

"How do we do that?" Hector shouted out toward the new leaders, breaking the silence.

"There are enough of us here that know something," Addy responded to Hector. Addy and Evan were playing off each other as a team. "How many people here remember the faces of some of the people that fought against us tonight?" Every single one of the survivors raised a hand. "They're the ones responsible for killing Christopher. Some of you probably even know a few of their names. Who here can name names?" A handful of the survivors raised their hands this time. Addy committed each one to memory. "That's great," Addy said. "All we need to do is gather the information that we have."

Evan chimed back in now. "The others can help us too," he said. "The other rebels in Europe and Asia and South America that fought with us, that fought for Christopher. They can help us. They won't want Christopher's death to go unavenged either."

Addy nodded with enthusiasm. "We have one last battle to

fight together—for Christopher. We know how to do this. We'll keep our enemies' names and what we know about them. They need to know that they can't get away with this."

"Stop them," Jared said again to Maria, hoping that she could do what he knew in his heart he could not. "You have to stop them."

But Maria saw the look in Addy's and Evan's eyes and she knew that she was powerless. "I can't," she said and her voice trembled.

"Try!" Jared shouted at Maria, grabbing her by the shoulders and shaking her.

Maria shook her head. "They won't listen to me," she told Jared. "Anything I say will only make it worse. They're young," she said, as if that were an excuse. *All they know is violence*, she thought to herself. *How could we have expected anything different?*

So Jared pushed Maria aside. "Stop this!" he shouted as he stormed toward Evan. "You'll regret this!" Jared raised his hoarse, whiskey-soaked voice as loud as his tired muscles would let him.

"Who are you?" Evan asked as Jared rushed toward them.

Jared had no answer. Who was he to them? He was the villain in their fairy tales. "You will regret this," Jared repeated instead of answering Evan's question. "I promise you that if you do this, you will regret it."

"What do you know about it, old man?" Evan said to Jared. "You didn't know Christopher. You wouldn't understand." Then Evan turned his back on Jared and asked the room, "Who is with us?"

Of the twelve survivors, nine of them agreed to help Addy and Evan. Brian and two others refrained, but none of them did anything to stop what was happening right before their eyes. Internationally, the percentages of rebels who joined Addy and Evan's cause were lower, but enough people joined the cause to make it work. It worked quickly and efficiently because when everything relies on forgetting the past there is little difference between being given knowledge and not being allowed to forget. Internationally, those that agreed to raise arms alongside Addy and Evan were mostly people who had met Christopher when he had visited Indonesia and Istanbul. Christopher had left his mark. The three mothers looked on in disbelief, mourning their son and mourning their inability to make these other children understand the consequences of what they were doing. Addy and Evan were so young and so passionate and they wanted so much. The three mothers knew that begging Addy and Evan to stop would only spur them on. The young don't listen to the old when it comes to passion. Every generation believes that they are the first to feel the things that they feel. That left only Jared to beg Addy and Evan to stop the madness before it became something that they couldn't control. But no one listened to Jared anymore. He fell to his hands and his knees in the middle of the room and repeated the words over and over again, "Don't do this. Let it go. For God's sake, let it go." But the young rebels walked around him as if he didn't exist.

The survivors gathered around Addy and Evan instead, wanting to hear more. They knew it wasn't over because how could it be over? They had one more mission. One more, Evan promised them, and *then* it would be over.

Sixty-eight

"So that's how the War started?" the young girl asked, barely able to cover the skepticism in her voice.

"You think I'm telling you stories?" the old woman responded to her.

"I don't know. It's just seems too—"

The old woman cut her off. "It seems too easy? Too fast?" The girl nodded her head. "You think that because it's so hard to end a war, it should also be hard to start one." The old woman remembered the bloody details that she was glossing over—the battles, the losses, the victories. Sure, there was more to the start of the war than she was letting on, but none of it mattered. The war was inevitable from the moment that Addy and Evan, the new war's Adam and Eve, decided to fight on.

"Shouldn't it be hard to start a war?" the girl asked.

"It should," the old woman told her, "but it's not. It never has been. Someday, maybe, it will be."

"If that's how the War started, then which side are we on?" the girl asked. "Are we on Addy and Evan's side or are we on the other side?"

The old woman sighed, wondering if it even mattered. "As time goes on, it becomes harder and harder to remember. It's been two generations already since the old war ended and the new war began. With each passing generation, the two sides seem to triple in size, no matter how many people are killed. Both sides know all too well how to make a war grow."

"I still don't know if I believe you," the young girl said.

The old woman looked past the girl and into her house. She wondered if she should open the old chest she kept in her bedroom to show the girl what was inside. Maybe those old journals would make the girl believe. But no, the old woman decided, the journals should stay hidden. The girl would have to decide what to believe on her own. "Why don't you believe me?" the old woman asked.

"Because the story is too sad to be true," the young girl said.

"How would a story being sad make it any less true?"

"Well, if the story is true, then that means that everything was pointless. It means that everyone was either a bad guy or a failure."

"Is that what you think?" the old woman asked.

The girl shrugged again. "Well, there doesn't seem much point in trying to end the War if it's only going to lead to another war."

"Listen," the old woman told her, "I'm going to teach you the most important thing you'll ever learn." The girl leaned in toward her. "Are you ready?" The girl nodded vigorously.

The old woman began slowly, trying to find the right words. "You can't judge people by the outcome of their actions. There's far too much chance in the world for that. If you judge people only by the outcome of their actions, you will grow up to be cynical and disappointed."

"Then how should we judge people?" the girl asked, confused.

"Judge them on what they try to achieve and how much they risk in trying to achieve it. Judge them based on the courage they have to muster to roll the dice when it counts and not on how those dice land."

"What does that do?"

"It takes all those people that you want to call bad guys and failures and turns them into heroes—every single one of them."

The young girl thought about it. She thought about the stories the old woman had told her. She thought about Joseph and Maria and Christopher. She thought about Michael and Reggie and Brian. Then she thought about Addy and Evan and even Jared. "Can they really all be heroes?" the girl asked the old woman.

The old woman's heart throbbed, knowing the type of War-torn world the young girl was going to have to grow up in, knowing all too well about the paranoia and the loneliness and the sadness that would surround her for her entire life. "Wouldn't you like to live in a world full of heroes?" the old woman answered the girl.

"That would be nice," the young girl replied, looking up at the old woman with a smile full of naive hope.

PHOTO BY KEVIN TRAGESER

Trevor Shane lives in Brooklyn with his wife and two sons.